CHASSE
THE LAST WIZARD SAGA
SONG 2

TONY SHILLITOE

Cover art by Kirsi Salonen
Cover design by TS

Millswood Books

ISBN: 978-1-7641847-9-3

For my childhood self
who was afraid to become
the warrior I needed to be.

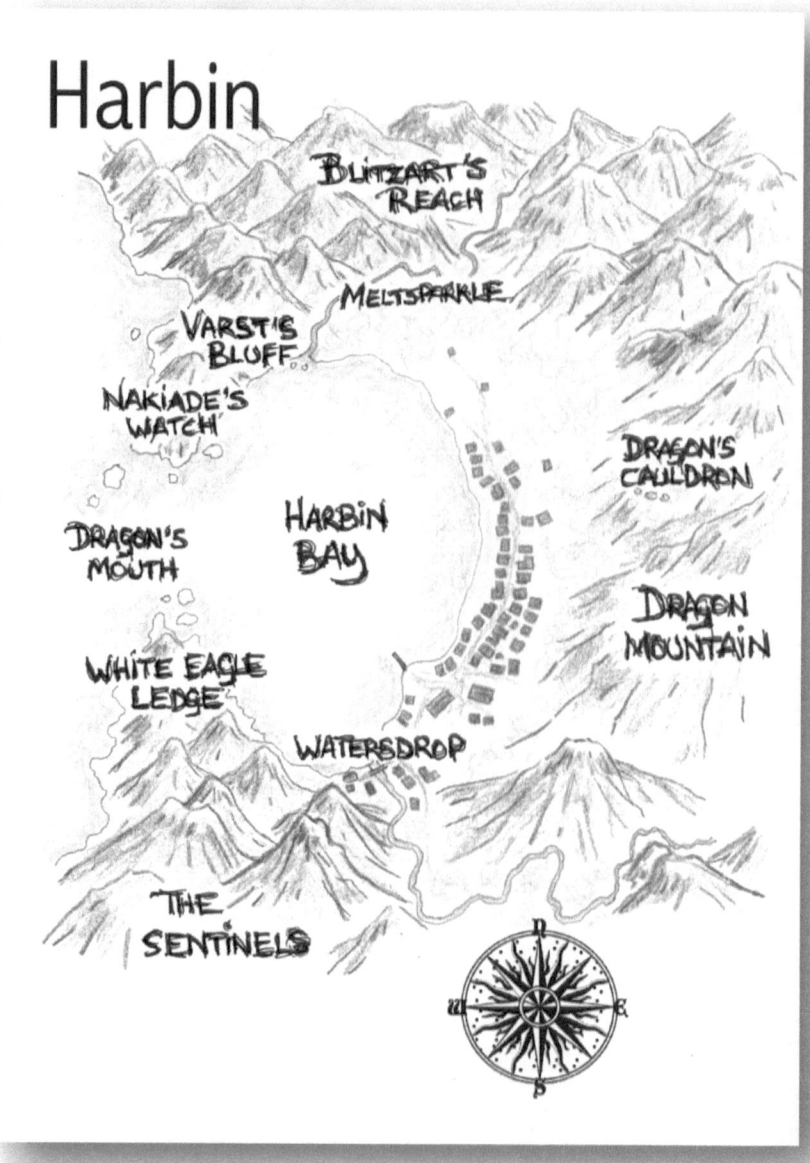

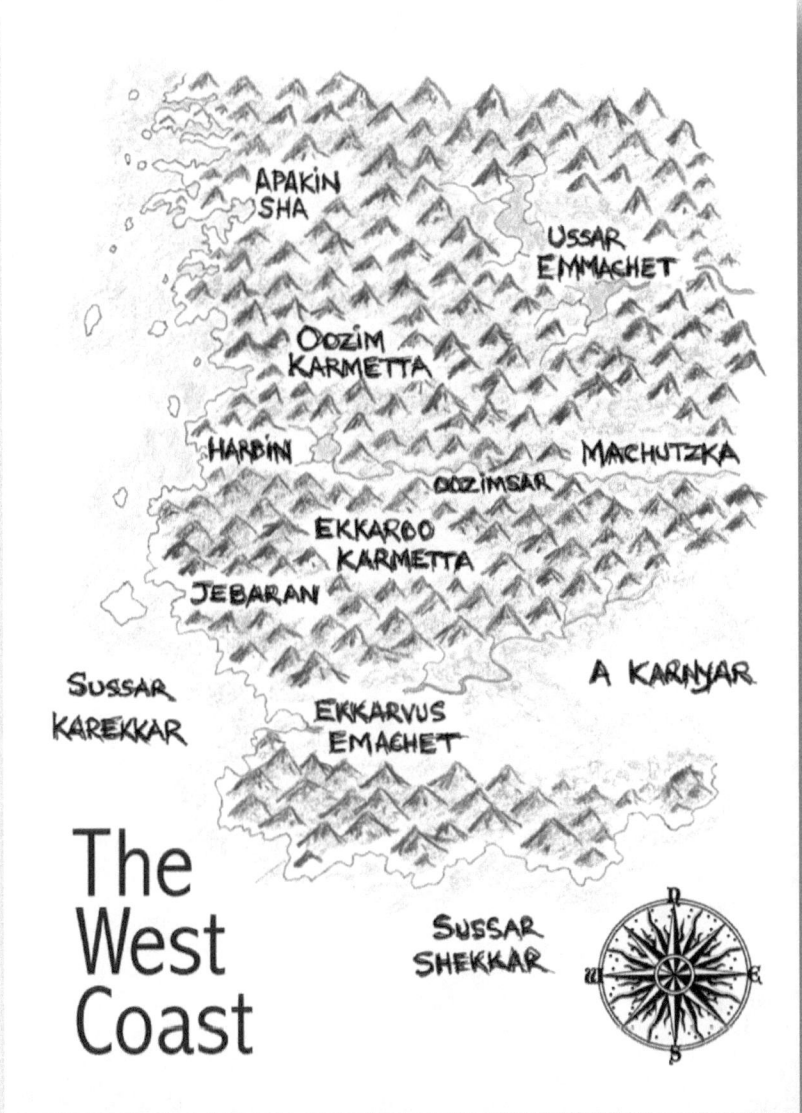

One

Kevan limped onto the jetty, the scars pulling against his skin reminding him that the past remained close. The rising sun touched his shoulders and he knew the day would be warm, but the chill morning air whispered that the end of summer was near. At the jetty's seaward end, he gazed across the blue water towards Dragon's Mouth. A wave exploded in a white plume over the distant rocks and Kevan waited for the next to follow. Dark blue ocean rollers pulsing through the isthmus between White Eagle Ledge and Nakiades' Watch carried memories on the soft breeze of dragonship journeys.

The jetty's wooden planks creaked beneath the weight of approaching steps and a voice spoke over Kevan's left shoulder.

'They will come back.'

Kevan turned and studied Jon's weathered face framed by his straggly blond hair and beard, the face of a warrior who had seen twenty-six summers and ten journeys on the dragonship. 'Yes,' he agreed. 'They will.'

'What will we do then?'

'Talk.' Kevan looked back out to sea. 'Make peace.' A lone grey and white tern dipped to the ocean, disappeared among the crests, and rose with a sparkling prize in its beak. 'Rebuild,' he added. He shifted his gaze to three fishing boats bobbing on the water closer to shore, one with a glowing lantern. The daily rhythm of catching, cleaning, sharing, cooking, eating went on for the village fishermen, uninterrupted by wider events or the cares of the man entrusted with leading the village. He clapped Jon on the shoulder, and said, 'Come. We will gather the men. There's plenty of work before Blitzart's icy breath returns.'

'What about Remi and Thados?' Jon asked, naming the two boys who were eligible to join the Dragon Fang in the coming Spring.

'Bring them,' Kevan said. 'They can begin their initiation early by working with us before Blitzart's breath freezes the land.'

'We should build our own dragonship,' Jon suggested.

'And we will,' Kevan agreed. 'We will.'

'Are you going to find Tamesan?'

Chasse paused at the door. His mother was baking bread on the hearth, her auburn hair tied back in a loose ponytail, her arms covered in freshly-ground white flour, and she was awaiting an answer. 'I asked Father if I could go up the mountain today,' he replied.

'Watch out for your little brother.'

'Is he out?' Chasse asked.

'He followed Kevan this morning,' Eesa explained, 'but I know he will wander elsewhere.'

'If I see him, I'll send him home.'

'What is that?' Eesa asked, spying a shiny black rod in Chasse's left hand.

'This?' he asked, lifting the rod. 'Tamesan asked me to take it to her.'

'Yes, but what is it?' Eesa persisted.

'An object the Herbal Man left behind.'

'Why does she want that?'

'Perhaps it's a keepsake,' Chasse suggested.

Eesa shook her head, as if Chasse's explanation didn't satisfy her. 'Don't spend all day on the mountain. I'm sure your father has work for you. And tell Tamesan I need her help to prepare for Procra's Feast.'

'I will,' Chasse promised, as he opened the door.

Chasse stepped into the morning air, stretched his arms wide and tilted his neck to ease his muscle tightness before he sucked in a deep, cool breath. The sun peering over the flanks of Dragon Mountain sprayed golden rays across the village and he luxuriated in the warmth on his cheek and neck. While he missed the comradery of the Warriors' Hall, sleeping in his childhood room brought comfort and treasured memories and kept the horrors of the dragonship journey partly at bay. He knew circumstances would change, and why, but he was content to spend a few weeks being more a child and less a warrior and less troubled by the onuses of manhood. Besides, there were matters to attend before he could resume his adult responsibilities. He ran his hands down the sides of his long red locks, shook his head, and headed for the village.

Chasse was aware of the planks moving beneath his boots and the stream thundering into the ocean as he crossed the wooden bridge over Watersdrop, and he looked down the shallow slope to the jetty at his father chatting with Jon. No doubt they were discussing plans for the village with so many people gone after the dragon encounter. At the close of summer into autumn, the village was normally bustling with women preparing for Procra's Dance, cooking and gathering and fashioning garlands and dresses for the unmarried women to wear on the evening when the single dragonwarriors chose their wives, but few villagers remained to celebrate and even fewer single eligible men and women were available to make choices. Many huts and cottages were empty since the Herbal Man and his dragon emerged from Dragon Mountain and Harbin was a ghostly memory of itself.

Chasse savoured the cool chill of the morning air in his nostrils and down his throat and sighed. If the Herbal Man and his dragon hadn't disrupted Harbin, he would be preparing to choose Kerryn for his partner at Procra's Dance – but Kerryn escaped with her parents, like most families who were terrified that Claryssa the golden dragon was going to kill them. No remaining girl of age in the village attracted his interest. Besides, he no longer felt ready for that change to his life after the summer disaster. Ghosts circled far too close to make him feel he was ready for manhood.

Spotting a ginger bushy tailed squirrel scampering into the bushes, he remembered why he was out early. He gazed up at Dragon Mountain, its snowy peak and the crags and cliffs and forested slopes, before he headed for the trail that scaled the lower section.

The familiar track twisted between trees and boulders and he clambered over rocks and fallen boughs that cluttered the path. Not so long ago, he was jealous that his sister, Tam, was sneaking up the mountain to learn the Herbal Man's secrets. Then he became an initiate dragonwarrior, and when he sailed with the Dragon Fang and beheld the brutality of battle Tam's gallivanting around the mountainside seemed trivial. Not so, anymore; not after Claryssa the dragon and Eric the Herbal Man changed Harbin forever.

Chasse stopped at a rocky outcrop and climbed onto a granite boulder like he did as a boy to stare across the bay towards Nakiades' Watch where the gulls were white spots against the blue sky and ocean. His home was beautiful, a landscape of ocean, trees, snow and mountains, rich with wildlife and his people's history, but his heart was troubled with darkness because the Harbin men kept a terrible secret from the women and children and he understood why. His whole boyhood was a trial leading him to the day when he could stand proudly among the dragonwarriors as they sailed south to fight dragons and bring home treasure, but he never imagined that, lurking behind the summer adventure, the truth would become his nightmare. Instead of heroes, the dragonwarriors were cruel sea-borne raiders who wreaked havoc and death on tiny communities along the coast to the south and returned home to boast of dragons they never saw and battles they never fought.

And he was witness to the one time it all went horribly wrong – the one time the southern people were waiting to exact vengeance on the Dragon Fang. Routed in a ruthlessly executed ambush, more than thirty Harbin dragonwarriors died in the desperate fighting or shortly after from their wounds and the dragon-hunting myth and fabricated heroism were exposed for all to see. Chasse was grateful that his father and he escaped death, although Kevan was sorely wounded and needed care when they returned to Harbin, and while Chasse avoided injury in the battle the scars inside his soul ached every night. He dreaded sleep. He dreaded the nightmares. He feared the truth.

He fought down his anger and sorrow. 'I will never do that again,' he whispered to the breeze. 'I will not be a raider, a false hero, not for anyone.' He slid from the rock to resume his climb.

Tam was waiting for him in the dragon's cavern. Chasse grinned, remembering his sister's defiance and determination as he walked. Even though she was a sun cycle younger, he sometimes felt she was wiser and more courageous than he ever could be. Despite their parents' protests, Tam spent nights on the mountain, alone, reading and learning what she could about the Herbal Man's treasures and his parting gifts, and today Chasse was joining her to learn more. The dragon's egg left in their trust was an amazing legacy that he still couldn't fully comprehend. Neither could he fathom how they would protect the egg or what they would do when it hatched. If his father or any dragonwarriors knew the secret he was keeping with his sister, they would storm up the mountain to claim the egg as a prize. Tam also told him that there were more gifts awaiting them in the caverns because she held three iron keys to three doors. Today they would open the doors.

Sensing movement between the trees leading onto the plateau, Chasse paused. Bears foraged across the mountain and his warrior training warned him not to take chances, so he crept forward until he could see the flat space where the Herbal Man's charred hut was a stark reminder of the conflict that took place a moon cycle earlier. The memory of Trask wreathed in dragon's flames flashed before his eyes and he almost expected to find a charred body in the patch of seared earth, but he knew that his father and Jon and other warriors carried Trask's corpse down the mountain the day after the Herbal Man and the dragon flew west while the dragonship, filled with terrified people, sailed south. The remaining villagers assembled at Watersdrop three days later to sing the Words of Passage for Trask as was traditional for burying the dead.

Chasse spotted his little brother crouched before a bush at the far side of the clearing, intently observing the ground. Curious, he crept across the dry grass and whispered, 'Jaysin, what are you-'

'Sh!' Jaysin hissed, turning his head sharply to glare at Chasse before returning to the focus of his interest.

Chasse followed his brother's gaze to a blue and black butterfly with white wingtips perched on a wilted yellow flower. 'Interesting,' he said dismissively. Insects were commonplace and often annoying.

'More than interesting,' Jaysin replied excitedly. 'It's a Snowtip butterfly. They are rare on this mountain. They live further north, in secluded valleys. They don't come this far south. I wonder why it is here?'

'Mother wants you to go home,' Chasse said, ignoring Jaysin's commentary.

'Not yet,' Jaysin replied.

'I say right now,' Chasse urged. 'Why are you up here anyway?'

'Why are you up here?' Jaysin countered.

'Meeting Tamesan,' Chasse said. 'And you are going back home.'

'I'll come with you.'

'You'll go home,' Chasse said firmly.

'What is that?' Jaysin asked, pointing at the rod in Chasse's hand as he stood.

'Go home now!' Chasse ordered.

Jaysin hesitated, as if he was intending to defy his brother, but he turned and obediently trudged across the patches of dead grass without looking back.

Chasse waited until he was convinced Jaysin was heading home before he continued across the plateau, passing dead trees and denuded bushes that were part of a lush forest, but when the Herbal Man and his dragon left the unusual plants and shrubbery on the plateau withered and died, as if mourning the old wizard's departure.

Chasse reached the foot of a goat path ascending a high cliff and braced himself. Although he was familiar with the narrow and steep path, he didn't like negotiating it because it was steep and treacherous, so he climbed carefully, until he reached a wide ledge where the view opened a panorama to the west over Harbin Bay, across Dragon's Mouth and away to the Great Ocean.

Thin smoke columns rose from the fishing huts and the Warriors' Hall hearth fires, and tiny figures traversed the village. He guessed that his father was one figure in a group of three close to the Warriors' Hall. He turned and eased into a cleft that opened into a cavern where he shook the Herbal Man's black rod to generate light.

The glow illuminated ancient drawings on the rough stone walls, the artistic records of the world as it was for the Dawn People, the first people to live on the mountain. He recognised a bear in one picture and a wolf in another, and he paused to examine an illustration detailing people bowing before a circle of light that he assumed was the sun, before his eyes were drawn to another drawing of a flying creature, like Claryssa, the wizard's dragon. Beneath the dragon, people were scattering in many directions and a pile of bodies lay to one side, presumably the dragon's victims. The image reminded him of the brief and futile clash between Claryssa and the Dragon Fang dragonwarriors. The old legend of Nakiades and his battle with the dragons masked the truth about dragons and their brutal power. Faced by a real dragon, the warriors were outmatched and overwhelmed.

Chasse descended a zig-zag staircase cut through the rock to a landing and descended again into a tunnel that led to the chamber housing the dragon egg in a nest. A glowing crystal in the ceiling lit the chamber with an amber hue and Tamesan stood beside the nest, waiting for him. Chasse shook the rod to dissipate its magical light.

Tamesan hugged him, and in the amber glow his sister's red hair was dark, and her skin tan. When she released him, she asked, 'You sent Jaysin back down?'

'How do you know he was on the mountain?'

Tam laughed as she said, 'He knows about this place.'

'I didn't tell him,' Chasse said.

'Neither did I,' Tam replied, 'but he knows. He's not a danger. He won't tell anyone or put the egg at risk.'

'How do you know he won't?'

'Jaysin is keen to know everything I've learned and more. He's excited that there is a dragon egg here, and he swore to keep our secret safe.'

'You spoke with him?'

'Yes,' Tam confirmed. 'Here.' She handed Chasse a dark brown leatherbound book.

'What is this?'

'A record of the Herbal Man's studies.'

'You know I can't read,' Chasse reminded her.

'But you'll have time now and I'll teach you,' Tam said, as she retrieved the book from him. 'It's not so hard,' and she gestured for Chasse to follow her. She led him from the woven yellow grass mound with the precious egg at its centre to the far wall and instructed, 'Watch.' She pressed her left hand against the rock.

Chasse was puzzled by his sister's action, until the amber ring on her left hand glowed like the crystal in the ceiling. An amber line of fire traced the outline of a door in the wall, the stone groaned and the door eased open.

'What just happened?' Chasse whispered.

'Magic,' Tam replied. 'Eric's gift to me.'

The revelation astonished Chasse. 'You can make magic?'

'Some. Come on,' she urged. She led Chasse into a short corridor, clicked her fingers and tiny lights sparkled along the walls revealing three wooden doors, one on either side of the corridor and one at the far end.

'How did you do that?' Chasse asked.

'The light?' Tam rhetorically replied. 'It's in this book.'

'You do magic from a book?'

Tam laughed, her green eyes sparkling with mischief. 'It's possible, but here Eric wrote that if I click my fingers in the corridor or chambers behind the secret door the lights will shine. It's not really my magic. It's Eric's. You could do it. Like the wand you're carrying.' Chasse looked at the rod in his hand. 'Eric left magic for us,' Tam continued. 'We have to learn how to use it.' She rattled the iron keys on her belt and asked, 'Left or right door?'

Chasse shrugged. 'Left?'

'Left it is.'

Tam tried the first key unsuccessfully. The second fitted the lock. They heard a heavy clunk as she turned the key and, when Tam pushed, the door swung lightly, despite its heavy construction. She clicked her fingers and lights sparkled around the walls and in the ceiling, revealing a room containing armour and weapons and clothing. 'The book says this is the warrior's chamber,' she explained.

Chasse stepped into the room, picked up a silver and gold helmet and rotated it, the light glittering on its surface. 'This is beautiful,' he said. 'I've never seen anything like it.' He put on the helmet and reached for a battle axe. Light sparkled along the blades and the handle shone like gold. The grip was woven with soft black leather.

'I think this is your treasure room,' Tam said, as she admired a dark green cloak draped over a chest.

'This axe is so light,' Chasse remarked. He swung it and spun it in his hand. 'And yet I can feel the weight and force in it. No one has an axe like this.'

'You do,' Tam said. 'It's yours.'

Chasse shook his head. 'I'm not the one who should have this.'

'Why not? You are a dragonwarrior,' Tam asserted.

'There's no honour in being a dragonwarrior after what I saw.' Chasse lowered the axe and rested it against a wooden table. 'If that is what it requires then I'm no dragonwarrior.'

Tam put her hand on his shoulder. 'No,' she said. 'You're right. You are more than a dragonwarrior. You're my brother and your responsibility is to protect our home. This is the path Eric told you was yours to follow. He gave you this chamber to become the protector you are meant to be.'

Chasse scanned the armoury, noting the craftsmanship in everything. It was genuinely a great warrior's trove. He faced Tam. 'I will do what I must, but I will never use these things for what our people did in the past.'

'Eric knew that, like I do,' Tam said. She picked up a thin bladed sword and twirled it, stepped back and announced, 'Time for a challenge.'

'What are you doing?' Chasse asked.

'You could never beat me before,' Tam reminded him. 'I don't think your dragonwarrior training will have helped.'

'Put it down,' Chasse urged.

'Scared?' she taunted.

'Scared I'll hurt you.'

Tam tapped the sword point on Chasse's forearm, saying, 'You're scared I'll hurt you.'

'Tam!' Chasse protested, but she tapped his wrist with her blade and poked out her tongue. 'This is your fault,' he warned, as he chose another sword and tested its weight. 'Are you sure you want to do this?'

Tam smacked her blade against his, grinning as she asked, 'Why are you waiting?'

Two

When Chasse emerged from the forest, the afternoon sun was crouching on the crest of the western ocean, throwing golden rays across the treetops and making the snow glow on the mountain peaks. He crossed Galt's goat pasture, watching a murmuration of black birds sweep and twirl and dive and roll across the forest canopy as they readied to roost. Galt, who was herding his goats into their shelter, waved, and Chasse acknowledged him, but his head was spinning from revelations on the mountain. Tam could do magic. She opened an invisible door and lit a corridor with a click of her fingers. She had keys to a chamber containing a mighty warrior's treasure – armour, weapons, clothing – a gift that the Herbal Man promised to Chasse. The exquisite equipment was unlike any that Chasse encountered and now it belonged to him. What could he tell his father? Would his father expect the hoard to be shared equally among the dragonwarriors? Should he even tell Kevan about the treasure?

He twisted an amber bracelet that Tam gifted him before he left. 'Wear this always,' she advised, when she slid it on his wrist, and she raised her wrist to reveal that she wore an identical bracelet. 'I have one for Jaysin as well,' she informed him.

'What does it do?' Chasse asked.

'It binds us,' she replied. 'It can do much more, but I haven't learned what or how yet.'

'How did you get them?'

'Eric left them for us,' Tam explained. 'Promise me that you will always wear it.'

Chasse nodded and replied, 'I promise,' but the bracelet's purpose remained an elusive mystery.

At the village, Chasse headed for the Warriors' Hall where he was sure he would find his father and the dragonwarriors. Kevan and Jon looked up as he entered and Kevan beckoned for him to join the eleven men at the long central hearth. 'You were meant to be here earlier,' Kevan rebuked, as Chasse sat on a log.

Chasse apologised, expecting to explain why he was late, but Kevan turned to the group to say, 'Eesa and the women are preparing for Procra's Feast in five days. We should have held Procra's Dance by now, but the dragon attack prevented it, and with the others leaving there are no eligible maidens coming of age.' He looked around the circle. 'Besides, of those of us who remain, there is only my son who could choose.'

'And Kurtis,' Jon intervened, nodding to a thickset dragonwarrior on Chasse's left. 'His wife left on the dragonship.'

'She may return,' Raven said, looking at Kurtis.

Kurtis shrugged and replied in a resonant voice, 'I don't think she will, but I'm not interested in taking another wife. Not yet.'

'There are also seven women whose husbands sailed on the ship and left them behind,' Kevan said. 'And there are three single women we should consider eligible.'

'There is only your son,' Jon reminded Kevan.

'One warrior and ten women to choose from,' Kogan teased, grinning at Chasse. 'You're a very lucky young man.' The dragonwarriors chuckled, but Kevan's eyes rested on his son.

Chasse was afraid as he spoke. He needed Tam's resolve, but he feared his father's rebuke. 'I won't choose,' he announced, returning his father's gaze. 'It's not the right time.'

'Are you certain?' Kevan asked.

Chasse nodded. 'Yes.'

'We need a celebration, though,' Raven argued. 'The last few days have interrupted our traditions and way of life. A celebration will bring us together.'

'It is good that Eesa and the women are preparing for Procra's Feast,' Jon suggested. 'Blitzart will sweep down early this winter.'

'How do you know that?' Lynel asked.

'The Dragon Heart prophesied it during last winter's storm,' Jon explained. 'He said it was a new cycle where Blitzart and Shaddho would gain power for a time over Varst's realm and we would see longer, colder and darker winters.'

'Last winter was the hardest I remember,' Raven agreed.

'If the Dragon Heart is correct, then worse is to come,' Jon pronounced gloomily.

'Maybe that's why he ran away with the others,' suggested Kogan.

'Who will be the new Dragon Heart?' asked Lynel. 'We need someone to advise on the ways of Varst and Procra and their children, and to bring blessings and to sing the Words of Passage.'

'The Dragon Heart had no apprentice,' Jon reminded the group. 'No one has learned his ways and his art.'

'There is much for us to discuss and do,' Kevan agreed. 'We must prepare for Blitzart's coming. We should merge the celebrations for Procra into one feast this time. Without the Dragon Heart to guide us, we must use our time wisely.' He paused before adding, 'And we must find a new Dragon Heart.'

A cold mountain breeze whispered between the wooden buildings and the few occupied huts glowed with hearth fires and oil lamps when Chasse emerged from the Warriors' Hall with his father and Jon.

'You will continue training in the Warriors' Hall after Procra's Feast,' Kevan informed Chasse as they walked towards their home, and to Jon he said, 'Every man will train during winter. When the others return, we will need to be ready.'

'I will ensure we are ready, Dragon Head,' Jon affirmed.

Kevan clapped Jon on the shoulder. 'You are a good man. Thank you.' After Jon bade Kevan and Chasse goodnight and headed for his cottage, Kevan placed a hand on Chasse's shoulder, and asked, 'Is your sister down from the mountain?'

'No,' Chasse replied.

'The Herbal Man is gone,' Kevan said. 'She has no reason to be there.'

'She is taking care of his goats,' Chasse explained.

'She can bring them down to Galt's pasture. She should be helping her mother.'

Chasse roused his courage to tell his father that Tam was accepting more important responsibilities than tending goats, but before he could speak a piercing cry rent the night and sent a shiver up his spine.

'Banni,' Kevan said calmly. 'Her child is gravely ill. She was bitten by a black snake this afternoon.'

Chasse turned towards Banni's cottage, pulled by his sister's love for her friend, but Kevan took hold of his arm, saying, 'The women will see to this.' As his father spoke, Chasse spotted two torch-bearing figures approaching Banni's cottage. The door opened, light flooded out, and the door closed after the women entered, followed by another cry and a choked sob.

'Can we do anything?' Chasse asked.

'Wait at home,' Kevan replied. 'That's all we can do.'

Chasse followed Kevan up the rise onto the Watersdrop bridge. He knew Tam would want to be with her friend, and as he looked up at the mountain, thinking of his sister, a small bright light appeared and disappeared between the trees, descending the path that he followed earlier. 'Tam is coming,' he murmured.

'How do you know?' Kevan asked.

'There,' Chasse replied, and he pointed towards the light moving through the lower forest.

'The child is healing!' Eesa announced when she entered the cottage, where her husband and eldest son waited expectantly.

'A good sign,' said Kevan. 'Varst smiles upon us.'

'Procra smiles upon us,' Eesa corrected. 'Where's Jaysin?'

'He went to sleep a while ago,' Kevan replied.

'It feels like it's almost dawn,' said Chasse, yawning.

'It is,' Eesa confirmed. She hoisted a water bucket onto the kitchen table and began to scrub her arms.

'Is Tam still with Banni?' Chasse asked.

Eesa looked up, surprised. 'How did you know your sister was there?'

'We saw her light coming down the mountain,' Chasse explained.

Eesa looked at Kevan, who confirmed the fact, before she explained events. 'She arrived with a potion and herbs and used them to help Jara. I did not know the girl had learned so much from the old man.'

Chasse eased past his mother and opened the door.

'Where are you going?' Eesa asked.

'To see if I can help,' Chasse replied.

'There is nothing for a man to do,' Eesa told him. 'Caring for Banni and her child at this moment is not the place for a warrior.'

'Wise words,' Kevan agreed. 'You should go to bed, Chasse. You'll have plenty of work to do later today, so I advise you to sleep before I call for you.'

Chasse felt compelled to help Tam, but his parents maintained their commanding gazes, so he acquiesced and said, 'I want a quick breath of air before I go to bed.' Kevan nodded permission and Chasse stepped outside.

At the edge of the cottage garden, listening to water cascading over

Watersdrop and the ocean roar against the cliff, the energy of the waves reverberating through the earth, Chasse felt Shaddho's dark wings enfolding the world and he shivered. The golden dragon, Claryssa, and her awesome demonstration of power before she and the Herbal Man flew west, crystallised for him the immortal supremacy of the great dragons of the Harbin pantheon; Arkamroth the sun dragon, Blitzart the winter dragon and Shaddho the dragon of death. The people of Harbin lived a fragile existence at the mercy of the great dragons and they were grateful that Varst, the creator, held the dragons from wreaking random havoc on the village. But their presence was everywhere; Arkamroth in the sun and fire, Blitzart in the winter chill, and Shaddho in the darkness.

His father urged Chasse to sleep, but since his first fateful summer journey as a dragonwarrior sleep only opened Shaddho's jaws in Chasse's dreams where images of the slaughter on the southern shores tormented him and left him wide-eyed in the darkest hours.

He was afraid to sleep.

And the talk in the Warriors' Hall of the cancelled Procra's Dance and the loss of Kerryn ached in his heart. He was certain that he would choose her for his wife when the feast was held, but she fled south with her family on the dragonship after the wizard and his dragon fought the Dragon Fang and he knew that she might never return, leaving him to wonder if he would ever choose a partner.

And there were the marvels on the mountain and the secret that Tam and he were keeping: the dragon egg and the wizard's treasures.

Sleep was impossible.

Chasse turned from the ocean to stare at the dark silhouette of Dragon Mountain looming over Harbin outlined by the moon with silver light. Soon, the rising sun would turn the silver to gold as Arkamroth chased Shaddho to the west, and the fishermen, and Galt the goatherd, would rise from their beds and set to their early morning duties.

Chasse yawned, shook his arms and rolled his shoulders. His body ached from the day's exertion. Exhaustion pressed down. He needed sleep but he did not want sleep. Sleep was the enemy waiting to unleash his troubles, his nightmares, but he could no longer fight sleep. Dejected, he trudged into the cottage.

'Father wants you at the jetty.'

Chasse squinted against the light.

'He wants you there now.'

Chasse blinked and recognised Jaysin pulling his right arm. 'I'm awake,' he protested.

'Good,' Jaysin said and added, 'I'm going.'

Chasse sat up in his bedding, rubbed his eyes and face, and yawned. Dull light filtering through the smudged window glass made him blink. He dressed, brushed out his red hair and tied it in a ponytail, and entered the main room. Finding it empty, he poured a mug of water from the pitcher, drank, and stepped outside.

He looked for Jaysin, but his little brother had vanished into the village or up the hillside. Clouds pressed low across the harbour and shrouded the mountains and a cold breeze drove grey waves towards the bay's northern reaches. Fishermen were mooring their boats and offloading their meagre catches. His father was at the end of the jetty with Raven and Lynel.

Chasse stepped back into the cottage, took his hide coat from the hook at the back of the door to rug himself against the chill air, and walked across the bridge and down through the village to the jetty. He answered greetings from fishermen and waved to women who were busily scaling and gutting fish on a bench near the shore.

'Most of the day is already gone!' Kevan called as Chasse walked across the jetty planks. 'You're not a bear. Hibernation comes after Procra's

Feast.'

Raven and Lynel were grinning as Chasse reached them, and Raven said, 'Your father was already busy when the sun rose.'

Chasse ignored the taunts and asked, 'How is Banni and her child?'

'Nothing's changed since last night,' Kevan told him. 'When we are done here, you can tell Tamesan she has work to do for her mother, once Banni is settled. For now, we have our own work.' He pointed across the bay. 'The Dragon Fang each take a day's turn keeping watch on White Eagle Ledge. Kurtis is there today. Tomorrow is your turn. You'll be here before sunrise waiting for Ashka to row you to the promontory. He will fetch you back at sunset. Until the winter storms arrive, we will set watch in case someone sails into the bay, or our people return.'

'Are you expecting the others to come back?' Chasse asked.

Kevan shrugged. 'If they only sailed a short way in fear of the dragon, they might return before Blitzart's breath freezes the world, but if they sailed south to gather more warriors to bring against the dragon they will not return until next summer.' He looked towards the mouth of Harbin Bay. 'Whether they return or not, we must be vigilant against anyone coming into our waters.' He turned to Chasse. 'It is time to restore order in Harbin. The Dragon Fang will assemble in the Warriors' Hall from tonight and sleep there, as we always do. Your training will continue. There are traditions to uphold. You are not yet fully a man.'

'I will see Tamesan before I move my belongings back to the Hall,' said Chasse.

'And give her my message,' Kevan insisted. 'She must help her mother as soon as she can. Now, go with Jon to cut wood for the winter stockpile.'

Chasse walked from the jetty, noting rain creeping across the distant ridge above White Eagle Ledge, and he shivered at the thought that it could be raining tomorrow when he took his turn on watch. At the beach, he deviated towards Banni's cottage. He knew Tam would not listen to what he had to say on his father's behalf. The Herbal Man's treasure was far too important for her to abandon over winter. If he could, he would stay with her to guard the dragon egg, but he knew Kevan would never allow him to do that. He had to find a way to retrieve the Herbal Man's gifts and explain them to the other men. There were more weapons and items in the chamber than he could ever use, so he would share them, but first he wanted to choose gear for himself.

Alys emerged from Banni's cottage as Chasse approached. She smiled demurely, and said, 'Your sister is very wise in the ways of healing. She learned a great deal from the Herbal Man.'

Chasse acknowledged Alys before he opened the door and peered around the edge.

'Chasse!' Tam whispered, and she gestured for him to enter quietly. Chasse stepped inside before he realised that Banni was sitting in her bed breast-feeding her daughter. 'Sorry,' he apologised and he went to withdraw, but Tam said, 'Don't go, Chasse.'

'I don't mind,' Banni reassured him. 'Come closer and meet Jara properly.'

Chasse hesitated. Women breastfeeding, discretely allowing their babies to suckle under the cover of shawls or swaddling while they sat and watched their friends at work, was not uncommon in Harbin and he was familiar with his mother feeding Jaysin when he was a boy, but he felt awkward in Banni's presence and he couldn't grasp why.

'Come on,' Tam urged, and she took Chasse's arm to lead him to Banni's bedside. 'Look how beautiful she is.'

Chasse studied Jara's cherubic, pudgy face and tiny fist pressed against Banni, keeping his focus on the child and not on the breast, but he did notice how pale and worn Banni appeared. 'You named her after Jared?' he asked, although he already knew the answer.

Banni smiled as she answered, 'Yes.'

'She's very sweet,' Chasse offered, unsure of what he was meant to say about a child. 'She is cured of the snake bite?'

Banni looked at Tam and smiled, before she answered Chasse with, 'Jara is already much better. Your sister is sent by Procra herself to heal us.'

'We'll leave you to finish feeding,' said Tam, as she pulled on Chasse's arm again. Outside the cottage, she asked, 'What message does Father have for me?'

'You know he sent me?' Chasse asked.

Tam laughed and replied, 'Tell Tamesan that she is required to help her mother prepare for Procra's Dance.'

Chasse grinned. 'Almost,' he confirmed, 'except that there won't be Procra's Dance because there's no one to do the choosing.'

'What about you?' Tam asked. 'It's your turn.'

'And who would I choose?'

Tam met her brother's challenging blue-eyed gaze, nodded, and said quietly, 'No. I guess not.'

'It's all right,' Chasse assured her, accepting Tam's curiosity. 'I'm not ready to choose.'

'You would have chosen Kerryn.'

Chasse shook his head. 'I'm not so sure I would, now.'

'Why?' Tam asked.

'Things have changed,' he said. Remembering his earlier sense of loss for Kerryn, he glanced up at Dragon Mountain and added, 'We have – responsibilities.'

'I will watch over the egg during winter,' Tam assured him.

'Have you asked Father and Mother?'

Tam smiled. 'They will say no. You know that as much as I do. If we tell Father there is a dragon egg on the mountain, he will want to smash it. He wanted to go up the mountain when he learned that Claryssa was there. The only reason no one else has gone looking is because we told them that Eric and Claryssa left for good.'

'But what if Father stops you from going?' Chasse argued.

'He can't stop me,' Tam said. 'I come and go as I need.'

'You know that's not true,' Chasse warned.

'I'm not a little girl, Chasse. I promised Eric I would protect his gifts to us, and I will.'

Unconvinced, Chasse shook his head and asked, 'How will you persuade Father? Or Mother?'

'I don't think I can persuade them,' Tam replied. 'But I have to do what I must.'

'You can't stay on the mountain alone,' Chasse insisted.

'I won't be alone,' Tam said.

'I can't stay with you,' Chasse argued. 'I want to, I really do, but-'

'You are a dragonwarrior, a member of the Dragon Fang,' she finished for him. 'You have to stay here. There is a lot of work for you and the other men to do, and I need you to keep an eye on Banni and Jara while I'm on the mountain.'

'Then why won't you be alone?' Chasse asked. 'The egg?'

'No,' Tam replied. 'Jaysin will be with me.'

'That's impossible,' Chasse asserted. 'Mother will never let him stay with you.'

'I won't ask her,' Tam said. 'But when the time comes, and she asks where Jaysin is, you will tell her he's with me and that he is safe and learning new skills.'

'Father will come up the mountain,' Chasse said. 'He'll be furious.'

'He won't come up the mountain. Blitzart is bringing a long and bitter winter and it will begin earlier than anyone expects. That's why you have so much work ahead of you. Gather all the food and firewood you can, and quickly.'

'Jon told us that the Dragon Heart prophesied a bad winter,' Chasse recalled. 'Did you hear that?'

'No,' Tam said. 'Eric told me.'

'When?'

'Before I came down the mountain last evening.'

'He's here?' Chasse asked.

'No,' Tam said. 'You saw him leave.'

Chasse was puzzled by his sister's cryptic reply. 'Then how did you speak to him?'

'Through the Seeing Waters,' Tam explained. 'The Seeing Waters allow people to speak across great distances and see things, sometimes things that are to come.'

Still confused, Chasse asked, 'I thought you said the Herbal Man and Claryssa were dying?'

'They are,' Tam confirmed, 'but not yet. They're tired and have found a place to be at peace. That's all they ever wanted here.'

A voice calling Chasse's name interrupted and Chasse saw Jon's lithe figure approaching. 'The Dragon Head said I'd find you here,' Jon explained as he arrived and he handed an axe to Chasse. 'We have wood to collect.' He acknowledged Tam with a polite smile, and told her, 'Eesa wants to see you in the Long Hall.'

'I'll go there now,' Tam replied. She smiled cheekily at Chasse and headed for the centre of the village.

As Jon watched Tam go, he said, 'Young Marron was sorely disappointed to be rejected by your sister.'

'She was never going to accept anyone's offer,' Chasse replied, hefting the axe onto his shoulder. 'And she wasn't of age. My sister is a free spirit, and she likes it that way.'

'That doesn't sit easy with your parents,' Jon observed, as the pair walked to the trees. 'There are traditions and expectations.'

Chasse wanted to say that he saw enough in the past weeks to know some Harbin traditions were hollow, but he shifted the conversation to the looming prospect of a long and bitter winter.

Three

Chasse pulled his leather overcoat tighter around his neck and chest and huddled against the wet rock, frustrated by droplets dripping from his hood onto his cheeks. The rain was settling in, turning the world grey, and he saw no point in keeping watch on White Eagle Ledge when he couldn't see a stone's throw across the isthmus.

He woke before dawn in the Warriors' Hall, as his father ordered, and met Ashka at the jetty so that the fisherman could row him to the promontory to take the role of sea-watcher for the day, but as the boat slid through the still water the morning air was brittle, thick fog shrouded Dragon Mountain, and the sun was barely a glowing smudge through the gloomy clouds.

'I wanted to be a dragonwarrior when I was a lad,' Ashka said through his straggly grey beard as he pulled on the oars.

'Why didn't you become a dragonwarrior?' Chasse asked between yawns.

'I was born to be a fisherman and that's what I am,' Ashka replied. 'Just like you were born to be a dragonwarrior.'

'You could have asked to be a dragonwarrior.'

'And risk the wrath of Varst and my father?' Ashka asked. 'Hardly, lad. I didn't dare ask. No one dares. That's the order of things.'

Chasse understood. A natural order existed in Harbin. His father frequently reminded him that the village survived through generations because people fulfilled their allotted obligations and destinies, and that Tam, despite the good she was doing for people, was disrupting the order. He said the dragon's appearance was clear proof of the havoc she caused by her disobedience. If she wasn't the Dragon Head's daughter, she would have been banished. Chasse did not tell Tam what Kevan said, although he guessed their father expressed his displeasure to her in private conversations. If he was being berated by their father, he would be ashamed, whereas Tam seemed to care little about what Kevan, or Eesa, thought about her wandering on the mountain and learning the ways of the Herbal Man.

He pondered the impending combined Procra's Feast and season leading into winter. The more that he considered Kerryn the more he realised he might not have chosen her. She would be a good wife, a good partner for a dragonwarrior because she would be compliant, but she lacked his sister's spirit, and he no longer thought he wanted a partner who was simply pretty and compliant. A woman like Banni had more appeal because she showed resilience and determination in raising Jara alone, and he knew that his sister admired her. Perhaps if Kerryn was more like Banni...

The rain intensified, clamouring on the rocks, forcing Chasse to curl tighter under the overhang, his boots caught in the torrent pouring from the stone lip. He shivered, his teeth chattering, and he reached into a cleft by his side that was filling with runoff to extract an ivory horn which he upended to empty of water. Raindrops beading on his hood, he studied the horn's etchings of warrior and dragon figures and symbols portraying a glorious past, his fingers tracing the cold, wet surface. 'This is not a warrior's life,' he muttered, staring through the rain. 'Is this what we must endure, Ecg?' he asked of the Harbin god of strength. 'Is it to be cold and wet and death and abandonment and endless work all the time?' The thrumming rain gave him no answer. He shivered again, hugged the horn to his chest and closed his eyes.

The same nightmare. Trapped within a dark, swarming press of warriors, being forced towards a wall of raging flames, he was never sure whether he was really hearing screams and battle cries or just believing the noise should be there. Because the nightmare was familiar, he knew what was happening and what would happen next and he did not want to repeat the events, but he could not escape. He was afraid, and yet he remained mildly curious, as if his spirit had to know what transpired. The press parted, and a bedraggled woman reached for him with desperate arms, eyes begging, mouth open as if about to speak before an axe cleaved her face. And an old man looked up from the ground, face caked in dirt and blood, and a spear impaled him. And the swarm rushed in, and the woman was consumed, and he was pushed and shoved and, no matter how hard he tried to swing his sword to fight off the writhing bodies, his arms were dead and useless, his stomach churned, and the scene morphed into a marsh of corpses and bloodied water and panic. He was trying to run in the marsh, but his boots were caught by tendrils threatening to drag him down, and the flames closed in. The dragonship's prow loomed out of the smoke and mist miasma, taunting him to reach it, but he couldn't get to it because the marsh was holding him. And then he was clambering aboard the ship, smelling fear and panic, and Marron slipped, and his arm fell between the ship's hull and the jetty, and Marron's face contorted in agony.

Chasse woke, kicking frantically, heart racing, escaping the dream's clutches but not its terror when he saw that his world was dark, damp, and swamped in the noise of waves surging against the rocks. A gull cried through the fog. Chasse wiped moisture from his face to focus. A light bobbed in the ocean. The gull cry became a voice calling his name. He eased from under the overhang, muscles stiff, and stood in the cold evening air, numbness permeating his cramped legs. Staring at the swaying light, he comprehended that Ashka was there to fetch him to Harbin. He returned the ivory horn to the cleft and climbed down to the verge where the waves heaved and foamed, grateful the rain was no longer falling.

'I can't come any closer to the rocks!' Ashka yelled above the din. 'You have to swim a few strokes away from them!'

Reluctant as he was, the chill deep in his bones, Chasse plunged into the heaving water and swam to the skiff, where Ashka hauled him aboard, the boat rocking precariously. Chasse huddled in the bow, surprised that he slept so long on White Eagle Ledge, while Ashka rowed across the bay towards the village lights.

Saturated and shivering, Chasse entered the Warriors' Hall to find the eleven dragonwarriors sitting at the hearth with three additional men.

Kevan rose at Chasse's entrance and said gruffly, 'Get dry clothing and join us here.'

Glad to be allowed to change out of his sodden clothes, Chasse went to his sleeping space and put on fresh garments, but he was curious as to who had joined the warriors in the Hall. When he returned to the hearth, he recognised two men – dragonwarriors who fled when Eric and Claryssa routed them on the mountain.

'You know Alan and Petar,' said Kevan.

Chasse acknowledged the warriors. Alan was the young warrior who he disarmed, bound and left on the mountainside the fateful day Tam and he warned the Herbal Man that the Dragon Fang were coming for Claryssa. Petar was an older, red bearded man who, Chasse recalled, liked to keep to himself.

'And this is Suran,' Kevan added.

Suran was dark-haired with a trimmed dark beard and tanned skin, the look of a southerner. His build suggested youth, but his expression and features belonged to an older man. Suran met Chasse's gaze without a smile or acknowledgement.

'They sailed in while you were meant to be on watch,' Kevan informed Chasse, and the severity of his gaze and accusation made Chasse tighten in the pit of his stomach. His point made, Kevan addressed the guests. 'We will make spaces for you to share the winter with us, and you can help prepare for the return of our people.'

Chasse sat and listened to the men's conversation, although he had clearly missed the discussions around what transpired when the dragonship sailed away in fear of the dragon, and they must have already discussed why the three men came to Harbin. He would ask his father to tell him later, or in the morning, what he had missed. For now, exhaustion ached through the fibre of his muscles and he was hungry. As if reading his mind, Jon rose and brought a bowl of goat meat stew, which Chasse eagerly and gratefully accepted, but while the warm food sated his hunger it made his body beg for sleep, so that when the hearth talk became mundane speculation about the coming winter and observations on the need to prepare for a harsh and long period Chasse excused himself and sank onto his bedding where sleep quickly enfolded him.

'Get up, lad, and bring a spear!' Jon ordered.

Chasse sat up groggily.

'Bring a bag of dried fruit and nuts. We will be waiting outside.'

Chasse threw aside his bedclothes and stretched, twisting his back and wrists as he stood. The sleep was solid, and the nightmare only visited once and so gently that he only recalled that it came but did not disrupt his sleep. Sun rays angling across the open space and filtering from the smoke hole in the roof revealed he was the only one remaining in the Warriors' Hall. He dressed, aware that his clothes were cold and smelt damp. He filled a leather bag with a handful of dried fruit and handful of seeds and nuts from the store, selected a spear from the weapon rack and headed outside.

A low blanket of mist covered the water across the bay and sunrise gilded the mountain flanks. The fishermen were unravelling and setting their nets, their breath steaming in the cold air, while their wives set up the scaling tables and buckets in preparation to clean the catch that the men were sure to bring ashore within a couple of hours.

'Varst is smiling on us this morning,' said Jon, as Chasse joined him and Raven. 'We only need Fler to be generous with her creatures today.' He handed Chasse a large leather bag.

'Where are we going?' Chasse asked.

'Hunting bear,' Raven replied.

'Have you hunted bear before?' Jon asked.

'No,' Chasse confessed.

'Then, this morning, you will learn a new set of skills,' Jon assured him. 'Follow us and move quietly.'

Chasse fell in behind the two men as they headed to Harbin's northern fringe, keen to be initiated into the Dragon Fang's annual hunting responsibilities. Bear meat and fat were two of many staples to tide the warriors and people through winter, along with goat meat and milk, fish, herbs, dried fruits, seeds and nuts. While cutting wood and keeping watch on White Eagle Ledge were necessary, if mundane, duties, hunting was daring and risky and a brown or black bear pelt cloak was a symbol of manhood. If he was lucky this morning, he might claim a pelt as his own.

Traipsing across the grass and entering the tree line at the base of the first rise, he wondered what his father and the three men who arrived the previous day were doing and where they were. He expected his father to admonish him for failing to keep watch and allowing the men's boat to enter the bay unheralded, but Kevan didn't wake him, and he left the Hall before Chasse was roused by Jon. Chasse assumed that his father was either very angry or he was punishing him silently. He wanted to ask Jon and Raven what occurred when Alan and his companions arrived, but Jon insisted on silent travel into the woods, leaving Chasse without answers.

He trailed Jon and Raven up the slope into the denser forest, watchful and wary that his spear did not brush against bushes or drag across the loose shale to make sound that might alert animals and birds. Raven stooped to search the earth for spoor, pinched and sniffed a sample of damp soil, rose, and he indicated that they should head diagonally across the slope.

The northern mountain face was familiar to Chasse. Tam and he were frequently warned by their parents to avoid it because it was bear territory.

'The bears mind their business, and we mind ours,' Kevan told them.

'If we are meant to be minding our business, why do you hunt the bears in Autumn?' Tam questioned, always wanting to know more than anyone.

'Natural balance,' Kevan told her. 'Procra and Fler provide the bears to sustain us, so long as we don't drive them away and don't kill them indiscriminately.'

'Is the same rule true for the bears?' Tam asked.

Chasse smiled at the memory. He recalled his father's exasperated disbelief that Tam could dare ask such a question and their mother intervening and urging Tam to accompany her to the Long Hall to alleviate the deteriorating conversation between father and daughter. That's why he loved his sister. She had a special courage and a mind that did not accept the status quo without questioning it.

A firm grip on his arm snapped Chasse back to the moment. Raven gestured for him to squat and look to his right. Through the mass of leaves and branches, he saw Jon crouched behind a large bush observing a glade. Moments later, a brown bear emerged, sniffing the air and tentatively moving into the open. Raven pointed to Chasse's right and indicated that Chasse should shift several paces in that direction. Raven held his fingers to his lips to emphasise the need for silence before he slinked to Jon's left.

Heart pounding, Chasse crept through the trees, ensuring his boots didn't scuff the earth or crush twigs, keeping a wary eye on the bear, and, when he reached a thick bush at the glade's edge, he hunkered down, gripping his spear, reminding himself of the throwing technique he repeatedly practised long before he entered the Warriors' Hall. He was nervous because practising how to throw and impale stationery targets was not the same as attacking a live, moving animal.

As he focused on the bear, a second creature emerged from the undergrowth; a brown cub padded into the glade and pushed beneath its mother's belly. The mother bear licked the cub's head before she stepped over it and sniffed the air again. A swarm of tiny gnats whirled over a bush to the bear's right.

Jon gestured for withdrawal. Chasse eased from his position, observing the bear as he navigated a path to meet with the other two warriors, and they moved silently away from the glade and circumnavigated the area, Raven resuming his tracking role.

Chasse knew the lore from his training. The only bears to be hunted were males. Killing females and cubs was dishonourable and threatened the viability of the bear community, but the encounter with the mother and cub was promising. The bears were foraging, getting ready for winter. There would be a boar somewhere.

A short while later, Raven halted again and indicated to Jon and Chasse to spread right and left. As he crept to the right, Chasse spotted their quarry squatting in a stand of Purpleberry bushes, savouring a handful of berries in his right paw. The black bear seemed pleased to be enjoying a rare feast of forest fruit, but he stopped eating and sniffed and surveyed the immediate undergrowth as if he was aware the hunters were stalking him. The air was tranquil. A small green bird flitted through the branches above the bear. Chasse stood perfectly still.

A spear flashed through the trees and struck the bear's right shoulder and the bear roared and reared. Chasse responded by hurling his spear at the animal's exposed chest, but to his chagrin the spear failed to penetrate the bear's hide and bounced harmlessly into the underbrush. Raven leapt forward and plunged the point of his spear deep into the bear's midriff, but the bear smacked him aside, sending the warrior tumbling into the bushes in a flurry of leaves. Hampered by the spear, the bear dropped to all fours and bellowed as the shaft twisted and stabbed deeper. Chasse unhitched his hand-axe and sprinted at the bear, dodging its sweeping claws and striking its left shoulder before he leapt to the side and out of the creature's reach. In pain, struggling to regain its balance, the bear didn't see Jon coming from behind. The warrior struck the bear's head twice with his axe, forcing the bear to collapse on its side. With a flurry of blows from Jon and Chasse, and a last push on Raven's spear by Jon, the fight was over.

'Good work,' Jon commended, clapping Chasse on the shoulder as he caught his breath. 'See to Raven.'

Raven was seated on his butt in the bushes, wiping blood from long raking wounds across his right ribs and chest. His jacket and jerkin were shredded 'You need a healer,' Chasse said, as he squatted beside the warrior.

Raven grinned and replied, 'A little water, some herbal compress, and I'll have trophy scars to brag about.' He shifted to a serious expression to add, 'But I ruined my favourite winter jacket.'

'Come and learn how to dress a bear, Chasse,' Jon called. 'Fler has gifted us a healthy, rich animal. This pelt will make a fine replacement winter coat for you, Raven.'

Chasse squatted beside Jon and the warrior handed him a sharp knife with a carved bone handle depicting a dragon's claw. 'This winter you will craft your own hunting knife. Every dragonwarrior does so after his first journey on the dragonship. Your hunting knife is a sacred tool that will be blessed by the Dragon Heart and you will carry it for the rest of your life.'

He drew another hunting knife from his belt and held it before Chasse. 'This is the knife I made when I was your age. I keep it keen and use it every day.'

'Then whose knife is this?' Chasse asked, turning the one in his hand.

'My father's,' Jon replied. 'One day, you will keep Kevan's knife for him.' He stopped to look at Raven, who sat beside Chasse, clutching his side. Blood seeped between his fingers. 'Will you be all right?'

'I will do what I can not to die,' Raven replied curtly. 'Let's see if you can teach Kevan's son how to dress a bear.'

Jon nodded and said to Chasse, 'First, help me lay the bear on its back.'

With the bear in position, Jon instructed Chasse as he made a long and precise incision from the tail to the bear's jaw and continued with deft cuts along the bear's limbs to methodically remove the hide. He asked Chasse to hold and help him turn the corpse as he shifted to different body parts. The sun climbed higher while the laborious process continued, and Jon asked Chasse to fetch water and tend to Raven frequently throughout the procedure.

'I am not a child,' Raven complained.

'Neither are you Nakiades,' Jon said. 'You've lost enough blood for one man. We should take you to the Hall.'

'Finish the task,' Raven urged. 'I'm hungry.'

After the hide was removed, the three warriors ate nuts and dried berries, and Jon checked that Raven was not worsening from his injury before he set to butchering the bear into meat portions, again teaching Chasse how to cut what parts and where, and guiding him to slice sections into equal portions for sharing as they steadily filled the leather bags that the three warriors brought on the hunt.

The middle of the day was well past, and the butchering task half-done, before Jon wiped his hands and asked Chasse to return to the village to fetch two more men. 'There's too much for us to carry and Raven won't be useful for the heavy task,' he said. 'We will probably have to carry him down too.' Raven protested, but Jon reiterated his instruction and sent Chasse on the errand.

Chasse cut across the brow of the northern slope, descending steadily, stopping only to step onto a flat rock on the western side where he took in the spectacular bay view. The plinth was a place he knew Tam frequented because it also allowed a view up the mountain slope towards the plateau where the Herbal Man's hut stood before it was incinerated. The clouds were higher than when he left the Warriors' Hall in the morning and they carried a bruised hue, reminding him the seasons were changing and the rains were coming. He looked up the slope, wondering if his sister was in the village helping Eesa or in the Herbal Man's cave learning magic, and when he shielded his eyes against the dull sunlight he noticed two figures weaving between rocks on the path leading onto the plateau. His nerves jangled. The figures were too big to be Tam or Jaysin. Someone was higher up the mountain than anyone normally ventured, apart from Tam or himself. *Who?* he wondered. *What are they looking for?*

He left the rock and hurried down the mountain, running hard, leaping over fallen branches and rocks, startling animals and birds as he descended, until he broke into full stride across the goat pasture. He found Kurtis, Lynel and Kogan stacking wood against the wall of the Long Hall and he asked them to help Jon and Raven.

'You need to show us the way,' said Lynel when he realised that Chasse was turning to go.

'On the northern slope, a third of the way towards the end of the tree line,' Chasse replied.

'That's a lot of country,' Kogan reminded him.

'Then start,' Chasse begged. 'Head up the northern slope. I'll catch up and show you. I have to find my sister.'

'We'll wait,' Lynel said, gesturing with his thumb at the Long Hall. 'Your sister's inside.'

Chasse ran to the front door and entered to find the Long Hall bustling with activity as the women prepared for Procra's Feast. When he spotted Tamesan sitting with Eesa, weaving garlands of blue, purple and orange flowers into strands of dried leaves, he acknowledged his mother and said, 'Tam, I need to speak to you.'

'Secrets?' Eesa asked.

Tam put down her flowers and accompanied Chasse away from the earshot of others. 'What's wrong?' she asked.

'Someone is searching the plateau.'

Despite Eesa's adamant protests, Tam excused herself from her task in the Long Hall, strode out of Harbin and headed up the mountain. Chasse started after her, but Lynel called him back, reminding him that he was meant to lead them to Jon and Raven. It irked Chasse to leave Tam to climb to the plateau alone, but he had no choice. Frustrated, he told the men to bring leather sacks to carry the fresh bear meat, before he jogged along the beach, followed by the warriors, and began ascending the northern slope. The climb felt like an eternity. Tam was taking a risk heading for whoever was on the plateau and he should be protecting her.

By the time he reached Jon and Raven, Chasse was decided. 'I have to go higher,' he told Jon.

'But we need your help here,' Jon said.

'I brought the others to help,' Chasse replied. 'My father wants me to find out who is on the plateau.'

Jon laughed and said, 'Your father is on the plateau. He went up there this morning with Alan and Suran.'

'Why?' Chasse asked.

'Alan wanted to show Suran the damage caused by the dragon.'

Flustered by the explanation, Chasse floundered for an excuse before saying, 'Father expects me to meet him.'

'He said nothing to us about that,' Jon replied.

'Tam told me when I spoke to her,' Chasse lied. He looked to Lynel and improvised. 'Lynel saw me speak to her.'

'He's telling the truth,' Lynel confirmed, looking up from Kogan who was tending to Raven's injuries. 'He kept us waiting.'

Jon said, 'Then you best go.'

Chasse thanked Jon and ran into the forest and climbed towards the plateau, his weary legs slowing his progress. Though he was now less concerned for Tam's safety knowing that their father was on the plateau, he was driven by a nagging disquiet something was afoot that threatened the Herbal Man's legacy. *Why would a stranger like Suran be interested in what happened with a dragon in Harbin?*

Not concentrating, Chasse veered around a pile of rocks and almost collided with Suran and Alan. The three stared at each other before Alan laughed, and said, 'This feels familiar. I still owe you for that little embarrassment that you and your sister inflicted on me the last time we met like this.'

'Why are you up here?' Chasse asked. 'Where's Father?'

'One question at a time,' said Alan.

'Where's Father?' Chasse asked.

'Your father is looking for your sister,' Suran said with a measured deep voice in his unfamiliar accent.

'We saw her further up this path, but she ran into the trees,' Alan added. 'Kevan told us to head back down and he went to find her alone.' He chuckled. 'She's hard work, your sister.'

'And, to answer your second question, we are up here because I wanted to see the truth behind the stories that your people told when they came to our town,' Suran said.

'They didn't believe we were attacked by a dragon,' Alan explained. 'That's why they sent Suran back with Petar and me – so Suran could see

35

the truth for himself.'

'There's nothing left to see,' Chasse argued. 'The dragon's gone.'

Suran glanced at Alan before saying, 'The dragon had to be living somewhere. And we know dragons have treasures.'

'There's no treasure,' Chasse refuted.

Suran raised an eyebrow. 'Really? How do you know?'

'We searched,' Chasse replied.

'Who?' Alan asked. 'Who searched? No one we asked last night in the Warriors' Hall searched up here.'

'I searched,' Chasse said. 'Tam and I searched.'

Alan laughed, shaking his head. 'You expect me to believe anything that you or your sister would say about the Herbal Man or his dragon? You were the ones hiding them.' He put his hand on his sword hilt and leaned forward menacingly. 'And I bet you're hiding the treasure now.'

Chasse stepped back. If it came to a fight, he thought he might be able to beat Alan, but Suran was an unknown entity, and the way he stood, balanced and assured, suggested that he was an experienced and capable warrior. Chasse did not want a fight. 'There's no treasure,' he repeated anxiously. 'The old man destroyed everything before he left. If you've been on the plateau, you've seen that for yourself.'

'The dragon wasn't hiding in a little hut,' Suran said. 'There's a very big cave up there, somewhere, and I will find it.'

Approaching footsteps interrupted the confrontation and Kevan appeared, descending the path. 'I can't find a daughter, but I find a son,' he said, grinning as he looked at Chasse 'You are meant to be hunting bears.'

'We killed one earlier,' Chasse replied. 'Raven was injured. Jon and the others are carrying the meat and pelt to the village.'

'Then, well done!' Kevan declared. 'Tonight, we will celebrate a good hunt. And tomorrow night is Procra's Dance.'

'I thought we were holding Procra's Feast,' Chasse said.

Kevan laughed and threw an arm over Alan's shoulder, saying, 'This young man is eligible to take a wife and he has a woman in mind. A match is cause for celebration.'

'I thought you would choose a wife,' Alan said to Chasse.

'There is no one to choose,' Chasse replied. He turned to Kevan to ask, 'Did you talk with Tam?'

'I couldn't find her,' Kevan said. 'Do you know where she was headed?'

'No,' Chasse replied. 'But I will keep looking for you.'

'No,' said Kevan. 'You will come and learn how to prepare for Procra's Dance and Feast.'

'I'm not choosing,' Chasse argued. He glanced at Alan, wondering who Alan intended to choose out of the eligible women because no one came readily to mind.

'That doesn't mean you can't learn how it's done,' Kevan retorted. 'Down we go.'

Four

Finding a moment to speak to his father was awkward with the men in the Warriors' Hall, but when Kevan headed for the entrance Chasse put aside his sharpening stone and spear and followed Kevan outside. Evening was settling across Harbin, the sun dissolving in the west, the sky streaked with patches of purple and cobalt, stars glittering softly.

Chasse shivered. It was going to be a cold night. 'Father,' he called to the broad silhouetted back.

Kevan turned. 'Have you finished sharpening the spear?'

'I have to talk to you.'

'I'm meeting your mother,' Kevan said. 'Walk with me.'

Glad to be invited, Chasse fell into step with his father as they crossed the centre of the village, heading for the bridge over Watersdrop. 'What do you want to talk about?' Kevan asked.

'Do you know why Alan and Petar and Suran are here?' Chasse asked.

'To find the dragon's treasure,' Kevan replied. 'Why?'

'There is no treasure,' said Chasse.

Kevan stopped to face Chasse. 'How do you know?'

'If there was treasure, Tam would know where it is. I've been with her and we haven't found treasure.'

'And you wouldn't lie to protect Tam or what she knows,' Kevan said slowly.

Chasse flinched at his father's sarcasm. Kevan so often doubted his children's words against adults. 'I will always protect my sister,' he asserted.

'Even against the Dragon Fang?' Kevan challenged. When Chasse was silent, Kevan added, 'The old man and the dragon are gone. There's no harm in letting Suran satisfy his curiosity.'

'Who is he?' Chasse asked.

'When our people sailed south to escape the dragon, they sheltered at a town the local townspeople call Jebaran. I pointed it out to you when we sailed past it at the start of summer,' Kevan reminded Chasse. 'Suran is a hunter from Jebaran. When he heard there was a dragon, and that it defeated the best of our Dragon Fang, he wanted to see for himself what the dragon did.' Kevan paused to catch his breath. 'We tell many tales about dragons, but as you learned we never fought any. We didn't believe they existed: except, of course, in Nakiades' legend.'

'Instead, you raided villages,' Chasse accused.

'Yes,' Kevan said, his eyes fixed on Chasse. 'We raided. And you know why we did that. It gave us supplies we don't have in Harbin. And kept alive our tradition.'

'And cost us lives,' Chasse said, although he dreaded his father's response to such a blunt statement, especially when Kevan drew a very deep breath before answering him.

'Yes,' Kevan admitted. 'It seems that we can no longer rely on raiding by surprise. The southern people waited for us to arrive and they had aid from a powerful protector farther to the east.'

'What will you do now?' Chasse asked.

Kevan ran his heavy hand through his thick auburn hair and scratched the back of his head briefly before replying, 'We will learn to live differently. We will change our reason for sailing south.'

'There is no need for Suran or the others to search the mountain,' Chasse insisted. 'The Herbal Man sealed the entrances to his hide-away.'

'Then we will break in. You obviously know where the entrance is.'

'You won't find the entrance, Father. The Herbal Man sealed it with magic,' said Chasse. 'No one can break in.'

'And you know all this because?' Kevan asked.

'Because the Herbal Man told Tam what he did before he left,' Chasse explained, and he hesitated before adding, 'And me.'

Kevan shook his head. 'Magic. Dragons and magic.' He snorted. 'If I hadn't seen the aftermath, or heard the same story told by Jon and Raven, I would say madness has touched our village.' He looked up at the sliver of moon low in the western sky, before he asked, 'Where is this entrance?'

'You know where it is,' Chasse replied. 'Under the ruins of the Herbal Man's hut. But you can't see it. And you won't find it. And even if you did, you couldn't open it.'

'Then there must be treasure if the old man went to great lengths to hide it so well,' Kevan argued.

'There's no treasure,' Chasse reiterated.

Kevan scuffed the earth with his boot. 'I will let Suran search,' he affirmed, without looking at Chasse. 'I gave him permission. If the entrance is expertly protected, there is no harm in Suran searching, is there?' He paused, before adding, 'I have an important meeting with your mother. Go back to the Hall,' and he turned and headed for the Watersdrop bridge.

Chasse watched until Kevan's silhouette reached the solitary figure waiting on the bridge with a lantern before he retreated to the Warriors' Hall, his thoughts racing through the information that his father shared. If Suran and the others were allowed to search, he had to alert Tam. She hadn't come down from the mountain and the impending night almost certainly meant that she would wait until the morning. *Can I wait until then to tell her*? he wondered.

The men were readying for Procra's Dance, so there was little chance they would venture up the mountain until the day after tomorrow. Tomorrow night, everyone was gathering in the Long Hall to celebrate Procra's Dance. Chasse was curious as to who Alan intended to choose as his partner. As much as he assessed the eligible women, he still couldn't fathom who Alan would choose.

Chasse stopped outside the Warriors' Hall entrance when he remembered that he promised Tam he would check on Banni and her child. The air was rapidly chilling, and his breath formed white clouds in the light spilling from the door. He decided and diverged towards the cottages. Banni's window glowed from candlelight, so Chasse knocked.

'Who is it?' Banni called.

'Chasse,' he answered. 'Is everything all right?'

He heard shuffling, a beam being lifted, and the door opened. Banni's profile appeared against the hearth. 'Come in,' she invited. Chasse entered and Banni closed the door behind him. 'Come by the fire,' she urged and she gestured to one of two stools arranged before the small fireplace. Chasse glanced at a bundle in a large basket close to the hearth. 'She's sleeping,' Banni told him. 'Have you eaten?'

'I have,' Chasse lied, knowing that an evening meal was awaiting him in the Warriors' Hall. He sat.

'Tamesan asked you to keep an eye on me,' Banni said, as she sat beside Chasse and leaned over her child's bedding.

'Yes,' Chasse confessed. 'Only if you don't mind.'

Banni met Chasse's gaze and replied, 'I like it. Thank you.'

'If you need anything,' he offered and faltered.

Banni smiled. 'I know who to ask. I should be fine. I might need someone to fetch wood for my store. Most other winter stock I can organise. The women are being very kind.' She adjusted a corner of the bear fur covering Jara, looked up at Chasse and asked, 'Are you to choose tomorrow night?'

He blushed and said, 'No.'

'I didn't think so,' Banni said. 'I only wanted to be sure that what I thought was correct.'

'There is no one for me to choose,' Chasse explained. 'I mean, there are single women, but I'm not ready to choose.'

'I think that's very sensible,' Banni said. 'Are you warm enough?'

Chasse grinned. 'Your fire is very warm,' he told her, but he stood and continued with, 'I better get back to the Warriors' Hall. I'll come by tomorrow with wood.'

Banni rose and opened the door. 'Thank you for checking on me,' she said, as Chasse stepped into the evening.

Chasse walked through the fog drifting into the village from the sea. Many cottages were empty, abandoned because people fled from the dragon, but light shone in the windows of those who remained, especially the fishermen's huts along the shore. The fearless dragonwarriors and most of their families escaped, leaving everyone else to their fates. The irony was obvious to him.

Inside the Warriors' Hall, the men at the hearth were eating and drinking, Kevan among them. Seeing Chasse enter, he called, 'Where have you been?'

'Visiting Banni,' Chasse replied.

'Isn't she too old for you?' Kogan teased.

'Dafid's wife was ten summers his senior,' Raven chimed in.

'And look what happened to Dafid,' quipped Jon, and the men laughed.

Chasse reddened, but he did not join the banter as he sat in the circle. Kevan asked, 'And?'

Chasse reached for a bowl of food and replied, 'She's fine. So is her child.'

Talk ebbed and flowed around who was to do what work the following day to prepare for Procra's combined Feast and Dance. Chasse listened to learn who Alan was going to choose, but no one was named and he was unwilling to broach the question.

Kevan stopped Jon, when he said he was retiring to his bed, to say, 'I have one announcement.' The men ceased their quiet conversations. 'In the absence of the Dragon's Heart, I have asked Eesa to lead the rites. Tomorrow, when the sun is low on the western horizon, I will officially install Eesa as Dragon Heart of Harbin.' He looked around the circle of faces lit by the glowing embers and tiny dying flames. 'Does anyone oppose this decision?'

'A woman has never been Dragon Heart,' said Petar.

'I think it is a good decision,' Jon asserted. He looked at Petar.

'I'm not opposed,' Petar said. 'I was merely referring to our tradition.'

'Anyone else want to speak?' Kevan asked. No one spoke. 'Then it will be done,' he concluded.

'We should sleep,' Jon said, rising. 'Tomorrow night we feast and celebrate.'

Chasse crossed the hall to his bed, removed his boots and belt, loosened his clothes, climbed beneath the skins and fur blankets, and let tiredness seep through his limbs, but his thoughts wrestled with his desire to sleep.

His mother was to be Dragon Heart, the first woman to hold the honour. He wondered if that would have happened before the Herbal Man and his dragon wreaked havoc on Harbin.

He hoped Tam was safe in the cave on the mountain and wondered if she would come down to celebrate Procra's Feast. She spent the previous winter on the mountain with the Herbal Man and his dragon when everyone in Harbin thought she perished in the blizzards, so he knew she could do it again, if she prepared well.

And he started thinking about Banni and how the men teased him. *Why do they do that*? he wondered. Banni was two summers older and already a mother. She was Tam's friend and she was a widow. He remembered her dark blond hair glowing in the firelight of the hearth in her cottage. He liked her smile. She was a calm person, friendly. Jared, who chose Banni for his wife, loved her in the brief time they were together. *She must still grieve for him*, Chasse thought. *Why am I thinking of her now*?

He rolled onto his left side and pulled his bedclothes tighter, willing himself to stop thinking and to sleep, but sleep kept its distance for a long time, and the nightmare lurked at the edges.

The children were playing Knock, a game familiar to Chasse. The game involved throwing spherical pebbles to see who could land their pebble closest to a braided quoit without landing in the quoit's circle. The person whose pebble landed closest was the winner and earned the right to throw the quoit to a new location for the next round. Anyone whose pebble landed or rolled or was knocked into the quoit's embrace sat out the next round of the game. He remembered the game could be fiercely contested, players deliberately trying to knock each other's pebbles into the centre. Boys often fought over contentious actions.

He spotted Jaysin squatting in the lee of the Hall, watching the children. Jaysin never played with the other children. Chasse knew the others saw Jaysin as strange, different, and so they didn't invite him to play, but Chasse knew it wasn't as simple as his little brother being bullied or ostracized by his peers. Jaysin fostered the distance and the disconnect by showing no interest in games, or fighting, or hunting, or even work skills. He preferred to observe butterflies, animals, people. He made up songs and stories. Like Tamesan, he wandered the hillsides, and his indifference to Harbin childhood frustrated their father and mother.

Chasse lowered the stack of straw he was carrying to the Long Hall for the pending Procra's Feast and approached his brother, and Jaysin looked up and smiled. 'Why are you watching?' Chasse asked.

'I'm counting who wins the most games and who is made to miss the most rounds,' Jaysin replied.

'Why are you doing that?'

'It tells me about people,' Jaysin explained.

'Like?'

'Freya is the most popular girl,' Jaysin said. 'Brin is the least liked boy because he's the best at this game, but he hardly ever wins it.'

'Why doesn't he win?' Chasse asked.

'Everyone else knocks his pebble into the centre whenever they can.'

'And Freya?'

'The rest of the boys knock her pebble close to the quoit whenever they can. Even Brin. She's not as good at the game as might seem by the number of times she wins.'

Chasse ruffled Jaysin's hair. 'Want to help me with the straw?'

Jaysin shook his head. 'I'm not a dragonwarrior.'

'You will be, one day.'

Jaysin looked up at Chasse, his face serious, as he said, 'I'll never be a dragonwarrior. You know that.'

'Of course you will,' Chasse replied, grinning. 'Another summer or two of growing and you'll be ready to learn the dragonwarrior ways. I'll teach you.'

Jaysin looked back at the game, no longer interested in Chasse's conversation. Chasse considered how he might engage his little brother, but finally he shrugged and patted Jaysin on the arm, gathered his straw, rose and continued his task. Before rounding the corner of the Long Hall, he looked back to where Jaysin was sitting, but the boy was gone. *Jaysin is right*, Chasse mused. *He is not destined to be a dragonwarrior because he lacks the necessary spirit, energy and courage.* Childhood was escaping Jaysin, and manhood was going to be even more elusive.

Chasse was pleased to see Tamesan helping their mother arrange dried flowers around the walls when he entered the Long Hall. He lay down his load of straw and approached Tam, grinning as he said, 'I wasn't sure if you'd be back today.'

Tam glance sideways at Eesa, before replying, 'Why wouldn't I be back?' Her expression warned Chasse to choose his words carefully.

'Can we talk outside?'

Tam asked Eesa if she could leave to talk with her brother. Eesa smiled at Chasse and said, 'I'm still disappointed you were denied a chance to choose this summer.'

'There will be other summers,' Chasse reassured her, before he led Tam from the hall. Outside, he said, 'Father gave Alan and the stranger permission to search for the dragon's treasure.'

'He told you this?' Tam asked.

'Last night,' Chasse confirmed. 'They're busy today and tonight, but I know they will continue searching tomorrow.'

'I will go up the mountain after tonight's feast,' Tam determined. 'I'll take leftovers to add to the winter food stock.'

'Father won't let you go.'

'He can't stop me,' Tam defiantly replied.

Aware of a presence behind them, Chasse and Tam turned. 'What are you two scheming?' Eesa asked, a smile gracing her lips.

'Wondering who Alan will choose tonight,' Chasse replied.

Eesa chuckled. 'We are all waiting to find out.'

'Are you sure no one knows?' Chasse asked.

'He has been tight-lipped with everyone,' Eesa said.

'Not even guesses?' Chasse persisted. 'There are ten who are eligible. Or at least that's what I heard.'

'Ten?' Eesa queried. 'Who told you that absurdity?'

'The men were discussing it in the Warriors' Hall,' Chasse explained.

'Men!' Eesa said with disdain. 'They think any woman without a man nearby is eligible to be chosen.' She shook her head. 'There are only three women who could be chosen tonight. Lena, Corba and Anai. None have been chosen before.'

'And Alan knows that?' Chasse asked.

Eesa stared, as if his question was absurd. 'If he doesn't, he will discover it soon enough.' She turned to Tam. 'I need you to check if there is enough water.' She glanced up at the sky and the darkening clouds. 'We will celebrate in the Long Hall. The rain is coming in.'

Chasse gazed at the northern hills where rain was sweeping across the trees and ridges. 'I have a job to do before the rain arrives. Excuse me,' he said. He ran to the woodpile behind the Warriors' Hall, loaded the wooden wheelbarrow and wheeled it to Banni's cottage and unloaded the contents by her back door. He was sure Banni was inside, caring for Jara, but he didn't interrupt. He wheeled the barrow back to the Warriors' Hall woodpile and went inside. As he sat beside Raven, who was polishing his belt buckle, heavy rain began beating on the wooden roof.

The villagers came through the downpour to assemble in the Long Hall, bearing the last of their offerings to place in the shared food stockpile. Procra's Feast marked the final opportunity for the villagers to organise and share their food supplies before the snows arrived and the long winter set in, and everyone arrived with baskets and bags to fill. The fishermen brought crates of dried and smoked herring, salmon and cod, and their wives carried jars of pickled seafood, and cakes, biscuits and bread. The dragonwarriors brought in leather bags filled with cured bear and elk meat, and cages containing squirrels and rabbits. Galt and his dragonwarrior sons bore bags of goat meat and milk. The dragonwarrior wives supplied seeds and nuts and herbs and plants gathered from the forest and from their small garden plots, and they also had bread and cakes and biscuits laid on the long sharing trestles. The women maintained a roaring fire in the central hearth and unburdened villagers gathered around it to ward off the encroaching evening cold as they talked of families and winter plans.

Kevan, Jon and Raven presided over the food tables, thanking individuals for their generous contributions while Jon's wife, Nomi, coordinated another group of women, including Banni with Jara wrapped in a tight bundle on her back, who were dividing the abundant produce into baskets for sharing between the villagers. A third group was putting the last touches to the long banquet table dominating the hall.

Chasse saw Tam helping Nomi and he wanted to join her, but dragonwarrior tradition dictated that he remain with the men surrounding Alan. He searched for his mother in the throng and finally realised she was the figure wearing a new black bear skin and dragon claw headdress at the end of the Long Hall where the Dragon Heart always stood. Her transformation from the Dragon Head's wife to Harbin's Dragon Heart was complete and Chasse was proud.

On cue from Kevan, the Dragon Fang collectively grunted, bringing silence into the hall, and Eesa began the traditional song to Procra and procession, shaking reeds rhythmically as she circumnavigated the food table. Everyone joined in the singing, filling the hall with harmony and joy, until Eesa sat at the head of the table. With Kevan and Jon flanking her, she offered the traditional blessing and the feast commenced.

Chasse ate with the warriors, listening to stories of hunting and considerations for the winter training, but part-way into the meal Kevan rose and called everyone to order. 'We have, again, been blessed by Procra and her daughter Fler,' he said, 'and what we eat and share tonight will shield us from Blitzart's brutal anger when his icy breath coats our world with white, and darkness stays longer than daylight. Brothers and sisters, tonight is a night for celebration!'

Cheers filled the hall.

As the noise abated, Kevan continued. 'And, tonight, we combine Procra's blessings into a single celebration. Tonight, dragonwarrior Alan, son of Edrin, will choose his wife!'

Another round of cheering echoed in the hall.

Alan walked to the central hearth where the warriors traditionally stood while each was introduced by the Dragon Head before they chose wives.

Kevan spoke as Alan faced the assembly. 'Great Varst and Procra, look upon this son of Harbin, son of Edrin, Edrin who sailed eighteen journeys on the dragonship before entering Varst's Paradise, this dragonwarrior who has sailed on the dragonship for five journeys, who has brought honour and wealth to Harbin, who has shown what it means to walk in the footsteps of Nakiades and not be afraid of the great dragons. Give this warrior your blessing as he chooses his wife, a daughter of Harbin who will give him strong children, a warm hearth and a home.' The people applauded and eyes in the crowd focused on the three unmarried women as Kevan asked, 'Alan, son of Edrin, who will you choose tonight?'

Alan smiled and replied with gusto, 'I choose Tamesan, daughter of Kevan and Eesa!'

A collective gasp rippled through the hall.

As Chasse looked to his sister, who was staring at Alan as if she misheard him, a cry of 'She is not of age!' rang above the murmurs. Eesa strode towards Alan. 'You have insulted the gods!' she accused.

'How?' Alan asked. 'How do you know the gods have not guided me to this point for a reason? Who is it who says Tamesan is not ready? This is her fifteenth summer. In fact, the end of her fifteenth summer.'

'I say she is not ready!' Eesa declared.

'You are a mother trying to keep her child a child!' Alan accused.

'I am Dragon Heart of Harbin!' Eesa retorted. 'I speak for the gods, and the gods say she is not ready.'

'You are not the law of Harbin,' said Alan. 'He is the law,' and he pointed to Kevan. 'I will take the decision of the Dragon Head.'

Before Kevan could respond, Amarti, the oldest woman in the village, interrupted with, 'Best look to your children, Dragon Head of Harbin.'

Kevan searched the faces in the Hall and realised that Tamesan and Chasse had vanished.

Five

The driving rain and darkness made climbing difficult. Sodden earth slid perilously beneath his boots, wet stones slipped from his grasp, and without the right clothes the bitter cold chilled him through to his bones, but Chasse persisted because he knew where his sister was going and Alan's shock announcement in the Long Hall motivated him. *Did anyone else know Alan was going to name Tam*? *Did his father know*? Tam would never accept the offered arrangement. *Is this why Alan returned*, he wondered – *to take Tam away with him*? He stumbled and slid into a muddy runnel, cold water sluicing through his coat and shirt before he could get to his feet. He shielded his eyes from the rain with his hand and cursed Blitzart for making human lives miserable. 'Leave us alone for one more day!' he begged as he caught his breath. 'One more day!'

He was unsure how far Tam was ahead but when he saw her leave after hearing Alan name her he followed, yelling after her shadow as she ran through the village. He thought he could catch her, but she was always quicker, more agile, and she knew the mountain path better than he did, and by the time he reached the forest at the edge of Galt's pasture Tam had disappeared into the night.

At the steepest section between the rocky outcrops, he stopped to shelter against a boulder. He knew he couldn't linger. It was highly likely Kevan ordered the men to pursue Tam, especially if he sanctioned Alan's request. *Father won't give Tam away*, he told himself. *She is a summer too young to consent, like our mother said. It doesn't make sense.* Chasse sighed. *Father needs to know the truth*, he decided.

He braced and recommenced scrambling up the mountain through the torrential downpour, his breath coming in wheezes, his legs aching. When he reached the gentler slope onto the plateau, he looked down the mountain towards Harbin, but the night and rain sealed the world around him. He trudged across the muddy ground, boots sinking in the sludge as he skirted the Herbal Man's hut ruins, until he reached the base of the goat path to the cave of the Dawn People.

The difficult section of the climb lay ahead. The goat path was awkward in daylight, but in darkness and rain he couldn't imagine how Tam negotiated it. He wiped his muddy boots against a rock edge, shivered as rain ran down the back of his neck, pressed against the cliff and edged cautiously up the path. He wished that he wore drier clothes. He wished he could see instead of feel. He wished that he could feel because his hands and fingers were numb from the cold. He wished that he wasn't climbing.

Halfway up the narrow path, his left foot slid off a rock and he desperately dropped to his knees to avoid toppling over the edge. He stayed on his knees, calming his nerves, summoning the courage to keep climbing, afraid he would discover that Tam fell like he almost fell. He rose and pressed on, hands scrabbling along the rockface for every crevasse and jutting stone he could find to keep him balanced and secure, until he reached the ledge and the mouth of the Dawn People's cave.

He stepped through the knee-deep pool formed by the incessant rain and emerged in the cave's dry confines, grateful to be underground, where he took stock of his situation. He was soaked to the bone, numb from the cold, and blinded by the absence of light. Even though he remembered the way through the cave to the stone steps leading to the Herbal Man's secret chambers, he was shaking with fear and cold.

He shuffled through the cave, feeling his way, bumping into walls and stalagmites, searching for the stairwell entrance, frustrated because he thought his memory was better than it was proving to be. He almost fell through the stone doorway when he found it, but he began the zig-zag journey, glad to see an increasing amber glow as he descended. He found Tam sitting on the edge of the dragon's nest, staring at the pink egg.

As Chasse approached, Tam said, without turning, 'You shouldn't have come.'

'You knew I would,' he replied. He climbed onto the nest.

Tam nodded. 'Yes. I knew you would.'

'What do we do now?' he asked, aware of the heat radiating from the egg.

'We begin by getting you warm,' Tam said, rising. 'There are clothes that will fit you in the warrior chamber.' She held out a hand to help Chasse stand and led him to the wall where she used her amber ring to open the invisible door, clicking her fingers to light the corridor. She unlocked the warrior chamber door, clicked her fingers to ignite the lights and ushered Chasse inside. 'I will be in the next chamber. Join me when you are changed.' She pulled the wooden door almost shut as she withdrew.

Chasse surveyed the chamber's treasure like he did the first time, but this time his eyes rested on a pile of clothes along the rear wall. He stepped over the armour and weapons and searched the collection of coats, jackets, trousers and assorted finery, choosing items that would keep him warm and protected from the rain and weather if he had to return down the mountain. He settled on thick brown trousers, a light grey tunic, and he was impressed by the texture and pliant feel of a dark blue leather cloak. He stripped off his sodden clothes and dressed in the items he selected.

Satisfied that he was dry and warm, Chasse left the chamber and entered the room opposite where Tam was peering into a silver bowl atop a marble pedestal. The walls were hidden behind shelves of books and glass bottles and flasks. Two benches, left and right, were covered with a plethora of objects and a large book lay open on one bench. 'What are these things?' Chasse asked.

Tam lifted her gaze from the bowl and replied, 'It's a library and a laboratory. This is where Eric made the medicines for our sick and injured people,' Tam explained as she approached a bench. 'It's also where he stored all the things he knew.' She put her hand on the book. 'Remember I promised that I would teach you to read? This is why. Eric, and hundreds of people like him, recorded their ideas and thoughts and recipes and experiences in these books, so that other people, like you and me, could read and learn them, and then record in our own books what we learn and know.'

'I still don't understand it,' Chasse admitted, shaking his head. He bent forward to examine the pages of the large book. The odd cream flat sections were marred by countless dark scribbles, like scratches on a dagger blade or a face. He recognised a drawing that looked like one of the flasks on the bench, but he wondered why anyone would draw a flask when it could be seen.

'When I teach you to read,' Tam said, 'all this will make sense.'

'Why were you staring into this?' Chasse asked as he studied the pedestal and bowl. Water shimmered within the bowl.

'Those are the Seeing Waters,' Tam told him. 'I told you I could talk with Eric through them.'

'How?' he asked, seeing only the bowl's silver base in the clear water.

'I don't know, yet,' Tam apologised. 'I can't make it work. I have to wait for Eric to contact me.'

'You're not going to be safe here. Alan will come looking for you.'

'Do you know why he named me?' she asked.

'No,' Chasse replied. 'He didn't tell any of us what he was planning to do.'

'Petar and the stranger knew,' Tam said. 'I saw their faces when he made his announcement. They were laughing.'

'I bet it's about the dragon treasure,' Chasse suggested. 'Maybe they think they can get to it through you.'

'Why choose me as a wife to do that?'

'Because, as Alan's wife, you would have to obey him,' Chasse said. 'You wouldn't have a choice but to show him all this.'

Tam laughed. 'I always have a choice. We all do. A man has no right to tell me what I can and cannot do.'

'I don't think Father would agree with you,' Chasse argued. 'Neither would Mother. It's how things stay in order. Everyone has a role in our village, and some have greater authority, like Father as the Dragon Head.'

'Oh, Chasse,' Tam said. 'Do you really believe that?'

'Why wouldn't I believe it?'

Tam carefully shifted a bunch of dried herbs to make room to sit on the edge of the bench, and said, 'If Kerryn was there tonight, and you chose her as your wife, would you have made her obey you, Chasse?'

'It's what a wife is expected to do.'

Tam dropped her head a moment, lifted it and asked, 'Have you come to tell me that I should go down to the village and accept Alan's proposal?'

'No!' Chasse denied. 'I came to protect you.'

'From what?' Tam asked, spreading her arms wide. 'By your logic, I have nothing to be protected from.'

'But Alan,' Chasse stumbled. 'I mean, you don't want to marry him. Why would you do that?'

'Because you told me that is what I am expected to do,' Tam said. 'Because I'm a woman and I should obey a man.'

'It's not the same,' Chasse argued.

'How is it not the same?'

Confused and annoyed by Tam's persistence, Chasse said, 'Because you're my sister.'

Tam snorted and stood. 'So, there are different rules for different women. Every woman should do as they're told because that's what men expect of them, but I don't because I'm your sister.'

'Stop it!' Chasse begged, infuriated. 'This is a stupid conversation.'

Tam glared. 'This is not a stupid conversation, Chasse. If I did what you think is right, I would be married to Alan now, or someone like him next summer, and scaling fish while I meekly wait for the dragonship to come home, believing that all you fine warriors are bravely fighting dragons to save the rest of us from – I don't know, from whatever we have to be saved from, which we both know isn't the truth. But I defied Father and chose to learn from Eric and be something different. I chose my path. I did not let a man choose it for me.'

'That's not what I meant.'

'Then, what did you mean?' Tam challenged.

Chasse shrugged. 'Let it go.'

Tam took a deep breath. 'I didn't mean to get angry with you.'

'It's all right,' Chasse said, and he looked around the chamber. 'We have to keep Alan and everyone away from here.'

'Alan, yes, but especially Suran,' Tam asserted. 'He is behind all that is happening.'

'How do you know?'

'He's the one after the treasure. He wants to find this place. Alan is helping him, but I think Alan has a different motive for being here.'

'Like what?'

'I don't know yet,' Tam said. 'Are you hungry?' Chasse nodded. 'Come with me.' She led Chasse to the egg chamber and to a small table laden with bags and jars. 'I have most of what I need for winter,' she explained. She rummaged in one bag and drew out purple tubers. 'You've had these before.'

'Cassa,' he said. 'Of course. Mother uses them in stews.'

'I'll make a soup,' she said. 'I have no meat.'

'I can get you some from our stockpile.'

'No,' Tam replied as she began slicing the cassa into a metal bowl. 'I don't eat the flesh of animals anymore.'

'Why not?'

'It's wrong. They live like we do.'

Chasse grinned and replied, 'They don't really. They're brutes. They don't think like we do, or feel what we feel, or build the things we build.'

'They feel,' Tam argued. 'And they do think. You met Claryssa. She's more intelligent than any of us.'

'She is a dragon,' said Chasse dismissively. 'I'm talking about goats and bears and wolves.'

'They have feelings. Look at how they care for their young,' Tam contended.

'Father says that's animal instinct. They do it because they only know that's what they have to do.'

'They do it because they understand how important it is to raise and care for their young.'

'I'll still eat meat,' Chasse said. 'It gives us strength and energy.'

'And I won't,' Tam replied. She poured water into the green bowl of sliced cassa, knelt and placed the bowl on the floor, held her hands over it, and whispered words in an unfamiliar tongue while Chasse watched. The water began to steam.

'How are you doing that?' he asked.

She ignored his question. When she was satisfied the water was hot enough, she rose, and said, 'It will be ready in a few moments.'

'You didn't answer my question,' Chasse complained. 'How did you heat the water?'

'A spell. Eric used it all the time to heat things.'

'But when did you learn it?'

'I saw him do it when he was here. And I read and learned it,' she explained. 'That's why reading is so powerful, Chasse, and why I will teach you to read. Fetch two goblets from the shelf over there,' she added, indicating a section of the wall. 'The broth is ready.'

Chasse fetched the goblets and held them while Tam filled them, and they sat close to the dragon egg, its radiant warmth comforting them as they sipped the broth.

'You have to go back to Harbin in the morning,' Tam said. 'Father will be searching the mountain and I need you to keep him from coming up here.'

'I'm staying to protect you,' Chasse said. 'What if Alan or Suran find the cave entrance?'

'If you stay,' she argued, 'Father will keep searching and he will be caught in the blizzard.'

'What blizzard?'

'Blitzart will breathe across the mountain tomorrow evening,' Tam said. 'The snows will be deep.'

'How do you know?' Chasse asked. 'More magic?'

Tam grinned and replied, 'Eric said the snows would come early before he left. But Amarti and Mother also spoke about it this afternoon when we were preparing the Hall. The older fishermen know the weather patterns and they said snow-bearing clouds growing in the north were heading this way. No magic. Just knowledge.'

'I still have to stop the others from searching,' said Chasse. 'You have no escape if they find the cave entrance.'

'I opened the third door, the one at the end of the corridor,' Tam replied. 'It's not a room. It's the opening of a very old tunnel.'

'Did you go in?'

'A little. It goes a long distance, twisting and turning.'

'I wonder where it ends?' Chasse mused. 'It must be another way out.'

Tam held out her hand to take his goblet. 'If you are still hungry, there are dried fruits, nuts and seeds in the small brown sack at the end of the table. I'm going to read by the egg. You should join me. I'll teach you.'

Chasse handed over his goblet and stood beside his sister. 'I will,' he said, 'but, first, I want to look through the items in the warrior room. Is that all right?'

'Of course it is,' Tam replied. 'You know where I will be.'

Chasse headed for the chamber, clicking his fingers as he entered, smiling because he could activate the lights and pretend he was casting a magic spell.

The first time Tam brought him to the room he was attracted to a battle axe and he found it leaning against a pile of armour where he left it. He picked it up, amazed again at how light it was in his grip, and he rolled and twisted the weapon in his hand, pretending that he was under attack. He ducked, weaved and swung the battle axe and emerged triumphant, ready for the next opponent.

He chose a metal shield emblazoned with an odd rearing animal with a long neck, skinny legs and a thick body. Again, he was surprised by the shield's lightness, his familiarity with shields being limited to the heavy wooden ones sometimes used by the Dragon Fang. He was trained to use a spear, but the battle axe felt easier and deadlier, and he danced around the chamber, battle axe in one hand, shield on the other arm, fighting and vanquishing imaginary foes.

Chasse lost track of time as he played with the equipment and tried on pieces of metal armour that were less cumbersome than the Harbin leather guards worn by the dragonwarriors, until he remembered his promise to Tamesan. Embarrassed by his infatuation with pretending to be a great warrior, he returned the gear to where he found it and retreated to the egg chamber.

Tam was seated by the egg with an open book on her lap and a small glowing sphere floating above her head, her red hair glowing in the light, and as Chasse climbed onto the nest beside her she said, 'This is the first book Eric used to teach me how to read. It tells us which herbs are best to use for healing medicines.'

'Why would I want to know that?' Chasse asked.

Tam chuckled. 'You might not, but you will have something far more valuable by learning how to read this.'

Six

Tam's prediction of snow, confirmed by the fishermen, was accurate. Chasse had to hurry. Stone glistened and trees dripped with moisture from the overnight downpour, but the bright sunlight creeping across the crest of the mountains glowed gold along the ridges and tree lines and the sky was intensely blue. Across the western ocean, the vestiges of night retreated beneath a low horizon of grey clouds, but dark, ominous clouds were closing in from the north.

Chasse stepped onto the goat path, remembering his perilous climb the previous night, and began the steep descent to the plateau. His clothes were warm, courtesy of a spell Tam applied to dry them before Chasse began the return journey, so he left the borrowed clothes that he wore overnight in the chamber where he found them. His sister's growing magical prowess fascinated and excited him, but it also disappointed him that her talent was one of the reasons she was hiding in the cave. He was heading down the mountain to confront the other reason.

From the base of the goat path, he trudged across the sodden plateau, remembering how it was filled with trees and bushes when the Herbal Man lived there. Every Harbin warrior's dream was to meet a dragon in battle but when they did meet a dragon on the plateau, they were outmatched and sent running in fear. No one imagined the extent of the power residing within a dragon until that day.

As Chasse reached the perimeter to recommence his descent, he was confronted by Alan, Petar and Suran who emerged from the trees, carrying spears.

'Where have you been?' Alan challenged.

'Searching for my sister,' Chasse replied.

Suran stepped forward and grabbed Chasse's sleeve. 'Dry,' he announced.

'After last night's rain?' Alan asked. 'How did you manage that?'

'I sheltered in a cave,' Chasse said, pulling his arm away from Suran. 'There are plenty around.'

'Perhaps you would like to show us exactly where this cave is,' Suran suggested.

'I have to get down to the village,' Chasse replied.

'I don't think you understood my request,' Suran said and his tone was threatening.

'What my friend is saying,' said Alan, 'is that we *insist* you show us the cave you sheltered in.'

'Perhaps your new wife is sheltering there,' Petar remarked, nudging Alan's arm.

Alan focused on Chasse. 'I'm certain she will be.'

'I didn't find my sister,' Chasse denied, but he knew the situation was deteriorating. 'If I had, I would be taking her back down now.' As he spoke, he measured his chances. He could bolt into the trees, try to outrun them and head for Harbin, hoping his father or Jon or someone would intervene or that the three facing him would back off when he reached the village. It was risky. Fighting was not an option. There were three men facing him and he had no weapon. He could lead them to a cave or at least pretend to lead them to one and lose them in the forest, reverting to option one. 'I'll show you where I sheltered, since you don't believe me,' he offered. 'Then I need to see my father.'

'Your father is out on the slopes searching like everyone else,' Alan revealed. 'He wants me to have the wife I chose.'

'I doubt that,' Chasse said. 'Father wouldn't give my sister to you. She's not even of age.'

Alan laughed. 'The Dragon Head is keen to bring peace back to Harbin and all the people. Your sister is an offering to reassure those of us who had to escape the dragon that it is safe to return.'

Chasse wanted to refute Alan's statement, but he was afraid there was truth in his words.

'Your escapade last night has everyone concerned,' Alan continued. 'I remember how your sister disappeared last summer too, and we were all searching for her, believing she was dead. She seems adept at this charade.'

'We need to get on with searching,' Suran said irritably. 'Lead us to the cave.'

Chasse met Suran's gaze, saying, 'It's across the slope, close to the bear territory.'

'I think it's up that path you came down,' Suran intimated. 'You can take us up there.'

'There's nothing up there,' Chasse replied. 'That's why I came back down.'

Suran levelled his spear at Chasse's throat. 'I came here to find the dragon's treasure and I will find it. And you are going to lead us to it now.'

Chasse's stomach twisted as he fought his rising fear. Alan gestured for him to lead them across the plateau. Feigning bravado, Chasse ignored Suran's spear point and commenced walking.

As the group crossed the plateau, the sunlight faded sharply and shadows swept across the ground. Chasse looked up at heavy, dark clouds rolling over the mountain peak. Tiny sparkling crystals drifted earthward. 'I think we better head down,' he said, turning to the three men.

'I think if you stop talking and walk quicker we might find what we are looking for,' Suran retorted, and he prodded Chasse with the spear.

Alan turned to Petar. 'Find the Dragon Head and tell him we have his son and daughter. Bring him and the others here.' He glanced up as a snowflake settled on his cheek. 'Hurry,' he urged. Petar trotted away.

'If the snows come –' Chasse started, but Suran poked him with his spear and ordered, 'Walk.'

At the foot of the goat path, the world darkened, the temperature dropped and a cold wind gusted across the mountain face and struck the group, carrying a thick haze of snowflakes that stained the earth and stone and undergrowth, and the wind howled as it ripped across the jagged rocks. Chasse pleaded, 'We can't climb, not in this wind.'

'But you climbed it last night in the rainstorm,' Suran argued. 'What's the difference?'

'We'll freeze,' Chasse replied. 'This is Blitzart's breath. It won't stop. The snow's started.'

'You kept warm and dry last night,' Suran reminded him.

Chasse veered towards the path, planning how he could even the odds to protect Tam and the dragon's treasure, when Alan yelled, 'Stop!' Chasse followed where Alan and Suran were looking and he saw Tam at the northern end of the plateau through the lightly falling snow. 'Wait here,' Alan ordered, and he walked towards Tam, but she disappeared over the rim of the plateau into the forest. Alan ran in pursuit.

'She won't get far,' Suran said.

'Then we can go back down,' Chasse suggested.

Suran lifted his spear. 'You are still taking me to whatever you're hiding up here. Move.'

Chasse wanted to protest, but Suran's mood and spear warned him not to. He stepped onto the narrow path and started to climb, until a handful of paces up Chasse pressed his right shoulder against the rock and swung his left arm swiftly back. His arm missed Suran, who stepped back to dodge, but Chasse used Suran's retreat as his chance to attack. He kicked, catching Suran off-balance and sending him tumbling backward over the short drop. Chasse leapt down, kicked the spear from Suran's grasping hand and sprinted across the plateau, the mud treacherously trying to slow him, the windstorm building intensity at his back.

When he glanced over his shoulder, to his dismay, Suran was on his feet, spear in hand, pursuing. Chasse knew that if he could make it to the descent he could lose Suran because he knew the mountainside better than the stranger. The forest loomed through the swirling snowfall. His heat pounded. A few more steps –

A heavy object bit into Chasse's right shoulder and sent him sprawling over the lip of the plateau. As he slid face-down along the mud and shale and stones of the sloping path, he realised Suran had speared him because of the awkward weight and numbness through his shoulder. He stopped sliding.

Fighting pulsing pain, he opened his eyes and saw boots on the shale. He raised his head. His father stood over him.

'Where's Tam?' Chasse asked when his father sat beside his bedding in the Warrior's Hall.

'Your sister is on the mountain again, like last winter,' Kevan said gruffly. 'Only this time there's no Herbal Man to protect her from Blitzart.' He held a cup of broth toward Chasse. 'Drink this.'

Chasse took the cup in his left hand, unable to move his heavily bandaged right shoulder. 'And Alan?'

'Sailed away,' Kevan replied. 'Ran back to the others.'

'Suran and Petar?'

'Suran bolted when he realised that he speared you in front of me. I sent men after him, but he's a hunter and fleet of foot and hard to catch. He vanished into The Sentinels. I guess he's heading for home, but he's run into Blitzart's jaws. The snowstorm came. If he is still out there, he will need Varst's protection to survive.' Kevan urged Chasse to drink the broth, before adding, 'Petar stayed. He brought me to you.'

'They sent him to do that,' Chasse said.

'I know.'

'You were giving Tam away,' Chasse accused.

Sadness creased Kevan's eyes, and he shook his head. 'That was never my intention. I did not know Alan planned to take Tamesan back to be Marron's woman. I thought he was going to choose another woman.'

The revelation of Alan's darker plan to steal Tam away for Marron astonished Chasse. 'But you were helping him look for us.'

'I was searching for my son and daughter,' Kevan replied. 'I would not send Tamesan away with Alan. She is not of age. And even if I was that cruel, Eesa would have fought me and I would not win against your mother.' He smiled wryly. 'Rest. The wound is not bad, but it will be a few days before you can continue your winter training.' Chasse started to rise. 'What are you doing?' Kevan asked.

'I promised Tam I would watch out for Banni,' Chasse explained.

'I said rest. I will drop by Banni's cottage. You can keep your promise when your strength returns.' As Chasse eased back onto his bed, Kevan chuckled and said, 'You have your first warrior scar.'

'I was running away,' Chasse said, ashamed.

Kevan nodded, saying, 'You were doing what you knew was the best action in the situation. Suran is experienced. You would not survive if you chose to face him. You made a smart warrior's decision. A smart warrior knows when to fight and when not to. And you're still alive. Be grateful.'

Chasse watched his father walk across the Hall to the doorway, aware of Kevan's limp, legacy of his fight with Trask. His father bore many scars from battles and brawls, badges of honour and courage that a man could wear with pride because he faced his enemy. His own first scar, in the back of his shoulder, was best hidden.

A snowstorm descended on Harbin and raged for eight days, locking everyone inside. Huddled by the hearth, the warriors told stories and ate and drank when they were not curled under bear and wolf fur in their beds, smoke coiling around the rafters and hanging like grey clouds through the hall before sifting through vents.

Jon, Raven and Kevan took turns refreshing Chasse's bandaging and applying an unction to his shoulder while the storm raged, and his wound healed quickly.

'You can thank your sister for this paste,' Jon said, as he applied the green ooze on the third day. 'She has learned everything the Herbal Man knew.'

'You had some left?' Chasse asked, remembering how Tam helped the Herbal Man heal the wounded warriors when the dragonship returned from its disastrous journey.

'She brought it down when we carried you from the mountain,' Jon told him. 'She left a bag of medicine she thought would be helpful.'

'I thought she stayed on the mountain,' said Chasse.

'She returned when she knew you were safe,' Jon told him. 'Your father and mother begged her to stay because the snow was falling, but she said she had to go back. Your little brother followed her.'

'Jaysin?' Chasse asked. 'Did Father let him go?'

Jon laughed as he began wrapping a clean bandage over Chasse's shoulder. 'Not at all. Your little brother sneaked out of Harbin without asking. Kevan chased him up the mountain through the first snowfall, but he couldn't find him.'

'How does he know Jaysin made it to Tam?' Chasse asked, imagining Jaysin clumsily trying to climb the goat path.

'Tamesan met your father on the plateau and told him that Jaysin was staying with her,' Jon replied. He shook his head. 'I feel sorry for your parents. It's a curse having stubborn children. Make sure you don't run up the mountain.'

Knowing Jaysin was on the mountain with Tam made Chasse impatient but, trapped in Harbin by the storm and his injury, all he could do was sleep and eat until his wound healed and his strength returned. He was meant to protect his family, to be a dragonwarrior of merit, but instead he was a burden and he was filled with guilt. Sleep came easily enough, but he woke from restless dreams, though he was grateful that, for once, he could not recall the content of those dreams.

The snow was deep through the village, coating the buildings beneath its crisp white mantle, and in the brittle sunlight the snow's brilliance hurt Chasse's eyes when he ventured out of the Warriors' Hall for the first time. Even wrapped in his father's bear fur coat, the chill bit his cheeks and crept into the toes of his leather boots and his breath formed thick white clouds. He trudged past the Long Hall and Kadin the smith's iced-in workshop, studying the morning sun glittering in ice shards laced through the fishermen's nets. The bright blue sky was reminiscent of summer days, but the air was frosty and the world frozen.

Banni's front door was half-buried with snow piled almost to the eaves around parts of the cottage, but smoke rising from the chimney reassured Chasse that Banni and Jara were safe and warm within. He knocked, self-conscious that he wasn't bringing anything of merit or use to Banni, and he chastised himself silently for his forgetfulness in his rush to fulfil his promise to Tam. He would ask Banni if there was any item she needed and bring it to her. The door opened and snow tumbled onto the entry. 'Sorry,' Chasse apologised. 'I'll clean that up.'

'It will melt,' Banni reassured him. 'Come in.' The room was warm and the hearth crackled with fresh kindling. 'I'm heating porridge,' she said. 'Would you like some?'

'Thank you, no,' Chasse replied.

'Have you eaten?'

'Not yet.'

'Eat with me,' Banni offered. 'I have enough for two.' She collected bowls from her shelf and stooped over the steaming pot on the hearth to scoop a ladle of porridge into each bowl. She indicated that Chasse should sit on a stool near the hearth and, after he sat, she handed him a bowl. 'How is your shoulder?' she asked as she took her seat.

'Stiff, but much better,' Chasse replied. 'I can join in training tomorrow. How is Jara?'

Banni smiled as she said, 'Growing every day. Hold this.' She passed her bowl to Chasse, rose, and retrieved Jara from a woven mat on the floor. She held her daughter upright and said, 'This is Chasse.'

Chasse stared at the child's dark eyes, puffy cheeks and cherubic lips, and a memory of his little brother Jaysin blossomed. He was too young to remember Tam's arrival, but he was six summers when his mother let him briefly hold his baby brother. He remembered the warmth, the milky tang and baby odours that assaulted him as Banni held Jara towards him. 'She is healthy,' he noted. Chasse liked how her cheeks creased into dimples. Her smile was warm, enticing.

'I'll let you finish your porridge,' Banni said, putting her bowl on the floor. 'I'll eat after I feed Jara.' She held Jara in one arm as she pulled her stool closer to the hearth, sat, opened her top and let Jara snuggle against her breast.

Chasse focused on his porridge as he ate, listening to the crackling hearth and the child suckling. More family memories crowded in – meals shared in the cottage by Watersdrop, winter nights with Tamesan and Jaysin playing Straws and Guess Which. It was only his second winter as a warrior, but with the novelty and honour of the first winter gone he missed the childhood comforts of home and understood why men chose wives as soon as they could after their initiation into the Dragon Fang. He paused from eating to ask, 'Is there anything I can do for you? Anything you need?'

Banni looked up from her child. 'I think I have all I need for now,

Chasse. Thank you for asking.' She looked down at Jara, before looking up again to say, 'And the same is true for me. If there is anything you need that I can offer, please ask. If you want to come by to eat, you are always welcome.'

Chasse lowered his bowl and stood, saying, 'I better go. Father wants me to work today while the weather is good.' Banni eased Jara from her breast, but Chasse continued with, 'No need to get up. I can let myself out, Stay warm with Jara.' He smiled and withdrew, pulling the door closed behind him.

As he trudged to the Warriors' Hall, Chasse spotted his father coming from their home, so he deviated to intercept him, his mind shuffling through thoughts of Banni and how beautiful she looked in the hearth glow with Jara nestled against her.

Seven

Chasse assessed Raven's stance, his hips, his feet, his grip on his spear. It was going to be a lunge or a sweep. A lunge. He knocked Raven's point aside with his spear and flicked his point back, shearing past Raven's chin. Raven backpedalled, balanced, moved his spear to his left hand, and met his gaze. The hand shift was a new tactic. Chasse assessed Raven's hips again, his weight transfer. Another lunge coming. Different angle. When Raven lunged, Chasse deflected Raven's spear, but Raven spun his weapon through his hands, using Chasse's energy for greater speed, and the base of his shaft smacked Chasse across the side of the head, stinging, making his eyes water. Chasse stepped back and Raven used the advantage to drive the shaft below the pointy end of his spear into Chasse's groin. Chasse grunted and dropped to his knees, gasping for breath, surrounded by laughter.

'Enough!' Jon called over the hilarity.

Chasse rolled onto his side, holding his groin, trying to cope with the pulsing ache and pain, and Raven squatted beside him, saying, 'Sorry, Chasse.'

'He'll get up when his balls recover,' Jon said. 'Give Remi a turn.'

Chasse crawled out of the fighting space and leaned against the edge of the long hearth and, between deep breaths, he watched Raven talking Remi through techniques to defend himself with a spear, remembering how he went through the same lessons the previous winter. The other trainee, Thados, was also observing vigilantly. Thados was Tad's son and Tad was a quiet, respected, loyal and tough warrior who sailed on the dragonship for eighteen summers. Everyone expected Thados would be like his father.

The recruits took the number in the residual Dragon Fang to thirteen, but only five men were required to spend the entire winter in the Warriors' Hall. The seven married men slept in their homes. As Dragon Head, Kevan wasn't expected to spend most nights in the Warriors' Hall, but he alternated with sleeping at home. The Dragon Fang met for breakfast every morning and again before sunset every evening in a traditional ritual of organisation and comradery. During days when the weather allowed, they gathered supplies, hunted, trained outdoors, and in foul weather they trained inside, alternating between sleeping and eating.

Remi was given three opportunities to fight Raven, but Raven beat him down quickly every time. Thados was called for his turn. Thados fell quickly after his introduction, but to everyone's surprise he swept Raven's legs from under him in the second bout.

Chasse stood gingerly to watch the third bout. Raven readied, grinned as he nodded to Thados and the match recommenced. Raven waited for Thados to make the first move, but the brown-haired youth seemed content to let Raven attack first. Raven made three probing lunges, each time his spear being turned away, before he spun, feinted high and struck low. Thados blocked the attack and stepped back. Raven attacked again, using his strength to break past Thados' determined defence, sending the youth further back and off-balance, but before Raven could strike a finishing blow Thados was balanced and warded the attack. Raven stepped back, and said, 'You have your father's wisdom.'

Thados did not reply, but Jon stepped between the two and pronounced, 'Enough. Another storm is brewing. We have work to do.'

The warriors were assigned to duties – fetching more wood, gathering food, checking on villagers to see if anyone needed help, but, to Chasse, Jon said, 'Your father wants to see you at Watersdrop.'

Chasse obediently headed for the bridge where he found Kevan and

Eesa waiting.

'How was training?' Kevan asked.

The question made Chasse twinge in his groin, but he replied, 'Good. Thados is a fighter.'

Kevan grinned. 'He should be. His father trained him every day.'

Kevan's comment disheartened Chasse. Kevan spent some time with him teaching him warrior skills, but not often because Kevan was always busy with Dragon Fang matters, whereas Tad chose to invest time to prepare Thados for his manhood and that explained why Thados could hold his own against Raven. Chasse wished his father spent more time with him in the same way. 'Why did you summon me?' Chasse asked.

'I want you to go to the ledges above Meltsparkle and wait there. Take a hide tent and everything you need to spend five nights away from the village,' Kevan instructed. 'And take a length of rope from the Hall.'

'Why?' Chasse asked.

'It is time for the Trial of the Second Winter. Every dragonwarrior does this,' Kevan said. 'No more questions.'

'Before you go,' Eesa said, 'I have a question.' Chasse met his mother's gaze, conscious of her querying raised eyebrow. 'What is Tam protecting on the mountain?'

'She's not hiding anything,' Chasse replied.

'I didn't accuse her of hiding something,' Eesa said calmly. 'I asked what is she protecting?'

Chasse shook his head. 'Nothing.' Eesa smiled and Chasse knew his mother didn't believe him.

'The Herbal Man left his possessions with her,' Eesa said. 'I understand Tamesan wants to learn more of his skills and we do need a healer in the village, but why did she want Jaysin to go with her?'

'Company,' Chasse replied. 'It gets terribly lonely in the cave. Jaysin will learn some of what she knows.'

'I wish she would explain her intentions to me,' Eesa said. 'Secrets are not healthy.'

'Organise yourself and get to Meltsparkle before midday,' Kevan interrupted. 'Don't be late.'

Chasse retreated from the bridge, looking back as he trudged through the snow to see his parents were still talking. He knew he was lucky to be the son of the Dragon Head, and now also of the Dragon Heart, but the luck didn't translate into privileges or favours because he was treated like every dragonwarrior. He appreciated why his parents did not elevate him over the others, but sometimes he wished that he could access insights to leadership and being strong that only his father could give him to enable him to stand above others if a time came to do so.

He looked at the sky and out to sea to read the weather. His father expected him to spend five nights in the wilderness, albeit a short distance from Harbin. The sun was bright, but clouds were piling on one another to the north as they did before the last storm swept in and although the wind was not strong it was present, whipping foam across the waves as they rolled through the bay. If the wind gained momentum, a storm could become a blizzard and Tam told him the Herbal Man predicted a blizzard was on its way, one greater than any they had seen. He didn't want to be caught in bad weather, no matter how close to home he might be.

Within the Warriors' Hall, he filled a skin backpack with tent gear, dried food, water, kindling and touchwood to light a fire, and an ice pick, and wrapped the backpack in wolf pelts that would serve as blankets. He donned his cloak and hitched a coil of rope over his shoulder. Provisioned, spear in hand, he began the trek to Meltsparkle.

He was excited and curious. While he heard mention of the Trial of the Second Winter after being welcomed into the Dragon Fang, its activities were never shared with initiates, or anyone outside the Dragon Fang. Chasse knew it was a sacred ritual that brought him another step closer to full manhood, like reaching sixteen summers and taking the first dragonship journey, so he assumed that embarking on the Trial of the

Second Winter would separate him significantly from initiates like Thados and Remi.

At the village fringe, he encountered three fishermen on the water's edge working on an upturned dinghy and he intended to trudge by, but from beneath a grey cowl a fisherman shouted, 'Young Chasse, isn't it?'

'Yes,' Chasse replied.

The fisherman pulled back his work-stained cowl and Chasse recognised Mattias with his shaggy rust beard. 'Where would you be heading alone?' Mattias asked.

'The Dragon Head wants me to camp at the base of Meltsparkle,' Chasse said. 'What are you doing?'

'Fixing Berikan's boat,' Mattias replied, gesturing with his thumb at the weathered dory. 'It's got more patches than the old man.'

'I earned every one of them patches,' a craggy voice declared as Berikan put down his awl to grin at Chasse. 'You know there's another storm bearing down, lad?'

'I read the weather,' Chasse replied, glancing north.

'Seems like the Dragon Head can't read the weather if he's sending you out there,' Mattias said.

'The Dragon Head can't catch a fish,' remarked the third fisherman as he straightened to greet Chasse, and the three men laughed at his irreverent observation.

'It's your second winter, isn't it?' Berikan asked, hobbling through the seaweed towards Chasse. Chasse nodded. 'Trial of the Second Winter,' Berikan concluded, as he stood beside Mattias. 'Be strong, young man. You will be tested.' Chasse wondered what the old man knew of Dragon Fang lore, but before he could ask, Berikan continued. 'You're thinking what's an old fisherman like me know of the dragon ways?' He chuckled and shook his head, before explaining. 'I'm a fisherman because I like fishing. I like the sea. I know the sea, like I know my hands.' Chasse glanced down at the old man's gnarled, scarred hands. 'Amarti and I had two sons, and a daughter,' Berikan said. 'Like you, my sons were dragonwarriors. You didn't know that, did you?'

Chasse shook his head, mumbling, 'No.'

'It was another time, in fact the same summer you were born,' Berikan said. 'My lads.' He paused, reflecting, before saying, 'They did their Trials, their second winter initiation. Different mentors for both, but they stayed out on the mountain and learned the old ways.' He stopped again, and tears glinted in the old man's eyes.

'What happened to your sons?' Chasse asked.

'Both taken by dragons,' Berikan replied. 'Idran in his third summer, Steban in his fifth.' He squared his shoulders. 'I wanted them to be fishermen like me, but the Dragon Head decided they would be warriors. So, they were.' His head and shoulders sagged. 'So, they were,' he repeated.

'Hey!' Mattias interrupted, putting his hands on Berikan's shoulders. 'Come on you sentimental old fool, you have a boat to fix. Let the young dragonwarrior do as he's told.' Berikan allowed Mattias to steer him towards the boat, leaving Chasse staring at their backs.

The conversation troubled Chasse as he headed for Meltsparkle at the base of the imposing wall of Varst's Bluff because the nightmare stirred in his memory and taunted him about the mortality and brevity of a dragonwarrior's life. As a boy, he revered the Harbin dragonwarriors and his father, and he wanted desperately to be old enough to join the Dragon Fang on the legendary journeys aboard the dragonship, but his first summer journey destroyed the fabric of his boyhood fantasy and left him drenched in doubt and confusion. The life of the dragonwarrior was nothing like he imagined. It was full of drudgery, repetition, compliance and brutal, bloody killing. Berikan could not know that his sons were never killed while heroically fighting dragons. They died while the Dragon Fang plundered defenceless villages. His sons died preserving a lie. The same lie tormented Chasse's sleep.

He passed a ramshackle and abandoned hut on Harbin's fringes, half-buried in the snow, where Asmae the crone lived in isolation for the last summers of her life, and it sparked another concern. He sometimes wondered if his sister faced a similar fate, given her passion for the Herbal Man's ways and her penchant for spending time alone. Tamesan spurned the idea of being chosen by a warrior and living like her mother and, while Chasse liked the energy and hope in his sister's adventurous and free spirit, he was worried that she would come to regret her decision to remain outside what was expected of women in the village. She spurned traditional beliefs, but the traditional Harbin life was normal, certain and secure for everyone, and he couldn't understand why Tam didn't see it that way. He hated thinking she might grow old and die alone, like Amarti.

Sunlight sparkled on the stream tumbling from the towering heights of Varst's Bluff over waterfalls and cascades to the shore. The ocean waves roared against the rocks, throwing spray into the breeze, and white gulls circled further out, searching for the silver flash of fish. Chasse looked up at the soft blue sky, at clouds gathering in the north and the wind flicking the crests of the waves and washing through the tree canopies. The weather was fickle and he wished he wasn't sent to Meltsparkle.

With diligent searching, he located a rocky overhang several paces above the tide line that sheltered a recess in the cliff face from the snowfall and the wind's cutting edge. Scorch marks and smoke stains on the rock were evidence that others had camped in the same spot, so he leaned his spear against the rock, unhitched his backpack and the rope, and methodically set up his refuge, laying out the wolf pelts, his rations and a fireplace, before settling to wait for whoever was coming – if anyone was coming. Berikan said his sons had mentors. Chasse guessed it would be Jon or Raven who would come to train him.

He stared across the bay at the distant mist-shrouded peaks of The Sentinels. *Did Suran make it back to his southern home?* he pondered. He was told by Kevan that any journey in The Sentinels was perilous and that

Suran was more likely to perish than reach Jebaran.

He looked up at Dragon Mountain, cloud obscuring its white peak, and wondered what Tam and Jaysin were doing, and how his curious brother reacted when he first saw the dragon egg. He smiled at the likely scenario. Jaysin would be amazed and overwhelmed and he imagined his little brother sitting on the edge of the nest, studying the egg, fascinated by its warmth and colouration, pestering Tam with question after question as only Jaysin could. And he wondered how his parents really felt with two of their three children living like hermits on the mountain, neither conforming to Harbin's culture. *And now the eldest is sitting alone at the foot of Varst's Bluff,* he wryly mused.

Chasse kindled a small fire to occupy himself, aware that he would have to forage for wood before nightfall to sustain a fire through the night. He decided he would wait until after midday before he scouted for resources, in case his mentor was on his way. Clouds dominated the sky, dulling the sun and cooling the air, and the wind gathered force. Snowflakes swirled and landed on the rocks to be washed away by successive waves. The fishermen in the bay abandoned their work and rowed to shore.

Deciding he should prepare for his night vigil, he took his spear and empty pack and navigated the rocks and banks around Meltsparkle, climbing into the woods in search of firewood. Snow buried the landscape, but sporadic patches protected by the tree canopy revealed sticks and branches and he collected what he could to carry to his camp. He paused once, warily watching a shadowy shape slide between bushes higher up the slope, recognising a wolf on the move, but the animal did not reappear. He finished foraging and retreated to his campsite, where he was surprised to find his father waiting.

'You have enough wood for tonight?' Kevan asked as Chasse dropped his pack.

'I think so,' Chasse replied. He straightened to say, 'I didn't expect you to be here.'

'Why not?' Kevan asked. 'I am your father.'

'But I thought – I guess I thought you would be too busy to be my mentor,' Chasse replied.

Kevan stooped and opened the pack and began emptying the wood Chasse collected. 'It is the duty of every father to lead his son through the Trial of the Second Winter,' he said slowly. 'Only those whose fathers are not warriors of the Dragon Fang, or those whose fathers have crossed to Varst's Eternal Paradise, need other men to guide them.' He looked up and smiled. 'Fortunately, for you, and me, I am still here.' He shook the debris from the pack and laid it against the rock, before sliding a pack from his back and placing it beside Chasse's pack. 'Rekindle the fire,' he said. 'We'll talk. And then we'll go for a walk before the sun sets.'

Flames guttering low, coals glowing, Chasse looked past his father's shoulders at the grey world. The sun was a hazy sensation of light and he estimated it was halfway towards the western horizon. Snow continued to swirl, and the wind continued to beat the grey water and the rocks. His father talked through the early afternoon of his role as Dragon Head and how he earned it, why men and women had delineated roles for social stability, and why different people in the village had different duties or skills, like the fishermen, Galt the goatherd, Merrik the blacksmith, and Kan the chandler. He explained the dragonship journeys and why they were important for retaining Harbin culture.

'Not all our summer journeys are for taking things,' Kevan said. 'Sometimes we trade with the southerners. We swap what we can make for things we cannot make, like metal blades and pots.' He waited for Chasse to meet his gaze before saying, 'Every dragonwarrior knows these things. We don't defend the village or fight or trade for fun. We keep the traditions. We ensure stability as much as we exist for security. Do you understand what I mean?'

'Yes,' Chasse replied.

'I know you still have bad dreams,' Kevan said. 'I understand. I was like you after my fourth summer. It was a bad journey. My friend, Haren, was killed, cut down in front of me by an axeman. After I came home, I dreamed of Haren's death every night.' He stopped and put a hand on Chasse's arm. 'What you saw on your first journey was a harsh initiation, one I would not wish on anyone, but it will pass, Chasse. It will pass. To be a man, you must master your fears. You must push these dreams aside.'

Chasse swallowed, his anger bubbling because his father's explanation did not convince him that what he saw on the dragonship journey was right or necessary. 'I never thought –' he began, but he stopped, unable to express what was surging through his thoughts.

'Becoming a man isn't easy,' Kevan said. 'The truth of the world is kept from children and for good reason. But you are a man, now, and you have seen some of the world's truth. What makes a man strong, and worthy, is how he adapts and grows with the truth.'

Chasse wanted to challenge his father on the necessity to lie to everyone, but his father's earnest face held him in check. *Perhaps I will learn to be stronger*, he told himself. *Perhaps my nightmares will fade as Father's faded*.

'Enough talk,' Kevan announced. 'Walk with me. Bring the rope.'

Chasse followed Kevan up the lower part of the cliff above the rock shelter to where the Meltsparkle waters tumbled over a fall, but he kept repeating his father's advice and questioning its validity in the face of the death and destruction that he witnessed on his first journey. He couldn't justify the killing of innocent people to propagate a lie about dragon hunting. It was wrong. Surely it was wrong. If he was like his sister, he would speak out against the wrong. He would not be part of it.

Kevan walked a few paces beyond the fall and stepped onto a flat slime-smeared stone beside the bank, a handspan beneath the water. He moved from the stone to another and another, the stones forming a simple crossing in a shallow section of the stream, and he beckoned for Chasse to follow. They began an arduous climb up the wet, slippery rock face of Varst's Bluff, Kevan leading, moving slowly and methodically, resting frequently, until they reached a narrow, snow-covered ledge. When Chasse settled beside his father, Kevan said, 'This can be a place for a powerful view over the bay on clear days, but not today.'

Chasse looked out and saw they were sitting a short distance below the cloud ceiling and the view was obscured by falling snow and fog. Looking down, he was surprised by how high they climbed.

'This is Nakiades' Rest,' Kevan said. 'Only the Dragon Fang know this place. Until today, you would not have heard of it. But now that you know, it is another secret you must keep.' He shuffled along the ledge and disappeared around a thin buttress, his head reappearing to say, 'Follow.'

Chasse eased around the rock and discovered a gap opening into a tall narrow cave. Kevan blocked the entrance. 'Tie the rope securely to this.' He indicated a rusty metal spike a handspan from the floor. 'Make sure it will not come undone.' Chasse knelt and secured the rope to the spike, tugging to check the knot would hold. 'Good,' Kevan complimented. 'Now, we go down.' He took the rope and dangled it over the edge of a pit and let the end drop from sight. 'I'll call when I am at the bottom,' Kevan explained, before he stepped over the edge and descended.

Chasse waited, peering into the dark hole, wondering where his father was leading him, remembering his adventures with Tam and the Herbal Man's cave. When he heard his father call from the dark, he took hold of the rope and shimmied down.

At the bottom, as his eyes adjusted, he saw a dull circle of light to his left. 'This way,' Kevan's shadowy presence said. Chasse followed his father along a short, low tunnel towards the light, until the tunnel became an oval cavern, open to the grey daylight and the ocean's roar at one end, the light revealing a jagged array of rocky formations. 'Nakiades' Rest,' Kevan announced. 'Only men of the Dragon Fang come here. Here, we see what we know to be true. Look.' He pointed at a large flat stone in the cavern's centre.

Chasse approached the stone. A battered, corroded copper helmet, a long green spear, larger than any owned by the warriors in Harbin, a green copper sword, and three white objects lay on the floor – and bones. As he perused the artefacts, he asked, 'Why are these things here?'

Kevan stood beside Chasse, and replied, 'These are Nakiades' relics. These are how we know the legend is true.'

Chasse examined the objects, recognising in the helmet an item similar to the helmets in the Herbal Man's treasures, although the metal was different. The bones resembled huge fangs.

'Nakiades slew Blitzart's spawn on the peak above us,' said Kevan. 'Those are three of the dragon's teeth. The hole we descend to enter this place was formed by the dragon's acidic blood. Here is where Nakiades left his legacy for us to remember and fulfil. We are the Dragon Fang. We are the children of Na-Kia-Des and the people of H-Ara-Bin.'

Chasse listened as his father recited the words that completed the re-telling of Nakiades' legend at every celebration. Like all Harbin inhabitants, he knew the tale by rote, knew the origins of their people, but after his first summer journey, when it became all too apparent the reality of the summer searches for dragons was nothing like the legend, he doubted the tale's authenticity. Staring at the artefacts, he knew the legend had to be authentic – that Nakiades did face and fight a dragon.

'This is where Blitzart's dragon lived,' Kevan explained, as he walked to the opening, indicating for Chasse to follow. 'Nakiades made this the place where his dragonwarriors could come to remember their oaths and be close to him.' He pointed to scratchings and etched illustrations on patches of the cave wall. 'Every man leaves a mark.' He approached a crude drawing of a warrior holding a spear aloft. 'This is my mark.' Chasse studied the engraving. 'You will leave yours today, before we leave.' He walked to the cave mouth and waited for Chasse to join him.

The cave opened to the western ocean, although low clouds and snow and fog obscured the vista and the wind battered the rocks and howled across the cave entrance. Chasse shivered at the wind's bite and the swirling spray rising from waves hammering against the rocks below wet his face.

'When the sun sinks into the Great Ocean,' Kevan said quietly, 'Varst paints the horizon myriad colours and this place is lit with golden light. An irony of our lives is that beauty and terror are neither opposites nor enemies, but parts of the whole. For the Dragon Fang, this means that sometimes what we are expected to do when we journey in summer is terrible to behold, but it is done to sustain the beauty of where we live for all who live here. One is not possible without the other, and, as a warrior in the Dragon Fang, this is now your burden and your responsibility.' He was silent and Chasse respected the silence, until Kevan directed, 'Make your mark on the wall Chasse, son of Kevan, so others will see and know that you stood among the Dragon Fang.'

Eight

Kevan lay curled beneath his bear fur under the ledge, snoring, and Chasse watched his father's side rise and fall in the glow of the coals. He liked having his father with him. The importance of what they were sharing on Varst's Bluff nourished him and filled him with identity and purpose, but as tired as he was, sleep did not come easily.

For his mark on the wall in Nakiades' Rest, he drew a warrior holding a battle axe to represent himself, but he also drew smaller figures – a girl and a boy – and an egg shape. His father stared at the finished etchings and Chasse could tell Kevan did not understand his clumsy symbols, but his father asked nothing, as if his silence and acceptance of Chasse's drawing was an expected measure of respect. He merely put his hand on Chasse's shoulder and said, 'Now, we climb out.'

The afternoon and early evening visit to Nakiades' Rest and his father's lessons dogged him when he huddled in the warmth of his wolf furs. Whether or not he liked the idea of sailing south to raid and trade, the legend of Nakiades was real and his role as a dragonwarrior of the Dragon Fang and a protector of Harbin was defined. He wondered if the dragon that Nakiades killed was an ancestor of Claryssa, the Herbal Man's dragon. And was Tam nursing an egg that would, one day, destroy homes and kill people?

When sleep finally came, he stood in the middle of a burning village again, bodies lying around him, a woman and a child reaching for him before being swept aside. And, again, the dragonship loomed through eerie orange smoke and Marron fell between the ship and the shore, and arms grabbed him and dragged him upward – and he woke, panting and thrashing his legs, a weight on his arms holding him down and a deep voice saying, 'Chasse. Son. Wake up. Wake up.'

'Here,' Kevan said, handing Chasse a sliver of cured bear meat. 'You'll need your energy today.'

Chasse accepted the offering and chewed, staring past the smoky campfire across Harbin Bay towards The Sentinels. 'Sorry about last night,' he said.

'We all have those dreams when we begin,' Kevan assured him, as he stirred herbs into his mug of boiled water. 'There is nothing to be sorry for. There is only determination to master these dreams.'

'I don't want to have them.'

His father shook his head and replied, 'You don't get to choose when and what you dream. The gods choose what they want you to think and they plant those thoughts inside your dreams for you to learn about life. How a man deals with his dreams determines how strong a man he is.'

'Do you dream about death?'

Kevan gazed across the bay. 'After I first sailed south, I could not sleep when I came home. I was nearly killed by a warrior when we raided our first town. My father stopped him before he could strike me, but I kept dreaming for months that he split me open with his great sword and that I was lying in mud and water, slowly drowning and bleeding to death. Every time, in that dream, I would wake at the moment I thought I was about to die.

After the second journey, that dream went away. I told you what happened on my fourth journey with Harlen. So, then I had more terrible dreams, but eventually they also faded. I forced them to go.' He turned to Chasse. 'Sometimes, as I've grown older, I have dreams that feel like I am dying, but they are not like that other dream, not the same terror.'

'Will I get used to it?' Chasse asked.

Kevan shrugged and nodded. 'Yes, you will get used to it, son. But you must know that in every battle there is a sword or a spear or an axe or an arrow waiting for you. If your courage and skill hold true, and your luck, the death weapon will not find you. Sometimes, you will find its bearer first and slay him. Sometimes, a friend will do that for you. And, sometimes, the one bearing your death weapon won't recognise you in the heat of battle and walk right past. But you must enter every battle knowing this and do what you can to stay alive. The day you forget is the day the death weapon will find you. Varst protect you from that day.' He took another draught from his mug and stood. 'We have much to do. Bring your spear and your pack. We return here tonight, Varst and Blitzart willing, and, if not, we sleep in the woods.'

Pack hitched, spear in hand, Chasse followed Kevan on a steady ascent, shadowing the Meltsparkle ravine, clambering over rocks, trudging through waist-deep snow patches, scaling small cliffs. Chasse knew they were following a familiar path rendered invisible by snow and the rugged terrain, a path trod by generations of warriors, and he secretly hoped that he would, one day, lead his son on this path as Kevan was leading him.

They emerged on a plateau that reminded Chasse of the one on Dragon Mountain, though it was smaller, about the size of the Long Hall and walled by snow-clad trees. Kevan halted at a fallen log and scraped snow from it before he laid down his pack. He indicated that Chasse should do the same while he strode to the centre of the glade with his spear. 'Take off your cloak and bring your weapon,' Kevan instructed. Chasse obeyed and moved to face his father. 'You've been trained in the Warrior Hall. Let's see what you know,' Kevan said as he spun his spear into ready position. 'Defend yourself.'

Before Chasse could ask a question, Kevan lunged, forcing Chasse to knock the thrusting spear point aside, and he stepped back and tested his balance in the snow. Kevan lunged again, Chasse repeating his defensive actions. The snow grabbed his ankles, but he jumped a step back and readied for Kevan's next move. This time, Kevan came on relentlessly, twirling and spinning his spear, forcing Chasse to block a rapid flurry of thrusts and prods and sweeps as his father used his strength to effortlessly push him towards the glade's perimeter. Chasse dodged left, attempting to turn his father's momentum, but Kevan pressed him until Chasse stumbled over a hidden snag and fell backwards among the trees.

'Get up!' Kevan demanded, before he trudged through the snow to the centre of the glade. 'Again!' he ordered, and he waited for Chasse to recover and return.

Kevan attacked, pressing Chasse into an inexorable retreat as he desperately fended Kevan's blows and swings, high, low, left, right, fast, slow, probing, until Chasse found himself floundering among the trees again.

'Again!' Kevan ordered.

When Chasse reached the centre and readied to defend himself, he noticed that his father was breathing harder, the exertion apparently sapping his energy. This time, Kevan's attacks lacked the power and speed of his initial onslaught and Chasse defended with greater ease, but his father still drove him to the tree line, not with strength but with an iron will. Chasse measured his father's rhythm, the pattern in his attacks, and when his father lunged, instead of blocking he stepped aside and Kevan stumbled. Chasse brought the haft of his spear sharply across his father's shoulders, before swinging the end up, catching Kevan across the jaw and sending him collapsing to his right.

Kevan stayed on his knees in the snow to catch his breath before he stood to face Chasse. Blood trickled from a skin split along his jaw. 'That took you too long. Why?'

Chasse shrugged, but he was concerned that he cut his father. 'You told me to defend,' he said, unsure of the right answer.

Kevan wiped aside the blood from his neck with his sleeve before replying, 'Dragonwarriors do not defend. When you create an advantage against an enemy, you seize it. You always seize it. Children play at defending. Warriors attack, even when they are forced to defend. Winning in this game is to be the one alive when it is done.' He walked to the centre, regarded Chasse and said, 'Again.'

Chasse wanted to ask his father to rest, but an order was an order, so he prepared for a fourth round. This time he knew he was expected to find an advantage as soon as he could. Kevan was obviously tiring and that meant his father would make a mistake, mistime a stroke. Chasse would be ready to take advantage.

So, he was surprised that, when Kevan attacked, his father's strength seemed to have returned, and Chasse backpedalled again, furiously fending off blows. Until he recognised a pattern. He ducked a sweep, pushed his father's spear aside and struck low, remembering Raven's move against him, but instead of striking his father in the groin he felt a spear shaft thwack against his head. He rolled sideways, ear stinging.

Kevan placed his spearpoint against Chasse's throat. 'Your mistake was assuming that I was tiring,' Kevan told him.

'How did you know?' Chasse asked as he rose, rubbing his ear.

'All young men think like that,' Kevan replied. 'They confuse an experienced warrior's conservation of energy with exhaustion.' He walked to the centre across the slushy earth, took a stand and said, 'Again.'

His ear hurt, his ribs and legs and arms ached, bruises were forming on his shin and his elbow, and he had stinging cuts across the back of his left hand and neck. He was grateful when Kevan finally tired of sparring, the only consolation being that his father also bore bruises and cuts. As they finished, Kevan said, between deep breaths, 'Don't be hard on yourself. If you were beating me in this exercise, you would be Dragon Head.'

Chasse understood, but it frustrated him that he, at best in a fight, could only momentarily disable his father.

Kevan ordered him to create a fireplace but not to light a fire. 'First, we need food.'

'I brought supplies in my pack,' Chasse said.

'I mean warm meat,' Kevan replied. 'A dragonwarrior must be able to hunt in every condition. Without good food, you will lose condition, and then energy and strength, and you will die.' He squatted beside Chasse and etched a crude map in the snow with his knife. 'On the northern slopes of Varst's Bluff is a wolf pack. We call them the Shadow Hunters. In the old language, they were called the She'ah'do. They have lived on this mountain since Nakiades' time. Some believe they were here before the mountain. Every dragonwarrior must eat the heart of a member of the Shadow Hunters to add the strength of the Shadow Hunters to his own. This is done during the Trial of the Second Winter.' He waited to connect with Chasse's gaze, before saying, 'It is your turn. Eat the heart of a Shadow Hunter.'

'Are you coming with me?' Chasse asked.

'No,' Kevan replied. 'I have fed you for your entire life, either through your mother as your father, or as Dragon Head feeding everyone. Today, you will feed me. I will prepare a good cooking fire and wait for you to return. When you do, you will prepare the meat as I tell you, and then I will eat what you bring. Here is where you must hunt,' he added, poking his map with his knife. 'The weather is not good, so be quick.'

Chasse collected his spear and checked that his hunting knife was secure in his belt before he headed out of the glade and up the slope as the map indicated.

The first bear hunt with Jon and Raven showed him how a team of dragonwarriors could hunt and bring down a bear, but a wolf was more agile, a cunning creature and seldom alone. He knew the stories from last winter of how wolves were the hardest creature to hunt, how they worked as a team to bring down their prey, how the dragonwarriors also combined to keep the wolves away from Harbin, and he wondered how he was going to do what his father ordered — how any dragonwarrior, alone, could kill a wolf.

He crossed a snow-capped ridge bordering two valleys, pausing to enjoy a brief respite from the falling snow and to check his bearings when the sun appeared and drifted between dark clouds. As he surveyed the landscape, he spotted dark shapes loping between the trees further down the hill. He crouched behind a tumble of rocks poking from the snowdrift to watch the shapes — wolves forging through the snow, spreading out but heading steadily for a common point in the valley. He counted seven wolves before he saw their prey — a herd of larger creatures gathered at a tributary creek that fed into Meltsparkle, animals he knew by description much like elk, only larger and without antlers, that rarely ventured near Harbin. Men who hunted deeper into the mountains beyond Varst's Bluff sometimes brought their pelts and hides down from the mountain.

'Cartenya,' a voice whispered behind him. Startled, Chasse saw Kevan kneeling nearby. 'The wolves will take one,' Kevan said. 'Watch.'

'You followed me?' Chasse asked.

'Talk after,' Kevan urged. 'Watch the wolves. Watch how they work.'

Chasse observed the unfolding events in the valley. The wolves fanned out to come at the cartenya from separate directions, and by drawing an imaginary line Chasse determined which animal they were targeting.

'They know which one they are all going to attack,' Kevan whispered. 'They would have followed and studied the herd for the last couple of days. One cartenya must have an injury or is weaker than the rest. The wolves know this.'

The cartenya stopped drinking at the creek, lifted their heads and several looked around, alert, sensing danger, but the wolves seemed to sense the change in attitude because they all paused, lowering into the snow as if one command was given to all.

'They will drive the cartenya into the deeper snow,' Kevan said. 'They're checking the wind isn't carrying their scent to the cartenya.'

The cartenya began shifting along the creek, aware that something was wrong in their world, and the wolves moved again, this time making subtle changes in their direction, steering the nervous cartenya, as Kevan said they would, towards a snowdrift. As one, the wolves suddenly broke into a charge, leaping and plunging though the snow. The herd bolted for safety and ran into the treacherous snowdrift, the deep snow bogging them down as they plunged and jumped and struggled to escape. The last cartenya found its way impeded by the rest of the herd. As it slipped, and lost its footing in the trampled, cascading snow, the wolves closed in, a tide of grey washing over the hapless animal and dragging it down.

The fight lasted longer than Chasse imagined it would. One wolf hung grimly to the cartenya's nose to suffocate it, while the others pulled at its back and neck with their jaws, avoiding the dying animal's thrashing limbs.

'So, I was never meant to kill a wolf,' Chasse said to Kevan as they descended beneath the darkening sky. The air was still, as if frozen. No snow fell. Chasse's voice echoed across the mountain.

'You should already know that a single warrior is not going to bring back a wolf.'

'Then why command me to do it?'

'A small test of your obedience. If you accept an order to carry out a difficult, even impossible task, you are worthy of being led. And it is good for you to understand why the Dragon Fang must be a pack, not individuals. When we hunt in summer, we must be one, like the wolves. If we are not, we will fail.'

'And that talk about the heart of a Shadow Hunter?' Chasse asked.

Kevan laughed and put a hand on Chasse's shoulder to stop him. 'If you understand how to act from what you observed today, you have eaten the heart of a Shadow Hunter. You have consumed its wisdom.'

The sun spread a deep red glow across the western ocean when they reached the camp at the base of Varst's Bluff. Kevan started the fire and when the flames were crackling he produced a white carcass from his bag and laid it on the rock. 'Not exactly a wolf, but a fox is tasty enough. You have a promise to keep and I'm hungry.'

Chasse set to skinning the fox with his hunting knife and preparing the meat, awkwardly trying to imitate the techniques he witnessed when Raven butchered the bear, while Kevan sat under the ledge, whittling a chunk of wood and offering advice and passing comment on Chasse's skills. The meat sliced into smaller chunks, Chasse filled the small pot with water from the stream to boil, adding herbs from a small bag that Kevan handed to him, and when the meat was ready the men used their knives to hook out pieces, savouring the warmth and odours, and talked of village matters as they ate.

After the meal, Kevan leaned against the rock, pulling his bear skin over himself, and said, 'I leave before dawn. I will not wake you, and should you wake as I'm leaving I will not speak to you. I will take your pack with me. You may keep one wolf fur and your spear. You, however, must not return to Harbin for three more nights. The last part of the Trial is for you to spend three nights and three days alone to think on what you have learned, last winter, last summer and this winter. Do you understand?'

Chasse stared at the coals and replied, 'Yes.'

'What have you learned as a warrior?'

Chasse hesitated, reflecting on lessons from Raven, his father and others. 'To take opportunity,' he said. 'Not to show my enemy my fear.'

'And?'

'To stand with my brothers. To be like the wolf. To honour Nakiades' legacy.'

'Good,' Kevan said. 'And, as a man?'

Chasse looked up. 'To be honest. To face my fears. To protect Harbin.'

Kevan nodded approval. 'We have one more thing to discuss.' He cleared his throat and adjusted his bear skin. 'A warrior undertaking the Trial of the Second Winter has often chosen his wife. You have not.'

'I am not ready,' Chasse replied adamantly.

'It is not important when you choose,' said Kevan. 'But it is important that you understand what it means to be a husband. Those who make their choice before the Trial are advised on this matter by their mentors, like I am about to advise you.' He shuffled his feet, a nervous action Chasse noticed as he waited to hear what his father had to say. 'The strength of our community lies as much in the relationships between men and women as it does between the members of the Dragon Fang. Warriors trade and protect. Fishermen and gardeners and hunters bring food. Artisans make things. Women forage and cook and give us homes,' Kevan explained. 'But men and women, as one, give us children. They give us life and hope. They give us a future. This is why we encourage pairings, why we encourage young men to choose at Procra's Dance, why we encourage young women to accept being chosen.' He met Chasse's gaze. 'Your duty is to choose a woman who will create life with you and secure Harbin's future.'

'I promise I will choose,' Chasse said. 'It's, well –'

'There is no one you are ready to choose,' Kevan finished. 'It is as it is. But there will be someone. Perhaps she is among the girls who are not yet of age that you haven't noticed.' He met Chasse's gaze. 'Or perhaps it will be a woman who is a widow.'

Chasse blushed, but he quickly replied, 'I do not think of Banni in that way.'

A wry grin creased Kevan's cheeks. 'Perhaps there will be a woman for you when the others return.'

'Do you think they will come back?' Chasse asked.

'I'm sure they will,' Kevan said. 'Their lives are here.'

'But what if they are like Alan? What if they come back to challenge you? Us?'

'There will be strong talk,' Kevan acceded. 'There will be a desire to find the dragon's treasure and you will have to guide Tam how to best defray the rumours. But I am the Dragon Head and your mother is the Dragon Heart. The people will listen. There will be peace.' He coughed. 'But I have not finished what is to be said.' He coughed again. 'When you do choose a partner, you choose a life together. Yes, women and men have different roles and responsibilities, but you will respect and honour your wife and you will not treat her badly or disregard her. After loyalty to the Dragon Fang, and your obedience to the Dragon Heart and Dragon Head, your care is to your wife. You must not forget this. It is a private oath sworn between man and woman after Procra's Dance, witnessed by the Dragon Heart, and you will be judged by others as to how well you keep your oath. Do you understand?'

'I understand,' Chasse replied.

'When you return from the wilderness, you will be seen as a man, not as a young man learning to be a warrior but as a man of the Dragon Fang. Childhood fancies and games are done. When the Trial is over, return to the Warriors' Hall. That is your home until you choose a wife.' He leaned forward, his face and beard glowing from the coals. 'I am proud to call you my son, Chasse. And I will be very proud to call you a dragonwarrior of the Dragon Fang.'

Nine

Chasse woke to a white, howling circle. Shivering and huddled hard against frigid rock, with snow piled along the ledge covering the fireplace and reaching to his feet, he couldn't see beyond the edge. Blitzart was burying the world with his cruel, cold breath.

Chasse pulled up his hood, rose, stamped his feet and rubbed his hands together to restore circulation, but the chill was deep, aching and grasping his ribs. He was alone, his father long gone, and emptiness weighed on him as cold as the snow. His spear leaned against the rock where he left it. He still had his knife. He clutched a bear fur. Everything else was gone.

He couldn't stay on the ledge. He was too exposed and the cold would slowly kill him. Shelter was the goal. *But where*? he wondered. He ran through his memory of his travels during the past two days. There were no shelters along Meltsparkle ravine, no caves. *Cave*, he thought. *Varst's Rest*. But it wasn't an option. The climb was difficult in ordinary weather, and he no longer had a rope to descend into the larger cave. He would improvise.

Barely able to see an arm span ahead, buffeted by the swirling wind and snow, he struggled up the slope beside Meltsparkle and deviated into a stand of deciduous trees, their bare limbs coated with snow and ice. He chose the largest, thickest trunk and hacked at and broke boughs, and hurriedly cross-thatched them against the base of the tree trunk, building a shelter framework, his teeth chattering, his fingers and feet going numb. As he filled the gaps between the branches and boughs, the snow piled around his construction. He climbed inside and shovelled as much snow from the base of the tree as he could until the space was large enough to crouch in. He stowed his bear fur before he emerged to pack more snow against the structure, leaving only a hole to crawl through. He climbed in, wrapped himself in his fur, pulled his hooded cloak tight, and curled up to wait out the storm.

For a while, through gaps in his structure, he watched the wind harrying the snow and whipping across the landscape, but the gaps filled with snow and the dull light dissolved. He recalled the survival lessons his father taught him, especially if he was ever caught in a storm on the mountain. Find or build shelter quickly. Cover up. Stay warm. Use snow to build a shelter. Spread leaves on the ground inside the shelter — if there are any. Learn from the animals. Under the snow is better than out in the open. Drink. Don't sweat. He recited the lessons taught in the Warriors' Hall — how to find and make touchwood from fungi on the trees to burn, how to create a spark using his spear head and a stone, how to trap small animals and birds, where to find edible plants and which ones not to eat. He only had to stay away for three nights. Food was a minor issue. If he had to, he could go without. There was plenty of water. The real challenge was keeping warm.

He snoozed and woke several times, aware of the wind continuing to wail outside his tiny space. He poked his spear through the structure, testing the depth of the accumulating snow and he made breathing holes, although he knew they were closing shortly after he created them. He was cold, but his fingers and toes tingled and ached as his body warmth stabilised. He closed his eyes.

The world was dark and silent when he woke. He lay still, straining to hear, before he shuffled, took his spear and poked it through the snow ceiling. He listened again, but the world beyond his shelter was silent. He needed to piss. He crushed snow in his hands to drink and rubbed warmth back into his hands before he dug with his spear at the snow burying the entrance, and he was surprised by its depth.

He emerged into a white world, the dull sun glow through the clouds indicating it was mid-afternoon, and as he stepped out his boots sank into the uncompacted snow. He fumbled through his layers and sighed as he relieved the pressure in his bladder, watching his piss steam.

Relieved, he trudged towards a stand of evergreens. The air was bitterly cold and he knew he couldn't stay out of his shelter for too long. He hacked down twigs and thinner leafy branches and used his knife to skin string-thin strips of bark. He bundled his plunder and carried it to lay outside his shelter before he headed for another stand, selected a Batchwood tree and dug into the snow around its trunk until he exposed the small, solid purple berries of a Fler's Gift plant. He harvested the berries and retreated to his shelter.

His hands were cold and the snow on his clothes was melting from his body heat. He didn't need water on his clothes. Time was running out. He wiped the snow from his clothes before he set to improvising a pair of snowshoes from the twigs with leaves, twisting the bark strips into crude rope to bind his creation. Shoes finished, he cobbled together a flat construct to serve as a door to his shelter. He pushed his snowshoes and remaining wood into the shelter and backed in, pulling his makeshift door closed in his wake. He would have liked more room, but frantic necessity left his quarters cramped; not good for active living, but the less air to warm inside the easier it was to retain heat. He spread the remaining wood and leaves on the floor to provide insulation, punched new holes through the ceiling with his spear and rested.

The effort to walk a few paces through the soft snow and dig the berries left him more exhausted than he anticipated, although another of the lessons from last winter was to avoid soft snow. *Now what?* he pondered. *Am I meant to stay here for two days doing nothing? What did others do? Is every dragonwarrior brought here to survive a storm?*

The afternoon was waning when he climbed into his shelter and the snow-buried shelter was dark, so there was nothing to do except wait and think and hopefully sleep until the next sunrise. He retrieved a berry, popped it into his mouth, and chewed.

Chasse didn't remember going to sleep, but falling snow woke him. He wiped his face, listening as he reached for his spear in the dark. More snow fell, and he heard scratching and snuffling at the trapdoor. An animal was digging furiously at his shelter. A bear? More than one. Wolves. A chunk of the ceiling collapsed. Twigs and snow thumped against his shoulder. Panicking, he thrust his spear upward, once, twice, three times, the last strike ending with a yelp and his spear twisted violently in his hands, pushed down from without. He wrestled with the weight, but he had no room to pull the spear free. And then an avalanche of snow and twigs cascaded over him. As he released the spear and wrenched his knife from his belt, a growling mass pressed on him. He stabbed and thrust frantically, buried in hot breath, the stench of offal and damp fur in his nostrils, blood, his legs trapped, flailing his right arm and pushing with his left against a heavy bulk, stabbing, pushing, enveloped by yelps, growling, more yelps.

Until the struggle ceased.

The load across his chest and face was warm, heavy, panting, but immobile. He struggled to breathe under the dying animal's weight, forced to suck in shallow gasps. He tugged at the fur, but with his legs pinned he couldn't get leverage to move the wolf. If there were more wolves, they could take him now. Anger and sadness flooded him.

He listened. Apart from the wolf's laboured and slowing breathing and his own heartbeat thudding inside his temple and chest, the world was silent.

He imagined he could see stars blinking overhead in the sky's night tapestry, but the vision was unclear and uncertain because the stars seemed to vanish and reappear after a short absence. *Clouds*, he reasoned. *The weather's changing.*

The wolf's body heat was unexpected compensation in the icy night, but he knew it would be fleeting and when the wolf shuddered and stopped breathing it was only a matter of time before the dead animal was cold and he, too, stopped breathing. He tried to shift the corpse using his upper body strength and determination, but he was trapped. *Not how I expected to die*, he thought. *How odd.*

He relaxed and focused on how he could change the situation, how he could adjust his arms, how he could use his knife to hack at the corpse to lighten the burden pressing down on him or dig at the earth to make space to wriggle from under the animal. He wondered how long it would be before the wolf's heat dissipated, and whether he would freeze after that, or would the snow start falling and smother him. Or another wolf would come to feed.

The last option made him feel ill. *As long as I'm already dead*, he decided. *Don't let me be still alive.* He imagined what his father would say, finding his son under a dead wolf. *I killed a Shadow Hunter*, he thought with pride. *My death will be sung in the Warriors' Hall.*

Then his spirit sagged again when he wondered if they would ever find his body on the slopes of Varst's Bluff. *Will another dragonwarrior find my bones during his Trial of the Second Winter*?

He tried again to move the dead wolf. The animal was big, bigger than he remembered wolves being. He strained and pushed. Nothing changed. The animal's ruff pressed against his jaw. If his legs were free – he strained, but his legs were firmly buried beneath snow and wood. This was his fate.

Praying to the gods was not his way. Fishermen, like Berikan and Mattias, prayed to Procra and Fler for abundant catches, and the Dragon

Heart offered prayers and small sacrifices to them and to Varst at ceremonial gatherings. It seemed the gods were invoked when someone needed a blessing or was sung across the divide between this world and Varst's Paradise or thanked for favourable events. If divine intervention was possible, he needed it. Ecg was the dragonwarrior's god, the giver of strength and courage called upon by the Dragon Fang before battle.

'Oh, mighty Ecg,' Chasse whispered into the darkness. 'Give this warrior strength to push aside this dead wolf and I will be your eternal servant.' He waited, but nothing changed his situation. He tried to move the weight from his chest. 'Please, great Varst, help me,' he whispered. 'If you are watching, if you can hear me, help me,' he repeated three times. 'Or Fler,' he said. 'I'm sorry I killed one of your beautiful creations. If you help me, I will become a protector of your wild creatures.' He waited. The night was silent. His body ached. 'I don't want to die like this,' he begged. 'It's a stupid way to die. Please, Varst!' he cried. 'Please!'

He wrestled with the dead wolf until his energy faded. The cold cut into him from his back, from his arms, his head. Moisture settled on his cheeks and forehead. Rain. Snow. Snow again. *What will come first*? he pondered. *Will I freeze? Will I smother?* Childhood memories came and went. Games of Knock. Sword fights with Tam. Teasing Jaysin with dead fish. Wrestling with Marron and Derik. He thought of Kerryn and of Banni and Jara. *What will my mother sing for me when I am gone?* he wondered. *If I close my eyes, perhaps I will go to sleep and not wake*. He closed his eyes, but his mind raced across questions, thoughts, visions as the cold dug deeper. 'Let me sleep,' he begged. 'Don't make me linger.'

Sensing the glow through his eyelids, he opened his eyes, blinked against the intrusion of the warm halo, and saw the blurred image of a young woman. 'Fler,' he mouthed. 'Thank you.'

His skin luxuriated in the warmth spreading along his back and the soft aroma of brewing herbs teased his nose. He opened his eyes. Daylight. He rolled over towards the source of heat. A fire crackled. Beyond the low flames, a hooded figure sat facing him, silhouetted against a backdrop of snow-caked trees.

'Hungry?' the figure asked. Chasse eased into a sitting position. 'The broth will nourish you,' the woman said.

'Tam?' Chasse queried.

The young woman lowered her white hood, her red hair tied tightly, and she said, 'I can't stay long. There's another storm sweeping in this afternoon. You need to be ready.' She leaned forward to lift a metal pot from the fire with a stick and she poured broth into a small bowl which she handed to Chasse.

'How did you find me?' Chasse asked, as he accepted the warm bowl.

'We are bound,' Tam replied. She revealed her amber bracelet.

Chasse lowered his bowl to study the amber bracelet that Tam gifted him, his understanding fighting with his confusion.

'I've been learning how Eric communicated with Gramma,' Tam explained. 'I can't do it yet, but the bracelets allow me to find whoever is wearing them, and I know it sounds strange but they also tell me how the wearers are feeling.' She glanced at her bracelet. 'Jaysin knows where I am and he's happy because he's sitting with the egg. He's teaching himself to read. I felt your fear, so I came.'

'I thought you were Fler,' Chasse said. 'I was praying.'

'I can take you with me,' Tam posed, 'but you'll be trapped in Dragon Mountain for a long time.'

'I can't do that,' Chasse said. 'I have to stay one more night and return to the Warriors' Hall, or I will fail the Trial.'

'I knew that would be your answer,' Tam replied. 'But you don't have much choice. If you stay here tonight, you will freeze. I think our father will accept you going back to Harbin a day early when he witnesses what is about to happen. Here.' She handed Chasse a small bundle. 'Fler's Gift berries, a knot of Dragonroot, and an unction to apply to your cuts. Go back to the village. Apologise. Tell them what I told you and wait. When they see the blizzard tonight, they will know you were right to return.'

'But how will you get back to the cave?'

'If I leave now, I will make it in good time.'

'I can make snowshoes for you,' Chasse offered. 'They won't take long.'

Tam pointed to a bundle beside her, saying, 'I have some. Eric left several pair in the cave, good ones. Finish the broth and head down to the village,' she urged. 'I have to go.' She bent to pack items, threw snow over the fire, and donned her snowshoes while Chasse drank the broth. As Chasse handed her his empty bowl, she handed him a small bag. 'Flint and touchwood,' she explained. 'You should be home well before the blizzard arrives, but just in case.' She lifted a black gold-tipped staff from the snow. 'Take care, brother. Don't tarry.'

'Thank you,' Chasse said.

As Tam turned to leave, she pointed to her bracelet. 'Remember, we are bound.'

Chasse watched his sister ascend the ridge until she disappeared into the forest before he assessed his situation. He had his knife and the supplies that Tam brought, but his spear was missing. He surveyed the sheltered grove that Tam brought him to and walked to the edge of the trees to orient himself. He searched the landscape and spotted the stand of trees where he had sheltered a hundred paces away, parallel to the grove. There were drag marks in the snow and he immediately wondered how Tam moved him or how she lifted the wolf from him. *The wolf*, he remembered. He hooked the small bags from Tam to his belt and headed for the trees.

The wolf lay in the ruined hollow of his makeshift refuge, a huge animal with a dark grey pelt. It seemed that Tam used branches to lever the corpse off him, although he had no memory of her doing so – no memory of anything except the light. His spear was broken, the head buried in the wolf's chest, the shaft missing. Flashbacks of his desperate battle flicked through his mind as he studied the chaotic scene.

He looked at the blue sky. The air was motionless. If Tam was right, and he knew she would be, he had enough time to reach Harbin before the next storm came. He collected fragments of branches and twigs, made a platform for kneeling, drew his knife, and set to skinning the wolf. *I will return too early*, he decided, *but I will bring a trophy*.

Chasse was plodding through the snow, almost into the village, wolf skin draped across his shoulders and back, when the wind hit him like a giant hand and pushed him to his knees, and he was enveloped in white. Wind and snow roared over the crest of Varst's Bluff and Dragon Mountain, a great white whirling cloud thundering down on Harbin like an avalanche. Chasse fought to his feet, pulled the pelt over his hood, and stumbled on, buffeted and bullied by the wind, determined to reach the Warriors' Hall, struggling to find direction as all reference vanished.

When the wind hit, he was heading straight for the centre of Harbin, so he pushed on blindly, believing he was not disoriented. The snow deepened in a steep slope and he realised that he was walking into a drift piled against a cottage. He was at the village edge. He adjusted direction and trudged forward. A tiny flickering yellow light exposed another cottage to his left, guiding him. Shadows loomed in the white. He headed for the largest shadow, the Warriors' Hall, and banged on the door. When no one opened it, he banged again, pain shooting through his frosted fist. It opened, Chasse lurched in and the wind roared behind him a moment before the door heaved shut and the beam dropped to lock it.

A fire crackled in the long hearth and he smelt boiling meat and tubers. Strong hands took hold of his arms and guided him to the log seats, the wolf pelt was lifted from his shoulders, and a warm bowl of stew was thrust into his hands.

Raven's face appeared. 'You brought Blitzart's whole dragon horde back with you!'

'Look at this wolf skin!' Kurtis remarked. 'This is the coat of the leader of the Shadow Hunters.'

'You surely have a story to share,' said Raven sitting beside Chasse. 'We'll hear it when you've eaten.'

'Where's my father?' Chasse asked.

'The Dragon Head is home,' Raven replied. 'When we saw Blitzart's anger coming over the mountain, he ordered the married men to be with their families. This is a big storm.'

'But you have a wife,' Chasse reminded him.

Raven replied, 'I do. But there are only Petar, Kurtis Thados and Remi here. Jon and I will take turns staying in the Hall to keep them company during this storm. I am first. I'll go to my home tomorrow night, if the storm permits. Others will visit when they can.'

'It will last several days,' Chasse said.

'How do you know that?' Raven asked.

'My sister told me,' Chasse explained.

'I will let your father know that you are safe when there is a break in the storm,' Raven offered.

'I can do that,' Chasse told him. 'I owe my father an apology for coming down early.'

Raven laughed jovially, saying, 'No one will be happier than the Dragon Head to see that you are wise enough to leave the mountain in the face of a blizzard.'

Ten

Chasse was praised for his survival in the Trial of the Second Winter as each dragonwarrior learned of his adventure. He modified the story of how he killed the wolf, keeping only the core parts about being ensnared in the shelter and fighting his way out. He emphasised his luck in spearing the animal through the mass of branches, leaves and snow, avoided details about being trapped and thinking he was going to die, and he divulged nothing of Tam's intervention. The dragonwarriors badgered him about his poor skinning skills, how he amateurly hacked from a carcass what could have been the finest wolf pelt ever seen in Harbin, but when the hide was cleaned and set out to dry, he was complimented on killing a fine animal.

'The pelt is yours when it is cured,' Kevan promised on his first visit. 'You earned it. Wear it with pride.'

'You will be known as Chasse Wolf's Bane,' said Jon. 'Generations will admire this pelt and wonder what mighty warrior killed such a noble beast.'

'But, for now, you are Chasse the new man in the Dragon Fang,' Raven reminded him, lifting a spear, 'and you have training to continue. Bring a spear and join in.'

The long days in the Warriors' Halls during the blizzard were spent sitting at the blazing long hearth to keep warm, listening to stories of past summer journeys, hunting experiences and escapes from danger, learning new techniques for whittling and repairing equipment, honing fighting skills, sharpening blades and exercising. The dragonwarriors sojourning with their families endured the wild weather to make brief journeys from their homes to share time with Chasse, Petar, Kurtis, Thados and Remi who remained in the Warriors' Hall, taking turns to keep the hearth burning. During the nights, they curled beneath fur layers to keep the bitter cold at bay while they slept.

Sleep teased Chasse. It came easily, but it brought curious, sometimes fearful dreams. The nightmare of the summer tragedy morphed into a pastiche of dancing dragonwarriors being buried in deep snow breathed by a white dragon, Blitzart, but when he tried to escape the battle to reach the dragonship his feet were trapped in ice and a gigantic snarling wolf, fangs gleaming in firelight, barred his path. And the wolf sometimes had Marron's face and sometimes Suran's. And sometimes he dreamed he was standing in a yellow glow before the goddess, Fler, a wolf on either side of her, and one laying at her feet, and she was admonishing him. When he tried to explain that he was only protecting himself, the words wouldn't come because his voice was empty. And beyond the glow was a dark, forbidding dragon shadow.

'You were screaming again,' Petar mentioned, when Chasse opened his eyes one night. The hall glowed with hearth embers. Wind howled outside. 'The dreams are bad?'

'Bad enough,' Chasse replied, blinking.

'We all have them,' Petar said, sitting back.

'What do you dream?' Chasse asked.

Petar shrugged, and replied, 'I never remember much. The most I recall is being on a ship like the dragonship, but I don't know anyone. And a dragon comes and I wake up afraid.'

'Why did you help Alan and Suran?'

Petar was silent after Chasse's question and Chasse wondered if he was asking more than he should, until Petar cleared his throat to say, 'I thought it was the right thing to do. Marron made the plan sound like it would bring Harbin together. And if Suran was correct, and there was a dragon treasure, we would be rich beyond measure. I had to come.'

'And now?' Chasse asked.

'Now, I am here,' Petar replied. 'Your father is Dragon Head and I know what is right.'

What Chasse wanted to ask was, 'Can we trust you?' but he let the question pass.

'Are you ready to go back to sleep?' Petar asked.

'No,' Chasse said. 'I'll take my turn at the fire. You sleep.'

Petar moved to his bed and settled under his furs while Chasse rose, wrapped his cloak tight and shuffled to the hearth. He stirred the coals with the heavy poker, watching golden sparks spiral and vanish, before he lay another chunk of wood on top and coaxed it to catch fire. As he sat and stared at the flames, he wondered how much trust his father retained for Petar and how wary he should be of a man who seemed able to change allegiance as it suited his circumstance. He tried recalling if Petar sided with Trask against his father before Eric and Claryssa changed the course of events, but he couldn't remember.

Another recurring dream concerned his sister. Chasse couldn't fathom how she found him on the slopes of Varst's Bluff, how she travelled through the storm and snow, how she moved him from beneath the wolf's corpse. He fingered his amber bracelet. 'We are bound,' he silently mouthed. The Herbal Man's magic lingered on Dragon Mountain and Tam was inheriting it. He never imagined how powerful it might be.

In his dream, he stood on a precipice, staring into darkness, the depths drawing him over the edge, but even as he stepped off, unable to resist the inexorable pull, Tam put her hands on his shoulders and he was freed from the urge and he could turn to face her. And she was older in the dream, her face worn and tired, her red hair turned white, as if she had become Eesa and Gramma Harmi and Amarti. But she smiled at him, and he knew everything was all right.

He stoked the coals. Sleep was precious. He wanted to sleep. He surveyed the hall. Petar was already asleep. Kurtis snored softly in the far corner near the weapon stands. He saw the outline of his wolf pelt on the drying rack. This was his home. He was a man. His childhood was done.

The blizzard lasted ten full days and when the people of Harbin emerged from their homes they stared in awe at a world encased in snow deeper than any villager experienced and a sheet of ice sealed the shallow water of the bay. Watersdrop waterfall was frozen and the fishing boats were encased in ice thick enough for the fishermen to walk on. Children ran to the shore to slide and play on the ice. The village numbers were counted to check that no one perished and the dragonwarriors helped excavate snow from doorways and repair damage, while fishermen used warm rods and torches to free their boats and experimented with fishing through holes cut in the ice.

With the winter solstice nigh, Eesa organised the women to prepare for Blitzart's Feast. 'If Blitzart has any cold breath left, I would be surprised,' Eesa announced when she gathered the women in the Long Hall. 'We will celebrate loudly, even as few as we are.'

'Don't aggravate a dragon god,' Amarti warned in front of the women. 'I thought each blizzard we endured this winter was the last, but not so. Not so.'

Keeping his promise, Chasse visited Banni each day after the blizzard. He helped by shovelling snow from her roof and walls and repairing a section of the cottage damaged by the weight of snow. She offered him a meal when he completed the repair and apologised when she had to leave him to complete the work while she tended to Jara, but as she fed the child she said, 'Tell me about the Trial.'

Chasse lowered his spoon and replied, 'There's not much to tell. I came home early.'

'Because of the blizzard,' Banni said. 'You would have died if you stayed out there.' She adjusted Jara on her breast and asked, 'What do you do in the Trial?'

Chasse almost asked if Jared told her what was involved after he took the Trial, but he thought the question would stir her memories and sadness, so he replied, 'Mostly we learn from our fathers – how to be men.'

'Secret men's talk,' Banni acknowledged, nodding. 'Jared wouldn't tell me about it either.'

Feeling as if he betrayed Banni by keeping a secret, he said, 'My father talked to me about how to be a good husband, and what is expected of us as protectors of Harbin. And it is a small test of what we learn about staying alive in the wilderness. There are no secrets, really. I thought it would be harder.'

'The cuts and bruises on your face and neck tell me it was hard enough. And where did you get the wolf skin?'

Chasse fingered the edge of the pelt draped over the stool and gave Banni the same story that he told the warriors. 'I was very lucky,' he finished.

'It will keep you warm,' Banni observed, and she returned her attention to Jara, nursing her gently and pulling her cowl closer.

Filled with an unexpected compulsion, Chasse stood with the wolf pelt and draped it across Banni's shoulders. 'It's a gift for you,' he said, stepping back.

Banni's cheeks reddened. 'I can't take this,' she protested, sliding the pelt onto her lap.

'Why not? Chasse asked. 'It's a gift.'

'But you earned it. I know how much the men prize a fur like this, Chasse. You have to keep it.'

Chasse grinned shyly. 'I can't take it back. I've given it away. You have to keep it. That's our custom.'

'I can give it to you as a gift,' Banni said. 'That's not giving it back.'

'I will be offended if you do that,' Chasse warned good-naturedly. 'Now, I must go back to the Warriors' Hall. Jon has more work for me and I should train. Let me know if you need anything, yes?' He backed out of the cottage, smiling and closed the door. As he walked to the village centre, he shook his head, grinning, and thought, *Why did I do that? Because I felt like it*, he told himself. *Banni needs it more than I do*. He wrapped his arms around his chest and hurried to the Warriors' Hall to find his old cloak.

'Where is your wolf skin?' Kogan asked, when Chasse donned his cloak.

'Drying out,' Chasse replied.

'Drying out at Banni's cottage,' Lynel remarked, as he entered with an armful of kindling, and he winked at Chasse. Kogan laughed.

'She's looking after it for me,' said Chasse as he hurried from the presence of his mockers.

'It seems that way to me,' Kogan teased.

Why am I feeling embarrassed? Chasse asked himself as he plodded through the snow to the beach, but he knew why. He was fond of Banni. He liked how she smiled and was kind to him. He liked how her soft hair glowed in the light of her hearth. And Jara was very cute. Her chubby face and tiny feet entranced him.

'Where are you going?' Jon inquired.

Chasse stopped to look at Jon who was helping Carlin the fisherman patch a crack in his boat's hull created by the crushing ice. A pitch pail steamed in the sludge of mud and snow. 'I was – I don't know,' he said.

'It is a worry when a young man doesn't know where he's going,' Jon said, his hands blackened by pitch. 'It usually means he's either been hit too hard around the ears, or he's in love.'

Chasse blushed and stuttered, 'I was – I was looking for my father.'

Jon laughed and shook his head. 'How are you going to explain to the Dragon Head what you've done with your wolf skin?'

'How do you –,' Chasse started to ask, stopped, caught his breath, and said, 'It was mine to give away and Banni needs it more than I do.'

'I don't care what you do with what is yours,' Jon told him. 'Your father might care.' He chuckled. 'And, again, he might take no notice. You have nothing to explain, do you?'

Chasse flinched at the quiet challenge in Jon's question. He shrugged awkwardly and strode towards the fish drying racks where several women and men were hanging the morning's catch. *It's my pelt to give away*, he reminded himself. *Nothing more than that. I felt sorry for her.* He acknowledged greetings from the fishermen and women and walked onto the ice, heading for a familiar figure wrapped in skins squatting at a fishing hole, dangling a line.

Berikan looked up as Chasse approached. 'Come to learn how to fish now that you're a man? I can teach you a trick or two that you won't learn in that Warriors' Hall.'

'How far does the ice go before you can't walk on it?' Chasse asked.

'No further than this,' Berikan said. 'Orin broke through yesterday afternoon not more than twenty paces from here. Floundered like a seal, until we threw him a rope and dragged him out.'

'How long will it stay like this?'

'If no more blizzards blow in, it may be a week before it's all melted,' Berikan said. 'The sooner the better. I don't like fishing like this. It isn't natural.'

Chasse looked at Berikan's basket and counted three fish. 'Are the fish harder to catch?' he asked.

'Count the fish,' Berikan replied. 'I am pleased you survived your Trial.'

'Count the warriors,' Chasse retorted, grinning proudly.

Berikan tried to look annoyed, but a grin appeared. 'Congratulations, Chasse, son of Kevan. Harbin is better for you being a man. Soon, you will be Dragon Head.'

Chasse laughed and replied, 'That I will never be.'

'Varst and Procra will decide what you will or will not be,' Berikan said.

'For now, you are a dragonwarrior.'

'That's my choice,' Chasse said. 'Like Galt. He chose to be a goatherd.'

Berikan shook his head. 'Galt was a dragonwarrior for five summers, until Varst decided otherwise.'

'I didn't know that,' Chasse replied.

'Then it's good that you should know. Some men choose to be what they are. I chose to be a fisherman and Varst was happy for that to be so. My sons, as I told you, chose to be dragonwarriors and Varst was happy with that – so happy he took them from this life to be his warriors in Paradise. Galt's sons are dragonwarriors, as was his father, but Varst did not want Galt to be a dragonwarrior, so he changed his path after five summers.'

'He was injured on a summer journey?'

'In his heart,' Berikan replied.

'How can that be?' Chasse asked. 'A heart wound is death.'

'It was death dealt to Galt the dragonwarrior,' Berikan said. 'And it gave birth to Galt the Goatherd. Galt chose one path for his life and Varst delivered him into another. We don't all get to choose who we become.'

'But how did Galt survive a heart wound?'

'Not all wounds are from without,' Berikan said. He coughed and reeled in his line. 'I am done for today. You can help an old man by carrying his basket to shore.' He rose slowly to his feet, careful not to slip on the ice, gathered his lines, and walked vigilantly towards the village, Chasse following with the fish basket. At the shoreline, Berikan took his basket from Chasse, thanked him, and added, 'It is almost a full sun cycle to Procra's Dance again, but the young widow is a good woman and you would do well to choose her.'

Berikan headed for the scaling benches, leaving Chasse to stare at his receding back, astonished by the fisherman's observation. It was as if everyone in the village was talking about his friendship with Banni and matching them without asking either if there was even a chance of a match. It was idle speculation, the kind of discourse he knew was common in Harbin whenever a boy and a girl played together, or walked together, or talked to each other. All the village parents imagined pairings, even encouraged them between friends of families. His mother liked Kerryn when he was readying for his first summer of manhood, enough to tell him that she would be a good choice if he was so inclined. But Banni was a friend through his sister and he accepted responsibility for looking after her on Tam's behalf. The gossip was annoying, especially if people like the fishermen and women were sharing it.

He turned from the shore and trudged towards the Long Hall where his father was helping his mother supervise preparations for Blitzart's Feast. If his parents asked about the wolf pelt, he would tell them where it was. If they didn't, he wouldn't offer to explain. He needed to keep busy and give nothing to the gossips to discuss, for Banni's sake. And for his own.

Eleven

Denied the communal gathering the previous winter by the cruel weather, and despite the deep winter chill, the Long Hall was crowded for Blitzart's Feast. Everyone in the village attended, seated in long rows, feasting and drinking and telling favourite tales in the glow of the fireplaces. As Dragon Heart, Eesa spoke the words invoking Varst to send his daughter, Fler, to drive Blitzart away and renew the earth with abundance, and Dragon Head Kevan toasted the company and gave his blessing to the feasting.

The Dragon Fang sat with their families, and Chasse sat with Kevan and Eesa, conscious of his sister's and brother's absences. He wondered how Tam and Jaysin were spending the longest, darkest night in the winter, and if they were quietly celebrating the passing of Blitzart across the world's face. He remembered that Gramma Harmi died on the night of the Feast last winter and that Tam was absent, sheltering with the Herbal Man, everyone fearing she perished in the storm. And Tam was absent again this time, living on the mountain.

As much as he wanted to spend time with her, Chasse avoided talking directly to Banni throughout the evening, but he often glanced in her direction to see if she was happy without making eye contact. Later, when the feasting slowed, and people began to return to their homes, Banni rose with Jara in her arms to leave and Eesa approached her with a basket. Chasse noticed the interchange and was about to return his attention to Raven who was retelling the story of a wolf hunt when he saw his mother beckoning. He excused himself from the dragonwarriors and, when he approached Eesa and Banni, Eesa said, 'I told Banni that you would carry this for her,' and she handed Chasse the food-laden basket. Determined to hide his embarrassment, Chasse politely acknowledged Banni, but avoided looking elsewhere, and he dutifully followed her from the hall.

The brittle night air sparked on Chasse's cheeks as he walked silently behind Banni through the snow and moonlight to her cottage. Banni opened the door and entered, laying the sleeping Jara in her bedding before she searched in the dark to find and light an oil lamp. 'Thank you,' she told Chasse when she took the basket from him. 'I'm sorry that Eesa asked you to carry it here.'

'I don't mind,' Chasse said.

'But you were enjoying the stories.'

'Not really,' Chasse replied. 'Raven always reminds us how good and quick he is at tying a knot.'

Banni laughed at the absurd remark and said, 'Would you like a cup of warm goat's milk? Galt delivered a fresh pail to me this afternoon.'

'No,' Chasse declined, fighting his awkwardness. 'Thank you. I better help my father and mother clean the hall.'

'I think it will be a long time before anyone begins cleaning up. Your friends look like they are settling in for a long evening.'

'Then I best go make sure they don't stay awake all night,' Chasse said, and he headed for the door.

As he opened it, Banni touched his arm and stood on her toes to kiss his cheek. 'Thank you for being kind. I appreciate what you do for me.'

Chasse mumbled 'Good night,' and closed the door.

He stood outside the cottage in the cold air, touching his cheek, fascinated by the mixture of emotions coursing through his mind and body. The yellow glow in the window brightened and adopted an orange hue and he knew that Banni was relighting her fire. Being kissed was not a new experience – he shared experimental kisses with Kerryn when no one was watching – but Banni's kiss lingered on his cheeks like a warm coal in the winter night and her presence enfolded him.

When he re-entered the Long Hall and approached the table where the dragonwarriors were congregated, Kogan looked up and said, 'We thought you weren't coming back.'

'Why wouldn't I come back?' Chasse asked, taking a seat.

'He means,' said Kurtis, winking at Chasse, 'we thought you would stay in a warmer bed tonight.'

Reddening at the comment, Chasse shook his head, saying, 'My sister asked me to keep an eye on her friend and that's all I'm doing. Think whatever else you choose.'

'We are,' said Kogan, and the men laughed.

'Has your father asked about the wolf pelt yet?' Jon inquired with his eyebrow raised.

'No,' Chasse replied sharply.

'He will,' said Raven. 'Have a good story ready for when he does.'

'Another tale,' said Jon. 'How about you, Petar? Tell us about the journey south after the dragon took down Trask.'

Glad to have the attention diverted to someone else, Chasse listened as Petar related the frantic escape south to Jebaran, and how panic drove the people to seek refuge with former enemies. 'We expected to be refused, but the people of Jebaran took us in and they were keen to learn about what happened,' Petar explained. 'Like us, they also have tales about dragons, and the notion that a dragon still lives enthralled them.'

'As it did us,' said Jon.

Petar continued explaining how the refugees from Harbin were received and found sympathy, but he said nothing about Suran and Alan's or Marron's plans, even when he was pressed, so Chasse excused himself as tired and retreated to the Warriors' Hall, glad to be free of the narration of repetitive stories the men told whenever they were together, and glad to be out of the opportunity for them to torment him about Banni.

Chasse wasn't alone when he entered the Warriors' Hall. Thados was already in bed. Chasse tip-toed quietly to avoid disturbing the initiate warrior. He remembered his own exhaustion in the first winter between training and work, a good reason for Thados to be in bed early, even on Blitzart's Feast, but he knew the youth's early-to-bed habit was instilled by his father, Tad, who always left the feast early with his family. He checked the hearth and stoked the embers and added a log to retain the heat before he climbed into his bedding and pulled up the furs.

He was ready to sleep, but his mind raced with the moments spent with Banni and her kiss, his emotions running from her touch. He reminded himself that she was a widow, she was older, she had a child, but the reasons did not alter his thinking. *I'm not ready to choose*, he told himself. *Besides, Banni might refuse me and then I would look foolish.* He rolled onto his side, buried his head under a fur and murmured, 'I am foolish,' and he focused on sleeping, but Banni would not leave his mind.

The sun fought Blitzart's breath during the days following Blitzart's Feast, the sea ice melted quickly and the fishermen launched their boats, glad to return to doing what they knew best. Kevan called the Dragon Fang to order and announced that they were building a new dragonship. 'Jon will supervise the building. Raven will supervise the gathering of resources. Each of you is assigned to a leader. There is much to do and little time to do it in.'

'Without Laren and Obyr, how can we build a ship?' Raven asked. 'They hold the knowledge and they are not here.'

'I know a little of ship building,' said Petar. 'Laren and I are friends. He talked about technique often.'

'It's eight summers since the last ship was built,' said Tad. 'I've almost forgotten what we did.'

'I haven't forgotten,' Kevan reassured them. 'I am not a ship builder, but the fishermen know boats well. Berikan, Mattias, Danyel – they all know what is needed to make a vessel stable and float. They will advise us.'

'How long will it take?' Kogan asked.

'A long time,' Jon said. 'It is not a simple a process.'

'We might not be on the ocean for this summer,' Kevan said, 'but we will be for the next. That is what we will do.'

'But the others will come back,' Petar contended. 'You know this. And that means we will have the dragonship back as well.'

'They will return,' Kevan agreed. 'But it will not hurt for us to have a second ship. And it gives us a purpose for the summer to work together and learn. Or else you will all become fat and lazy goatherders.' His taunt drew laughter from the gathering. 'Is it agreed?' he asked.

Raven chose the three youngest warriors for the task of felling trees and preparing the trunks. 'Swinging the axe will build your strength and improve your skill with the weapon,' he told them as they climbed through the snow towards a stand of Barkwood trees. 'We will work in pairs, Remi with me.'

At the stand, Raven chose a tree and demonstrated the cutting technique they were to use, the blade angles and offset notches on opposite sides of the trunk to determine the direction of the tree fall, and he finished with, 'And when you make the last strike, yell "Away!" to warn the other pair that your tree is coming down; and move quickly in the opposite direction.' He explained how to trim the boughs and twigs to clean the trunk in readiness for hauling down the slope to the village and reminded them to sharpen their blades between cutting down trees. 'Work hard, my young warriors. We will have ten trees ready by sunset. Tomorrow, we will cut down ten more.'

Chasse gestured to Thados to join him, and the pair strode through the snow to a sturdy tree. 'This one,' Chasse decided. 'I'll cut the first notch.'

He hefted his axe, targeted where to strike and swung, the shock reverberating through his hands, wrists, shoulders and legs as the blade bit into the wood and chips spun away. He lowered his blade and made the second strike at an angle below the first, as Raven demonstrated.

Chasse knew how to cut wood. Kevan made him chop firewood as soon as he was big enough to handle the small wood axe. 'A man must be a good wood cutter,' Kevan told him. 'It builds strength and makes you useful to your family.' He grinned and added, 'And it's fun.'

In the beginning, Chasse relished the responsibility and the act of doing a man's job, proudly carrying his first armful of kindling into the cottage to place before the hearth and enjoying the accolades from his parents, but the task soon lost its lustre and became a chore. 'Why can't Tam cut wood?' he asked Eesa after one afternoon of chopping when his shoulders ached and blisters on his palms stung.

'Because your sister is learning how to make you a hearty meal and preparing a warm place for you men,' Eesa replied, adding, 'If you can't cut wood, no woman will want you for a husband.'

'I don't want a wife,' Chasse complained.

Eesa wiped the flour from her hands and patted her son's head. 'Oh, you will, young man, you will. And one day you will be glad that you know how to chop wood.'

Chasse shifted stance and swung again, searching for rhythm in his strokes, determined that he would not make mistakes in front of Thados. After all, he was the older man by a full sun cycle, a warrior who had completed the Trial of the Second Winter. He was responsible for Thados.

The first call of 'Away!' came from Raven as a Barkwood crashed to the earth, sending a flurry of snow skyward. By the time Chasse called 'Away!' for Thados' and his second tree, Raven was calling the warning on his and Remi's third.

'Break!' Raven yelled. 'Food is coming!'

Chasse gratefully lowered his axe and leaned on it as he looked down the slope at four women trudging towards them from the village, carrying baskets. His back, arms, legs and shoulders ached from chopping, and blisters were forming on his hands and inside his fingers faster than he expected. He thought his experience in collecting firewood for the Warriors' Hall and for Banni would have toughened him for this exercise, but it clearly did not. He glanced at Thados and saw the young man was sitting on a trunk, examining his blistered hands. It was harder work than he imagined.

As Chasse sucked in the air, he spotted two figures walking across the slope from the south, a woman and a boy, both using staffs and snowshoes to negotiate the snow, and joy filled his heart. 'I am going to meet my sister and brother!' he called to Raven as he pointed at Tam and Jaysin. 'I'll bring them here.' He lumbered through the snow, and Tam and Jaysin altered direction to intersect with him. Jaysin left Tam's side to jog awkwardly towards Chasse on his snowshoes, laughing, feet spread-eagled to avoid overbalancing, and he wrapped his arms around Chasse's waist. Chasse accepted the hug and disengaged as Tam approached, saying with a broad smile, 'I'm pleased to see both of you.'

'And us you,' Tam replied, embracing Chasse. 'Are you all right?'

'I'm good,' Chasse replied.

Tam looked past Chasse at the trio gathered among the trees. 'What are you doing?'

'We're building a ship,' Chasse said.

'A ship!' Jaysin cried, and he ran to the trees.

'That will take a full sun cycle or more,' Tam said.

'That's what Father said,' Chasse confirmed. 'It gives us purpose.' He looked directly at Tam, and asked, 'Are you staying?'

'I can't,' she replied. 'I came to ask you to come to the mountain when you can.'

'Why?' Chasse asked.

Tam's eyes lit with joy, as she said, 'We have a baby.'

Her revelation left Chasse momentarily confused, until he realised what Tam was really announcing and he whispered, 'The dragon?'

'Yes!' Tam replied. 'The egg has hatched! You have to meet Harmi!'

'Harmi?'

'I named her after Gramma. Eric would love that.'

'I'd love to come,' said Chasse. He glanced over his shoulder at the men labouring in the trees, and added, 'But I have to finish my work here.'

'The others can do that,' Tam insisted. 'This is something that none of them can see or do.'

'No,' Chasse replied. 'It's not that easy. I'm a man, a full dragonwarrior now. I have to act like one. I have to be responsible.'

'Of course you do,' she said, trying to curb her disappointment. 'I thought you should know.'

'Thank you,' Chasse answered. 'I want to meet Harmi. I really do. I will come when I can. If the weather holds off.'

'It will,' Tam told him. 'There will be one or two more snowfalls, but only light ones. Fler is already seeding the world.'

'Eric told you this?'

'No,' Tam replied. 'I am learning how to scry weather. I'm studying the texts Eric left that show how to read the weather and predict it ahead of time. I can tell what will happen by what has already happened and how weather patterns work.' She laughed and added, 'And a little clever guessing.'

'More magic,' Chasse said. 'How much can you learn?'

'It's not magic, Chasse,' Tam told him. 'And I don't know how much I can learn. That will depend on Harmi.'

'What does Harmi have to do with it?'

'When you visit, I'll explain.' She looked past Chasse's shoulder. 'I think Raven wants you to go back.'

Chasse saw Raven waving and Jaysin was walking towards Tam and Chasse. 'He has grown, hasn't he?' Chasse noted, assessing his little brother's gangly frame.

'In more ways than one,' Tam said. 'He learns everything quickly. When you visit, he can show you what he's learned. Eric was right. Jaysin is very different.'

'You are going to visit Mother and Father?' Chasse asked.

'And Banni. We have a short time before we go home.'

Chasse heard Tam's reference to home and knew she meant the cave and he felt an unexpected pang of disappointment.

'You shouldn't cut down the trees,' Jaysin said when he reached his brother and sister.

'Why not?' Chasse asked. 'We need them.'

Jaysin squinted up at him and said, 'Trees exist to live and to help us live. You should only take what you really need.'

Jaysin's sincere expression made Chasse smile. 'I will make sure there is no waste. I promise.' He looked at Tam with a mystified expression.

'I told you he is learning,' Tam said. 'We must hurry. Come to the cave when you can.'

'I never thanked you enough for saving my life,' Chasse said.

'You are here,' Tam affirmed. 'And we are bound.' She touched his bracelet, and it tingled through his wrist. 'That's all I need.' She ushered Jaysin forward, turning to Chasse to say, 'Don't forget. Come meet Harmi as soon as you can.'

Twelve

Chasse adjusted his backpack, leaned on his spear and stared across the bay, taking in the view from Nakiades Bluff to White Eagle Ledge. Yesterday he was on White Eagle Ledge, taking his turn on watch and, unlike his first experience, the day was mild and the sea a dark metal colour, rolling but not wild or rough. Clouds kept the sun away much of the time, but periodic patches of sunlight warmed his shoulders and back while he observed the terns and gulls wheeling around the rocks and cliffs, and sea hawks hovering higher, searching for prey. Spring was rising. Blitzart's grip on the world was fading like the melting snow. He had delayed his visit to Tamesan long enough.

He rose before dawn to begin the journey up Dragon Mountain with the pack of food preserves that Eesa made him carry to Tam and Jaysin. He thought his father would make it difficult for him to spend a day away from training and working on the dragonship, but Kevan encouraged him to go.

'I would come too,' he said, after he gave Chasse permission. 'Next time, I will. But you must go. See your mother. She will have things for you to take to Tamesan.'

'Tell her there is much to do,' Eesa told Chasse when he informed his mother that he was visiting Tam and Jaysin. 'I would appreciate her help for the Celebration of Fler next week. And take these condiments and breads. She must be hungry.'

Neither parent referred to Jaysin, apart from Eesa mentioning him in passing, and the omission puzzled Chasse. As he stood on the ledge, he pondered why his parents gave his younger brother scant attention.

Perhaps it was because he was so different, so less focused on what was expected of a boy, that they could not relate to him.

His mother's interest was in Tamesan because she was a girl, but Tam was no ordinary girl in Harbin and was not doing as Eesa expected – although he knew Eesa hoped that Tam would eventually come around to traditional ways.

He understood his father's dismissal of Jaysin. Jaysin showed no sign of being a dragonwarrior, which was a source of bitter disappointment for Kevan. But Chasse couldn't comprehend why either matter would make Jaysin's wellbeing less important to his parents, especially as he spent the winter on the mountain away from them.

He continued up to the plateau, noting how the snow was receding, the slopes cut with rivulets of melt water, green shoots and leaves and bright yellow and red buds emerging from the earth and branches. As he crested the path to the plateau, he was startled to find grass pushing through the thinning snow and bushes sprouting fledgling leaves, multicoloured birds flitting through the bare boughs, and buds and mosses greening the ruin of the Herbal Man's hut. Life was reviving on the plateau after the long winter and he felt energy in the air.

As Chasse approached the cliff base where the goat path commenced, Tam appeared in a shimmer of light from the rocks and came forward. He stopped, staring at the apparition, until Tam said, 'No climbing this morning. This is much easier. Follow me,' and she vanished into the light. Her disappearance astonished Chasse. He stared at the light, uncertain of what to do, until Tam reappeared and said, 'Take my hand.' Chasse accepted her extended hand and allowed her to guide him forward, but he closed his eyes as he entered the light and energy tingled through his body. 'You can open your eyes now,' Tam whispered.

Chasse opened his eyes and in the amber light he saw that he was in the egg chamber. 'How?' he asked.

'This is real magic, Chasse,' Tam explained. 'I made a portal. A simple one. My first one ever.'

'Wait. I'm confused,' Chasse admitted. 'We were outside. How can we suddenly be here?' He turned to the cavern wall behind him. There was no door, no way to enter.

'Think of a portal as a doorway,' Tam said. 'Only it isn't restricted to height or proximity or a building structure. It's determined by the resonance in the elements and how the elements connect with our minds and our desires.'

Chasse shook his head. 'I still don't understand. How did you learn this?'

'Come on,' Tam said and took his hand. 'I'll show you, later. First, come and meet Harmi.'

Chasse unhitched his pack, put down his spear, and let Tam lead him to the nest. The egg no longer dominated the centre. Instead, a light grey ragged mound filled the space. When Chasse mounted the nest, the mound stirred, and a small lizard-like head rose to face him. Bright blue eyes opened.

'Harmi!' Tam announced.

Chasse studied the creature studying him. The amber light from the overhead crystal gave the baby dragon's grey scales an interesting tinge, like coals glowing along the ridges.

'Like the sun rising over Dragon Mountain,' Tam whispered.

'How did you know what I was thinking?'

Tam laughed and replied, 'I didn't, but I guessed you were thinking something like that because that's what I think when I look at her.'

'She's not the same colour as Claryssa,' Chasse observed.

'She will be,' said Tam, 'one day, when she's very old. Dragons change colour as they age. She's light grey now, and she will become darker grey and possibly even red until she is fully mature, and then she will gradually lighten and turn golden, like Claryssa.'

'How do you know all this about dragons?' Chasse asked.

'She reads!' Jaysin declared as he ran into the room and climbed onto the nest. The dragon faced him, tilted her head and he patted the dragon's snout. 'That's how I know, too.'

'You can read?' Chasse asked.

'Tam taught me,' Jaysin said proudly. 'She can teach you.'

'Chasse started to learn the last time he was here,' Tam told Jaysin. 'We can continue his lesson today.'

'I can teach him!' Jaysin said, climbing down from the nest. 'I'll get the book about dragons. He can learn about Harmi.' He headed to the wall and touched it. The hidden door glowed and opened and he disappeared into the corridor.

'He has a ring like yours?' Chasse asked.

'No,' Tam replied. 'He taught himself how to do that.'

Chasse was more confused than ever. 'How could he do that?'

'I don't know,' Tam replied. 'He reads a lot and he learns very quickly.'

'But so do you,' Chasse said.

'Not like Jaysin,' Tam replied, reaching to stroke Harmi's cheek. 'I've only been able to do things since Harmi hatched. I wouldn't have made the portal without her. We're connected.'

Chasse watched Tam caress the baby dragon, wrestling in his mind with everything unfolding before him like a bizarre dream. Dragons were the spawn of the gods. Dragons existed in Harbin stories and fables. But Nakiades did fight and kill a dragon. He saw the relics. That's why the Dragon Fang sailed to battle dragons every summer to settle Nakiades' debt. But there were no dragons. The Dragon Fang really only raided and plundered villages and towns. The dragon reason was a lie. And yet there was a dragon and it lived above Harbin in Dragon Mountain. And it was golden and powerful beyond imagining. It was the last dragon and the Herbal Man was the last wizard. But they left, and in doing so they left behind an egg. And here was Harmi, a dragon, and his sister sat with it as if she was its mother. And it gave her magical powers.

'Chasse?' He turned to Tam. 'Jaysin wants you to read a book with him,' she said. Chasse looked to his left to find Jaysin sitting beside him with a massive book covering his lap, opened to the first page of an illustration of a dragon's head.

'This book tells us everything there is to know about dragons; how they came to be, what they like doing, the names of the most famous ones, where they lived, who their wizards were,' Jaysin announced, and before Chasse could respond Jaysin went on. 'This word here is dragon. See? That is the symbol for the sound "d", this one for "r", this one is "a."'

Chasse looked at Tam for an explanation. 'I know,' she said. 'I taught him a little about reading in the first week that he was here, but he's taught himself ever since. I don't know how he does it.'

'Chasse,' Jaysin urged. 'Are you watching?'

Tam lifted her gaze from the Seeing Waters pedestal to face Chasse and said, 'I haven't heard from Eric.' She sighed. 'I hope he and Claryssa are safe.' She gestured for Chasse to follow her out of the cavern into the corridor and into the chamber where the books and scrolls and a variety of items were stored and she pointed at the left corner where Jaysin was curled on a makeshift pile of clothes serving as a bed. A large tome lay open on the ground beside him. 'Our little brother spends a lot of his time right there, either reading or asleep.' She led Chasse to two stools beside a large granite stone in the opposite corner and asked, 'Are you cold?'

'Not too bad,' Chasse replied.

Tam placed her hands on the stone until it glowed like a large coal and Chasse felt the emanating warmth. 'A useful piece of magic Eric taught me,' Tam said. 'Everything has energy, but the energy needs to be coaxed to be useful.'

'How much of this can you learn?' Chasse asked.

'I don't know,' Tam replied. 'As I said before, that is up to Harmi. She carries all the knowledge of the magic I can learn. Eric told me that a wizard is bound for life to his dragon, so I am bound to Harmi. Our lives are intertwined, now, until we die.'

'But you're not a wizard.'

Tam smiled shyly and said, 'It seems I am.' Seeing Chasse's perplexed expression, she explained. 'When I chose to guard the egg, I chose to become a wizard. I bound my life to Harmi's life.'

'Why would you do that?' Chasse asked.

'Why did you swear an oath to the Dragon Fang?' Tam asked in return.

'To protect my family,' Chasse replied. 'To protect Harbin.'

'And to follow in Nakiades' footsteps and hunt dragons,' Tam continued. 'We all know the Dragon Fang oath. And you take it because it means you have purpose. It defines your manhood. Protecting the egg was my oath and it has defined me.'

'Does that mean you're never coming back to live in the village?' Chasse asked.

'Not in the village,' Tam replied. 'Where would Harmi stay?'

'We could build a hall for her.'

Tam grinned. 'A Dragon Hall to go with the Long Hall and the Warriors' Hall,' she said sceptically. 'I'm sure Father and Mother would approve.'

'They would do it for you,' Chasse argued.

'Perhaps,' Tam replied. 'We will see when the time is ready. But I have a bigger problem for now and I need your help.'

'What?'

'Harmi is hungry. She needs fresh meat.'

'You want me to hunt for you?' Chasse asked.

'Not yet,' Tam replied. 'Eric kept goats for a reason. There's a door in the main chamber to the goat cave. The goats come and go onto the plateau through a narrow tunnel to forage.'

'How did you feed them through winter?' Chasse asked.

'That's why I was up here so much,' Tam replied. 'I had to cut and store grasses and grains for the goats, as well as set up for Jaysin and myself. And Harmi.'

'You want me to prepare a goat for Harmi?'

'I need you to prepare at least two, please,' said Tam. 'Harmi is small, but she has a big appetite.'

'How long before she can hunt for herself?'

'At least several moon cycles,' Tam replied. 'She has to grow and develop strength in her wings to fly. Until she can fly, a dragon baby stays in the nest and is fed by her mother or by her wizard.'

'How many goats in the cave?' Chasse asked.

'I don't know,' Tam replied. 'I'll come with you. I have to show you which goats to kill.'

'You know you will have to learn how to kill and butcher them,' Chasse said. 'I won't always be able to come up here.'

'I can't kill an animal,' Tam replied squeamishly.

'If you want to feed Harmi, you don't have a choice. I can show you what to do.'

'I'll choose which ones, and I'll leave you to do what you know,' Tam said. 'I can't watch.' She led Chasse into the central chamber, past the sleeping dragon, to a small wooden door, and she produced a brass key to unlock the door before she unhitched an oil lantern from a hook and lit it. 'No magic?' Chasse asked.

'I left my staff at the nest,' Tam said apologetically.

When she opened the door, Chasse smelt the goat stench. He followed his sister into a low-ceilinged cavern. Eyes glittered before the lamp light revealed patchwork goats that came forward to nuzzle Tam.

'We keep the nannies and the younger ones. This one,' she said, touching a black and white animal, 'and this one,' she added, indicating a brown goat with a white blaze along its snout. She took Chasse's arm, and said, 'Please don't let them suffer.'

'I can't do it in here,' Chasse said. 'It will spook the others. Where is the tunnel to outside?' Tam raised her lamp and pointed to a cleft in the cave. 'I'll take this one first,' said Chasse, indicating the black and white goat. 'Do you have rope?'

'I don't know,' said Tam. 'I can try coaxing the goat outside with food.' She crossed to a small bag in the corner, drew out a handful of dried grass and lured the goat into the tunnel. Several more joined in, pushing at her hand for the food, and the small procession weaved through the narrow tunnel into the daylight.

Chasse followed in their wake and when they were outside he laughed at the gathering and said, 'Now what? They're all out here.'

'I will distract the others,' Tam offered.

'Thank you,' Chasse said and he sized up the goat he had to slaughter.

Tam's request gave Chasse responsibility and challenge, a test of his manhood. The difficulty was that he had never killed a goat, but he didn't want to look foolish or uncertain in his sister's eyes. He drew his hunting knife and crept behind the target. Aware of his presence, the goat bleated and started, but Chasse leapt and tumbled to the ground with his arms wrapped around the animal, wrestling to his feet as he held the struggling creature. The rest of the herd, frightened by the trapped goat's frantic bleats echoing across the plateau, bolted into the tunnel. Chasse fumbled, until he had a solid grip on his knife and the goat's jaw, made a swift cut across the goat's neck and held the shuddering animal until it was still.

'You said you wouldn't let it suffer,' Tam protested, tears streaming down her cheeks.

'How else was I meant to do this?' Chasse asked, annoyed by his sister's complaint as he caught his breath.

'I don't know,' she said. 'Painlessly?'

'Everything I've seen about dying doesn't happen painlessly,' Chasse retorted, wiping his blade on the goat's hide. 'You know that as well as anyone does. You saw my friends dying when you were helping the Herbal

Man. Death is always painful and I hate it. At least this goat died quickly, not like some of my friends.' He shook his head and looked away. 'I'm sorry,' he apologised, guilt usurping his anger. 'That wasn't necessary. But, if you want to feed Harmi, you have to get used to this. This is what it will take until she can hunt for herself.'

'I'll fetch the other goat,' Tam said resignedly and she turned to enter the cave.

'It won't come easily, not after seeing and hearing this,' Chasse said. 'You'll need a rope.'

Chasse butchered the meat as best as he could remember and was finished by nightfall. Having watched Raven with the bear and tried his hand at imitating the skills on the fox that he prepared for his father, he still felt clumsy and uncertain, even though he knew the meat didn't need careful preparation to feed the dragon. He cut a portion of leg to boil for Tamesan, Jaysin and himself, and filled a bag with the rest. Walking through the cave made him self-conscious of his cargo, but he accepted that it was part of what had to be done and he passed through, trying not to look directly at the goats.

As Chasse placed the bag against the wall in the cavern, dry grass rustled and Harmi's reptilian head appeared over the rim of the nest, her nostrils flaring, blue eyes focused on the bag. A sharp thrill tingled Chasse's nerves as he recognised the dragon's predatory expression, the carnivorous creature rising, driven by hunger and a desire to tear into raw meat, and for an instant he glimpsed the dragon that Harmi would become. He retreated from the bag to avoid interfering with Harmi when she crept over the rim and hopped onto the cavern floor, her tail sliding across the stone as she approached the bag. She stopped, and Chasse saw she was staring at Tam who was entering the cavern from the corridor.

'This is the first time she's eaten meat,' Tam said. 'She's very excited.'

'I can see that,' said Chasse. 'I need to wash before she mistakes the blood on me for part of her first meal.'

Tam looked at Chasse's hands and clothes and said, 'Jaysin is awake. He can show you the entrance to the hot springs.' Harmi started nuzzling Tam, nudging her towards the bag. 'I have a child to feed,' said Tam. 'Go wash and change into the spare clothes in your chamber. Then we can eat.'

Thirteen

Jaysin was bent over another book beside Harmi's sleeping form, reading beneath the glow of a hovering spherical globe that highlighted his auburn hair and pale skin. He turned a page to continue, oblivious to Chasse and Tam observing him.

'Does he ever stop reading?' Chasse asked, leaning forward to warm his hands on a warming stone that Tam conjured.

'Only to practise something he learns,' said Tam, 'or to ask me a question.'

'He needs to get out in the air more for his health,' Chasse suggested.

Tam smiled. 'You sound like Father. Jaysin spends time outside. He loves studying the insects and birds and animals, and he collects herbs for his experiments.'

'He must have a connection with Harmi, like you,' said Chasse. 'That's why he can do the things he's doing.'

'No,' she refuted. 'He doesn't.'

'How do you know?'

'Harmi told me.'

'Isn't she still like a baby?' Chasse asked.

Tam replied, 'No. She's a very old intelligence inside a baby dragon's body. That's how dragon lore is passed down. They have their mother's dragon knowledge within them from the moment they hatch. Harmi knows everything Claryssa knew, and Claryssa knew what her mother knew. Every dragon generation knows what was learned before them and they pass on all they learn, as well as everything they were born with, to the next generation.'

'Like how we share Nakiades' legend,' said Chasse.

'Not at all like what we do,' Tam corrected. 'We have to learn our history and our knowledge. Dragons are born with it.'

'That would be amazing!' Chasse exclaimed. 'To know everything straight away? Imagine what you could do.'

'It's terribly confusing,' Tam replied. 'Suddenly, you know why things are like they are. You understand the connections, the energy sources, the joy and the pain that can come from certain decisions. You know more than you want to know.' She saw Chasse begin to speak, and said, 'You have another question, and I will answer it. I told you that Harmi and I are connected. Completely. Everything she knows, I know. Every thought she has, I hear in my head. Everything she feels, I feel. That's why I knew you were back in the cavern with her food. I felt her hunger and her excitement at seeing and smelling the meat. We are two, but we are also one. And it works both ways. She's sleeping now. She sleeps a lot. But if I was suddenly afraid, or in danger, she would feel it and know and she would wake. See? It is amazing to know so much, to know everything that has happened in the past. But it is also an awful burden. And that's why it is confusing.'

'Can you see the future?' Chasse asked.

Tam laughed and replied, 'No, Chasse. We can't see what hasn't happened. We can only predict what might happen from the evidence we already have. We can learn from the past to make better decisions to avoid the old mistakes.'

'Look!' Jaysin interrupted excitedly. He held up a small, glowing stone. 'I can do it too!'

'I'm impressed,' Tam said. 'Don't make it too hot.'

'What's he doing?' Chasse asked.

'You saw me create a warming stone. Now, he can do it,' Tam explained.

Chasse looked with amazement at the stone glowing in Jaysin's hand.

'Can I learn how?' he asked, turning to Tam.

Tam met his inquiring gaze and said, 'I don't know. First, you need to learn how to read. Then we can see what you can do. Take a book with you tomorrow morning when you return to the village and practise.'

'I haven't got time to practise,' Chasse said. 'There is already enough to do with building the ship and hunting and training. And there's no one to show me if I can't work it out or remember what Jaysin and you showed me.'

'I have something else to show you that I learned last night.' Tam reached for his wrist and touched the amber bracelet. Inside Chasse's mind, she projected, 'Harmi has shown me how we can be in contact through the bracelets. It's how Eric and Gramma could speak to each other.'

Chasse's eyes widened with shock. 'I heard you in my head!' he blurted.

'Yes,' Tam said. 'That's how it works. So, I can help when you need. I'll give you a good book to learn from. I'll teach a little of it to you tonight, before we sleep. I also have potions and herbs that I want you to take to Mother. Tell her I will come down to help everyone prepare for the Celebration of Fler, and I will explain, then, what the potions and herbs are used for.'

'You are becoming the new Herbal Man,' Chasse said.

'In a way,' she answered, 'I already am Eric.'

Chasse stood on the plateau, staring at the shimmering portal and the images of his sister, her red hair glowing in the light and his brother Jaysin standing beside her. They waved and vanished. What he witnessed and learned in the visit left him caught between awe and perplexity. He slept restlessly, dreaming of a dragon sweeping over Dragon Mountain, and blood on his hands and voices in his head he could not control. Tam made him promise to keep the secrets of Harmi's existence, Jaysin's growth in magical aptitude, and the cavern of treasures. He was becoming a vessel of many secrets; Tam's secrets, the Dragon Fang secrets, his secret care for Banni.

Tam asked how Banni was faring and he assured her that he was taking care of Banni.

'I visited her last time I was in the village,' Tam said. 'She spoke very highly of you. She appreciates your help.'

He wanted to ask if Banni said anything more, whether she told Tam that she wanted him, but he was too embarrassed to ask. Instead, he promised to keep helping her when she needed. Everything he was learning was a secret he had to keep. Manhood was full of secrets.

His backpack was heavier than when he ascended the previous day, filled with Tam's gifts for their mother and a book Tam gave him to practise reading, titled *Animal Habits and Habitats*. She said it was a record that Eric created because it was a collection of notes about various wildlife around Harbin.

'You will find it useful, for yourself and for the Dragon Fang,' she said, while she showed him how to match words with illustrations. 'It might help everyone develop better understanding of how, when, where and what to hunt.'

He accepted the book to make Tam happy, but he felt no desire to read it. He had more than enough to learn to be a dragonwarrior and he was confident the men already knew what to hunt and when.

He glanced up at the sun gleaming in the bright blue sky before he headed for the path to Harbin. It was early enough that he was sure he would be in the village well before midday, so he descended carefully, wary of the slippery rocks and mud, using his spear to balance. Snow still covered much of the slope, but the melt was rapidly revealing the rocks, trees and earth.

What he didn't expect was the blow from behind. The force sent him sprawling against rocks and tumbling down a short slope, the weight of his pack preventing him rolling quickly to his feet. Head stinging, he flailed his arms and clumsily rolled onto his side to find a masked figure standing over him with a makeshift tree branch as a club. His spear was out of reach, dropped when he fell. He did have his knife.

'No stupid moves,' the masked man warned. 'I have no qualms in killing you.'

Even muffled by the cloth mask, the accent was familiar, but Chasse couldn't place it.

'Take the knife out of your belt and throw it to the side. Slowly,' the figure instructed.

Chasse reached for his knife, assessing his chances if he chose to fight. The backpack impeded his movement. He might get a throw, but knife-throwing wasn't likely to do anything more than create a brief distraction. He had no advantages. He eased the knife from his belt and tossed it aside.

'Get up, slowly and carefully,' the attacker ordered.

Chasse struggled against the backpack weight as he rose. His head ached. Pain throbbed in his right shoulder and ribs from the fall.

'Now, back up to the dragon treasure,' the stranger said, gesturing with the club.

Suran, Chasse realised. *The southern hunter survived the blizzard*. He glanced at his spear. It wasn't close enough. But if he was going to protect Tam and Jaysin, he had to take the risk. He dodged left, reaching for the spear, but the club cracked hard against his right ribs, and he grunted with pain as he cartwheeled to the ground. The agony and breathlessness crippled him.

'You really are an idiot,' Suran said, standing over Chasse. He kicked Chasse in the ribs, making him snap into a curled position, fighting to breathe through the intense hurt pulsing in his side. Suran grabbed

Chasse's backpack and hauled him to his feet. 'This is nothing like the pain I will make you feel if you keep being so stupid,' Suran hissed through his teeth. 'Walk,' and he pushed Chasse forward.

Chasse fought the burning in his side, breathing shallowly to avoid the pain shooting through him. Tears welled. He whimpered.

'Keep moving,' Suran ordered. 'You are not a man. A man doesn't cry. You are a child. You are nothing.'

The goading made Chasse start to turn, but the club cracked across his shoulders and he collapsed to his knees, crying.

'Get up,' Suran snarled. 'Get up or I will kill you.

Chasse wanted to yell 'Kill me, then!' because without him Suran would not find the dragon cavern, but he didn't want to die, not yet, not like this, not without a fight. He braced and pushed to his feet, the backpack straps and the effort sparking sharp spasms through his chest and back. He groaned, faltered, and stepped forward. Each step up on the path sent more spasms through his being. He spat a gob of blood onto a rock and stopped, overwhelmed by dizziness, but Suran pushed him hard from behind and he stumbled.

'This time, boy, no father to save you or your sister,' Suran said. 'You shouldn't have survived the spear, but I've practised since then. I blame the poor workmanship of your Harbin spears for that error. It shows in the weakness of your men.'

Chasse grimaced against the agony. And then he heard a voice in his head, asking, 'What happened? You're hurt.' The intrusion startled and confused him. As he struggled to control his thoughts and pain, the voice coaxed, 'Relax, Chasse. Calm down. Think what you need to tell me.'

'Suran,' Chasse thought. 'The Jebaran hunter. He's back. He caught me. I can't get away.'

'I'm coming to you,' Tam replied. 'Do what he asks. I'm coming.'

'No,' Chasse projected. 'He's dangerous, Tam. Hide. I won't show him anything.' Tam did not respond.

Chasse went to turn his head, but Suran pushed from behind, saying, 'Almost there. Don't get ideas, boy.'

Every breath was agonising, every step sent jabbing jolts through his side and chest. Chasse climbed onto the plateau and raised his teary eyes. Sunlight glittered on patches of snow. The Herbal Man's ruined hut seemed cloaked in greater swathes of green than when he passed it earlier. Despite his predicament, the world looked radiant, renewed.

'Move!' Suran ordered, prodding Chasse. 'This time we go up that path and you won't play any tricks.'

Chasse lowered his eyes and limped across the plateau towards the goat path, thinking through his options, knowing that Suran was expecting him to attempt something and was ready to beat him down. His father warned him against confronting a seasoned hunter like Suran, told him that he was lucky to survive the first encounter. *Why am I so pathetic as a man*? Chasse reflected angrily.

'Stop!'

Chasse halted at Suran's order and saw his captor staring past him at the cliff. Tam was waiting at the base of the goat path, the black staff upright in her left hand, one end on the ground.

'You know why I'm here,' Suran said. 'Take me to the dragon treasure.'

'There is no treasure,' Tam replied calmly. 'Release my brother.'

Suran's club struck the back of Chasse's legs and Chasse buckled and dropped to his knees. 'Take me to the treasure or I will kill your brother, and then I will make you take me anyway.'

'You don't have to do this,' Tam reasoned.

'I gave you a chance,' Suran said.

Chasse couldn't see Suran behind him, but he did see Tam swiftly lift her staff and point it in his direction and a short burst of light flashed across the gap. Suran screamed as Chasse toppled reflexively to his left, grunting when the impact jolted through his torso. He smelt burning flesh. And passed out.

'Chasse? Can you hear me?'

Chasse opened his eyes, blinking against the dull light.

'I want you to drink this.'

A smooth, cool surface pressed to his lips. He recognised Tam's red hair at the edge of his vision. He parted his lips and let the sweet, sticky syrup spread across his palette and tongue and ooze down his throat.

'It will dull the pain.'

Chasse swallowed, breathed in and winced.

'A few moments first,' Tam advised. 'Stay still. Breathe softly through your nose.'

Chasse desperately wanted to fill his lungs with fresh air, but he obeyed and drew shallow breaths, feeling the liquid permeate his stomach and chest.

'You will go to sleep,' Tam said. 'Rest is important.'

He was outside. The sky was patchy white clouds and soft blue. He was on the ground.

He opened his eyes slowly. The room was dark. Soft orange hearth fire glow illuminated the lower half of a wooden wall. It was his boyhood bedroom. The memory of being carried flickered like bare tree branches moving silently across an ashen sky. He wasn't lying entirely flat; his head was raised. Rain clattered on the shingle roof.

Smooth, cool. Pressed against his lips. How many times had this happened? He let the soothing liquid enter his mouth. Sleep. Sleep was everything. Sleep was all.

Shafts of daylight angled from gaps between the wood. Dust motes spun in the light, blinking and glittering.

'I have broth for you. You must be terribly hungry.'

He turned his head. Eesa knelt by his bed.

'Tamesan says you should be able to sit up carefully today, even get out of bed.'

'Where is Tam?' Chasse asked.

'Gathering herbs. She will be back soon,' Eesa replied. 'Here.' She held the broth forward.

Chasse accepted the bowl. The aromas tantalized his taste buds and he sipped, savouring the warm flavours. 'This is good,' he said. 'How long have I been sleeping?'

'Close to four days,' Eesa said. 'Tamesan said the medicine would do that.'

'How did I get back down here?' Chasse asked.

'Your brother came to fetch your father and the men,' Eesa explained. 'They carried you down the mountain.'

'What about Suran?' Chasse asked.

Eesa used her hand to brush aside Chasse's fringe, as she said, 'The stranger is dead. You saved your sister's life.'

Chasse lowered the bowl to meet Eesa's gaze. 'I-' he muttered, but he was lost for how to explain what he knew happened. 'I didn't-' he started and stopped.

'Your father is very proud,' Eesa said, 'as am I. Twice, now, you have confronted death and beaten it down. You are a true Dragon Fang warrior.

Everyone speaks of your honour and courage.'

'How is the patient?' Tam interrupted, appearing behind and above Eesa. 'Hungry, I see.'

'I have to finish organising for the celebration,' said Eesa, rising, and she said to Tam, 'When you are ready, I'd like your help in the Long Hall.'

'I won't be long,' Tam promised as Eesa left the room. She sat on the edge of Chasse's bed and asked, 'How are you feeling?'

'Awake,' he replied, lowering the bowl. 'What did you say to the others about Suran?'

'I told them that you saved my life,' she said.

'But I didn't,' Chasse argued. 'You saved mine. You killed Suran. I saw it.'

Tam's expression became calm and serious. 'I can't tell them the truth, Chasse, and neither can you. No one here can know about Harmi – not yet.'

'How would they know about Harmi if they knew you stopped Suran?' Chasse asked.

'You know the answer,' Tam said. 'Without Harmi, I have no magic. They would ask me to explain how I threw a spear so accurately and hard that it went right through Suran, or if not throwing it then how I pushed a spear through him.'

'Is that what you told them? That I speared Suran?' Chasse asked.

'Yes.'

'And that is the story I have to keep telling?' Chasse asked.

'I need you to do that. For me,' Tam pleaded. 'For Jaysin. And for Harmi. We need to keep the truth to ourselves a little longer.'

'Until Harmi can fly.'

'Yes!' Tam replied. 'You understand.'

'I need to get up,' Chasse said, easing up slowly, feeling pain creep across his chest.

'Slowly,' Tam advised as she assisted him to stand.

'I might need clothes too,' Chasse said, looking down at his bare legs.

Tam laughed and said, 'I'll find clothes for you. And then I'll walk you to the Long Hall. Slowly. You have a lot of healing to do.'

Fourteen

After the Celebration of Fler, like the snow, the days melted into Spring and the bleak Harbin landscape became green and colourful. The village hummed with activity, the dragonwarriors cutting and shaping wood for constructing a ship, Kadin and his son, Beni, firing the kiln to forge copper rivets and gussets and nails, artisan men and women weaving goatskin squares into a sail, Berikan and Amarti and the fishing folk catching and cleaning and mending. Chasse wandered through the activities or sat and watched and learned and sometimes helped with a variety of light duties, feeling useless while his ribs and cuts and bruises healed, although Kevan insisted that he take his turns on watch at White Eagle Ledge.

'Sitting and watching,' Kevan said. 'No easier task in the village.'

As with the wolf, the dragonwarriors wanted Chasse to retell the story of Suran and how he defeated the older, experienced man in hand-to-hand fighting.

'He was tough to survive the blizzard in The Sentinels,' Kogan noted one evening around the hearth fire.

'He was a seasoned hunter,' Jon said. 'He would have known, better than any of us, how to survive those conditions.'

'He was greatly admired in Jebaran,' said Petar. 'He will be mourned.'

'But Kevan's son bested him,' said Raven. 'We are stronger than the strongest of their people.'

'I was lucky,' Chasse insisted. 'If he hadn't tripped, I would not be telling this tale.'

'How you win in battle is not important,' Kevan said. 'Only that you win.'

'Where did you find the strength to push the spear through the man?' Petar asked. 'That is not easy to do, even for a very strong man.'

'He was protecting his sister,' Jon offered in explanation. 'If I was protecting my wife, I could push a spear through three men!'

'As could I,' Raven agreed. 'Protecting what you love gives a man strength he did not know he had.'

Chasse listened to the conversations, the statements of strength and passion, the accolades offered to him for acting as a true warrior of the Dragon Fang should act, and he avoided adding details to the tale to ensure that he made no mistakes when asked to retell what happened. 'Suran ambushed me on the plateau. At first, he had the upper hand, and I thought I would die, but he slipped on a wet rock, so I took my chance and stabbed him with my spear.'

Individuals asked about his ribs and injuries, but he told them he didn't remember the pain or what happened when Suran attacked him, only what he did when he had a chance. He knew the others talked about the story, perhaps doubted how he related it, but there was no alternative evidence. Suran attacked him. He killed Suran. Tam found him and sent Jaysin for help. When the men arrived, they found Suran on the ground impaled through the chest with Chasse's spear. No one could question the facts.

He visited Banni to help with small chores and she stopped to chat with him when she was walking by. He was self-conscious of talking to her, but no one mentioned it in the Warriors' Hall or teased him like before. It was as if the village accepted and protected the relationship as part of the seasonal milieu. Jara was growing quickly, making talking sounds, walking, and eating morsels of food, although Banni was still breastfeeding and would do so until Jara was at least two or three summers, as was expected.

Tam came down to the village every two or three days, bringing herbal remedies, pastes and lotions, and visiting people who asked for or needed her attention. She tended cuts, blisters and minor injuries the men received through working on the ship, gave Amarti a herbal mix to ease her bowel discomfort, checked in on Jon's and Raven's wives who were pregnant, and made sure Chasse was recovering.

'How long will this take?' Chasse asked when Tam pressed her head against the side of his chest to listen to his breathing.

'From what I can tell, you were very lucky,' she said, straightening and taking a glass vial from her bag. 'The bones are mending quickly and your lung is recovering, although it will never be exactly as it was.'

'Why?' Chasse asked.

'A tiny part of it died.' She looked at Chasse's face and said, 'I'm sorry, but you should know. But not very much of it. You may never really notice a difference.'

'I can breathe easier now than I could two days ago,' he said.

'Good,' Tam said, 'but it will be at least a few more days before you can start doing normal things. And no fighting for some time. A hit in the right place will break your ribs again.'

'But I should be training,' Chasse said.

'You know there will be no dragonship journey this summer,' Tam said. 'And you can do many activities to build your strength and flexibility other than fight.'

He could not argue. His sister's reputation as a healer was widely accepted in the village and everyone considered her a better one than the Herbal Man. She was sought and feted when she visited. Chasse heeded her advice and declined when the younger warriors invited him to duel as part of training. Instead, he practised improving speed and fluidity in his moves with a spear and with a sword, stopping when a move pulled or pinched. He worked on his strength without straining his sides, focussing on his legs and arms, and by the time the people of Harbin were preparing for the next celebration – Ecg's Feast – Chasse could move freely without discomfort.

On the day of the Feast, Kevan sent Chasse to keep watch on White Eagle Ledge and Chasse returned at sunset to join the eating and conversations. Being the only boys turning sixteen summers in age, Remi and Thados were welcomed into the Dragon Fang at Ecg's Feast to begin their warrior training, but because they were already training the Feast was a formality acknowledging their role as dragonwarriors. Tam came down from the mountain to celebrate and told Chasse she was staying overnight in their family cottage, but Jaysin was absent. Later in the evening, Chasse walked Banni home, offering to carry Jara, and he left the pair at Banni's door to return to the Long Hall.

As Chasse headed for his seat among the Dragon Fang, Eesa intercepted and took him aside. 'Is Banni all right?' she asked.

'Yes,' Chasse replied. 'Why?'

'Will you ask her to be your wife at the next Procra's Dance?'

His mother's question startled Chasse and he blushed, before saying, 'She has Jara.'

Eesa smiled and asked, 'Why is Jara a problem?'

'She's not,' Chasse said, struggling to explain. 'I'm not ready to choose.'

'So, you don't like Banni?' Eesa asked.

'I like Banni very much,' Chasse replied. 'Tam asked me to take care of her because they are friends, that's all.'

'And she would be a good match,' Eesa said. 'Your sister was wise to encourage you.'

Chasse looked past Eesa at Tam who was sitting in a group of younger women. 'I don't think that is Tam's intention,' he said.

'As Dragon Heart, I am sanctioning this choice, should you make it,' Eesa said. 'People have talked, and everyone agrees it would be a good pairing.'

'Has anyone asked Banni?' Chasse queried. 'It should be her choice as well. What if she does not want to be my wife?'

Eesa raised an eyebrow and said, 'You sound like your sister. A man asks. A woman can say yes or no. That is how it is always done. If you want to choose Banni, be a man and choose her.' She patted Chasse's shoulder and walked to join the older women.

Chasse watched his mother go, his mind in turmoil from the conversation. The village had already decided he would marry Banni when neither Banni nor he mentioned a relationship of that kind between them. Ignoring calls from Kogan to join the warriors' table, he beckoned Tam to speak to him.

Tam excused herself from her group and joined Chasse. 'What is the matter?' she asked.

'Has Banni spoken to you about me?' Chasse asked.

'In what way?'

Chasse glanced at the table where Eesa was talking to Amarti before he replied, 'Has she said anything about me choosing her?'

Tam's expression flicked through brief incredulity to a smile. 'Banni likes you,' she said. 'She appreciates what you do for her.' She chuckled and added, 'She sees you as a brother, as my brother.' She looked across at the table of women and said, 'The village is gossiping, isn't it?'

'Our mother encouraged me to ask Banni to marry at the next Procra's Dance,' Chasse explained.

Tam's expression became serious. 'Has anyone thought of asking Banni what she wants?'

'That's what I said. That's why I asked if you knew how Banni felt.'

'You should ask Banni yourself,' Tam suggested.

'I don't know how to ask,' Chasse said. 'And you told me she sees me as a brother, so I would be stupid to say anything to her. I like her. I don't want to make her think I'm helping her because I want something more from her.'

'What about Kerryn?' Tam asked.

'Kerryn is gone.'

'She might return,' Tam suggested.

'I know the others might return, but I am no longer interested in Kerryn. As I told Mother, I'm not ready to choose anyone. I'm like you. I will choose if and when I am ready.'

'Then don't let anyone pressure you into making a choice. And don't pressure Banni. She is still mourning Jared. She likes your company. Enjoy that. Be yourself. Make your own choices.' Tam touched Chasse's arm, as she withdrew to return to the women's table.

Chasse stood by the wall, contemplating his sister's advice, until Kogan yelled, 'Tell us the wolf story again, Chasse Wolf's Bane!' Chasse waved Kogan aside, said 'Goodnight,' and exited the Long Hall.

The Warriors' Hall was dark and cold when he entered, the long hearth left to cool while everyone went to celebrate Ecg's Feast, but he was content to be alone. He grabbed a bear fur, threw it over his shoulders and left the Hall, heading for the jetty. A lamp glowed in a fisherman's hut – Caemun's – and the bay shone silver under the moonlight. He passed the shadowy woodwork skeletons of the fledgling ship and the fish drying racks and climbed onto the jetty, walking along the clinking planks to the end where he stood, staring towards the mouth of the bay.

Dragon's Mouth, he mused. *I feel like I am caught in the dragon's mouth*. He glanced up at the moon and at the light on Nakiades' Bluff. The air was chilly, his breath exhaling in warm clouds lit by the moon. The water lapped gently against the jetty pylons. *Everyone expects me to ask Banni. Except Tam. And probably Banni. I like her. I like the way she talks, the way she smiles, the way she plays with Jara. I like her*. He scuffed his boot against the planks. *Why do I like her*?

Hearing the planks creak, he turned to see the moonlit figure of his father approaching, and he waited until Kevan reached him.

'My son is troubled,' said Kevan quietly.

'Small things,' Chasse replied.

'Eesa said that she spoke to you about Banni.'

'There's nothing to talk about,' Chasse said. 'Mother knows that I care for Banni because Tam asked me to do so. Gossips are making more of something that isn't there.'

'A village thrives on gossip,' Kevan remarked. 'I would not disapprove if you did show affection for her. She is young. The gods were cruel to take her husband. She will marry again, eventually.'

'Tam said she is still in mourning,' said Chasse. 'I will respect that.'

'As you should,' Kevan agreed. 'But you do have feelings for her.'

'Does it matter?' Chasse asked, annoyance brewing. 'What matters is what she is thinking. You told me to respect the woman I choose.'

'Be calm,' Kevan said. 'I did not come to anger you, only to see if you were all right.' He gently placed a hand on Chasse's shoulder. 'Are you ready to recommence training?'

Chasse flexed his shoulders and rotated his right arm, saying, 'As ready as I could be. The ribs are healed.'

'Good,' said Kevan. 'Go to bed. Tomorrow morning, you and I, and the two lads will go hunting. You can help me teach them. They can learn the craft from Chasse Wolf's Bane.'

'I'm not sure I have much to teach them,' Chasse said.

Kevan laughed, saying, 'They don't know that. Reputation is as much bluff as it is action. To them, you are already Chasse Wolf's Bane. Let them think that. No more stories of luck from you. The best warrior stories are tales of courage and strength and you will tell your stories that way for the benefit of those who come after you. Agreed?' He patted Chasse's shoulder. 'Be the man you are. That is what Harbin expects of you.'

Fifteen

The White Eagle Ledge sea watcher's horn echoed across the mountain, startling birds into flight and stopping the hunting party. Chasse looked at Kevan. 'Higher ground,' Kevan recommended.

'This way,' Chasse replied, leading the party up the slope to a rocky outcrop he knew would give them a view across the bay.

'Who is it?' Remi asked as they climbed.

'Every chance it will be our people returning,' Kevan said. 'No one else sails these waters.' He clambered up the rocks, following Chasse.

'There,' said Chasse, pointing. 'Two sails. One red sail. The other is white.'

Kevan followed his direction. 'Two ships,' he murmured.

'Why would they bring two?' Chasse asked.

'They were crammed tight to leave,' Kevan reasoned. 'Maybe they acquired another ship to bring supplies as well. Either way, we better get to the village to meet them.' He scrambled down the rocks with the two young warriors in pursuit.

Chasse let the others forge ahead because he considered climbing the mountain to talk to Tam, but he knew she would have heard the sea watcher's horn and be observing the ships sailing into Harbin. He looked up at the plateau, but he decided to do as expected of him and descended in the wake of the others.

By the time they reached the village, the villagers were gathering along the jetty and the shore and the Dragon Fang were armed and waiting. Chasse noted that the second ship was a different design and a much larger vessel than the dragonship. While it had one mast rigged with a

149

square white sail, it also had a second mast with additional sails furled on three cross spars and a long bow spar that had a sail furled along its length. It stayed in deeper water.

'Deep draught,' Berikan said as Kevan and Chasse stood beside him at the jetty. 'That strange ship can't go into the shallows like a good dragonship.'

'Have you seen a ship like it?' Chasse asked.

'Not me,' Berikan replied. 'Your dragonwarrior friends may have seen them when they sailed south.'

'I saw one like it,' Kevan said, 'when we traded in the bigger towns two summers ago.' He pushed past the villagers and strode onto the jetty with Chasse, Remi and Thados, where they joined the other dragonwarriors.

When the two ships were closer to shore, the dragonship was rowed forward to dock at the jetty and familiar faces smiled and called greetings. Lance was close to the ship's prow, giving orders, with Alan beside him, and the Dragon Heart stood amidships shaking a handful of berries as he sang the village's traditional landfall appreciation to Varst. Chasse was also curious about a figure in a hooded cloak beside the Dragon Heart.

Men clambered onto the jetty and Kogan, Kurtis and Raven helped them to moor the ship. At a quick measure, Chasse counted thirty warriors on the dragonship, but there were several faces he did not recognise.

'Where are the women and children?' Jon yelled over the hubbub.

'On the big ship!' Lance responded as he headed for Kevan.

'Are they coming ashore?' Kevan asked when Lance reached him.

'When we have ensured there is no threat,' Lance replied.

'The dragon is long gone,' Kevan assured him.

Lance smiled as he said, 'Alan confirmed that when we rescued him.'

'Rescued?' Kevan asked.

'We know what happened,' Lance said. 'But I would prefer if we met in the Warriors' Hall to resolve the conditions for our people to return.' He looked Kevan squarely in the face and said, 'I presume your hospitality will allow that?'

Chasse saw his father's expression momentarily sour, but Kevan forced a smile and replied, 'Let me lead you to the hall.'

The hooded figure from the dragonship approached, and Lance said, 'My remiss,' as the figure used his left hand to lower his hood, revealing his dark eyes and hair. 'You know Marron.'

Chasse felt the tension between the men in the Warriors' Hall and reasoned it was due to the uncertainty of returning. He studied the ten men seated along the hearth. Kevan, Jon, Raven, Lynel and Petar were on one side, facing Lance, Neal, Alan and two strangers. Chasse and the dragonwarriors who remained in Harbin were gathered behind Kevan, and those who arrived – including Marron with his hood again masking his face in shadows – stood opposite. The strangers who were not members of the Dragon Fang wore armoured garments of leather and metal, an unusual combination Chasse decided, since the dragonwarriors preferred leather for protection, lightness and flexibility. Kevan welcomed everyone and he promised that a feast would be held that evening to celebrate the return of the Dragon Fang and the villagers.

Lance acknowledged Kevan's welcome before he introduced the two strangers who were wearing the foreign leather and metal armour. 'These men represent Jebaran whose people very kindly allowed us to winter with them. Matihaka Asmara.' The man with braided greying hair nodded. 'And Hesha Karzekk Mikane.' The dark-haired man, his hair tied in a ponytail, also nodded, but something in the second man's features made Chasse think he was familiar. That they had multiple names was also fascinating.

'We are ready to welcome everyone home,' Kevan said. 'Everyone's houses were kept safe. It has been a bitter winter.'

'Thank you,' Lance replied. 'But the world for us is very different than when we left last summer. There are important matters to address before we are happy to return.'

Kevan was perplexed as he asked, 'Like what?'

'First, there is the matter of the Dragon Heart,' said Lance. 'Your wife assumed the mantle. It is not hers to have.'

'That is easily resolved now that the Dragon Heart is returned,' said Kevan. 'Eesa did what she could to serve a purpose.'

Lance accepted Kevan's offer. 'Then there is the matter of the Dragon Head,' he continued. 'Before we left, Trask defeated you.'

'Trask is dead,' said Kevan flatly.

'But there is no successor,' Lance stated.

'I am the Dragon Head,' Kevan said.

'But you are not the Dragon Head,' Lance insisted. 'You were defeated by Trask.'

'Who challenges me? You?' Kevan asked brusquely. He rose from his seat, surveying the warriors, and said, 'In the absence of Trask, and anyone else challenging me after the dragon came, I reclaimed my role as Dragon Head of Harbin. Who, here, denies my claim?'

'I do.' The response, in a foreign tone, came from Mikane, who stood to face Kevan. 'I deny your claim.'

Kevan stared at the man, assessing his athleticism and capacity, and replied, 'You are not a dragonwarrior. Your claim is invalid.'

'As is yours,' said Lance. 'A defeated man cannot be our Dragon Head. It shows weakness, and the Dragon Fang does not tolerate weakness.'

Chasse heard mumbled conversations around the Hall. Kogan leaned against him, and whispered, 'We stand by your father.'

'Then who is the Harbin man who claims to be Dragon Head?' Kevan asked. 'Let him speak, if he exists.'

'I am.' Marron lowered his cowl and stepped forward. 'As the son of the last Dragon Head, I claim the position of Dragon Head for Hesha

Karzekk Mikane.'

Kevan's initial surprise was replaced with disdain. 'What foolish claim is this?' he asked. 'The son of a Dragon Head has no automatic claim and you cannot claim the role for another. The position must be won by combat.'

'And Mikane has challenged you,' Marron said. 'Fight him to reassert any claim you think you might have. Prove you are the Dragon Head.'

'The stranger has no right here,' Jon said, standing beside Kevan.

'He has the right to avenge his brother's murder,' Lance said, standing beside Mikane.

'What has his brother to do with this?' Kevan asked.

'Suran,' said Mikane in his foreign accent, and Chasse understood why Mikane looked familiar. 'You know the name. My brother came here in peace with two of your men. One of your men returned to us with his tale of how he was treated. I see the other seated here.' He nodded at Petar. 'But my brother has not returned and I do not see him in this company.'

'That does not mean anyone murdered him,' Jon said.

'Then where is he?' Mikane challenged. 'Take me to my brother.'

'He headed south, into The Sentinels,' Kevan explained. 'We haven't seen him since.'

'Why would my brother leave, unless he was being hunted by your people?' Mikane asserted.

'He came to plunder a dragon treasure that does not exist,' Kevan said. 'He attacked my son. That is why he was not welcome.'

'You knew my brother,' Mikane said, looking at Petar. 'Where is he?'

Petar stood, looking in turn at Kevan and Chasse, and Chasse saw Petar was frightened. 'Your brother —' Petar began and hesitated.

'Tell me the truth!' Mikane ordered.

Petar glanced at Chasse again, before saying, 'He was killed.'

Mikane's face flushed with anger. 'Who killed him?' he demanded.

'I did,' said Kevan, before Petar could speak. 'I killed your brother.'

Mikane's hand gripped his sword, but Lance held his arm, saying, 'The challenge stands, Hesha Karzekk. You know your brother's killer.'

'There was no murder,' Jon said, glancing at Chasse. 'The Dragon Head was protecting his son. Suran was in the wrong.'

'Do not tell me who was right or wrong!' Mikane snarled. 'I will have my revenge. My brother's blood demands it.'

'Then it is settled,' Lance said, nodding to Marron. 'Mikane and Kevan will battle to determine the new Dragon Head of Harbin, and who is just in the eyes of the gods.'

'This is a trick!' Jon accused.

'This is our law,' said Lance. 'Do you want me to get the Dragon Heart to adjudicate?'

'He is tainted by your lies. He will say whatever you want him to say,' Jon argued.

'Enough!' Kevan interrupted. 'The law is the law.' He sized up Mikane. 'If this is what you want, we will meet outside and let Varst decide.'

'One spear, one sword, one knife, no armour,' Lance said. 'The winner kills or forces the loser to yield.'

'I will be waiting,' said Mikane. He led his followers out of the Warriors' Hall, leaving the door open.

'You do not have to do this,' Jon argued.

'Eventually, this was going to happen,' said Kevan.

'Not with a stranger,' Raven retorted. 'He has no right in our village.'

'If Marron wants to challenge you, then the one-armed spawn of Trask should be fighting you,' Jon asserted.

'Varst will protect me,' said Kevan. He moved to the weapon rack to select a sword.

Chasse followed his father. 'Why did you say you killed Suran when it was me?' he asked.

'Because you would not be able to fight this stranger,' said Kevan.

'He defeated his brother,' Raven asserted.

'By luck,' Kevan replied. He turned to Chasse. 'Correct?' Chasse looked at the others dejectedly and nodded. 'By luck,' Kevan repeated. 'There is no room for luck in this type of combat. You would be outmatched in every way.'

'But it should be my fight, not yours!' Chasse declared.

'You are not Dragon Head,' Kevan replied. 'Whoever wins this will be Dragon Head of Harbin.'

'Then let me fight,' Jon demanded. 'I have a right to make a claim.'

Kevan put a hand on Jon's shoulder and said, 'There will be a time for you to be the Dragon Head and I hope that you will be, one day. But it is not today. Today the burden is mine to carry.' He picked up his spear and headed for the door. Jon, Chasse and the remaining dragonwarriors followed him outside.

The village square between the Warriors' Hall and the Long Hall was filled with people talking and jostling for a view. The dragonwarriors formed an inner circle in the shape of an arena and Mikane waited in the circle. With his leather armour removed, Mikane's physique was formidable, the muscular build of a strong, seasoned warrior. He spun his sword briefly in a demonstration of skill before he stuck it into the earth and took up his spear when Kevan entered the circle to face him. Kevan stuck his sword in the ground and gripped his spear.

Lance stepped into the arena, held his hand high to call for silence, and spoke. 'People of Harbin. Before you stand two men who lay claim to the title of Dragon Head. This battle will determine who will hold that role. You are here to witness that the combat is fair and according to tradition. Varst, and Varst alone, will pass judgement on these two men. When I step out of the circle, the fight begins.' He nodded to Mikane, glanced at Kevan, and stepped out of the arena. As he did, the people began urging on their chosen combatant.

Chasse searched the crowd until he saw Eesa among the Harbin women, her face stern, eyes fixed on Kevan. He felt an urge to go to her, and he wished Tamesan and Jaysin were with them, but he was expected to remain with the dragonwarriors. He remembered how Ethen held him back when Kevan fought Trask, telling him that a dragonwarrior did not take sides when the Dragon Head was challenged by a contender. So, he watched as Trask beat his father. He even watched when Tam and Jaysin intervened. And he ran from the village when Tam told him to run. Like a coward. The memory haunted and goaded him. He stepped forward to the edge of the ring. If his father needed him this time, he was ready.

He observed how the combatants studied each other, waiting for the other man to make the first move, while the crowd yelled tactics and demanded action. Chasse anticipated Kevan would attack first, especially after his advice during the Trial of the Second Winter, and an instant later Kevan lunged, a probing assessment with his spear that Mikane easily knocked aside. As if satisfied with what he saw, Kevan began to circle, forcing Mikane to adjust a step, but then he lunged, stopping Kevan's advance.

And the fight commenced in earnest.

Mikane followed his thrust with a reverse swing, spinning under Kevan's sweep to smack Kevan's legs with his spear, scoring a cut across his shins and evincing a cheer from the crowd. Instead of reacting and retreating, Kevan barrelled into Mikane and sent him stumbling back, fighting to regain his balance. Kevan stabbed at Mikane's groin, but Mikane was quick and strong. He deflected Kevan's spear and used his elbow to club Kevan's head. Kevan backpedalled, flailing his spear deliberately to thwart any follow through, and the two squared again, reassessing each other.

'How could a slow, old man kill my brother?' Mikane taunted. 'Suran was strong, fast, skilled. You, on the other hand, are feeble.' Kevan did not respond as he began, again, to stalk his quarry. 'You must have tricked him, somehow,' Mikane said. 'Stabbed him in the back, maybe. Or did you make all your warriors ambush him.'

Kevan ignored the goading accusations as he closed in. He attacked Mikane and their spears flashed and clattered while they warded each other's blows and returned the like, until they locked hands and arms in an embrace that prevented either moving. Their arm muscles and leg muscles bulged as they wrestled for the upper hand. Mikane attempted to sweep Kevan's leg with his own, but Kevan stayed upright and strong. Chasse saw sweat streaming from the men's brows and necks, the thin line of blood on Kevan's shins, heard them grunting and breathing harshly. Unexpectedly, Mikane collapsed backwards, planted his foot into Kevan's stomach, and he hurled Kevan over as he rolled, coming to his feet, spear ready. Kevan rolled as he landed and scrambled to his feet, in time to use his arm to ward a spear thrust. He swung down at Mikane's hand. There was a loud crack and Mikane retreated, shaking his injured hand. Shouts of approval and encouragement echoed through the village.

Mikane grinned, twirled his spear expertly around his body in a show of bravado and stalked Kevan. He thrust twice, both attempts deflected, before he back turned and swept the spear low. Chasse recognised the move and knew his father would block it and anticipate the return reverse high sweep – all the Dragon Fang practised the move – but no one expected Mikane's extraordinary manoeuvre.

As Kevan blocked the low sweep, Mikane buried his spear tip into the ground and used the weight behind Kevan's block to vault past his opponent. He landed on his feet, lifted his spear and stabbed Kevan under his ribs. The thrust and withdrawal were so quick that many spectators did not see the wound, until Kevan waved his spear awkwardly with his right hand to ward Mikane away and staggered back. Mikane charged past, swinging his spear sharply across Kevan's right hand, forcing Kevan to drop his weapon. His opponent disarmed, Mikane skipped in, kicked Kevan in the chest to send him backward onto his behind, snatched up Kevan's spear, and walked cockily away as Kevan slowly got to his feet. Mikane twirled the two short spears theatrically before he stuck them in the earth, took up his sword, faced Kevan and said, 'I'm ready to finish this, old man.'

Chasse saw his father touch his side and examine the blood on his hand, and it reminded him of the same wound that Trask inflicted on Kevan. That time, Kevan was beaten and already on the ground. This time, Kevan was still standing. Mikane had not won yet.

Kevan retrieved his sword. He wiped sweat from his brow and left blood streaks across his forehead and cheek as he closed the gap between Mikane and himself.

'A man who doesn't know when he's beaten is either very foolish or very dangerous,' Mikane said. 'Let's see which you are.' He danced a couple of steps forward, spinning his sword as he did before the fight. He lunged and dodged Kevan's sweep, thrust and parried Kevan's reply, and skipped a couple steps away.

'Losing blood tires a man,' Mikane said. 'Throbbing pain makes him desperate because he knows he doesn't have much time left.'

Kevan closed in and swung and Mikane deftly warded his blade. Again, Kevan swung and again Mikane deflected the attack. The third time, Mikane twisted Kevan's blade inward so that it narrowly missed him, stepped forward and punched Kevan sharply in the face with his free hand, sending Kevan reeling backward, blood streaming from his nose.

'The last time your warriors came raiding our towns and villages we taught you a lesson,' Mikane said, circling Kevan. 'While you've been living your secluded lives in this backward village, we've been learning from the Kermakk. We've grown stronger.' He danced aside as Kevan swung, retreated a few steps, and said, 'You are the past, old man. Your ways are over. Your people belong to us.' And then Mikane moved in a flurry, a blur of motion, and when he stepped back Kevan dropped his sword, and collapsed as if his legs lost their will to stand. Cheers and gasps rose from the crowd.

Chasse felt as if a spear was thrust through his own gut as he watched his mother run into the circle and drop to her knees beside Kevan and he wrapped his hand around the handle of his hunting knife, anger flooding him.

Above the chatter, Lance yelled, 'Varst has spoken! Mikane is Dragon Head of Harbin!'

His announcement was greeted with cheers, mostly from the returned villagers and strangers, but the warriors behind Chasse were silent. Chasse began to draw his knife, but a hand firmly gripped his right shoulder and Jon said quietly, 'This is not the time to do anything foolish. You are a dragonwarrior. Your father would expect you to act like one.'

'Tonight, we celebrate the rebirth of Harbin!' Lance announced. 'We welcome our new Dragon Head and a new order!'

Chasse sucked in his breath to quell his seething anger and deep sorrow, shrugged Jon's grip and walked forward to kneel beside his sobbing mother. 'This is my fault,' he muttered.

Eesa turned reddened eyes on him. 'Why would you say that?'

'Mikane wanted revenge for his brother's death.'

'His brother?' Essa queried.

'Suran.'

Eesa's eyes widened and she locked her gaze on Chasse. 'Your father did this to save your life,' she said. She looked down at Kevan and whispered, 'I understand.'

Dragonwarriors gathered around Essa and Chasse, and Jon said to Chasse, 'Help us carry Kevan to the Warriors' Hall. We will prepare your father for singing on.'

Eesa wiped her eyes and looked up. 'Thank you,' she whispered to Jon, and she put her hand on Chasse's shoulder as she struggled to her feet. 'Go, Chasse,' she said quietly. 'Help prepare your father for his journey.'

Chasse swallowed, tears welling, and rose to stand with Jon. Across the shoulders of the dragonwarriors, he saw Marron smiling and his rage burned.

Sixteen

'Becoming a man is a painful process,' said the Dragon Heart as he washed blood and earth from Kevan's face. 'Life and death circle you, even when you think you hold them in your hands. Procra and Fler nourish life. Ecg protects it and takes it away. And Varst, Almighty Lord, oversees all of this and makes his own determination as to who will live and who will die.'

Jon and Raven washed Kevan's legs while the Dragon Heart repeated his litany, the men reverently cleaning the body on a wooden table in the corner of the Warriors' Hall as they readied Kevan for Eesa and her helpers to dress him before singing the Words of Passage. Chasse soaked his cloth in the warm water before applying it to the wound in Kevan's side, washing away caked blood and dirt. There were more scars on his father's body than Chasse knew he had, forming a tapestry of his father's struggles and challenges. He touched the scars from earlier wounds as he cleaned, remembering the ones he knew came from Trask, and he wondered how and when his father earned the other scars.

Chasse couldn't explain his emotion. Emptiness – as if his nerves were dead. The corpse was his father and not his father. Kevan was large, strong, a life force, a mighty warrior. Chasse wanted him to sit up and tell everyone to step back and leave him alone, that there were tasks to do and training to complete. He wanted him to say, 'I will meet you on the slopes of the mountain. We will hunt together.' He shouldn't be dead. This death was unfair, too soon. He was beginning to know his father, to learn from him. Where there was a burgeoning purpose, a direction opening before him, now there was a void. He wanted to cry, but he knew crying was not the action of a dragonwarrior. He would be strong. He would do his duty. He would be the man his father expected him to be. But he wanted to cry, to grieve, to mourn deeply.

'This is yours, Chasse Wolf's Bane,' Jon said, and he handed Chasse Kevan's bone handled hunting knife. 'May you carry it with the same honour and grace as your father and his father before him.'

Chasse took the knife and stared at its hardened edge, the scratches and grooves along the blade, the bone worn smooth and discoloured by generations of sweat. He knew that one day the knife was to be his, but not now, not today, not this soon. He had so much more to learn from his father.

'We carry Kevan, now, to his home,' said the Dragon Heart. He laid a red cloth across Kevan, covering him head to foot, and Jon, Raven, Kogan and Chasse took corners of the tabletop and lifted it from its trestle legs to bear Kevan from the Warriors' Hall.

When they stepped outside, a large group of dragonwarriors were waiting to quietly watch them pass as they bore their burden across the village to Watersdrop and over the bridge into the cottage. Eesa and Tam opened the door, allowing the men to shuffle through and place Kevan on the table.

Chasse was quietly pleased to see his sister, but he retained his grave expression to honour his task. Jaysin lurked in the bedroom doorway, staring at the red cloth. Eesa thanked the Dragon Heart for bringing her husband to her before she said to Chasse, 'Take Jaysin with you. It is not his place to be here. Ask Banni if he can sleep at her cottage tonight.'

Chasse gestured silently to Jaysin who crossed the small room with his eyes fixed on the body, and the men stepped aside to let five women enter the cottage. 'We'll leave you to talk with your brother,' Jon said quietly as they crossed the bridge. 'We'll see what the new Dragon Head expects of us.'

Chasse waited for the dragonwarriors and Dragon Heart to walk away before he said to Jaysin, 'I'll show you where father and I went hunting.'

'I don't like hunting,' Jaysin replied.

'We won't hurt any animals,' Chasse promised. 'I'll show you where the Shadow Hunters live.'

'What are Shadow Hunters?' Jaysin asked.

'A special pack of wolves. No one can catch them,' Chasse replied. 'Come on.'

Chasse led Jaysin across the village towards Nakiades' Bluff, nodding as people offered polite condolences, determined to show courage by not crying or screaming with anger. He considered going to the Warriors' Hall to collect his spear, but he decided it would be safe to walk the slopes during the morning. He had Kevan's knife if unexpected danger arose.

When they reached the outer buildings, Chasse stopped to watch boats being rowed to the shore from the Jebaran ship. The distance made recognition difficult, but he was certain that the people aboard the rowing boats weren't women and children but more Jebaran warriors. He hesitated, wondering whether it would be prudent to return to his companions.

'What's wrong?' Jaysin asked. 'I thought we were going to see the wolves.'

'We are,' Chasse replied. He looked one more time at the incoming boats before he led Jaysin into the forest.

The trees were vibrant with fresh growth, the earth moist and in places rocky under foot, so different to his experience during the Trial of the Second Winter. Birds flitted between the branches, squirrels scampered along them, and a fox crouched and melted into the bushes. Jaysin was attentive to the creatures, pointing them out and naming them for Chasse's benefit.

'How do you know so much about them?' Chasse asked, when they spotted an ermine scurrying into a burrow.

'I study them,' Jaysin replied. 'And there are books in the Herbal Man's library that lists the animals and all their habits and habitats. Tam gave you one, remember?'

Chasse blushed at the reminder of an unfulfilled promise. 'Do you read every day?' he asked.

'Every moment I can,' Jaysin replied. 'There's so much to know.'

'Including magic,' Chasse said.

'I love learning magic!' Jaysin replied. He sighed and shook his head. 'I just can't show anyone.'

'Why not?' Chasse asked as they climbed a short slope.

'Tam said it would scare people and they wouldn't feel safe around me,' Jaysin said.

'They would be fascinated,' Chasse said.

Jaysin shook his auburn locks and Chasse noted how much longer Jaysin's hair had grown while he was secluded on the mountain with Tam. 'They wouldn't like it,' Jaysin said. 'I know they wouldn't. Sometimes, when I see the games the other kids play, I can think of better ways to play the games, only when I try to share my ideas they laugh and tease me. It's better not to show people new things.'

'Can you show me some magic?' Chasse asked.

Jaysin's eyes widened. 'What would you like to see?'

'I don't know anything about magic,' Chasse said. 'Wait,' he added, remembering what he witnessed Jaysin learning in the cave. 'I know. Make a stone warm.' He picked up a small flat stone. 'Like this one.'

Jaysin grinned, saying, 'Easy.' He cupped the stone in his hands and held it out.

Chasse took the stone and felt heat. 'I'm impressed.'

'Everything contains energy,' Jaysin explained. 'Even when a thing is still, energy remains in it. Heat is energy. Light is energy. The trick is learning how to coax the energy into action.'

'And you learned this by reading the Herbal Man's books?'

'Yes,' Jaysin confirmed, but his smile faded.

'What's wrong?' Chasse asked.

'Why didn't you stop that man from killing Father?'

Chasse felt as if his breath was punched from his lungs. 'It wasn't my choice.'

'That's a silly answer,' Jaysin said. 'When Trask tried to kill father, Tam and I stopped him. You should have helped us then, too, but you didn't.'

'I tried to talk Father out of fighting Mikane,' Chasse said. 'I honestly did. But he wouldn't listen. He said it was the right thing to do, to fight Mikane, and I had to do the right thing by not interfering.'

'You all could have stopped it,' Jaysin said, tears welling. 'Father didn't have to die. You could have stopped it.' He sank to the ground, unable to contain his sorrow.

Chasse felt his own grief rising as he knelt beside his brother. 'Don't cry,' he said quietly. 'Men don't cry.'

Jaysin looked at him with his watery eyes and said, 'That's also stupid. People should cry if they need to, especially when they are sad.'

'Did Tam tell you that?'

Jaysin sniffed and wiped his nose with his arm before replying, 'No. I know it without anyone telling me. It feels right to cry when I need to. Father and Mother and you always say, "Don't cry", but sometimes I need to cry. Otherwise, it hurts much worse to keep it locked inside. I don't understand why you aren't crying for Father.'

Chasse sat beside Jaysin and put a hand on his shoulder in the way he knew Kevan would put his hand on his son's shoulder. 'To be a man,' he said, trying to use the expressions Kevan and others used with him, 'means keeping control of your emotions as much as you can.'

Jaysin shrugged Chasse's hand from his shoulder. 'Then I don't ever want to be a man.' He dropped his head and sobbed.

'Come on,' Chasse urged, trying to divert Jaysin's thoughts. 'The Shadow Hunters are over the next ridge.'

'What will happen to Mother?' Jaysin asked, without raising his head.

'I —,' Chasse began, cleared his throat of his pressing emotion, and said,

'She will be fine. She's an important person in the village.'

'I don't think so,' Jaysin said, looking up. 'With Father gone, no one will protect her. We have to take her with us.'

'To the mountain? She wouldn't do that. She won't leave Harbin.'

'She won't be safe,' Jaysin argued.

'Everyone loves and respects her,' Chasse reasoned. 'She will be all right.'

'She won't have Father. Or you,' Jaysin said. 'You'll live in the Warriors' Hall and go away on the dragonship. She will be alone.'

'But you will be there. And Tam will visit.'

'I'm never going back.' Jaysin met Chasse's querying gaze. 'I mean it.'

'And where will you live?' Chasse asked. 'On the mountain?'

'Yes,' Jaysin replied. 'With Tam and Harmi.'

'People will miss you.'

'No one will miss me.'

'I will miss you.'

'You know where I will be,' Jaysin said. 'You can visit whenever you want.'

Chasse heard Jaysin's steely resolve and knew that he meant what he said. His brother was an odd mix of emotions and thoughts and he was changing in ways Chasse didn't understand. 'I'll show you the Shadow Hunters,' he said, holding out his hand to draw Jaysin out of his mood. 'Come on.'

Jaysin accepted the proffered hand and followed Chasse up the slope to the ridgetop, where they crouched among the bushes to observe the wolf den on the side of the adjacent hill. 'There!' said Jaysin excitedly. 'I see them!'

Chasse squinted, struggling to see what Jaysin obviously could see, until a grey wolf pup trotted onto a flat rock. A second appeared, a white one, and it sat beside the first. The pups were sniffing the air and savouring the scents. Fascinated by the vision of the pups, Chasse wasn't aware of Jaysin's movement until his brother appeared several paces down the slope. 'Jaysin!' he called softly. 'What are you doing?'

'Going to see the pups,' Jaysin replied eagerly, and he continued descending through the trees.

Chasse scrambled after his brother. 'Come back! They'll tear you apart!' he yelled, but Jaysin moved through the vale and up the slope with unanticipated agility and speed, and by the time Chasse reached a stand of bushes and trees close to the den Jaysin was on all fours with five wolf pups dancing around him, ears flattened and tiny tails wagging as they sniffed and licked his arms and face. 'Jaysin!' Chasse hissed. He drew his father's hunting knife and anxiously searched the glade and den mouth for the adult animals, but Jaysin sat on his haunches and held his finger to his lips, warning Chasse to be quiet. A pup climbed onto Jaysin's lap and he stroked it. Two chewed his boots. The other two rolled nearby in a mock fight.

Chasse was enthralled by the vision of his little brother playing with the Shadow Hunter pups, until a larger shape loomed in the den entrance, a she-wolf, and she was snarling. He clutched his knife, summoning the courage to save his brother, but he knew he could not single-handedly kill a wolf with a hunting knife. His escape during winter was happenstance. Two such turns of luck in a lifetime were unlikely.

The appearance of a second, larger black wolf from the bushes flushed him with terror. Two wolves. Jaysin was dead for certain, and he was as good as dead if he was stupid enough to attack. *Why this cruelty, Varst?* he begged. *My father? Now us? What have we done?* Frozen with fear, he watched the wolf mother stalk Jaysin from the den mouth while the bigger animal observed. He was honour-bound to protect Jaysin. That was a dragonwarrior's oath — to protect the people of the Harbin, especially family, but he was being challenged to give his life to uphold the oath: first, with his father facing Mikane, and now with Jaysin hunted by wolves. He had already looked death in the face enough times. *Am I marked to die*? he wondered. *Why*? He couldn't save Jaysin, not in the situation before him. The wolves would tear them apart. They would both die.

As the wolf mother closed in on Jaysin, growling and sniffing, Jaysin calmly held out his hand. The wolf hesitated, snarled and warily sniffed Jaysin's fingers. And then licked his hand. And moved closer to nuzzle his arm. Jaysin patted the wolf's ruff as if he was stroking one of Galt's goats and the wolf rubbed against him, sniffing his hair, before she picked up a pup in her mouth and carried it into the den.

Awed by what he was witnessing, Chasse stayed in the bushes, aware that movement would divert the wolves' attention to him and he knew they would not react to him like they were responding to Jaysin. He wasn't sure if he was far enough downwind to avoid detection. In the rush down the slope to stop Jaysin, he forgot the basic hunting safety techniques.

The second wolf, the male, padded around the perimeter of the glade and lay near the den mouth, observing Jaysin. Chasse noticed that his brother made no overtures to the bigger wolf, choosing to sit patiently while the she-wolf collected another pup and carried it into the den. The wrestling pair stopped their game and followed their mother in, but the pup curled on Jaysin's lap was asleep and unaware of what was happening. The mother wolf returned and approached Jaysin, sniffed his shoulder and licked his face, before she hoisted the fifth pup from his lap to carry it in. Two pups peered from the den mouth as the mother wolf re-emerged and padded to Jaysin. She sniffed his hair as he remained still, before she nudged him, at first gently and then firmly, so that he stood. He began to walk towards Chasse, slowly. As if satisfied the human was leaving, the mother wolf trotted into the den, but the vigilant male watched with amber eyes until Jaysin entered the bushes before he loped into the undergrowth.

'Stand quietly and walk with me,' Jaysin whispered as he passed close to Chasse. 'Don't look back and don't stop.'

Chasse obeyed his brother's instruction, still fathoming what he had witnessed as he fell into step behind Jaysin. The brothers walked in silence until they reached the top of the ridge, at which point Jaysin stopped to peer across the gulley at the den. 'I'd never seen the Shadow Hunters,' he said. 'They're beautiful.'

'How did you do that?' Chasse asked, his pulse pounding.

Jaysin kept staring across the hillside as he replied, 'Every creature has a culture and a language. If you learn it, you can treat them respectfully and they will do the same.'

Chasse shook his head. 'You can talk to wolves?'

Jaysin grinned. 'Not like you and I talk. No. But you can communicate with them and they with us. In simple ways.'

Chasse kept shaking his head as he asked, 'And how did you learn this?' He hesitated and added, 'You read it, yes?'

Jaysin shook his head, saying, 'No, and yes. The Herbal Man has a book called *Animal Lore* and I read it, but you have to live with the animals to learn their culture.'

'You haven't lived with wolves,' said Chasse. 'How could you learn wolf culture?'

'I've spent time with them,' Jaysin said. 'While I wandered the mountains. You haven't seen everywhere I've been.' He pulled up his sleeve to reveal a scar on his forearm. 'They're not all friendly, at first.'

'You were attacked?' Chasse asked in disbelief.

'Warned,' Jaysin told him. 'The first wolf I tried to speak to didn't like it. But I learned. When I approached her the next time, she was more tolerant because I wasn't disrespectful.'

Chasse let the concept resonate in his mind, but none of Jaysin's chatter was making sense. 'We better go back to Harbin,' he said. 'I have work to do.'

'I will check in on Harmi,' Jaysin said.

'Alone?' Chasse asked, but he corrected himself, saying, 'Of course alone. Should I tell Tam?'

'She knows,' Jaysin replied.

'We will sing the Words of Passage for Father tomorrow. Will you come down for that?'

'No,' Jaysin said. 'I'll spend time thinking of him on the mountain. I don't believe in the Words of Passage. There is no Paradise.'

'Why not?'

'It isn't logical. It's like the story about Nakiades fighting the dragons. It's a made up story so that people can make sense of stuff they don't understand.'

'Nakiades' story is real,' Chasse asserted.

'For you,' Jaysin said, 'but you're a dragonwarrior, so you have to believe it.'

'I know it's real,' said Chasse, thinking of the cavern within Nakiades' Bluff.

'How do you know?' asked Jaysin. 'Because someone told you it is true?'

Chasse wanted to prove what he knew. He wanted to tell Jaysin there were relics in a cave belonging to Nakiades. But he was sworn to secrecy. The adult world was all about keeping secrets. Instead, he shrugged and said, 'I'll walk with you across the slope to Dragon Mountain.'

'I'll teach you how to communicate with wolves!' Jaysin said excitedly. 'You won't have to hunt them anymore.'

Seventeen

Chasse was surprised to see Banni hurrying towards him as he crossed Galt's pasture, the goats separating as he walked between, and she began yelling before he reached her. 'Chasse! You have to leave! You have to leave now!'

'What?' he asked. 'Why?'

'Mikane and Marron,' Banni said. 'They're forcing Tamesan to take them to the dragon treasure.' Chasse felt his anger explode and he started to march past Banni, but she grabbed his arm. 'Chasse! No! You can't! There's too many of them!'

'How many?' he asked.

'At least fifty,' she said. 'More foreign warriors came on the other ship. Mikane's older brother is leading them.'

'Older brother? Asmara is his brother?'

'No,' Banni replied. 'Another man came with the new warriors.'

Chasse remembered what he saw before he led Jaysin up Nakiades' Bluff, the boats rowing to shore. 'What are Jon and Raven doing?'

'Mikane disarmed them and the others who were here with you and ordered them to stay in the Long Hall,' Banni explained as she steered Chasse to the goat shelter. 'Mikane sent his brother with a group to look for you and Jaysin on Nakiades' Bluff.'

Galt emerged from the shelter, holding a rust and white kid, but when he saw Banni and Chasse he returned inside without speaking.

'What about my mother?' Chasse asked.

'Eesa is with the women in the Long Hall. She sent me to find you,' Banni replied. 'She's safe.'

'I have to save Tam,' Chasse asserted.

'You can't, Chasse,' Banni insisted. 'Tamesan told me to tell you that the best you can do for now is not get caught. Find a place to hide.'

'I have to warn Jaysin,' Chasse said, realising where the threat would turn. Alan and Petar knew the dragon's cave was on the plateau or nearby and they would search there. 'What about you?' he asked.

'They have no interest in me or any of the women, but I'll do what I can for Tamesan and Eesa,' Banni promised. She gripped Chasse's hand and said, 'Stay safe,' before she leaned up and kissed him.

Startled by Banni's unexpected kiss, Chasse blushed, and mumbled, 'Please keep an eye on Tam. I'll do what I can.' He turned to avoid lingering on Banni's gaze, saw Galt wink from the corner of the shelter, and he headed for the mountain slope.

Aware that he was being hunted and that the path up Dragon Mountain was obvious, Chasse took a circuitous route, climbing small embankments and cutting through thicker stands and bushes, vigilant for movement or sound that would reveal men searching for him. From Banni's information, they were anticipating intercepting Jaysin and him on Nakiades' Bluff, so it was fortuitous that Jaysin returned to Dragon Mountain and Chasse had not returned to Harbin by the way they left. As much as he wanted to hurry, he knew haste without care would lead him into trouble as it did when he clashed with Suran. The memory made him move with greater caution, wondering if the strangers who arrived had hunters like Suran among them.

He reached the plateau and hid in the bushes, observing the area, listening, watching for signs that might betray anyone waiting for him. He would be exposed on the goat path, but it was the only way into the cave that he knew. He drew his hunting knife and ran across the plateau and reached the goat path without incident. A quick search of the surrounds showed no one was on the plateau. He climbed.

At the top, he paused to survey the landscape and spotted a small party emerging from the trees along a ridge between Dragon Mountain and Nakiades Bluff. He had arrived before the searchers. That meant they wouldn't expect him to be on the plateau and that gave him time. He slid into the cleft and made his way by touch and memory across the cavern of the Dawn People to the steps.

Harmi was awake and staring with blue reptilian eyes as he descended into the chamber. Unsettled by the dragon's intense gaze, he looked for his little brother, but Jaysin wasn't visible. 'Jaysin!' he called as he reached the last step. Harmi cocked her head. She was sitting in the nest, and she was significantly larger than he remembered. His wrist tingled and, glancing at his bracelet, he saw it glowing softly.

'I'm here,' Jaysin replied, walking through the doorway to the goat cave and carrying a bucket.

'Are you feeding Harmi?' Chasse asked, crossing the chamber to Jaysin.

'I was feeding the goats,' said Jaysin.

'Tam is in trouble,' Chasse announced.

'I know,' Jaysin replied, as he put down the bucket at the foot of Harmi's nest.

'How do you know?' Chasse asked.

'We've been talking about it,' Jaysin replied. When he saw Chasse's incredulous expression, he tapped his bracelet. 'We are bound.'

'Then why don't I hear what you're saying?' Chasse asked, showing his bracelet. 'Tam told me we were bound.'

'Because we only learned how to do it over a longer distance today,' Jaysin said. He grinned and continued, saying, 'Go over there.' He pointed to the far side of the chamber.

'I have to rescue Tam,' Chasse insisted.

'Please,' Jaysin pleaded.

Chasse walked quickly away. When he reached the chamber wall, he pivoted. 'Now what?'

'Hello.'

Jaysin's voice echoed in Chasse's head. He reeled and touched his forehead. 'What did you do?'

'I'm sending you my thoughts,' Jaysin replied. 'You try.'

As absurd as the concept seemed, Chasse focussed on Jaysin and thought, 'Can you hear me?' He remembered Tam's communication when Suran attacked him. He closed his eyes and focussed again, but an unexpected blanketing, formless sensation filled his mind, stifling his thought. He opened his eyes and asked, 'What was that?' He saw Jaysin staring at Harmi.

'Harmi told me to be quiet,' Jaysin explained.

'She can do that?' Chasse asked.

'Apparently,' Jaysin said, grinning. 'I didn't know. I thought she could only talk to Tam.' He approached the dragon and Harmi leaned forward to let him stroke her grey snout.

'I'm going to my chamber,' said Chasse. 'I have to do something to help Tam.' He approached the hidden door and hesitated before he placed his left hand on the stone. Nothing happened.

'Think about opening the door,' Jaysin prompted.

As Chasse imagined the door opening, his bracelet tingled, the door glowed amber and opened. He smiled at Jaysin who was grinning at him, but his elation was mixed with mystification that he could open the door with magic. Within the corridor, he remembered that Tam used a key to open the warrior's chamber, but he discovered the door was open, as he left it. He clicked his fingers and the ceiling crystals lit.

He began by selecting the battle axe, its grip sublime as he lifted it, the blade shining in the crystal light. Though he was unfamiliar with wearing metal armour, he selected a breastplate, armguards and a helmet from the equipment. Much to his surprise, each piece fitted perfectly, the armguards feeling as if they adjusted to enclose his forearms as he put them on. He found a set of silver gloves, the metal in tiny rings flowing like liquid as he lifted them. Like the armguards, they were snug and light. He spun the axe through sweeps and arcs and, satisfied with what he chose, he made to leave, but he discovered Jaysin in the doorway.

'What are you doing?' Jaysin asked.

'This is all I have,' Chasse replied. 'If I can save Tam, I will.'

'There are too many for you to fight alone,' Jaysin argued, reminding Chasse of Banni's warning.

'Then I have to be cunning,' Chasse declared.

'Like a Shadow Hunter,' Jaysin said.

'Wolves hunt in packs,' Chasse replied. 'I thought you would know that.'

'Young wolves have to make their own way,' said Jaysin. 'They leave the pack until they can create one of their own or join a new one. That's us.'

His younger brother's unusual wisdom fascinated Chasse. 'You read that?'

'No,' Jaysin replied. 'It's what I've seen.'

Chasse entered the corridor and headed for the main cavern, Jaysin following in his wake. 'If you can send your thoughts to Tam,' he said, 'tell her I'm going to find a way to get her out of Harbin safely. And Mother.'

'What about everyone else?' Jaysin asked.

Chasse stopped as they entered the main chamber, glanced at Harmi who was watching them, and said, 'If I can do something that will help the others, I will. I just don't know what, yet.'

'A distraction,' Jaysin said. 'Something that will lure the others away from the village.'

Chasse nodded. 'You're a tactician too?'

'I can show you a book called *The Dancing Warriors*,' Jaysin said. 'It has a whole lot of tactics and ideas for winning battles and skirmishes. I'll show you.'

'You know I can't read,' Chasse replied. He looked at the dragon again, and said, 'Do what you can to keep this place safe while I fetch Tam. Here.'

He pulled Kevan's hunting knife from his belt. 'This was Father's knife. You might need it.'

Jaysin took the bone-handled weapon and perused it as he twisted it in the light. 'I don't know how to fight,' he said, handing the knife back to Chasse.

'Keep it for now,' Chasse urged, pushing Jaysin's hand away. 'Can you learn any magic that will help?'

'I know a book on the shelves. It's called *Arts of Arcane Warfare*. I'll read it,' Jaysin said.

'Can you communicate with Tam now?'

'Yes,' Jaysin replied. He closed his eyes as if entering a trance, but his expression shifted to disappointment.

'What is it?' Chasse asked.

Jaysin opened his eyes. 'They're forcing her to lead them here,' Jaysin said angrily. 'They're already climbing the mountain.'

'How far up?' Chasse asked.

Jaysin focussed before replying, 'Almost halfway.'

'Tell Tam I'm coming,' Chasse said, and he jogged past the dragon's nest under Harmi's watchful gaze.

'Tam says you should stay,' Jaysin called, but Chasse hitched his battle axe on his back and ascended the steps, disappearing into the darkness.

I have to save Tam, Chasse silently told himself. *I failed Father. I can't fail my sister.*

Chasse halted at the peak of the goat path to check if anyone was on the plateau. The area was empty. A bank of white clouds loomed along the southern horizon above The Sentinels and gulls wheeled over White Eagle Ledge. He wondered if anyone was on watch and who it was. He searched the trees and bushes and shadows at the perimeter of the plateau to be sure that no one was hiding in waiting before he descended, moving as quickly as the treacherous path allowed, surprised that his new armour wasn't hindering his agility or speed.

When he reached the base, he ran to the closest trees. Jaysin's idea of a distraction was good, only Chasse didn't know how to create a viable distraction. He could kindle a small fire and let them think that Jaysin and he were camped on the hillside. That ruse might draw some away. But when he thought about it, if there was a hunting party searching for them, only the hunting party would divert. The group coming up the path with Tamesan wouldn't change course. They didn't need to. He should have asked Jaysin to ask Tam how many were escorting her. He would have to find out for himself. If he had more time, he could hurry down to the village, organise Jon and the loyal dragonwarriors, and return to challenge Mikane's warriors, but he knew the loyal dragonwarriors were outnumbered and stood little to no chance of success in a battle. He had to be the lone wolf – hungry, determined – and use his instincts to attack his quarry and survive. The problem was how. He resolved to sneak down the slope and observe the ascending party to ascertain the number and how Tam was being guarded. Then he could decide on his tactics.

He moved swiftly through the fresh and lush undergrowth beneath the trees, wary of loose rocks and slippery patches, shadowing the path, conscious of Watersdrop babbling in a nearby ravine as its melt water tumbled and poured over rocks. When a bevy of green birds rose squawking a short distance down the slope, he stopped to listen. Unable to detect human movement, he edged along a short bank and concealed himself in a large bush a small distance above the path where he had a clear view. His heart raced. He unhitched the axe. His bracelet tingled.

Two men came into view, Jebaran warriors with metal breastplates and swords and braided hair. Alan followed, and then came Tam, hands bound, Mikane at her side. Behind was Marron in his hooded cloak, and following him were more warriors, eight as they appeared in single file around the bend in the path. Thirteen men. Twelve seasoned warriors.

Chasse's heart sank. Who had he ever beaten in a real fight? How could he release Tam without fighting? He watched the party pass below his hiding place while he ruminated on what he could do to even the odds or isolate Tam to rescue her. He should have gone down to Harbin and somehow brought support, but he knew that strategy would be too late to save Harmi or Jaysin. Tam's captors would be on the plateau soon. Then he had an idea.

He hitched his axe onto his back before he slid down from the bank, stepped onto the path as the trailing party members began to round another bend, picked up a stone and hurled it so that it rattled against a rock. The last two men turned and when they saw Chasse standing on the path they shouted and gesticulated. He waited until they began pursuit before he bolted down the path, rounded the corner where he first saw them appear, and veered into the undergrowth. He sprinted between two trees, picked up another stone and flung it down the hill to clatter along the path, drawing his pursuers after its sound. Then he clambered up a small rise onto a rocky outcrop and checked where the rest of the party was situated.

They were gathered at a flat section of the path, listening. Chasse counted. Mikane sent two more men after his stone distraction. That left six warriors and Marron. As he assessed the numbers, Mikane urged the group on, pushing Tam in the back to force her forward. Time was short and the opportunity to rescue Tam was not improving. He headed for the next bend where the path narrowed, climbed a steep section between rocks and waited.

Two warriors appeared in single file ahead of Alan, Tam and Mikane. Studying the situation, Chasse doubted a second attempt to draw more men away would work. *Now what?* he pondered. *Wait? Run? Fight?* He unhitched his axe, weighed it in his hand, hesitated, and stepped into the path of the lead warrior.

The man stopped and stared up at him, until Mikane yelled, 'Get him!' Encouraged, the warrior unsheathed his sword and started up the rocky steps.

Chasse had the advantage, being on higher ground, so he waited until the warrior stabbed at him before he swung his axe. The warrior read his attack, ducked, and swept at Chasse's legs, forcing Chasse back. Sensing an opportunity, the warrior tried to step up, but Chasse struck him hard across the left shoulder with his axe, sending the warrior tumbling into the second man.

Alan stepped past both men, spear ready and climbed towards Chasse, yelling, 'No escape this time, boy!' Chasse knocked aside two probing thrusts, before he realised that Alan was distracting him from the movements of the warriors who left the path to climb through the bushes to flank him. When Alan made his next thrust, Chasse focussed into his swing and his axe sliced neatly through Alan's spear. Stunned by the destruction of his weapon, Alan retreated and Chasse withdrew.

A warrior emerged from the trees to block Chasse's escape as he reached a flat section of path, but Chasse knocked him backward with his axe and he pushed past a second warrior before the man could react. Free of the attackers, he sprinted hard.

He was on the final slope before the plateau, his legs burning from the exertion. His remaining option was to block them at the top of the path, but his mind raced with the reasons why that was a hopeless plan. He lunged up the rise and sucked in his breath when he halted and turned, his nerves jangling, his muscles aching, his chest sore, the axe resting in his palms.

'Run, Chasse. Don't do this.' The intrusion in his head from Tam startled him. 'You can't beat them. There are too many.'

'I have to try,' he thought in answer. 'I have to.'

'Please do what I say. I will be all right. Run. Now.' The first figure appeared below him, a warrior. And another. And Alan. They were coming for him. 'Please!' Tam pleaded. 'For all of us. Go. Trust me. Run. Now.'

A spear arced towards him. Chasse stepped aside to let it whistle past and skid along the plateau grass. The first warrior was a few steps away. He spotted more men emerging from the trees a hundred paces to his right. He had no chance to fight and win. He ran.

Eighteen

With his back against the rough stone in the shallow cave, Watersdrop thundering in his ears and spray dampening his skin, Chasse examined his cuts and bruises. When Tam ordered him to escape, he ran to the Watersdrop gorge where he lost his pursuers in the tangle of cliffs, rocks, waterfalls and bushes, because Tam and he explored all the nooks, clefts and crannies for refuge in the gorge's higgledy-piggledy descent as children and he knew which ones would baffle those chasing him. This cave sat behind a tall waterfall, reachable only by plunging into the cold water and wading waist-deep through the fall to a rock ledge entrance.

After he was certain he was safe, Chasse tried reaching Tam by thought, but she did not respond. She said she was safe before he bolted. He barely fought off the warriors he intercepted on the mountain, so he had no choice but to trust her, although it peeved him that he could not save her.

He touched the handle of the battle axe lying on the stone before his crossed legs. It was a fine weapon, and with it in his hands, and the light and agile armour, he felt he could match anyone, but the truth was he lacked skill. He lacked experience. He lacked courage. Even though he cut through Alan's spear, and he knew he might beat Alan in a one-on-one encounter, if it came to a fight with support around him Alan would win. Most other seasoned warriors would beat him one-on-one.

If Tam was keeping access to the dragon cavern from Mikane and Alan, he reasoned she must have a plan for Jaysin and herself. *But what about everyone left in the village?* he wondered. *Our mother? Banni? Jon? Raven? What is going to happen to them if Mikane and his people don't get the dragon treasure they seek? And what can I do about it?* 'What can I do about it?' he murmured, as he watched water pouring into the pool at the cave mouth. He imagined his father's face reflecting in the shimmering haze of the waterfall's spray and said, 'What would you do, Kevan, Dragon Head of Harbin? What would you want me to do?'

'Are you safe?'

The interruption startled him, but he recognised Tam's presence. 'Yes,' he replied.

'Where are you?'

'In the cave beneath the fifth fall. How did you get away from Mikane and Alan?' Chasse asked.

'I haven't,' Tam projected.

'Where are you?'

'In the dragon cave.'

'You led them there?'

'I had no choice,' Tam replied.

'But Harmi?'

'She's safe. Jaysin took her through into the chambers behind the hidden door. Oh, wait.'

'What? 'Chasse asked. 'Tam? Is everything all right?' When he received no answer, he asked again, 'Tam?'

'It's all right. Marron was being – Marron,' Tam said.

'What's he doing?' Chasse asked.

'It doesn't matter. I'm fine.'

'Where are the others?'

'Trying to find a treasure,' Tam replied. 'Some are in the goat cave. They're finding goats.' Chasse imagined Tam laughing. 'Mikane is making them take whatever they can find. He doesn't believe there's no treasure, but he can't –'

'Tam?' Chasse projected. 'Tam?' He waited before trying again. 'Tam?'

When she remained silent, he took the axe and crawled to the cave entrance, slid over the rock ledge into the water, and waded to the bank. He hesitated, after he climbed out of the stream, deciding between the village, or the mountain, before he chose the mountain and began the steep ascent out of Watersdrop gorge.

'Chasse? Where are you?'

Chasse stopped. 'I'm at the edge of the plateau. What happened?'

'They're marching me down to the village,' Tam projected.

'Who? How many?'

'Mikane and Marron, and two others,' Tam replied. 'They left four in the cavern to keep searching.'

'I'll come for you,' Chasse said.

'No. Save Jaysin and Harmi,' Tam insisted. 'Be careful.'

Chasse waited for more information, but Tam was silent. She wanted him to rescue Jaysin and Harmi, but he thought she said they were safely behind the hidden door. Maybe she was afraid the men remaining in the cavern would find the door. Four warriors. She wanted him to do something about them. *How?* he wondered.

He crossed the plateau and climbed the goat track. As he neared the top, he unhitched the axe and moved warily, anticipating a warrior on watch. And one was. The man spotted Chasse as he negotiated the last kink in the climb. Lower than his opponent, but having the element of surprise, Chasse swung at the warrior's ankles and the axe bit. The warrior yelped and hopped back, and Chasse charged, catching the man off-balance, and with a second swing the warrior grunted and collapsed against the wall, groaning and clutching his thigh. Chasse kicked the man's sword over the edge, saying, 'I'm sorry.' The warrior stared back at him, grimacing with pain.

Chasse stepped past the wounded man and moved into the dark

recesses of the Dawn People's cave, listening as he approached the steps leading into the dragon chamber. Three against one was impossible. He knew his best chance was to isolate them. *I've beaten one*, he reassured himself. *I can beat the others*.

'Watch out!' yelled the wounded man at the cave mouth, his voice echoing.

The warning sparked dread in Chasse, but he summoned courage and descended. Halfway down, he came face-to-face with the next warrior, a thick black bearded man with broad shoulders. 'Attack is the best defence,' he remembered his father urging. He barrelled into the warrior and sent him stumbling down the steps with Chasse bounding after him. Before the man could rise, Chasse struck with his battle axe, chopping across the warrior's shoulder. The warrior screamed and clutched his wound and collapsed, thrashing his legs to keep Chasse away. Chasse strode around him and entered the dragon cavern.

In the amber glow, two Harbin dragonwarriors were waiting for him. One was Alan, the other Neal. Both squared up to confront him.

'There's no need to do this,' Chasse said, easing to his right. 'You know there's no treasure. You've seen it for yourself.'

'Lie after lie after lie,' Alan replied, rolling his spear in his hand. 'You and your sister. Your father must have been so disappointed. Even your little brother. What a weak, pathetic excuse he is.'

Chasse's anger rose, but he refused to be drawn recklessly into a fight. 'You should be defending Harbin from Mikane and his people,' he argued, continuing to circle right, keeping the dragon nest between the warriors and himself. 'You are dragonwarriors.'

Alan gestured to Neal who circled in the opposite direction to trap Chasse. Chasse needed an advantage to reduce the odds. The nest. He measured the distances between himself and the warriors, ran and jumped, landing on the mass of twigs, dried grass, feathers and assorted materials. Now they would have to climb to attack him. 'That won't help you,' Alan sneered.

'We don't have to fight,' Chasse replied.

'That's what all cowards say,' Alan retorted as he approached the base of the nest.

'My brother is not a coward!' cried Jaysin, who appeared before the wall with the hidden door.

'Where did you come from?' Alan demanded, turning to Jaysin.

'Leave us alone!' Jaysin yelled angrily.

'Grab the boy!' Alan ordered. Neal headed for Jaysin.

Urged by the threat to his brother, Chasse jumped from the nest to attack Neal, taking the dragonwarrior by surprise, enough to knock him off balance and with a second sweep of his battle-axe he knocked Neal against the wall. Before Neal could recover, Chasse struck him squarely across the left knee with the flat of his blade and Neal collapsed, holding his shattered knee.

As Chasse spun to confront Alan, he was horrified to see a spear flash towards Jaysin, pass through him and clatter against the wall. Jaysin did not flinch. Alan gasped. The astonished dragonwarrior drew his sword and advanced.

And Harmi appeared beside Jaysin. Small as she was, no larger than a tall man, she still looked like a dragon and her presence froze Alan.

'Your turn,' Jaysin whispered inside Chasse's mind.

'Drop your weapon, Alan!' Chasse ordered as firmly as he could muster, awestruck by what he witnessed. Alan glanced at Chasse but returned to staring at the baby dragon. 'Yes,' Chasse affirmed. 'There is a dragon here. And you saw what a dragon can do. Go, while you can. And tell Mikane and Marron that we are coming for our sister if they don't let her go.'

Alan looked as if he was considering an attack, but Chasse knew the vision of the spear passing harmlessly through Jaysin had unnerved him, and the dragon's sudden arrival amplified the man's fear. 'There's no point fighting,' Chasse said. 'You can't hurt the dragon.'

Alan screamed and threw his sword at Harmi. As with Jaysin, the sword passed harmlessly through the dragon. Alan stared, his face in disbelief, before he backed towards the steps.

'You can't let him leave!' Jaysin urged.

Chasse ran to intercept Alan's retreat, but the dragonwarrior drew his hunting knife and faced Chasse. 'You agreed to let me go,' Alan stated.

'I can't let you leave,' Chasse said, fighting his nerves.

'You can't stop me,' Alan snarled, and he lashed out with his knife, the blade skimming past Chasse's chin. Stepping back, Chasse balanced and waited for Alan's next stroke. 'Your fancy axe and armour doesn't make you a warrior,' Alan taunted. 'Even with this, I'll take you down, boy.' He faked a lunge and Chasse retreated another step, unsure of his chances. 'This time, I will kill you,' Alan sneered and charged.

Chasse swung, but Alan ducked beneath the blade and hit Chasse full on the stomach with his shoulder, sending Chasse sprawling backward, clutching his axe. Alan's momentum was meant to bring him on top of Chasse, but Chasse remembered what Kevan taught on the slopes of Nakiades' Bluff and rotated with the force, pushing Alan past so that he could roll to his right and avoid being pinned. He scrambled to his feet to face Alan as he rose.

Alan composed himself and stalked Chasse, searching for a flaw in his guard. He slashed at Chasse with his knife, but Chasse dodged, deflecting the sweeps with his axe. 'I don't want to kill you,' Chasse said, catching his breath. 'Please.'

Enraged, Alan charged again, but this time Chasse knocked Alan's leading arm aside, sidestepped and kicked Alan in the backside, using Alan's energy to drive him to the floor at the foot of the nest in front of the image of Harmi. Startled, Alan swung his knife at the dragon and the image shimmered. He swung again, straightened, and said, 'There is no dragon.' He turned to Chasse. 'There's no dragon here,' he reiterated. 'I don't know what trick you managed to play, but it's done,' he growled. 'And so are you.'

Chasse sensed his opponent's surge in confidence and braced on the balls of his feet. Alan circled, but Chasse held his ground, letting Alan come within the reach of his axe, waiting, anticipating. When Alan charged, Chasse dropped to his knees and swung. Seeing the tactic, Alan jumped, too late to avoid the blade that cut deep into his shin, but his mass and movement wrenched the axe from Chasse's grip. Chasse rose, drawing his father's hunting knife, heart racing, expecting Alan to come again, but the dragonwarrior stayed curled on the floor, clutching his shin and moaning. Chasse retrieved his axe, stood over Alan and said, 'I'm sorry.'

'Mikane will slaughter you,' Alan threatened between gritted teeth. 'You are dead. You just don't know it.'

'I'll tie you up and bandage the wound,' Chasse said.

Alan kicked viciously with his left leg, missing Chasse, and screamed, 'Don't touch me!'

'I don't have a choice,' Chasse replied. 'And neither do you.' He searched the cavern for rope or anything suitable to restrain Alan and Neal, the latter still sitting against the wall nursing his shattered knee. Grinding stone drew Chasse's attention to the secret door and Jaysin emerged, trailed by a larger shape.

'You *are* a warrior,' Jaysin said with pride. Harmi trotted past Chasse.

'How did you –?' Chasse began and hesitated.

'Not me,' Jaysin said. 'Harmi. What are you looking for?'

'Something to tie these men up,' Chasse replied.

'Lots of rope in the goat cave,' Jaysin replied. 'I'll get it.' He headed for the opening.

'Get that thing away from me!' Alan cried.

Harmi sniffed the air near Alan. 'Harmi!' Chasse called, but Harmi ignored him and approached Neal. The terrified dragonwarrior pushed to his feet, only to buckle in agony from his crushed knee. Harmi nudged him and he scuttled away on his hands and his right knee. 'Harmi!' Chasse called again. The dragon looked at him, disappointed, before she snorted and climbed onto her nest.

'Rope,' Jaysin announced, dragging a length from the goat cave.

Neither Alan nor Neal obliged with letting Chasse bind them, until Harmi hopped down from her nest and advanced on them, at which point Chasse crudely suggested that he thought she was hungry. 'We feed her goat meat,' he said, 'but I think she wouldn't mind a change in texture.' The men acquiesced. Unsure of the truth in Chasse's threat, they were unwilling to test its validity.

Chasse bound Alan's shin, and then he asked Jaysin for the light wand, before he climbed the steps to find the third warrior unconscious, blood from his cut shoulder coagulating on the stone. He applied dressing to the man's shoulder and bound his legs and wrists, struggling at first to sit him up because of the man's bulk.

He ascended to the cave of the Dawn's People to discover the fourth warrior was gone, a blood trail leading onto the path. Worried the warrior had escaped to warn Mikane, Chasse started down the path, but he stopped when he saw the warrior's motionless body lying directly below on the plateau. Regret flooded him. He didn't intend to kill anyone.

Chasse returned to the dragon cave to check that his prisoners were securely bound and their injuries attended.

Perched on the dragon nest with Harmi, Jaysin asked, 'Now what?

'Now, I rescue Tam,' Chasse replied.

Nineteen

From the ridge that overlooked Watersdrop and the bridge to his family cottage, Chasse monitored Harbin. Six fishing boats in the bay were surrounded by circling entrepreneurial birds. People laboured along the foreshore and the jetty, mending nets, gutting and cleaning fish, repairing boat hulls. Galt's goats meandered across the meadow and Galt sat in the shade of a tree watching his herd. Three women bearing baskets crossed the space between the Long Hall and the Warriors' Hall, trailed by five children. A dozen warriors were chatting outside the Warriors' Hall. The village seemed peaceful, normal, except for the strange twin-masted ship anchored offshore and the warriors who were clearly not dragonwarriors but men from Jebaran. He searched for familiar figures, recognising the villagers, but he couldn't see his mother or Tam.

Men emerged from the Warriors' Hall as the women arrived and they held the door open until the women entered. The men headed for the jetty, acknowledging the Jebaran warriors by the Warriors' Hall as they passed. Chasse recognised Jon and Petar, and possibly Jak as the third dragonwarrior. The hooded figure was Marron. He watched the group walk onto the jetty and stop to talk. Marron pointed to Dragon Mountain. Chasse guessed Mikane told Marron that he found the dragon cave. He focused and projected, 'Tam? Can you hear me?' He waited, anticipating a reply, but Tam was silent. 'Tam?' he asked again.

'I'm here,' Tam replied. 'Where are you?'

'Above Watersdrop. Where are you?'

'Helping in the Long Hall.'

'A feast?' Chasse asked. 'I didn't think we would be holding Varst's

Sacrifice.'

'It's for my pairing with Marron,' Tam replied. 'He intends to get what he always wanted.'

'When?'

'Tomorrow night.'

'I won't let that happen,' Chasse promised.

'Don't do anything stupid, Chasse,' Tam urged. 'I can escape if I need.'

'And go where?' Chasse asked. 'Mikane knows about the cave. And Alan has seen Harmi.' He waited for Tam to reply, but she was silent again. 'Tam?'

'We have to leave.'

'And go where?' Chasse reiterated.

'There is a way,' Tam projected. 'I was hoping we would not have to do this, but Eric said it was inevitable. I can't keep mindspeaking. People are staring.'

'So, what do I do?' Chasse asked. 'Tam? Tam? What do I do?' Tam did not answer. He twisted his bracelet and tried again, but she was unresponsive. 'Now what?' he muttered.

He returned his attention to the men on the jetty. Marron was heading into the Long Hall. 'Marron is coming,' he projected to Tam, but he received no indication that she heard him. He was angry that Marron was haunting his sister and frustrated that he could do nothing about it. He surveyed Harbin a short while longer before he decided to sneak across the hillside to the goat pasture. Galt would know what was happening.

The sun squatted in the west when Chasse emerged from the forest. Galt was busily urging his herd towards the wooden shelter and he didn't see Chasse until Chasse was a few paces away. 'You scare a man creeping up on him like that,' the goatherd complained. 'You shouldn't be here,' but he beckoned for Chasse to follow him into the shelter. Beneath the thatch roof, he said, 'I'm sorry that you lost your father. He was a good man.'

'Thank you,' Chasse replied quietly.

'The new Dragon Head is still searching for you,' Galt informed him.

'Do you know what he intends to do?'

'He still thinks you and your sister are hiding a dragon's treasure on the mountain,' Galt explained, and he paused before asking, 'Are you?'

'They've seen the cave,' Chasse replied. 'They know there's no treasure.'

'He doesn't believe it,' Galt said. 'I heard him tell Jon that they found a clue and your sister is refusing to tell them the truth.'

'Where is my mother?' Chasse asked.

'Eesa is with the women in the Long Hall. Do not be too concerned. The Dragon Head is not treating her unkindly,' Galt said.

'But he's letting Marron take my sister,' Chasse noted sourly.

'Young Marron has always coveted your sister,' Galt replied, nodding. 'In a way, Varst and Procra have guided him back here for a reason.'

Chasse shook his head, and began with, 'The gods have –' but he stopped when a twig cracked and Galt's eyes shifted to the shelter's entrance. Chasse spun, unhitching his battle axe, and faced Kogan and Raven.

'You shouldn't be here,' Raven said quietly.

'I don't want to fight,' Chasse said.

'Neither do we,' Kogan answered. 'Best you put down your axe and come quietly.'

'Are you siding with Mikane?' Chasse challenged.

'We obey the Dragon Head,' Raven replied matter-of-factly. 'That's what dragonwarriors do.'

'But he's brought strangers. They're not dragonwarriors,' Chasse argued.

'Not yet,' Raven said, 'but they will be.'

'How?' Chasse asked.

'Jon and Raven will train them like they trained you,' Kogan explained.

'I came here to save my sister,' Chasse said. 'I have no fight with my friends.'

'If you're disobeying the Dragon Head, then you do have a fight with us,' Raven said. 'You know that.'

'You served my father,' Chasse said.

'True. And Trask too, if briefly,' Raven agreed. 'We answer to the Dragon Head and Mikane is now the Dragon Head.'

Chasse shifted his stance, preparing to fight. 'Where did you get the fine axe and armour?' Kogan asked.

'Does it matter?' Chasse retorted.

'So,' said Raven nodding. 'There is a treasure, isn't there?' He turned to Kogan, who met his questioning look, before he turned back to Chasse to say, 'If you run, now, we haven't seen you. Call it paying my respect to your father. But know this, Chasse Wolf's Bane, when we next meet, you will either be one of us or we will have no choice but to take you to the Dragon Head.'

'You can leave the fine axe,' Kogan suggested.

'No,' Chasse replied defiantly. He met Raven's stare and said, 'I will go, and I will remember your kindness and all that you taught me.'

'Don't come back,' Raven warned. 'There's no place for you here if you cannot accept the new Dragon Head.'

Chasse thanked Galt and walked between the two dragonwarriors, but he was wary in case there was a trick in their offer to let him leave. As he headed across the pasture towards the forest, Kogan called, 'I will have that axe if you come back!' but Chasse ignored the taunt and melted into the trees. Once he was sure that he was out of sight, he angled across the hillside, closer to the slopes of Nakiades' Bluff and hunkered down to wait for nightfall.

Chasse watched a fox trot across a small clearing ahead of his hideaway, hunting small game or insects and the animal stopped and raised its muzzle to sample scents before vanishing into a bush. The sky steadily darkened, and stars appeared, dull at first, brightening as the sunset faded. His plan was simple. If she let him, he would stay in Banni's cottage until late, and after midnight he would sneak to wherever Mikane or Marron were keeping Tam prisoner and free her. He was confident Banni would know where Tam was housed.

Evening settled across the bay and village. The last fishermen carried lamps from their boats to their huts and cottages and lights flared within. A pair of warriors appeared from the forest and headed for the Warriors' Hall. Lanterns flickered to life on the Jebaran ship in the bay.

Satisfied the village was quiet, Chasse crept down the slope and along the fringe of Harbin until he was close to Banni's cottage. He checked that no one was watching before he crossed the open ground to Banni's door and listened. Light seeped from the doorsill, but the cottage was quiet. He knocked gently.

A moment later, Banni's voice asked, 'Who is there?'

'Chasse.'

The door opened enough for Banni to look out, before she said, 'Come in,' and she ushered Chasse inside.

The cottage room was warm, flames crackled in the hearth, and Chasse smelled stew bubbling in the cooking pot above the fire. Jara sat on a pile of fur playing with a woven bangle and the child watched him with round shining eyes.

Chasse approached the fire, rubbing his hands to warm them, and said, 'I'm sorry to intrude.'

Banni smiled. 'I was worried,' she said. 'They're hunting you.'

'They have Tam,' Chasse said.

'I know,' Banni replied. 'Marron intends to take her for his wife. He's told everyone that he doesn't have to wait for Procra's Dance because the new Dragon Head and the Dragon Heart both sanction his choice.'

'Where is Tam?' Chasse asked.

'I'm not sure,' Banni replied. 'There is talk Marron will take over your home because it belongs to Tamesan.' She breathed before saying, 'The Dragon Heart is taking Marron as his apprentice.'

'Marron as Dragon Heart?' Chasse asked. 'But he always wanted to be the best warrior in Harbin.'

'He can't be a warrior with one arm,' Banni said.

'True. He's choosing another path to become important.'

'What are you going to do?'

'Rescue Tam,' Chasse replied. 'We have to leave here. It's not safe for us.'

'But there are too many,' Banni argued.

'That's why I will find her tonight, when everyone is asleep. If Marron intends to take our house, I guess she is staying there.' Chasse looked around the small room and asked, 'Can I sleep on the floor?'

'Are you hungry?' Banni asked. 'I have stew.'

Realising that he hadn't eaten throughout the day, Chasse replied, 'Please.'

'I'll get furs for the floor while you eat,' Banni offered, as she took a bowl and ladled stew into it. 'Here.' She handed Chasse the bowl.

The warm food made his mouth water, and he scooped the stew greedily into his mouth, savouring the flavours while Banni went into her bedroom. She returned with a familiar dark grey wolf fur that she lay on the ground near the hearth, saying, 'This will keep you warm.'

'What about you and Jara?' Chasse asked.

'I have more, and Jara sleeps with me,' Banni explained. 'We keep each other warm. There's water in the bucket by the door.' She pulled a stool beside the hearth. 'For now, we can talk.' She indicated a second stool for Chasse. He followed her direction and sat and finished the last scoop of stew. 'Where will you go?' Banni asked.

Chasse met her quiet gaze, and said, 'I don't know. Tam says there is a place, but she didn't say where.'

'I wish you didn't have to leave.' She reached out and touched Chasse's hand and he felt her touch thrill along his arm.

He blushed and replied, 'I wish I didn't have to leave either. I wish I was a stronger warrior so that I could fight Mikane and stop this happening.'

'You are all you need to be,' Banni said. 'I like who you are.' She withdrew her hand. 'I'll take Jara to feed and you can see if you can sleep.' She stood and leaned over Chasse to kiss his forehead. 'Be careful,' she said as she straightened. 'Give Tamesan my love. Tell her she has been a good friend and that I will miss her.' She lifted Jara from the floor and withdrew to her bedroom.

Sitting on the stool, staring into the hearth fire, Chasse was elated and confused. Banni's affection made his heart race and his mind spin. If they weren't leaving, if Suran and Mikane and the strangers hadn't come, if there was no secret on the mountain, if his father was still Dragon Head – he wished all of the things away because he could then be with Banni, eventually. But they were real and the past could not be changed. He was certain that Tam would be at their home with their mother. To be safe, when he woke, he would circle along the fringe of the village to Watersdrop and his home. Mikane would have guards at the house to keep Tam from escaping so he would need a plan for dealing with them.

He unhitched his axe from his back and studied the blade in the glow of the fire. The edge was keen, honed expertly, and showed no sign of wear or damage from his use. He used it to defeat four warriors. Before he had the axe, he doubted that he could win a fight with any experienced warrior. On his first dragonship journey, when they were ambushed and defeated, he ran from battle. His father, Jon, Raven, Alan – they all could easily beat him down. *Until now*, he mused, turning the axe in his hands.

Chasse placed the weapon on the floor and arranged the wolf fur. He was glad that he gifted it to Banni. When he was gone, the fur would remind her of him. He was grateful for Banni's stew because it strengthened him for the challenge ahead. He lay down, pulled the fur around his shoulders, and stared at the flames shuddering in the hearth.

The dream was on him before he could resist its pull and he was afraid before the swirling smoke and chaos enveloped him. Shapes, shadows, figures lunged and moved through the dark and light, lightning, flashes of flame, a shape of a dragon looming in the sky and a blade swept past his face. Two shadows, warriors, stalked him in the dark, flashes revealing their presence. And the light suffused into an amber glow and more warriors appeared, surrounding him, closing in. He reached for his axe, but his only weapon was his father's hunting knife and it felt large and clumsy in his hands. He knew there was only one outcome.

'Chasse.'

Hands gripped his shoulders. He opened his eyes to darkness.

'Chasse.' Warm arms enfolded him. 'You were dreaming,' a voice whispered. 'Sh.'

Chasse relaxed, fear easing from his nerves. Banni saved him from his nightmare. He could smell her closeness, feel her hair across his cheek, her body pressed against his, her arm across his chest. He was safe. He closed his eyes.

'Where are you?'

Chasse opened his eyes. The room was dark, the hearth cold. He felt for Banni, but she was gone.

'Chasse?'

'Tam?' he projected.

'Where are you?'

'In Banni's cottage,' he replied. 'Why?'

'Leave!' Tam urged. 'Now!'

'Where are you?' Chasse asked, grabbing his axe as he rose to his feet.

'Never mind. Go up the mountain. I will find you. Go!'

Chasse fumbled his way to the door, opened it and stepped outside. The first light that caught his eyes were flames rising from the Warriors' Hall. He stared, making sense of what he could see, and he realised that a disaster was unfolding. Shadows appeared and disappeared, bearing buckets from the ocean. Shouts and yells echoed in the brittle air, and lamps and candles flickered in the huts and cottages as people woke to the fracas. His first impulse was to run to help extinguish the flames, but he knew that Tam knew what was happening and she had ordered him to leave. He glanced at Banni's bedroom door, lingering, before he closed the cottage door and headed for the forest.

He climbed the moonlit slope, jogging between the trees and bushes, scrambling over rocks, slipping in stones and loose earth, weaving towards the path to the plateau. At the usual ledge, he gazed over Harbin and saw a tower of flame crackling along the length of the Warriors' Hall, the fire flickering across the façade of the Long Hall and the roofs of the closest buildings. *What have you done?* he thought.

'I did what I had to,' Tam said quietly, startling Chasse as she joined him on the rock ledge. 'They could not hold me. He could not do what he intended.'

'Who?' Chasse asked.

'Marron,' Tam said with distaste. 'And now he won't ever do anything like that to anyone.'

The icy tone in her voice astonished and chilled Chasse. He wanted to know what it was that she did to Marron, but he was afraid of the answer. Instead, he asked, 'Did you start the fire?'

'Yes,' Tam replied, 'but no more talk. We have to leave. Mikane and the others will come for us and we can't be found. Come.'

Chasse looked down at Harbin where his boyhood dragonwarrior dreams were turning to ash before he hurried after Tam.

Twenty

Chasse rummaged through the equipment in the chamber, selecting what he could carry and what would be useful. He exchanged his rough tunic and trousers for a set of finer clothing that was cleverly inlaid and padded to add warmth. He embellished his armour with greaves and pauldrons that he stuffed into a leather backpack. He found a silver buckled belt with pouches and slots for knives and he chose two finely crafted daggers to accompany his father's hunting knife. He also chose a gold handle sword with a dragon etched into the metal and odd markings along its blade, kept his battle axe, and found a metal spear that was lighter and stronger than the shafts of the dragonwarriors. He packed a small coil of rope into the backpack before he left the chamber to join Tam, Jaysin and Harmi in the second chamber. 'What do I do with Alan and Neal and the Jebaran warrior?' he asked.

'The others will find them,' Tam replied. 'Have you got all you need?'

'Almost too much to carry,' Chasse replied. 'What about the magic stone door? Alan and Neal saw it.'

'They can't see it to open it,' Tam replied, as she led Chasse into the corridor. 'Of course, they can dig through the stone eventually, but that will take them a long time.'

'Food and water?' Chasse asked. He was conscious of bruising on Tam's forehead and he noticed a puzzling strand of grey in her dark red locks near the bruise.

'We'll forage for food and water,' Tam said as she hitched a backpack onto her shoulders over a thick hooded emerald cloak. 'There will be plenty. That's where your dragonwarrior training will come in handy.'

'I want to take more books,' Jaysin complained as he struggled to lift his pack onto his shoulders.

'We can't eat books,' Chasse said.

'Time to go,' Tam told them, and she ushered Harmi and Jaysin into the corridor.

Following, Chasse said, 'You haven't told me where we are going.'

'To the other side of Dragon Mountain,' she replied. 'After that, I don't know, although Harmi is teaching me what we might find. She's trawling through her collective memory and that's not easy for a baby dragon.'

'The tunnel leads all the way through the mountain?' Chasse queried. 'Who built it?'

'It doesn't go that far,' Tam reassured Chasse. 'The Dawn People originally built it. They mined metal. It does go deep into the mountain and it's rough. We have to find the end. First, though, I'll seal the chamber doors so the others can't find them.'

'How?'

'A spell Eric left for me.' Tam closed the door and held her hand against it. Her amber ring glowed and the door shone and became part of the stone corridor. She repeated the spell on the warrior's chamber door. 'That should keep the treasures safe,' she told an astonished Chasse. She squeezed past Harmi and Jaysin to unlock the wooden door at the end, and when she clicked her fingers a small light sphere appeared and hovered in the tunnel. 'It will be a tight squeeze for Harmi,' she said. 'I'll lead. Jaysin and Harmi follow me. Chasse follow behind. Here.' She pulled a familiar black rod from her belt and asked Jaysin to pass it to Chasse. As Chasse accepted it, Tam said, 'You'll need it. Harmi's bulk will block my light. Let's go.'

Tam and Jaysin entered the tunnel and Harmi squeezed through the door, her wings folded tightly across her back, her body brushing the tunnel walls. Tam's light created a halo effect around Harmi. Chasse shook the light wand and as he watched the dragon's tail drag along the ground in his path he wryly accepted that he was about to spend his journey staring at Harmi's rump. He pulled the door closed behind him.

The rough and winding tunnel switched back on itself as it descended into the heart of Dragon Mountain and numerous narrow branches veered into darkness. Crystals glinted in the stone and colours danced when Chasse's wand highlighted them. Harmi stopped several times and twisted to manoeuvre around tight bends and squeeze through narrow sections, and Chasse wondered what they would do if the dragon reached a point where she could go no further.

And then they reached crude steps that rose sharply beneath a low ceiling and it was obvious that Harmi could not negotiate the way forward. 'Now what?' Chasse yelled, unable to see Tam or Jaysin.

'This is the end,' Tam replied in mindspeak. 'We go out here. Step through the light.'

Tam's instruction puzzled Chasse, until Harmi shuffled and vanished, and he was left staring at a shimmering blue haze blurring the steps. He closed his eyes and stepped through.

When Chasse reopened his eyes, the world was grey, sunlight suffused through the morning fog, and the nearby trees were malevolent shadows. Tam and Harmi stood on the shore of a lake, its water silent and flat and stretching and dissolving into the fog. Jaysin squatted before a burrow in the roots of a tree, coaxing a small grey animal to emerge from its sanctuary. 'Where are we?' Chasse asked.

'Harmi says this is the eastern side of Dragon Mountain,' Tam explained.

'You said you can only make a portal to a place where you've been,' Chasse said. 'How does Harmi know this place?'

'Claryssa knew this place,' Tam replied. 'Remember? Harmi has the collective knowledge of her ancestors, including Claryssa. She found this place in her memories.'

'Then we can portal to other places that she can remember from her ancestors,' Chasse said. 'We don't have to stay here.'

'There is a limited range for portals,' said Jaysin, who approached bearing a small animal in his arms. 'Harmi knows we can't open portals over long distances.'

'What is that?' Chasse asked, staring at the creature's short, grey erect ears and large round dark eyes above its pink nose.

'I don't know,' Jaysin replied. 'This is the first one I've ever seen. I don't think they live on our side of the mountain.' He grinned and added, 'Now I know. Harmi says it's called a muvarna. They live in the valleys and only come up this far when the weather is warm enough to have babies in the burrows.' Jaysin winced, said, 'Ew!' and stared coldly at the dragon.

'What?' Tam asked.

'She said they're very tasty,' Jaysin explained, hugging the little creature closely. 'Bad Harmi.'

'She won't eat them,' Tam assured Jaysin. 'She's learning that she doesn't need meat.'

'But you made me slaughter goats for her,' Chasse reminded Tam.

'That's when I thought there was no choice but to feed her meat because she's a dragon,' Tam replied. 'But I stopped giving her the goat meat the next day and fed her grass and berries and whatever I could find that wasn't an animal and she was fine. She can eat like the rest of us.'

'So, where to from here?' Chasse asked. 'If Mikane and his men figure out we came to this side of the mountain, they'll come searching for us.'

'Beyond the lake is a river that cuts down through the mountains into a forest and Harmi says that leads to where other people live. We should head there,' Tam explained.

'Is it safe?' Chasse asked as he watched Jaysin return the muvarna to its burrow. Tam seemed to ignore his question, but he realised she was communicating by mind with Harmi and waited.

Tam finally said, 'Harmi's collective memory confirms what I feared would be the situation from stories that Eric told me. We have to be very careful where we choose to stay or visit. Dragons and wizards were outlawed and hunted and killed by the rulers of places beyond the mountains and they probably still are. It won't be safe for Harmi.'

'Dragons are hunted everywhere, from what we know,' Chasse replied. 'That's not news.' He surveyed the landscape, seeing trees and mountains emerging from the fog, the lake widening. 'It's early and I'm tired, like we all are, but we should go as far as we can to the far side of the lake, at least to where the river you mentioned starts. Even if Mikane works out that we are on this side of the mountain, it will take them two or three days to get around here, which means we could rest on the other side this afternoon and tonight, and start the journey tomorrow morning.'

Tam called Jaysin and focused on Harmi, the dragon unfurling her juvenile wings to stretch, and said to Chasse, 'We're ready.'

Chasse breathed on the sparks until a tiny flame took hold in the tinder nest. He lowered it reverently into the cluster of twigs where he fostered its growth on a clump of touchwood with more breathing. When the flames spread, he leaned back in the dim evening light to admire his work.

'That's impressive,' said Jaysin, squatting to stare at the fire.

'I can show you how to do it,' Chasse replied. 'You should know these things at your age.'

'Father kept offering to teach me,' Jaysin said. 'I don't need to know.'

'Except now you do,' Chasse said. 'Now you are in the wilds.'

'You're here to do it,' Jaysin replied. 'I still don't need to know.'

'What if I'm not here?'

'Then I won't be here either,' Jaysin replied definitively, and he stood and walked away.

Chasse watched his brother move through the evening shadows to the riverbank. His hair was longer and becoming dark red and he was growing taller and lankier. Jaysin was tall for a lad of almost twelve summers and he was outgrowing his dark grey trousers and heavy green vest, even the black, fur-lined cloak he brought, and yet he possessed none of the traits Chasse associated with growing into manhood; no desire to fight or wrestle, no curiosity for survival in the wild or in weapons, no interest in girls. He was locked inside his unique childhood where he played with animals and fostered his strange habit of reading and his magic. Even though his capacity for magic was fascinating, Chasse felt that it masked Jaysin's unwillingness to grow into a man. As the older brother, and now the man of the family, he had increasing responsibility for ensuring Jaysin also became a man. He just wasn't sure how he could encourage Jaysin in that direction.

Chasse assessed the campsite that they reached during the middle of the day. He offered to keep watch for the afternoon while the others caught up on sleep, and Tam and Jaysin gratefully accepted his offer, settling beneath the trees and napping for a while, but he noticed that Harmi sat and stared across the lake in the direction from whence they came for a long time after they arrived and he wondered what the baby dragon was considering while she was staring westward.

Chasse reflected on their situation. In a few short, frantic, and violent days, their home vanished, their father was dead, their mother was reduced to a common village woman, and they were fugitives, all because of one man's greed for treasure and another man's lust for Tam. Tam wore a bruise yet to be explained. Whatever she did to Marron, and however she set fire to the Warriors' Hall, she effectively shut the door on returning to the village or negotiating with Mikane and his followers who would want nothing less than revenge.

He tossed a small pebble into the lake and watched the ripples oscillate and reflect sunlight as they spread in concentric circles. He should have been brave enough to confront Mikane and fight for his family's honour. That's what a dragonwarrior would do. A true warrior would overcome his fear of dying and courageously confront his enemy. But he wasn't that brave and he wasn't a true warrior. When he was tested, he failed. He ran. Twice. This last time he betrayed his mother and Banni and ran.

Chasse flicked another pebble into the lake and Harmi turned her head and stared at the ripples. *Protecting Tam and Jaysin and the dragon is the right thing to do*, he silently told himself. 'I made a choice,' he murmured to the lake.

Tam emerged from the trees with herbs in her arms and broke his reverie. The evening was rapidly falling into night, the last traces of sunset vanishing from the mountain shoulders, and Tam was a silhouette taking colour as she neared the fire. 'You looked like you were lost very deep in thought,' she said after she lay her bundle on the ground.

'I was hoping Banni was safe,' Chasse responded. 'And Mother.'

'I hope they are, too,' said Tam as she crouched to sort through the herbs and tubers.

'We should have found a way to get them out of the village.'

'Mother would refuse to leave,' Tam reminded him. She put aside four large tubers. 'I asked her to come with me, but she said Harbin was the only place she knew and she was confident she would be safe.'

'When I know you and Jaysin are safe, I will go back for Banni,' Chasse vowed.

Tam looked up and said, 'We will all go back when it is time.' She shuffled the herbs. 'For now, we need to eat.' She pointed to her backpack. 'There's a pot hanging on the side. Can you fill it with water and bring it to the fire?'

Thankful to be given a task, Chasse fetched the bowl with water and placed it by the fire and he used small branches to fashion a makeshift tripod to suspend the pot. Tam put the four beige tubers in the pot, dropped broken herbs into the water and hung it on the tripod over the fire to boil, and sat again.

Chasse sat beside Tam and asked, 'You don't have to tell me, and I wasn't going to ask, but what happened between you and Marron last night?'

Tam met his gaze in the firelight and drew a slow breath before she said, 'Marron wanted me to do what men expect of women and I refused. He hit me, thinking that he could force me to obey him. I pretended to be hurt and collapsed, and when he stood over me I kicked him in the balls.' She laughed at Chasse's astonishment. 'You taught me that. Remember?' she asked.

'Painfully,' Chasse replied.

'I also got up and hit him with his spear. I knocked him out,' Tam explained. 'I wanted to spear him while he lay there, I really did. I should have killed him.' She stopped and stared at Chasse, and he felt her anger. 'Instead, I tied him up and left him in our home.'

'Where was Mother?'

'At Amarti's,' Tam explained. 'Mikane banished her from our home and gave it to Marron to be his when he became Dragon Heart.'

'And the Warriors' Hall?' Chasse asked.

'I thought it would distract attention from us,' Tam replied. 'I lit the fire after I escaped Marron.'

'I was coming to rescue you,' Chasse said quietly.

'I know.' Tam put a hand on Chasse's hand. 'But I'm glad you didn't.'

'You didn't think I could.'

'Not in the way you're thinking,' she replied. 'You're brave, like Father was brave. No one can doubt you, Chasse. But the odds were too great. You couldn't have won. You know that is the truth. You have nothing to be ashamed of, nothing to prove.'

Chasse heard Tam's words, but his heart was unsettled because he believed he did have something to prove as a dragonwarrior and he failed. He went to speak, but Jaysin interrupted with, 'What are we eating?'

'Umaki broth,' Tam replied. 'There are bowls in my pack. Fetch them.' Jaysin rummaged in Tam's backpack.

'I need to piss,' Chasse announced. He walked to the edge of the firelight and into the trees, but as he finished urinating he became aware of red eyes shining a few paces away in the dark and an icy chill spread through his guts. He drew his hunting knife. A second pair of eyes appeared. Whatever animals sat behind the eyes, he estimated they were larger than wolves. He took a step back, and another. A ragged hiss emanated from the animals.

'Stay where you are.'

Chasse recognised Jaysin's voice. 'Go back to the fire,' Chasse urged. 'I'll protect you.'

'No,' Jaysin said. 'Too late. Stand perfectly still.'

'What?' Chasse asked.

'Don't move,' Jaysin projected in mindspeak. 'Whatever they do, you have to stay still. Don't do what you think you ought to do.'

'What are they?' Chasse asked.

'I don't know.'

Jaysin's answer did not reassure Chasse. He swallowed as the first set of eyes moved closer and the vague silhouette of a four-legged creature appeared, at least half Chasse's height and long, like an oversized wolf, but not a wolf because its face was flatter, rounder. The animal came within an arm's length and he heard it sniffing. He tightened his grip on his knife.

'Please don't move,' Jaysin pleaded in his mind.

Ready to react, Chasse kept still as the animal closed the gap and sniffed his legs, his crutch, his chest, his chin. A rank offal stench assaulted his senses. Only a shifting patch in the night, Chasse saw the creature's head was bigger than his own and the eyes glittered from the distant firelight. The animal slunk around him, pushing against his legs, almost forcing him to move, but he braced to maintain his balance. The eyes of the second animal shone, but it kept its distance while the first moved to inspect Jaysin. Chasse knew that if the creature pushed against his brother, as it pushed against him, Jaysin would topple. Then what would it do? What would he do? He heard the animal sniffing again, drawing deep scents. All the time he strained to hear the animal move, but it was silent, as if its paws were not touching the earth. The animal merged into the dark and the distant pair of eyes winked out.

'We can go back now,' Jaysin projected.

Unshackled from his fear, Chasse backed out of the trees, his legs trembling. He breathed deeply, composing himself, before he strode to the fire where Jaysin was already telling Tam what happened.

'I've never seen them before, but they were like wolves but bigger and not really like wolves at all. They were studying us. They had already eaten, so we weren't really in danger unless we did something they didn't like,' Jaysin said quickly. 'I should have brought the *Creature Compendium* I found in the Herbal Man's library. They would be listed in it.'

'Could you communicate with them?' Tam asked.

'Almost,' Jaysin replied. 'Their images are different though, like a whole new language. They see things like a wolf – hunting and the natural world – but they used other images I haven't seen before. They're intriguing.'

'Will they come back?' Chasse asked.

'I don't think so,' Jaysin replied. 'Not those two, anyway.'

'I'm exhausted,' Chasse said. 'I need sleep. If you two share watch until the moon is high, I'll take over then. But I need to sleep.'

'You should eat first,' Tam said, lifting a bowl of broth. 'We'll keep watch until you're rested. Tomorrow, we head down the river gorge.'

Chasse accepted the broth, grateful for sustenance, but he shivered at the memory of the peculiar wild creatures prowling the night at the perimeter of their firelight. The world beyond Dragon Mountain was different and dangerous.

Twenty-One

The river flowed swiftly out of the lake before it cut a steep gorge through the narrow valley between the mountains and Chasse discovered the way becoming increasingly treacherous as the party headed east during the morning. The river bucked over rocks and plunged down cataracts, sending plumes of spray high into the air, forcing Chasse to lead the group higher up the slope to negotiate their way. Eventually, they shadowed the river by clambering across the rocks and cliffs and through the forest, much to Jaysin's chagrin.

'I thought you said there was a path,' he complained to Tam.

'I said we had to go this way,' Tam replied. 'I never said there was a path.'

Several times, they backtracked and climbed so the dragon could fit through spaces, and by late afternoon everyone was exhausted from the erratic journey.

'I say we camp here,' Chasse suggested as they climbed onto a small ridge with a view across the narrow river canyon. 'We need food and energy.'

'I'll gather berries and herbs,' Tam offered.

'I'll see what I can catch,' Chasse said.

'There's no need to kill animals,' Tam said. 'We will have enough.'

'For you,' Chasse replied. 'I need meat.' He glanced at Harmi who was curling to sleep beneath a large tree. 'She could do with something more robust than plants. Jaysin, stay here with Harmi and organise wood for a fire.' He strode into the trees with his spear.

The afternoon light faded and the air chilled as he crept through the forest searching for spoor, scratches on tree trunks, faint trails and dung. The indications were the forest was alive with a variety of creatures. He wanted a small catch, like two or three foxes, enough for a meal to feed three people, or a supplement for Harmi. Satisfied with finding a fresh dung heap, he hid in the bushes with his spear and waited for his prey.

The evening was closing in before four foxes appeared on the tiny trail to the dung pile, their white tail markings revealing them in the dull light. Chasse watched the creatures snuffle in the undergrowth, testing the area was safe before one trotted forward to relieve itself. Finished, it sniffed its droppings before sitting aside and licking its fur, while the second fox scampered onto the dung pile. Chasse moved with care to raise his spear. *Throw or charge*? he pondered. He charged out of the thicket and lunged, impaling the fox that was licking itself. Its companions vanished into the undergrowth.

Walking back to the camp, Chasse was proud that he could hunt and supply food. He remembered his father laughing at his first attempts to catch animals and his compliments when Chasse caught a squirrel.

'Catching the first is what turns a boy into a man,' Kevan said, patting him on the shoulder. 'Now you know. Hunting gives a man purpose in the village.'

As he approached the camp, Chasse was mildly surprised to see a glow through the trees, but when he entered the tiny clearing there was no fire to greet him. Tam and Jaysin crouched over a glowing stone and a pot emanating steam sat atop the stone. Harmi lay curled in the shadows.

'Where have you been?' Tam asked.

Chasse held up the fox by its tail and announced, 'I caught this one.'

'Why?' Jaysin asked. 'That's cruel.'

Chasse raised an eyebrow as he leaned his spear against a tree trunk, pulled out his knife and replied, 'To eat.' He began skinning the fox.

'You didn't need to do that,' Jaysin said. 'Tam made a broth.'

'Your dragon doesn't seem all that interested in broth,' Chasse argued.

'And this will give the broth more flavour and goodness.'

'I don't want Harmi to depend on meat,' Tam said. 'If you have to eat it, be my guest, but don't feed it to Harmi.'

Chasse felt as if he should argue why it was important to eat meat and how the dragon was a carnivore by nature, but he knew that he would be wasting his breath, so he skinned the fox, gutted it and searched for a stick to skewer the meat for cooking. When he was done, he looked at the glowing stone and asked, 'How hot is it?'

'You will be able to roast your meat,' Tam told him. 'I can make it hotter if needed.'

Chasse tested the heat rising from the stone before he placed his food on it. Jaysin was sipping his broth. Tam was feeding Harmi a collection of herbs and grasses. 'I'll stay awake until the moon is high,' Chasse said as he rotated the cooking meat. 'We'll split the watch into three parts each night. Normally, I'll take the last watch like last night, but tonight I will go first, after we eat.' He waited for acknowledgement as he smelt the roasting meat and his mouth watered in anticipation of his small feast. *They might not want the meat*, he decided, *but I will enjoy it*. He saw Harmi lift and tilt her head, staring at the roasting meat, her nostrils twitching. 'I'll share a little with Harmi,' Chasse said.

'She doesn't need meat,' Tam said.

Chasse met Tam's insistent gaze and nodded, but he saw the dragon was still eyeing the meat hungrily and he knew that his sister was going to have to give in eventually to Harmi's appetite.

'You should lay down your weapon,' Tam projected, calmly warning Chasse to follow her instruction.

Chasse twisted the cold metal spear in his hands as he inspected the warriors surrounding them in the shadowy undergrowth. Some held spears, some axes, and some held little shafts across thin wooden staves. None were big men. They were lithe like Jaysin's stature and clad in crude green garbs adorned with leaves and twigs for camouflage and feather necklaces. The morning light glowed on their foreheads and cheeks.

'Chasse!' Tam urged.

Chasse reluctantly lowered his spear to the earth, but he stayed ready to unhitch his battle axe if the warriors attacked. A man stepped forward, uttering nonsensical sounds that baffled Chasse and he looked to Tam for an explanation.

'I don't know what he's saying,' Tam said. 'I'm warning Jaysin to stay out of sight with Harmi.'

'How do you keep a dragon out of sight?' Chasse whispered.

Tam nodded towards the approaching warrior, saying to Chasse, 'I think he wants to look at your axe.'

Chasse faced the warrior, who spoke again as he held out his hand. The man's tanned arms were darkened with tattoos spreading up to his neck and disappearing under his green tunic at his shoulders. Chasse reached behind his back and unhitched his battle axe, expecting the young man to be suspicious of his movement, but the warrior smiled and held out his hand expectantly. Reluctant as he was to hand over the weapon, Chasse placed the axe handle in the warrior's hand. The warrior accepted the weapon and studied it, turning it to catch the morning light on the polished blade. When he held it up to show his companions, the warriors uttered sounds suggesting admiration. The warrior gestured for Chasse and Tam to follow him.

'What about Jaysin?' Chasse asked.

'Harmi and Jaysin will follow secretly,' Tam said. 'We have no choice.'

The warrior party escorted Chasse and Tam out of the river ravine and along a narrow, steep and forested valley, following a smaller creek tributary. The winding trail was worn from long use, but Chasse could tell it was only visible to a trained eye or someone who knew it was there.

Abruptly, a palisade of split and spiked branches, at least the height of three men and extending left and right to rocky cliffs on either side of the narrow valley, barred their way, and the stream spilled through a wooden grate at the base of the wall. Heads peered over the rim. The warriors exchanged words with the men on the wall before a door opened through which the warriors ushered Tam and Chasse.

Inside the compound was a meeting or assembly area, the earth trodden bare and hard, but the surrounding wooden buildings with thatch roofs and perched on stilts pressed in as if intent on consuming the open space. People in doorways and beneath the buildings stared and Chasse was surprised to see wolves scattered among the people. The warrior who confronted Chasse ushered Tam and Chasse to the front of the group and made them face a larger, central building.

A man and a woman emerged from the building and descended a set of wooden stairs. The man wore a long dark green robe, like a dress Chasse thought, and a single gold chain draped from his neck across his thorax. His greying hair was long, reaching to his waist, and streaked with dark strands, reminding everyone of the colour of his younger days. He held a gnarled, dark wooden staff in his left hand, and his arms, like the warriors, were black with tattoos. The woman, also heavily tattooed, wore a dark green dress that brushed the steps and the earth as she walked. Like her partner, her hair was long and grey, but it was braided with bright coloured beads and she wore coloured bangles on her wrists.

The pair stopped before Tam and Chasse to scrutinize them before the leading warrior spoke. He held up Chasse's axe and pointed at Chasse. The older man said something to his partner and she also spoke, and a young woman came forward from the crowd and gestured for Tam to go with her. Tam looked at Chasse before she trailed the young woman towards a separate building. The older woman followed them.

'Where are you taking my sister?' Chasse demanded, looking directly at the man who had to be the village's Dragon Head or someone equally as important.

The grey-haired man spoke in his unfamiliar tongue, and Chasse was herded by the warriors to the end of the meeting space. Hands swarmed his body, taking his sword, his knives and stripping away his armour, and the lead warrior tossed Chasse's axe to a man among those ushering Chasse aside. The men chattered as they passed his weapons and armour back and forth, examining them in detail, and then, to his astonishment, they stepped back and he was handed a wooden staff. The villagers were watching. The lead warrior faced him, also holding a staff. *Am I being tested*? Chasse wondered. *Or is this meant to be to the death*?

'What's happening?' Tam interrupted with mindspeak.

'They want me to fight,' Chasse replied.

'I'm coming back,' Tam said.

Chasse could not respond because the warrior with his tanned chest marked with horizontal scars deliberately cut into a pattern, his arms decorated with tattoos reminding Chasse of waves and lightning, advanced with clear intention to fight and Chasse recognised a formidable foe, a warrior whose muscular definition proclaimed strength and agility. He fended the warrior's first blows, moving back and to the side as he measured the man. There was nothing cocky in the warrior's style, no bravado. He was a seasoned fighter, balanced, quick, calmly confident. Chasse ducked a short sweep, but his shoulder stung as a returning blow struck home. He edged left, swinging his staff hard to force the warrior back, but the man parried Chasse's attack and drove the end of his staff into Chasse's inner thigh. The sharp pain shocked Chasse into rapid retreat as he blocked a flurry of attacks to the villagers' jubilant shouts. He steadied, swinging, lunging and blocking as they traded blows, but Chasse could not penetrate the warrior's uncanny defence. And then a sweeping staff smacked against Chasse's chest and he stumbled, sinking to his knees to avoid falling. The warrior stepped back and gestured for Chasse to return to his feet. Bruising pain throbbing in his thigh, his chest smarting from the last hit, Chasse rose.

The lessons from Raven and his father flicked through his memory as he prepared for the warrior's attack. He slipped under the first lunge, spun right so that his back was almost pressed against his opponent and punched back with his elbow, catching the warrior under his ribs. The man grunted and staggered as Chasse spun to his left, staff whirling in a low arc, and he caught the warrior sharp across his right arm, wood thwacking against skin, the warrior yelping. Confidence rising as the warrior retreated, Chasse waded in with a burst of blows, searching for a gap in his opponent's defence, driving one strike hard against the warrior's knee, but he misjudged the man's resilience and speed, and suddenly felt his legs swept from under him. He landed heavily on his back, the breath forced from his lungs, and he gasped for air as he rolled onto his side and struggled to his feet. The crowd cheered. To Chasse's surprise, the warrior lay down his staff, dropped to his knees, bent at the waist and lowered his head to the earth.

'You should do the same.'

Tam's telepathic message surprised Chasse. He searched for her in the crowd and found her standing with the older woman in green. She nodded. Chasse faced the prostrate warrior and dropped to his knees, placed his staff to the side and bent forward until his forehead touched the ground. He heard a murmur from the crowd, and sensed a presence, and he lifted his head to discover his opponent standing before him.

'You can stand,' Tam told Chasse. 'I think you have been accepted.'

'What do we do about Jaysin and Harmi?' Chasse asked when Tam handed him an orange earthen bowl of sliced fruits. 'They can't stay hidden.'

'Harmi found a cave on the ridge overlooking this valley,' Tam replied. 'It was in Claryssa's memories. She and Eric must have travelled through here. Jaysin and Harmi are sheltering there until we can leave.'

'What about food?' Chasse pressed. 'Jaysin can't hunt. I assume Harmi's too young to hunt.'

'They don't need to hunt. There are plentiful berries and tubers and herbs in these mountains,' Tam reminded him. 'How are your bruises?'

Chasse rolled his arm to examine a round purple mark on his tricep. 'Nothing bad,' he replied, and he rubbed the larger bruise on his inner thigh. 'They took my gear.'

'You impressed them with your skills,' Tam said. 'Even I am impressed.'

'Raven and Father taught me during winter,' Chasse replied.

As he lifted the bowl to drink the broth, the woven cloth covering the door entrance to their hut was pulled aside and three warriors entered, and they gestured for Chasse to accompany them. Chasse glanced at Tam, who silently projected, 'I'm here. Use mindspeak if you need me.' He handed his bowl to Tam and rose.

The sun was hovering above the western peaks when the warriors led Chasse through the village gate and onto a trail leading up a slope. He studied the trail they traversed, memorising the way, noting minor features, a rock shape or pile, a distinct tree shape, a view, in case he needed to find his way back.

The trail climbed steeply above the village before the group entered a shaded glade on a tiny plateau, where he immediately recognised the man with whom he fought among a half dozen men who were busy practising with various weapons.

The warrior smiled, approached, stood before Chasse, touched his chest and said, 'Keshaan.' He touched Chasse's chest with the back of his hand, saying, 'Ooa?' He paused, touched his own chest again and repeated, 'Keshaan.'

'Chasse,' Chasse replied.

'Chaez,' Keshaan repeated. 'Chaez.' He grinned and said, 'Fayme. Oh mechan bestra. Fayme,' before he led Chasse to two warriors who held the odd weapons with tiny spears. Keshaan took one long bent staff from a warrior, selected a tiny spear, slotted it on the string running from both ends of the bent staff, drew back the string, aimed and released. The tiny spear shot across the glade and buried deep into a tree trunk. The warriors cheered. Keshaan turned to Chasse and handed him the weapon, saying, 'Chaez. Oh nakki.'

When Chasse stared with confusion at the weapon in his hands, a second warrior with the same weapon stood beside him and demonstrated how he should hold the bent staff. Keshaan laughed and he helped Chasse to place his left hand at the centre where dried tendrils wrapped the wood and positioned the feathered end of the small spear on the string in Chasse's right hand. He motioned for Chasse to increase the tension by drawing the small spear back and mimicked aiming. Chasse copied the motion, released the small spear, and watched it flash past the tree and disappear. Keshaan patted his shoulder, handed him another small spear, and recommenced Chasse's training.

'Harmi says that, from your description, the weapon you were learning is what we would call a bow in our language, although no one in Harbin has one. The little spears are called arrows or shafts and people who use them are called archers. She says the memories that she carries of the weapon are a mixture of interest, anger and pain. Men used them against dragons, although they are mostly ineffectual because arrows cannot penetrate dragon scale unless magic is involved. Harmi says bows are better for hunting animals and for humans to kill each other.'

Chasse watched the firelight dance on Tam's face while he listened. Shadows played along the walls of adjacent huts and villagers traversing the compound were silhouetted against other fires. People ate and talked as they settled into the cold night. A small group of women and children sat at one fire crooning a song. 'Are we prisoners?' he asked.

'I told them that we must continue our journey in the morning,' Tam replied.

'How did you do that?' Chasse asked. 'Do you understand their language?'

Tam chuckled and said, 'No. While you were being trained, I was taken to Luani's hut. She is the young woman who first took me aside. We communicated as best as we could. She's the daughter of the Hukani. That is the title of the man and woman who lead this village, like our Dragon Head and Dragon Heart. She explained what I said to her parents.'

'How do you know they understood?' Chasse asked.

Tam shrugged and stared into the flames. 'I don't,' she replied. 'I guess we will find out in the morning.'

Twenty-Two

Chasse studied the shadowy crowd gathered at the gate, wondering if they were willing to stand aside when Tam and he made it clear that they were leaving. The air was close. Every sound echoed. Fog shrouded the forest and mountains in the slate blue pre-dawn. 'Keshaan still has my equipment,' Chasse noted as Tam joined him outside the hut.

'It won't matter, so long as we can leave,' Tam said. 'Come on.'

The prospect of losing weapons and armour irritated Chasse. They had a long way to travel and without weapons they had no protection from danger. He fell into step beside his sister as she walked calmly to the gate, but Keshaan and four warriors stepped out of the crowd to block their path. Chasse clenched his fists. It seemed obvious to him that they were not being allowed to leave.

'Chaez!' Keshaan called, and he gestured to a warrior who came forward to lay Chasse's axe at Chasse's feet. A second warrior approached and laid Chasse's spear and sword beside the axe. A third warrior placed Chasse's armour on the ground. And then Keshaan approached, carrying a bow and a quiver of arrows. He stood beside Chasse, hitched the quiver over Chasse's left shoulder and pressed the bow into Chasse's hand. 'Eshanta ma asenji!' Keshaan announced, and he locked eyes with Chasse. 'Eshanta ma asenji!' He stepped aside and the warriors cleared the path.

A familiar young woman came forward with two companions who handed Chasse and Tam their backpacks. The young woman smiled at Chasse, but to Tam she said quietly, 'Emaya ma asenji,' before she also stood aside. The gate creaked as the warriors swung it open.

'Time to go,' Tam said to Chasse.

Chasse put on his armour and bent to collect his weapons, and as he walked past Luani with his sister, Tam smiled and said, 'Kia ami sooana.' Luani's face lit with joy.

'What did you say?' Chasse asked as they passed through the gate.

'I said "Thank you, my friend,"' she replied.

'Luani taught you that?' Chasse asked.

'I learned it by listening and watching as everyone else talked,' Tam explained.

'Where to now?' Chasse asked, before he glanced over his shoulder at the wooden palisade and gate.

'Jaysin and Harmi are waiting by the river,' Tam informed him. 'We'll meet them and go on from there.'

Chasse and Tam followed the path along the narrow valley, stopping twice for Chasse to choose when forks appeared that they didn't notice the previous day. Chasse was conscious of the bow he carried, repeating in his thoughts what Keshaan taught him about technique. He could throw his spear twenty or thirty paces with accuracy, but the bow shot arrows a hundred paces or more and that meant he could hunt more effectively. But he had to master the weapon. And he had to learn how to make arrows in case he broke or lost any of the ten in Keshaan's gift quiver.

Chasse and Tam found Jaysin seated on a flat rock by the river, engrossed in a conversation with a pair of grey and white squirrels. The squirrels scampered into the undergrowth.

'Where's Harmi?' Tam asked.

'Fishing,' Jaysin replied. Tam raised a querying eyebrow, but before she could speak the water in the centre of the river bubbled and swirled and the dragon surfaced and waded to the bank, shaking droplets from her head. She hopped onto the earth and dropped five flopping fish before the astonished threesome. She snatched up the largest and began chewing.

'Looks like meat is still on her needs list,' Chasse noted wryly.

'We can eat fish,' Tam defensively replied. 'They're not sentient animals.'

'How do you know fish don't think or have feelings?' Jaysin asked.

'Do you know?' Tam countered.

'I can find out,' Jaysin said. 'I will find out.'

'How will you do that?' Chasse asked. He picked up a gasping, writhing fish and stared at its glassy eyes. 'I can't see much intelligence in this one.'

'I don't know, but I'll find a way,' Jaysin said. 'It makes sense that they are sentient.'

Chasse set to killing and cleaning his fish, saying cheerfully, 'We have a meal, thanks to Harmi. I gratefully accept the gift.'

Chasse led through the forest and up and down the slopes along the reaches of the river. With greater awareness that other people lived in the mountains after their encounter, he remained vigilant, stopping regularly to listen and survey the landscape, and he bent to study spoor to determine what animals lived and hunted in the gorge. Tam used each pause in their progress to pick herbs and collect plants and tubers and stored them in her bag. Jaysin walked beside Harmi, the little dragon waddling along and squeezing between rocks and trees on tighter sections of the path, but every time that Chasse or Tam stopped or deviated, Jaysin sank to his haunches to alleviate his exhaustion.

Mid-afternoon, the river current increased in speed until the waters squeezed into a cleft and plunged over a deep fall, showering the forest and mountains with mist. The path east seemed blocked until Chasse discovered a narrow stairway cut roughly into the rock. 'This is the way forward,' he said as he pointed to the crude steps. 'Be awake. Someone made these steps.'

'Harmi can't negotiate that,' Jaysin said. 'We have to find another way.'

'The only other way is to go back and climb out of the river valley,' Chasse replied. 'Tam?' he asked, turning to his sister for her opinion. Tam did not answer, her face set in contemplation. 'Tam?' Chasse repeated.

'Sorry,' Tam said, blinking. 'Harmi said she will meet us at the top.'

'How?' Chasse blurted.

'She's recalling a spell that Claryssa knew. Only we have to climb first and describe where we are. In fact, she'll see where we are through my eyes,' Tam explained.

'I don't understand,' Chasse said, unable to hide his confusion.

'She's going to translocate!' Jaysin exclaimed. 'Wow!'

'What is that?' Chasse asked.

'It's how Claryssa was able to get in and out of the cave on Dragon Mountain,' Tam explained. 'There was no cave entrance large enough for her to go in and out of the cavern, so she translocated.'

'I read about it!' Jaysin interjected. 'I started learning it. But Harmi already knows it!'

'I still don't understand,' Chasse said, shaking his head.

'Lead us to the top of the stairs and Harmi will show you,' Tam assured him.

The climb was steep and arduous because the steps were uneven and some so badly worn that Chasse had to turn his foot sideways to maintain purchase. He was conscious of Tam and Jaysin climbing in his wake, but they took their time and listened to his instruction, and eventually all three stood on a ledge high above the ravine.

Chasse asked Tam and Jaysin to wait while he explored the trail that led from the ledge to ensure it was navigable and that Harmi could follow it once they worked out how to get her up the steps, but when he re-joined his siblings Harmi was crouched on the ledge, staring at him with her blue reptilian eyes.

'You missed it!' Jaysin said. 'I have to learn that!'

'The path winds along the top of the cliffs,' Chasse told them, although he was still mystified as to what Harmi did to reach the top. 'It's well-worn and clear, so others must use it regularly. We need to be watchful.' He looked up at the eastern sky and added, 'There's also a storm brewing. We have to find somewhere to stay dry overnight.'

Shadows were deep across the mountains and valleys before Chasse spotted a rock overhang higher up the slope above the path they were following. He noted that an overgrown track led between the rocks and trees to the overhang, so he urged the others to wait until he inspected the site before he led them to shelter. They reached it as the first raindrops fell.

The space beneath the overhang was deep, almost a cave, and large enough that Harmi easily crept in, and curled up at the back and she was asleep before Tam created a warming stone.

'Does she have to sleep all the time?' Chasse asked.

'She's growing,' Tam replied. 'Dragons sleep most of the day, even as adults, but baby ones sleep every chance they get. The constant travelling is exhausting her.'

'It's exhausting me,' Jaysin chimed in. 'And I'm hungry.'

'And I'll make a broth,' Tam said, as she began unpacking items from her bag and backpack. 'But you can fetch water.' She handed a small ceramic pot to Jaysin who groaned as he accepted the chore.

Chasse watched his brother descend in the light rain to fetch water from a rivulet running from the mountains into the river gorge. 'How far are we travelling?' he asked as he stood beside Tam.

Tam looked up from tearing leaves for the broth. 'I still don't know. Harmi hasn't travelled through here and her ancestral memory only references Claryssa flying over the mountains, not walking through them.'

'But Claryssa and the Herbal Man came from somewhere,' Chasse argued. 'Where was that?'

Tam rose and said, 'Machutzka. I think I've pronounced it right. It's a town.'

'But where is it?' Chasse asked. 'How far?'

'It's further east, at the edge of the mountains,' Tam explained. 'I don't know how far. Dragons fly very fast. For us, it could be a long walk.'

'Maybe we should find somewhere to stay for a while,' Chasse suggested. 'We've travelled five days away from home. I don't think Mikane and his men will pursue us this far. In fact, they're probably grateful we've gone.'

Tam agreed. 'There's plenty of food here, but I'm not sure that this overhang will shelter us enough.' She added a handful of herbs to the broth.

'I will search for a better place tomorrow,' Chasse promised. He breathed in and added, 'That smells good.'

'I found Fireweed this morning. It adds zest to food,' Tam explained.

'Mother used it sometimes,' Chasse reminisced.

'Yes,' Tam replied.

Chasse peered down the slope in the direction that Jaysin descended, his thoughts drifting between wondering where Jaysin was and how their mother was faring under Mikane's leadership. The aroma rising from Tam's broth teased his childhood memories of home and Eesa and sometimes his father eating at the table and he wondered if running away, instead of confronting Mikane, was actually the right choice. He should have stayed to protect his mother. He should have stayed with Banni and Jara. He should have stood beside his father when Mikane challenged him. Tradition meant he couldn't, but was tradition more important than family? He didn't know. Tradition was flawed. He was aware that the rain was growing heavier. 'Jaysin's taking his time,' he remarked.

'Something's happened,' Tam said, lowering a ladle and touching her bracelet.

Chasse's bracelet tingled. 'I felt it,' he said. 'I'll make sure Jaysin's safe.' He took up his spear, pulled up his hood on his cloak, strapped on his axe and strode into the rain.

The earth was slippery, the rocks glistening with the steady rainfall as Chasse followed Jaysin's dissolving tracks to the rivulet. When he reached the channel of running water, he was shocked to discover the signs of a struggle in the soft earth and the pot crushed and abandoned. Heart racing, he searched until he found tracks and intermittent drag marks. He followed the trail, adrenalin driving his speed across the greasy ground.

The light was almost gone and he couldn't see the tracks clearly, the signs disappearing as the rain turned the earth to mud. The tracks stopped. *Where are you?* he projected to Jaysin, but his little brother did not reply. Just as he was deciding if he could go further, the rain stopped and he stumbled onto a very narrow but obvious path running across the face of the gorge and climbing onto a ridge. *Whoever has Jaysin had to follow this*, he concluded. The question was whether they traversed right or left. *Left*, he decided. Right would take whoever it was to the village they left in the morning.

'Chasse?' Tam's query entered his mind as he started to follow the path. 'What's happening?'

'Someone took Jaysin,' he replied.

'Who?'

'I don't know.'

'Where are you? I'll come,' Tam insisted.

'Stay where you are,' Chasse ordered. He spotted a flickering light a short distance ahead on the ridge. 'Wait,' he said, and he crept towards the firelight.

'Chasse?'

'Wait!' he insisted. 'Please.' He crept to the edge of a screen of bushes and found three men squatting at a campfire, roasting a small animal on a spit. Jaysin was propped against a tree at the edge of the firelight, his eyes shining as he watched his captors. 'I found him,' Chasse projected. 'He looks unhurt. There are three men holding him captive.'

'I'll come to help,' Tam said.

'No,' Chasse replied. 'Stay where you are. Keep Harmi safe.'

'What will you do?'

'I'll work that out,' Chasse replied. *Three against one isn't a good fight,* he pondered, as he assessed the men.

They seemed to be his age or not much older and they looked fit. They wore animal skin clothing – rough cut and with little evidence of the skilled sewing in clothes worn by Harbin villagers. Their hair was dark, long and loose. It was impossible to tell if they were experienced warriors or novices like himself. He might be able to bluff them with his appearance. He might not. He might be able to fell one and frighten the others. He might not.

One warrior rose, tore a leg from the baking animal and took it to Jaysin, but Jaysin shook his head, refusing the offer. Perplexed, or perhaps annoyed, the warrior returned to the fireside and ate the meaty morsel. Another warrior rose and carried a waterskin to Jaysin and held it so that Jaysin could drink. When Jaysin was sated, the warrior put the skin beside Jaysin before he returned to eat with his companions.

Chasse considered the situation. His brother was a captive, but he was not being treated badly. They might only be taking him to their village because he was an intruder. They might not be wanting to fight. He noticed one man was examining Jaysin's bracelet.

Chasse rose, spear held low to be non-threatening, stepped out of the bushes, and calmly said, 'Hello.'

The warriors leapt to their feet, two reaching for spears, one raising a bow and taking aim.

Chasse held out his hands in a non-aggressive gesture, although he was ready to duck or dodge if the spears or an arrow were launched. 'I don't want to fight,' he said. He lowered his spear slowly to the ground, wary of a sign of attack, but the men held their defensive stances, watching him as he straightened and held out his hands again.

The shortest man spoke. 'Makko. Makko deahn.' The words meant nothing to Chasse, but he mimed eating in the hope that they would understand. The shorter man glanced at his companions, spoke a word, and all three lowered their weapons. The short man gestured for Chasse to join them at the campfire.

Chasse approached, ignoring Jaysin who he knew was staring intently at him, sat at the fire and accepted the offer of a small piece of meat, savouring the aroma and flavour and juice as he chewed. The warriors spoke to each other, and the short man spoke to Chasse, but the language barrier was solid. Remembering Keshaan's conversation, Chasse touched his chest and said, 'I am Chasse,' repeating 'Chasse' twice to emphasise his name.

He pointed at the short man who grinned and replied, 'Tayma. A Tayma.' The short man pointed in turn to his companions and said, 'Fahntoo. Ekkim,' and the men smiled and laughed. Tayma tapped his chest and said, 'A Tayma,' and pointed to Chasse and said, 'Da Chays.'

Chasse smiled, held up his scrap of meat and said, 'This is very good.' The warriors laughed and continued talking to each other, occasionally glancing at Chasse and nodding.

After eating a couple of bites, Chasse pointed to the bracelet on the ground beside Ekkim and indicated that he wanted to look at it. Ekkim glanced at Tayma, who nodded, so he handed the bracelet to Chasse. Chasse held it up and pretended to examine it in the firelight. He put the bracelet on the ground at his feet, took off his linked gauntlets and handed them to Ekkim.

Ekkim accepted the gauntlets. He slid one onto his right hand and held it up for his companions to view and they nodded approval. Ekkim turned to Chasse, and spoke, indicating that he considered the trade was good, and he slid his left hand into the second gauntlet, rolled his hands and proudly inspected his new trappings.

Chasse waited for Tayma to look in his direction before he said, 'What are you doing with the boy?' and he pointed at Jaysin. Tayma glanced at Jaysin and shifted his attention to Chasse, looking for a clue as to what Chasse was asking. Chasse said, 'I want the boy,' and he added a mime of taking Jaysin away with him. Tayma's expression became serious and he interrupted his companions who stopped to observe the interchange. Chasse repeated his awkward mime, saying, 'I will take the boy with me.'

'Fa!' Tayma said, anger creeping across his face.

Struggling to add weight to his request, Chasse mimed his kinship with Jaysin, holding his hands together to demonstrate the closeness of the relationship. Tayma's expression remained static momentarily, before he laughed and spoke to his companions who also laughed. Tayma uttered a string of phrases directly to Chasse, smiling, and then his face became serious again, and he repeated, 'Fa!'

Chasse reached over his shoulder and unhitched his axe, an action that brought all three warriors to their feet with their weapons. Ignoring the threat, Chasse placed his axe on the ground before Tayma. He pointed to the axe and to Tayma, and then to Jaysin and to himself. 'You keep the axe,' he said. 'I take the boy.'

Tayma stared at Chasse. He spoke to his companions and they lowered their weapons. Tayma glanced at Jaysin at the edge of the little camp and looked down at the axe. Firelight danced along the blade, making it shine. Carefully, Tayma picked up the axe and he scrutinised it like Chasse remembered studying it, turning and testing its weight and balance. He handed the weapon to his closest companion who also assessed it, and he straightened. Tayma spoke, and he raised his left hand to touch his palm on Chasse's forehead. Sensing he should do likewise, Chasse raised his hand and placed his palm on Tayma's forehead. Tayma spoke again and removed his hand. Chasse followed suit, unsure if he also was meant to say something, although he did not understand what he ought to say. The third warrior passed the axe to Tayma who bounced it in his hands, admiring the blade. Then Tayma looked at Chasse and pointed to Jaysin, speaking again, gesturing for Chasse to take his gift and leave.

Chasse smiled, said, 'Thank you, Tayma,' and he headed for Jaysin. He knelt and untied his brother's hands and ankles.

'You swapped your axe for me?' Jaysin asked, as Chasse helped him to stand.

'It was a very poor exchange,' Chasse quipped. He handed Jaysin his bracelet and stooped to collect his spear, before he ushered his brother into the night.

Twenty-Three

Chasse watched the eagle circling above the gorge in the afternoon light. Its effortless flight, riding updrafts and eddies, rarely beating its wings, showed the eagle's mastery of its world and the vision fascinated him. 'One day,' he whispered to the air, 'I will master what I need.'

He lowered his gaze, lifted his bow, drew back, and sighted along the shaft at the trunk twenty paces away. He tilted the point slightly, having learned by trial and error that arrows travel in a curve to the target, judged the light wind as being minimal and loosed the arrow. It flew to its mark beside three others. He reached down to pull another shaft from the ground and reloaded. Daily practice was building strength in his arms – his left from holding the bow steady against the pull of his right arm on the bowstring.

The decision to find a place where the four could live led him to a rock ledge that was the entry to a wide and deep cave beneath a high cliff. He nearly didn't find it because the cave mouth was screened by heavy foliage affording effective camouflage, and he only looked beyond the bushes and vines because a small brown animal scurried into the foliage. He reconnoitred as much of the space as he could see without a torch, startling birds and bats for whom the cave was a refuge, before he returned to lead Tam, Jaysin and Harmi to the potential sanctuary.

Tam conjured a floating globe to reveal that the cave walls were adorned with etchings and ochre drawings similar to those in the cave of the Dawn People: stylised animals, hunters, hand and figure silhouettes. They found a pile of old bones in a recess, remnants of a long unused fire pit and charcoal stains across the ceiling rock that were testament to the cave once being a home for ancient humans.

'Are we staying here for very long?' Jaysin asked when Tam began to unpack.

'For as long as we are safe,' Tam replied, looking at Chasse.

'What about the tribal people?' Jaysin asked.

'I found this by accident,' Chasse said to reassure Jaysin. 'No one has been in this cave for a very long time.'

'It's still a cave,' Jaysin whined. 'Can't we find a village? Somewhere there is a bed?'

Tam stopped unpacking to reply, 'You know the answer to that as well as any of us.'

Jaysin shrugged. 'I know. I hope it isn't for too long.'

'You'll have plenty of time to read the books you lugged along with you,' said Chasse, unable to mask his annoyance with his brother. He heard scales scraping against rock and turned to find the dragon selecting the best spot to curl up to sleep. 'I think Harmi has already made our choice,' he noted wryly.

The best discovery in the cave was a cleft that opened into a small chamber where a pool sparkled in a sliver of light angling from an overhead fissure. The moist walls glistened, ground water seeped in to keep the pool fresh, and Chasse knew rains would pour through the fissure to refresh the water. A dry channel ran through the cleft and across the cave floor to the entrance, which he determined was the runoff when the pool overflowed. The cave was the perfect place to hide.

Chasse focused, loosed the arrow and hit the target. He reached for another arrow and reflected on what transpired after they found the cave.

The dragon slept most of the time, waking only to eat, drink, excrete and urinate. Chasse cleaned out every dropping and fetched fresh meat to add to the plants that Tam and Jaysin harvested because what became obvious to everyone was how rapidly Harmi was growing, even while she slept. Within the first ten days of settling in the cave, she doubled in size, waking ravenous and consuming everything the trio provided before she returned to dragon dreaming, and she continued to grow as the summer days passed.

And then began the unexpected impact of Harmi's slumbering on Tam, because every time the dragon slept Tam was pulled into Harmi's dreams.

Chasse had glimpsed the potential of mind melding many times since Tam revealed it to him, but in the cave, as Harmi grew, the dragon's dreams assaulted Tam's conscious mind with greater vigour, until one evening, a few days after they settled into the cave, Tam collapsed to her hands and knees.

Chasse dropped the firewood he was carrying and ran to his sister, kneeling beside her. 'Tam?' he asked, seeing sweat beading on her brow.

'What is happening?' Jaysin asked as he arrived from where he was practising a spell.

'Harmi,' Tam uttered slowly. 'She's in my head.'

'She's asleep,' Jaysin said.

Tam sat onto her haunches, calming her breathing, and replied, 'But, when she's dreaming, I see her dreams as if they are my own.'

'That's awkward,' said Jaysin.

'What can I do?' Chasse asked.

'Nothing,' Tam replied. 'There's nothing you can do. I have to master this.' She drew a deep breath. 'This is part of who I am, part of who Harmi and I are together. I guess she sees my dreams too.'

'What is she dreaming?' Chasse asked.

Tam collected her thoughts, and answered, 'A mishmash of things. Sometimes she's flying, sometimes she's on the edge of a cliff, sometimes she's conjuring spells. Sometimes she's in places we've never seen, with stone buildings larger than the Long Hall and surrounded by stone walls. It's chaotic, like lightning flashes of memory and ideas exploding simultaneously.' She winced and sucked in another sharp breath, and Chasse put his hand on her arm. 'It's all right,' Tam assured him. 'It's not pain, merely surprise, like having an unexpected idea.' She grinned. 'It *is* an unexpected idea.'

'Ideas don't make you fall,' Chasse said.

'Harmi has powerful ideas,' Tam replied.

Over the ensuing days, Chasse saw Tam's random and startled reactions become subdued as she learned to control the effect of the dragon's dreams, but she withdrew more and more from daily interactions with Jaysin and with him. Instead, she spent long periods sitting cross-legged in contemplation at the cave mouth reciting phrases in languages Chasse had never heard. He also noticed that her red hair was softening in hue and the grey streak he first spotted in their escape from the village lightened and widened. When he dared to break her concentration to ask if she was all right, she glared, so he left her in peace and practised using his bow. Jaysin buried himself in his books in the cave, seemingly content to be left alone when the daily chores were done. And Harmi slept.

As for Chasse, his sleep was plagued with dreams and nightmares – nightmares lingering from the dragonship journey, the escape from Harbin and Banni. The worst one that recurred for several nights had him standing in snow in an open glade, his feet frozen to the earth while he watched Banni running to him with Jara in her arms. Figures sprung from the trees and became Mikane and shadows of dragonwarriors who were going to catch Banni before she could reach Chasse. And in the last instant, they morphed into wolves and leapt. He woke, trembling, infuriated, afraid, distraught.

Several days after arriving at the cave, Jaysin interrupted Chasse's bow training to excitedly announce, 'You have to see this!' He strode to Chasse. 'Look!' He held out his left hand.

Chasse peered at the smooth grey and black stone in Jaysin's palm and bemusedly remarked, 'It's a stone.'

Jaysin put his right hand over his left palm and removed it. 'And?' he asked.

Seeing the stone gone, Chasse said, 'You picked it up in your other hand.'

Jaysin rolled over his right hand and opened it, revealing an empty palm. Chasse looked from palm to palm. 'Surprised?' Jaysin asked, grinning delightedly. He placed his right hand over his left, lifted his right hand away and the stone reappeared in his left palm. 'And it's back!' he declared.

'How did you do that?' Chasse asked. 'Where did you put the stone?'

'I didn't shift it,' Jaysin said. 'Watch as I do it again.' He repeated his hand movements, the stone vanishing from his left palm and reappearing. Seeing Chasse's bewildered expression, Jaysin explained. 'It's an illusion. I don't make the stone disappear. You just think it has.'

'That doesn't make it any clearer,' Chasse complained. 'You learned this from your book?'

'It took practice,' Jaysin said proudly. 'Now I can try it on larger things.'

'I don't get how you can trick my eyes when I can see perfectly clearly,' Chasse said.

'I trick your mind,' Jaysin said. 'I make you think there's nothing in my hand, but the stone is still there.'

'You can't trick my mind,' Chasse argued. 'I control my thoughts.'

'Like when I speak to you?' Jaysin projected with mindspeak.

'That's communication,' Chasse retorted. 'I want to hear you.'

'Then try stopping me talking to you,' Jaysin projected.

Chasse glared at his brother and willed himself to block Jaysin's mindspeak.

'Is it working?' Jaysin asked. 'I don't think it is. I'm in your head and you can't stop me. You can't totally control your mind.'

'That's enough!' Chasse snapped angrily. 'Go do whatever you do with your magic! Stay out of my head!' He saw Jaysin's startled expression fade to disappointment, but his weakness at being unable to stop Jaysin entering his mind aggravated him, so he waited until his brother withdrew before he unleashed his anger on the target trunk. His first two shots missed, maddening him further.

Another host of days had elapsed since the incident with Jaysin. Chasse explored the area surrounding the cave and diligently practised with his bow every day. Although he found evidence of hunting groups passing below their cave, they remained undisturbed in their lair. The waning summer creeping into autumn brought increasingly colder nights and chilly mornings, but Tam and Jaysin's abilities to create warming stones without risking fire or bright fire-like glows meant that strangers would not be inadvertently attracted to light emanating from the cave and they could keep warm. There was plenty of game and plant life was abundant. They had fresh water. Nothing suggested Mikane or his men were still hunting them. There was no compulsion to move on.

Chasse lowered his bow and walked to the tree to retrieve his arrows. He inspected the wooden tip of each as he pulled them from the bark. Two required re-sharpening. One shaft was cracked and ready to break. He knew nothing of manufacturing arrows and he could only craft them from the memories of his brief interaction with Keshaan. Keshaan's people made arrow tips from sharpened stone, but they had only given him wooden arrows in the quiver, good enough only for hunting. He used his knife to sharpen the shafts, and hardened them over flame, but the wooden points hardly penetrated the target trunks and only his bowstring tensioning and draw strength improved the depth of each hit. He had to improvise making stone arrowheads, only he didn't know how.

Losing his axe to save Jaysin niggled at him. He did not consider the exchange to be the wrong decision, but he missed the axe because it was the finest weapon he owned, a gift from the Herbal Man's trove. He would have liked to master it. The dragon sword with its etched blade was a fine weapon, better than any sword in Harbin, but the axe was his favourite. 'So, I will master you,' he said to the bow as he slid it over his shoulder.

He hoisted the quiver over his other shoulder and headed up to the cave.

An anguished cry startled him. He peered into the gorge, hearing the river surging over the rocks far below, and waited. *I'm imagining things*, he thought. Then he heard the cry again; someone in trouble or in pain. He immediately thought of Jaysin. Did his little brother wander foolishly into trouble again?

He descended the hillside, winding between the trees and bushes to the edge of the gorge, and when he reached it a scream echoed below. He assessed the direction of the source and searched for a way down the cliff. With no clear path, he jumped from rock to ledge to rock and scrambled down short slopes. The scream was repeated above the river's rising thunder.

As he rounded a sharp bend, he spotted an animal on the opposite bank, a mottled four-legged creature the size of two men with a long snaking tail. It was pawing at a cleft in the rock, digging away clumps of earth and dislodging stone. Behind it, on a flat lump of stone, lay a ragged, bloody body, one arm dangling in the river. Chasse unhitched his bow and quiver and fitted an arrow to the bowstring. Another frantic scream rose above the din of the rushing water. The animal had someone trapped in the cleft.

Familiarity formed in his memory. The animal was like the creatures that Jaysin and he encountered in the dark. He aimed. The air currents above the gorge river were tricky, the distance about twenty paces. He fired. The arrow flashed across the river and bounced off a rock by the animal's head. The animal didn't notice. He nocked a second arrow, aimed and loosed. This one struck the target's hind leg and stuck and the animal whipped around, biting at the source of sudden pain, until it dislodged the shaft. Chasse's third arrow glanced off of the creature's skull. The animal's eyes flared, fixed on Chasse and narrowed, and it crouched. As Chasse quickly loaded a fourth arrow, his last with a sharpened point, and raised his bow, the animal leapt. Chasse's arrow pierced the creature's shoulder mid-flight and the animal dropped short of the bank, floundering in the water as the fierce current carried it into the rapids where it disappeared in a spume of watery froth and spray.

Across the river, a tousled head appeared from the cleft. The owner, a boy, emerged warily, searching for the animal. Two more children appeared, a girl and a boy, clinging to each other. They seemed younger than the first boy, but they shared the same dark hair and skin hue. The first boy knelt beside the mangled human corpse on the rock, pushing and prodding it, and the other two kneeled beside him, and they kept touching and caressing the body fondly, until the girl looked up and met Chasse's gaze. She tugged the older boy's arm and he stared across the space at Chasse. Chasse lifted his arm in a friendly wave, but the older boy urged the children to rise. The younger children scrambled up the side of the gorge and vanished among the trees, while the older boy stayed put. Chasse waved again. The boy did not respond. He knelt beside the body, his hands continuing to caress it, while he kept looking at Chasse.

Chasse considered crossing the river, but the current was strong and the water at least to his chest in depth from what he could see. The animal's fate was proof that he could not cross safely. He watched the boy for a few more moments before he shouldered his bow, waved again, and climbed out of the gorge to return to the cave.

Sometimes he could sleep without fear. Sometimes the dreams came and threw his sleep into disarray. Two came. He stood in the middle of the dragonship, surrounded by shadows of warriors who were intent on keeping him where he was. He glimpsed a mountain peak beyond the fringe of the red sail and it was on fire. A larger shadow stood before him. He couldn't see features, but he knew the man was Suran and behind him stood Mikane and behind him was Marron with both arms intact. And

behind Marron, though he couldn't see them, were his family. And Suran held his battle axe. And he was weaponless. And Suran struck.

He sat up, reaching for his sword, before he realised the cave was dark and he was escaping a dream. His heart pounded. He listened. The wind breathed at the cave mouth. No one was on watch. *We have gotten lazy,* he thought. He rose and went to the opening and stared up at the stars. The mountains were dark in a moonless night and he wondered if Shaddho's presence reached beyond Harbin.

Outside the valley, a wolf howled and another answered. He waited for the wolf conversation to continue, but the night returned to the sounds of the wind whispering through trees and over rocks. The air was cold. He wanted to return to his warm bed, but he decided he should keep watch, so he sat and leaned against the stone and listened as he watched. And closed his eyes.

The second dream was confusing. A red dragon – perhaps Harmi, perhaps not – was perched atop a white stone wall like a giant hawk, watching. Chasse looked down to see what the dragon was observing and gazed into a wide, treeless valley, where people milled. He sensed their fear of the dragon. And they were calling to him. And then he stood among them, looking up at the dragon circling overhead. The dragon landed and the people scattered, and he was facing the dragon with his bow. He loosed an arrow and it bounced harmlessly from the dragon's scales. And Marron was laughing at him.

Twenty-Four

Chasse led Tam into the gorge, choosing a pathway less chaotic and difficult than the one he created the previous afternoon. The mid-morning sun sparkled on the river and a rainbow glowed in the spray rising from the rapids. Birds swept between trees, twittering and chattering, and Tam stopped to admire and study them as they perched, but Chasse urged her to follow by reminding her of his tale. At the base of the descent, he pointed across the river to the stone slab where the body had lain, but it was gone. 'The children were hiding in that crevice,' Chasse explained. 'The creature was trying to get at them. It was lithe, like a wolf, but strong like a bear.'

'They either came back for the body, or something carried it away,' Tam suggested. She studied the torrent separating them from the far bank. 'No one can cross this. We should be safe.'

'We better get back,' Chasse said. 'Thanks for coming to see.'

He started to ascend the steep cliff to lead to the top when Tam called his name above the river's roar. He stopped and turned. Across the gorge, people were assembling on the bank. Three children stood at the head of six adults and they were observing Tam and him. He raised a hand and waved. No one responded, initially, until a female raised her hand and waved in return.

'You made contact,' Tam said.

'I'm not sure that's good or bad,' Chasse replied, descending to stand beside his sister. He studied the group on the opposite bank. 'Those are the three children who were being hunted by the animal.'

'The short man is gesturing,' Tam pointed out.

The man produce a bow and he tied an object to an arrow before he raised the weapon, aimed, and fired. The arrow, weighted by its burden, tumbled clumsily through the air and landed several paces from Chasse. Chasse climbed across the rocks to retrieve it and returned to Tam.

'What is that?' Tam asked.

Chasse untied the object from the arrow and held it up, unravelling two thin leather straps. 'It's a fang,' he said, marvelling at its bright white colour and size, bigger than a bear or wolf fang. He gazed at the bowman who lifted his hand in a friendly gesture. 'I think they're thanking me for saving their children.' The people began climbing out of the gorge, the short man at the rear.

'You've been honoured,' Tam said, studying the fang. 'Look.' She twirled it to show Chasse a rune inscribed in the enamel.

'What does it mean?' Chasse asked.

'It's an ancient form of writing,' Tam explained. 'If we were in Eric's library, I might be able to find a text to translate the rune's meaning.' She took the ends of the leather and tied them. 'Lean forward,' she said. Chasse bowed his head and Tam slid the leather over his head and hung the fang at his neck. 'There,' she announced. 'It's your amulet.'

'A what?' Chasse asked.

'It's a charm to protect you,' Tam explained.

'You think it's magical?'

'It might be. The people who gave it to you probably think so. Wear it.' She laughed. 'They call you Chasse Wolf's Bane back home. You'll need a new name when we learn the name of the animal that you drove away.' She touched his shoulder as she walked past and said, 'We should go back to tell Jaysin what happened.'

Chasse let Tam lead the return climb, admiring his sister's agility as she scrambled up the cliff. Her hair was tangled but free, as if defying her inner composure to remind him that she was no ordinary individual, but it was also much lighter in hue, as if it was fading from red into a golden tone.

She was in her sixteenth summer, but because of her increasing wisdom and manner she was more like an older sister, not his younger one. She understood far more than he could imagine.

As they walked between the trees, Chasse caressed the fang dangling against his chest. It was a special gift and he burned to know what the rune meant. If it was magical, it was another change to his world. Growing up, magic was the stuff of folklore, contained only in the tales of Nakiades and the dragon, but now it seemed as if magic permeated everything; the Herbal Man and his dragon, his sister, his brother, the bracelets they wore, perhaps even the fang amulet. He wanted to believe magic was nothing more than tricks and illusions, but he slept in a cave with a dragon. The world was not the Harbin world he thought he once understood.

Tam did not wake when Chasse called her name. He knelt beside Jaysin to examine her. Her breathing was regular, like it ought to be for a person asleep, but she did not stir when he nudged her arm.

'Is she sick?' Jaysin asked.

Chasse stood and answered, 'I don't think so.' He glanced at the looming somnambulant dragon form curled behind his sister's bedding in the cave's dull light. 'It's as if she's sleeping like Harmi.'

'I'll test her mind,' Jaysin said.

'What?' Chasse asked, startled.

'Sh,' Jaysin warned. He closed his eyes and his expression became fixed, before he gasped, 'Wow!' and he opened his eyes wide.

'What?' Chasse repeated.

'She's dreaming!' Jaysin said excitedly. 'She's sharing dreams with Harmi! Amazing dreams!'

'About what?' Chasse asked.

'It's all scrambled, but they're flying and then they're high above mountains and then deep inside strange dark forests, and there's flames and sheets of water!' Jaysin explained.

'You can see all that?' Chasse asked.

'Absolutely!' Jaysin replied.

'You can see what is in someone's head?' Chasse persisted.

'I told you I was learning how to do that.'

'You told me that you could trick people into thinking that something that was there wasn't there,' Chasse retorted.

Jaysin grinned mischievously. 'That was only the first step.' He shook his head. 'Actually, it's like the third or fourth step. Mindspeaking comes before that.'

'And the Herbal Man has all that written in the book you read,' Chasse said. Jaysin nodded. 'Is it safe?'

Jaysin shrugged. 'I'm not sure. I haven't finished learning.'

Chasse looked at Tam and again at Harmi. The dragon's grey scales moving gently as she breathed. 'If Tam is going to sleep like the dragon, we have a problem,' he said. 'We can't leave them alone, and we have to make sure they're both fed and given water when they wake.' He looked at Jaysin. 'You have to help me do some of Tam's work if you want us to eat. And we will have to share watch, day and night.' He ignored Jaysin's sour expression. It was time Jaysin learned to be an adult and to shoulder adult responsibilities, and he was, by circumstance and by age, Jaysin's mentor.

Chasse stepped onto the flat rock at the cave mouth and gazed across the gorge, sampling the air on his skin as he studied the clouds. Leaves across the mountain were rapidly changing to shades of red and golds and falling to the earth and clouds were snowy peaks towering above the mountains. Showers washed the rocks and earth and became small torrents tumbling down the slopes and cliffs into the gorge, swelling the river whose thundering voice grew louder. Birds abandoned their summer homes, flocks flying east and south to escape the impending winter, and the small forest animals gathered seed and nut stocks to tide them over the coming months of snow. Plants withered as the icy night air strangled them. Though some of the change was familiar, the weather on this side of Dragon Mountain was different to what Chasse understood in Harbin. While there were no storms sweeping in from the wild western ocean and the surrounding mountains gave shelter from the northern storms, he could sense snow was coming and soon.

When he heard Jaysin calling, he re-entered the cave, and asked, 'What is wrong?'

'Have you seen Tam's hair?' Jaysin asked. He raised his conjured light sphere to illuminate where Tam was lying. 'Her hair is going greyer,'

Chasse had noticed Tam's hair growing lighter almost daily, but he also saw that she was gaunt and pale from lack of food, despite Jaysin and he insisting that she eat in her rare waking moments. She spent no time exercising or being outside. She even took her rare toilet breaks a few paces from where she slept, leaving Chasse to clean after her while she staggered back to her dried grass bedding.

Unlike Tam, Harmi was always ravenous when she woke and there never seemed sufficient food to sate the dragon's hunger. While Tam steadily diminished, Harmi grew larger. The additional phenomenon was that, like Tam's hair, Harmi's scales were changing colour, from grey to dark rust to red, as if she was absorbing the hue from Tam's locks.

Chasse knelt beside Tam and checked her breathing and heartbeat. Both were steady and calm.

'Do you want to know what they are dreaming?' Jaysin asked eagerly.

'They're not dreaming,' Chasse replied.

'How do you know that?' Jaysin asked.

'I can tell without your magical intrusion,' Chasse said as he glanced at

242

the stock of plants and seeds and herbs spread across stone ledges. 'If we were home, we would be getting ready for Procra's Feast. The warriors would be hunting and the women would be foraging and preparing food and decorating the Long Hall.'

'We missed Procra's Dance,' Jaysin said, grinning. 'I guess we will miss Procra's Feast.'

'I think we should do something,' Chasse said. 'It's tradition.'

'Our traditions got us into this situation,' Jaysin retorted. 'I'm happier without them.'

'Snow is coming. I felt and smelt it outside,' said Chasse. 'We don't have much more time to get our stocks organised. You and I can go out together just this once. Tam and Harmi are safe. No one has found us in the past weeks. We'll do short trips for the rest of the day and check in each time we bring back food. And, tonight, you and I will celebrate Procra's Feast.'

Jaysin quietly replied, 'If that's what you want.'

Chasse nodded. 'That's what I want.'

The sky darkened throughout the day as the brothers foraged for nuts and fungi and plants, all scarce in the dying autumn. Chasse collected thin branches suitable for whittling and shaping into arrows, and he caught four small dark brown animals that he intended to skin and cook, much to Jaysin's disgust. 'You don't even know what they are,' Jaysin accused.

'They look tasty enough to me,' Chasse replied, his grin taunting his younger brother. 'A warrior needs meat.'

'Just another reason why I never want to be a warrior,' Jaysin retorted.

Together, they made four forays, the last focussed on digging as many roots and tubers as they could find. Spying a large bush of crimson Eagleberries on a ledge of a low cliff, Chasse left Jaysin to continue foraging along the narrow path, while he searched the cliff base for an approach to the ledge. He hefted his bag over the same shoulder as his bow and methodically worked his way up the rocks, climbed onto the ledge and edged toward his goal.

Chasse knew from his mother that Eagleberries, so named because the big birds prized them, were large crunchy and nutritious. They could be boiled into jelly when they began to rot and Tam used Eagleberry jelly in her herbal mixtures, making them a universal item. While he never cooked the berries, Chasse saw Eesa and her companions prepare them for Procra's Feast and he liked the opportunity to have one symbol of the Harbin Feast in their evening meal.

Jaysin's shrill shriek stopped him. He turned on the narrow ledge to peer in the direction of his brother's cry. At first, Chasse couldn't discern anything through the trees, but then Jaysin appeared, sprinting along the path towards the cliff, pursued by a large man with a staff.

'Chasse!' Jaysin screamed. 'Help!' The man swung his staff and caught Jaysin's heels, sending the lad sprawling. Jaysin rolled onto his back as the imposing figure loomed over him.

Chasse dropped his forage bag onto the ledge, unhitched his bow and fumbled for an arrow. The man reached for Jaysin. Chasse aimed and fired. The range being more than thirty paces, his height above his target, the rapidity of acting, meant his arrow sped past the man's shoulder, but it successfully distracted Jaysin's assailant. 'Run!' Chasse yelled as he loaded a second arrow. 'Go!'

Jaysin scrambled to his feet and ran, and the man started after him, but Chasse's second arrow sped accurately towards the target – until the man spun and knocked the missile aside with his staff and glared up at Chasse.

Chasse checked Jaysin's progress. His brother was disappearing into the forest, too far ahead for the man to pursue. Satisfied that Jaysin was safe, he loaded another arrow, took aim and returned the man's steady gaze along the shaft. He was surprised by how long the man remained watching him.

If the stranger decided to attack, Chasse could fire at least two arrows before the man reached the base of the cliff. He could fire at least two more if the man tried to climb. The stranger couldn't knock every arrow aside. Chasse hoped that his last shot convinced the man he was capable with a bow and attacking would be foolhardy. As if reading Chasse's mind, the man took several slow steps back and melted into the forest.

Chasse held his position, watching and listening to the forest for signs that the man might be sneaking closer, but the area was quiet. The confrontation was over. He lowered his bow. The man was easily the biggest he had ever seen, taller than any Harbin dragonwarrior and broad across his chest and shoulders.

Chasse hitched his bow and quiver, cut the Eagleberries from the bush, packed them in his forage bag, and warily climbed down the cliff, listening and watching in case the stranger was setting an ambush. He took the path part of the way to the cave, veering from it before he climbed the slope to keep his destination hidden.

Jaysin was waiting. 'Did you kill him?' he asked, as Chasse entered the cave.

'No,' Chasse replied.

'I didn't see him until the last instant. He wasn't there and suddenly he was. I was scared witless,' Jaysin explained. 'I left my bag,' he added apologetically.

'As long as you weren't hurt,' Chasse said.

'I'm all right,' Jaysin replied. 'Where did he go?'

'Back into the forest,' Chasse replied.

'He was huge,' Jaysin said. 'Like a walking mountain.'

Chasse smiled at his brother's exaggeration but he agreed, saying, 'He was definitely a big man.' He unhitched his forage bag, opened it, and announced, 'Eagleberries. Do you know to cook them?'

Jaysin shrugged, saying, 'Not really.'

'They're fresh enough,' Chasse decided as he examined one. 'We'll have them raw. Tonight, we celebrate in the old way.'

'Two people isn't really a celebration.'

'We're alive,' Chasse responded, laughing. 'That's cause enough for us to celebrate.' And then he sighed.

'What's wrong?' Jaysin asked.

'People,' Chasse said. 'I miss Father. And Mother.'

'Will we go back and rescue Mother?' Jaysin asked.

Chasse smiled and said, 'We will. When the time is right.'

'When will that be?'

Chasse shook his head and he looked at Tam and Harmi, before he quietly replied, 'I don't know.'

Twenty-Five

The silhouette in the cave mouth was striking and familiar; tall, solid and imposing. He held a staff in his left hand and a sword hung from his belt.

Chasse whispered to Jaysin, 'Take this. Whatever happens, protect Tam. Wake her, if you can.' He held his hunting knife handle towards Jaysin.

'But I —' Jaysin started to argue.

'Now!' Chasse hissed.

Jaysin crept to Tam's sleeping form and shook her leg, whispering, 'Tam! Wake up! Please!'

Chasse reached for his bow and nocked an arrow as the silhouette moved into the cave and became a shadow at the edge of the warming stone light. 'Stay where you are!' Chasse warned. The man continued to advance, the light exposing his thickly bearded face and shining on his metal staff. 'Stop!' Chasse ordered. The man stopped. 'We don't want trouble,' Chasse said as calmly and with as much authority as he could muster. 'Leave.' The man came forward. *I don't want to shoot anyone*, Chasse deliberated, but when the man closed the gap he let the arrow fly. Instead of knocking the missile aside, the man caught the shaft in his right hand, a finger breadth from his chest, and lowered it as he continued to approach. Startled, Chasse fumbled for another arrow.

Jaysin screamed, 'Chasse!'

Before Chasse could ward the attacking rush, the man swept Chasse's legs with his staff and brought him down hard against the floor on his back, his head hitting heavily against the stone. Pain thrumming through his head and shoulders, as Chasse grunted and pushed up on his elbows a burst of bright light temporarily blinded him. He squinted to make out a sphere floating at the ceiling among the worn stalactites, and a flurry of bats and birds desperately escaping the cave. He shook his head, sucked in air, and reached for his hunting knife before remembering that he no longer had it. He rose to face the intruder, knowing he could not win a hand-to-hand fight against a brute – and stared in amazement.

Jaysin stood before Tam's supine body, arms outstretched, holding the hunting knife with both hands towards the man, but the intruder was staring past Jaysin at Harmi's sparkling scales. Harmi's head rose, deep blue eyes opened, and the dragon gazed at the intruder. The man gasped, dropped to his knees, and stretched out his arms on the floor until his forehead touched the stone.

Chasse retrieved his bow and nocked an arrow, taking aim at the man's back.

'Stay your weapon.'

The mindspeak intrusion, the words clear but the accent alien, startled Chasse. 'Tam?' he thought in reply.

'She is waking. This man is not a threat to us. Put down your weapon, Chasse.'

Chasse looked at Jaysin, who had lowered the knife, and then he was filled with awe as he realised that it was the dragon mindspeaking to him. He lowered the bow and eased his grip on the drawstring.

'You can put it down,' Harmi told him. 'You won't need it.'

Chasse lay the bow on the ground. He noticed Tam stir and sit up. In the magical light of the floating sphere, Tam's hair was silvery white. 'What is going on?' Chasse asked.

'This man is a Lorekeeper,' Harmi informed him. 'One of the last.'

'Why is he doing that?' Jaysin interrupted, staring at the prostrate intruder.

'Lorekeepers worship dragons,' Harmi replied. 'He is paying respect.' Chasse detected a sensation in Harmi's telepathy, as if the dragon was chuckling. 'He is praying to me that I will spare his life and bring honour to him, so that he might tell others what he has seen.'

'He can mindspeak?' Chasse asked.

'No,' Harmi replied. 'I am reading his thoughts. You have much to learn from him. His name is Natias Hunda.'

'What have I missed?' Tam asked, as she stood and stretched her arms. When she spied the dark-haired stranger prostrated before Harmi, she queried, 'Natias Hunda?' The stranger lifted his head.

Chasse wondered how Tam knew the stranger's name. 'We are one,' Harmi reminded him.

Natias rose to face Tam, towering over her, and spoke in his tongue, 'Ka du mas io pada, Lek Madin?'

Tam replied, 'Chen fa orbay ni draca eb mas wen, Natias.'

Natias lowered his head respectfully and spoke again, while Chasse watched, bemused and confused by the unexpected exchange. 'I know his language,' Harmi explained. 'So, Tam can speak Menin too.'

'What did he say?' Chasse asked, seeing Natias fall to his knees again.

'Word for word?' Harmi asked rhetorically. He said, '"I never thought I would see a god, Great One. I have staunchly followed in my father's and grandfather's footsteps, keeping the ancient faith, always believing the gods would return, but perhaps not believing I would be the one to receive the blessing."'

'Mak, Natias,' Tam urged. 'Chen fa comon erra sheh.'

Chasse handed Natias a hunk of boiled meat and the big man gratefully accepted the offering, saying, 'Sha,' which Chasse was learning meant 'Thanks.' Natias sat on a ledge near the cave entrance, chewing his meal while staring at the rain blurring the vista, Jaysin was hunched over a book, a hovering sphere illuminating the pages, and he scooped portions from his bowl of seeds, nuts and berries, and Tam and Harmi were asleep.

While she was conscious, Tam explained to Chasse and Jaysin what she knew, and therefore what Harmi knew, about Natias. 'In the Old Kingdom, dragons were worshipped as gods by the Menuii, Natias' ancestors.'

'We have dragon gods,' Chasse said.

'But ours are not always good,' Jaysin intervened. 'And we never really see them, do we?'

'No,' Tam agreed. 'The Harbin dragons are purveyors of winter and darkness and fire. They are symbols of events, but not real creatures. The Menuii revered living dragons as keepers of great knowledge and power.'

'We should take Harmi to the Menuii,' said Chasse. 'She will be safe.'

'The Old Menuii Kingdom collapsed a thousand summers ago.'

'How?' Jaysin asked.

'War,' Tam replied. 'New kingdoms rose. The old were destroyed.'

'This is the way of men,' Harmi interceded telepathically. 'They kill each other for power.'

Chasse glance at the dragon, before he asked, 'If the Menuii are gone, how is Natias here?'

'Not every Menuii perished in the war, or in subsequent wars,' Tam replied. 'They found places in the forests and the mountains to hide and flourish. They followed the dragons and the wizards and fought to protect them when the Kermakk regime came to power and outlawed them. But it was a futile struggle because in the end the Kermakk and others hunted down and killed every wizard and dragon, at least those they could find and trap. And that meant they also killed every Menuii descendant they could find.'

'But they didn't catch them all, did they?' Jaysin asked. 'Eric and Claryssa escaped. Natias escaped too.'

'Natias' ancestors survived,' Tam said. 'They hid in the mountains, maintained their faith and that's why he is here.

'So, there are more of his people,' Chasse said warily.

'Not near here,' Tam said. 'His people live in Machutzka, the place that Harmi was leading us to, but Natias came here alone.'

Tam and Harmi were awake for a while after Natias' arrival, but they eventually succumbed to slumber, leaving Chasse and Jaysin to establish a relationship with the intruder. Jaysin tried communicating with words and sign language, but he eventually gave up and retreated to his reading, leaving Chasse to contend with Natias.

Chasse stared at Natias' broad back, contemplating what it would be like to live in the mountains, alone, maintaining faith in something that you weren't sure would be real. He could not do it. He was in awe of Natias' physical stature, his muscular strength and lightning reflexes. He could not imagine any dragonwarrior being Natias' equal in combat and he was grateful that he wasn't forced to fight Natias to save his brother and sister. Nevertheless, despite Tam and Harmi's assurances that Natias was not a danger, Chasse kept a watchful eye on him.

Natias withdrew to a corner in the cave to begin an exercise routine that lasted a long time, finishing with him repeating a set of movements with his sword. Exercise completed, Natias prostrated before Harmi's sleeping form, repeated a litany of phrases, said, 'Armeh,' to Chasse and Jaysin, and chose a space in the cave to sleep.

The weather turned sour after Natias' arrival. A thunderstorm broke overnight and rolled across the mountains, but it brought torrential rain instead of the snow that Chasse anticipated and, by daybreak, the world beyond the cave was flooding and water gushed along the overflow channel from the cleft pool through the cave and out into the valley. Tam and Harmi slept on, despite the weather, while Jaysin stayed fixated in his book until Chasse asked him to conjure the warming stone for cooking. Natias sat apart, staring at the dragon for most of the morning, until Chasse took meat to him.

Close up, Chasse studied Natias. The warrior's dark hair was tightly braided into multiple strands that were tied to form four locks that reached to his shoulders and his hair was coated with grease, making it shine. His bushy eyebrows sat above dark eyes that glistened like his hair and his full beard had a braid hanging either side from his moustache. A scar ran across the bridge of his broad nose and another scar carved a white path through his beard on his left cheek. His broad shoulders grew from his tightly sinewed neck and his exposed, chiselled forearms were covered with dark dragon tattoos. Even seated, he was half a body length taller than Chasse sitting beside him.

Natias finished eating and rose to stretch his arms and legs. He winked at Chasse before he walked into the rain and down the slope to the trees. A brief time later, the big man returned, shaking the rain from his shoulders and arms, and he beckoned for Chasse to follow him into the main part of the cave. Jaysin looked up from his reading. Natias bent and assumed a position with his legs stretched out and resting on his hands with his arms straight, and lowered and raised himself on his arms, repeating the action until he completed forty repetitions. He stood, flexing, and indicated for Chasse to take his place. 'I have no idea what you are doing,' Chasse said. Natias shrugged and again indicated that Chasse should copy his exercise.

'He wants you to do what he did,' Jaysin called.

Chasse glared at his brother and said, 'I understand that. I don't understand why.'

'Do it,' Jaysin urged.

Chasse lowered into the same horizontal position and began pumping down and up on his arms, surprised after several repetitions at how challenging the exercise was. He stopped and stood. Natias looked at him and raised an eyebrow. 'What?' Chasse asked.

'I think he's saying you didn't do as many as he did,' Jaysin suggested.

'Read your book,' Chasse retorted.

'I think you should do some more,' Jaysin said.

'You come and do them,' Chasse challenged.

'I'm not a warrior,' Jaysin replied, smirking.

Chasse met Natias' insistent gaze. 'These are not as easy as they look,' he said to himself as he resumed the position.

Chasse was glad that Tam was awake and hungry, but he couldn't stop staring at her hair. 'What is bothering you?' she asked, when she recognised his concern.

'Your hair,' he said. 'It's almost white.'

Tam caught a wisp in her hand and stared at it in the glow of the warming stone. She twisted it, before she rose and headed for the cleft leading to the pool. She conjured a bright sphere, its light spilling from the cleft, and studied her reflection in the water.

When she returned, Chasse saw wonder in her expression, and he said, 'It's been changing ever since you bonded with Harmi.'

'I loved my red hair,' Tam said quietly as she sat.

'It's like Harmi soaked all the red from your hair into her scales,' Chasse said.

Tam looked at Harmi lying by the wall and the red hue infusing her scales. 'We are one,' she whispered.

'Harmi told me the same thing the last time you were both awake,' Chasse said. 'I'm glad you're awake again. How long will this sleeping continue?'

'Until Harmi is ready,' Tam said.

'And what does that mean?' Chasse asked.

'Dragons grow quickly,' Tam replied and she yawned. 'They move from hatchlings to what we would call adult in a matter of months. Harmi said they had evolved to grow fast because humans and other creatures hunt baby dragons when they are most vulnerable, so dragons adapted over a long time to ensure their safety and survival. What takes us fifteen summers from baby to adult takes a dragon less than a sun cycle. But it comes at a cost – an awful lot of sleeping; for the dragon, and for its chosen wizard as the dragon grows and the bond is sealed.'

'You'll go back to sleep again,' Chasse said despondently.

'Yes, but not as often or for as long,' Tam replied. 'Harmi and I are bonded. To think and act together, we share our psyches, our history, our knowledge.' Tam laughed. 'She has very little to learn from me, but I am seriously struggling to make sense of her past. She remembers thousands of sun cycles.' She shook her head and stared into the middle distance, before she blinked and said, 'Her next growth step is learning to fly and, for that, she needs to be awake.'

'But she should know how to fly, shouldn't she?' Chasse queried. 'She has Claryssa's knowledge and the knowledge of the other dragons.'

Tam grinned. 'She knows, but she still has to practise before she can do things. Knowledge is only knowledge. Knowledge doesn't do anything. Applying knowledge is what is important. You need to know so that you can try to do, but you have to do to learn how to do something well. You know how to use your bow, but you still have to practise to use it well.'

Chasse recognised the truth in Tam's explanation. No skill was automatic. Knowing it was no guarantee of being able to do it. He gestured at Natias who was prostrate before Harmi, and said, 'I can't understand him. He keeps asking me to do strange exercises. I need you to translate for us.'

'I'm happy to do that,' Tam replied. 'I have access to his language through Harmi's knowledge and I can converse with him, but it will still take a little time to master Menin. You can ask Harmi to translate.'

Chasse looked at the dragon and Harmi faced him as if she expected him to mindspeak. He focused his mind at the dragon and said, 'Can you ask Natias why he wants me to do his exercises?'

Harmi shifted her attention to Natias, who suddenly sat up on his haunches, staring at the dragon, astonished. 'Harmi spoke to him,' Tam said to Chasse, chuckling. 'Imagine if Varst or Ecg spoke directly to you.'

Chasse pondered her comment. The Harbin gods spoke to no one, as far as he knew, except, apparently, the Dragon Heart: if the Dragon Heart was telling the truth. He never expected the gods to speak to him.

Natias shuffled on his knees and replied to Harmi, his normally bass voice a pitch higher, his words echoing in the cave.

Harmi kept her gaze on Natias, but she projected to Chasse, 'You might not like what he has to say.' She paused before explaining. 'He says he is bound by his oath to make you into a man capable of serving me.'

Tam grinned. 'What's so funny?' Chasse asked.

'You should talk to Harmi, Tam replied.

'But you're listening in,' Chasse accused.

'I don't have a choice,' Tam said. 'Go on.'

'Ask him what he means by that?' Chasse said to Harmi.

A hiatus was followed by Natias speaking to Harmi before Harmi projected to Chasse, 'Natias says you are a boy with a boy's body. He is astonished that I even let you accompany me because you are weak and slow and unfit to be in my presence. He says he must amend this. He will make you strong and fast, like him. He will make you one with the Menuii.' For the second time, Chasse sensed wry humour underlying the dragon's mindspeak. 'He wants my permission to shape you into a man,' she added.

'Your permission?' Chasse blurted aloud. He saw Natias turn to look up at him. 'Tell him I am a Harbin dragonwarrior. Tell him I know how to train and fight,' he projected to Harmi.

Natias turned to face the dragon. A moment later, he replied to Harmi, and then he rose to his feet to face Chasse.

'You told him?' Chasse asked.

'I gave him permission to train you as he chooses, and I said that you will do as he says,' Harmi replied. 'He said he will train you from now.'

Twenty-Six

From the morning after Harmi gave Natias permission to train him, Natias drove Chasse hard, forcing him to run, to jump, to do his crazy exercises, to carry loads up and down slopes, to crawl through the snow and mud, to throw logs as far as he could, left and right hand, to do flips and somersaults, day after day, three times every day. At first, Chasse found it to be fun because it was challenging and different, but Natias was manic in his insistence on perfection of technique and speed and strength. He made Chasse repeat the drills until Chasse could not move.

When Chasse told Tam what was happening, five days into the training, she replied, 'You will be stronger. Show him what a dragonwarrior is really made of.' What he wanted was for her to say, 'It's fine. You don't have to do what Natias tells you to do,' but she didn't. She threw a challenge at him to prove himself. So, he worked harder. But his body ached. Every muscle, every tendon screamed with pain. When he slept, he was so tired he didn't even have the old dreams. Except once.

The dragonship was filling with blood as the dragonwarriors perished around him, even his father. He was surrounded by a writhing horde, a darkness that took Shaddho's dragon form and opened its maw to swallow him. He screamed because he was going to die.

Natias woke him and he held Chasse's arms to stop him thrashing in his bedding. The big man spoke gently, a tone and words at odds to how he spoke to Chasse during the days, and he stayed beside Chasse's bed until Chasse fell asleep. Natias never mentioned the incident the next day. And the training continued.

Chasse's legs burned. His lower back ached. He wanted to throw up. The weight across his shoulders pressed down heavier with every step up the steep snow-caked embankment. The sludge gripped his boots as he lifted his feet and threatened to make him slip every time he put down a foot. He stumbled on a rock and slid to his knees, the sludge flooding his trousers, the weight bag tilting precariously left. With a brutish grunt, he pushed to his feet, felt the earth slide treacherously and fell. The weight rolled onto his head and pressed his face into the mud. Reflex kicking in, he struggled to shift the bag off his head, rolled onto his back and let the steady snowfall land on his muddy forehead and cheeks as he sucked in air. *I'll stay here*, he decided. He sensed a shadow move over him, opened his eyes, and he saw Natias staring down.

A big hand extended and Natias barked, 'Moff!'

'Leave me here,' Chasse gasped.

'Moff!' Natias repeated.

Chasse heaved a sigh, lifted his hand to be gripped by Natias and he was wrenched to his feet. Natias picked up the sack of sand and heaved it down the slope. Chasse watched it thud into a mound of snow.

'Ana,' Natias said, gesturing.

Chasse already hated the word. 'Again.' It was Natias' favourite pain word.

'Ana,' Natias repeated.

Chasse shook his head.

'Ana!' Natias ordered.

'No!' Chasse retorted, glaring.

Natias met Chasse's determined gaze, until Chasse looked away and took a step up the slope, but Natias grabbed Chasse's arm and pulled him in front of him. 'Ana!' he snarled.

'No!' Chasse yelled. He tried to pull his arm free, but Natias' big hand held him. 'Let go!' Chasse yelled.

'Ana!' Natias ordered.

'No!' Chasse screamed. He was startled when Natias thrust him backward, forcing him to fall onto his back and slide down the slope. Exasperated, he scrambled to his feet, demanding, 'What was that for?' Snow spiralled across the landscape.

'Ana!' Natias called in reply.

'No!' Chasse yelled. 'I'm going back to the cave!' When Natias stayed silent, Chasse trudged up the slope and moved to the side to pass, but the big man grabbed him and sent him sliding in the slush again.

As Chasse sat up, a staff landed in the mud beside him. He looked at the weapon, and up at Natias. 'If that's how you want it,' he snarled, anger boiling in his veins. He got to his feet, picked up the staff and plodded up the slope. He knew he was in the wrong position, downhill, Natias holding the higher ground, but when he realised Natias was weaponless his confidence flourished. 'You really want me to fight?' Chasse asked. Natias kept his silence.

Chasse went to walk past the big man, but Natias stepped in his way. Anticipating the move, Chasse spun his staff and swung at Natias' shins, but the staff only hit the sole of the big man's raised boot. Reacting, Chasse spun and launched a strike at Natias' opposite ankle and again the staff thwacked against the sole of Natias' raised boot, only this time Natias brought his weight down and trapped the staff. Chasse wrenched the staff from beneath the boot, lost balance and slid down the slope on his back. He lay there, sucking in his breath, assessing how he could overcome his antagonist. He had to use a ruse.

Resolved, he struggled to his feet, staff at his side, and climbed, shaking his head, saying, 'I can't beat you. You're too strong. I think we can work this out by talking,' but when he reached Natias he kicked with his left foot at Natias' right knee and swung his staff at Natias' crutch. His boot connected, but Natias grabbed the staff with both hands. Even though Chasse's knee blow buckled the man, Natias wrenched the staff from Chasse's hand and he struck Chasse as he tumbled and rolled across his back to his feet. Caught off-balance, Chasse took the full force of the blow across his left ribs and yelped as he crashed into the mud and slid down the slope again.

Clutching his arms to his ribs and gasping for breath, Chasse rolled onto his side. An object landed nearby. He opened his eyes and discovered the staff impaled in the mud like a spear. He sucked in his breath and he stayed where he was, unwilling to rise. He expected the big man to stand over him and bellow, 'Moff!' but the only sound was the breeze in the trees and the patter of snow. He closed his eyes. *Natias is slowly killing me*, he decided.

'Are you dead?'

Chasse ignored the voice.

Jaysin asked again, 'Are you dead?'

Chasse opened his eyes. Snow stuck to his lashes. He wiped his face.

'I guess not,' Jaysin said. 'Hungry?'

'Where is Natias?' Chasse asked.

'Worshipping Harmi. Again,' Jaysin replied.

Chasse eased into a sitting position, but he winced as his ribs were wracked with pain.

'What happened to you?' Jaysin asked.

'Natias made his point,' Chasse replied.

'I'll help you up,' Jaysin offered, taking Chasse's left arm.

'No,' Chasse said bluntly, pushing Jaysin aside. 'I'll be fine.' He pushed to his feet, groaning, the pain in his ribs making him grit his teeth and scrunch his eyes.

'You might have a broken rib again,' Jaysin said.

Chasse ignored his brother, took a step forward, lost his footing and fell, crying out as he landed.

'Oh, you definitely have a broken rib,' Jaysin exclaimed. 'I'll get Natias to help.'

'I don't want his help!' Chasse snapped. He struggled to his feet again, and took a defiant step, grunted as pain tore through his chest, and he took the next step, and the next, sweat breaking out on his brow as he climbed. He remembered the last time his ribs were broken by Suran and how long it took for them to mend. He made ten paces before he crumpled and lay on his right side, breathing sharply, every breath sending pain shards searing through his chest.

Heavy falls filled the cave entrance waist deep with snow from storms that lashed the mountains for ten days and the world was more in darkness than in light. Chasse woke from a dream that he was being lifted and carried effortlessly by giant arms before a dragon enfolded him beneath a wing and wrapped him in healing warmth. He was afraid the other dreams would come, but they stayed away, leaving him to rest. He finally woke from a long sleep to drink water and sip nourishing broth, and to relieve himself, and steadily his waking time extended to sitting up. His ribs no longer ached.

'I'm awake more than you,' Tam teased, as she passed him a bowl of greens.

'Why am I sleeping so much?' Chasse asked.

Tam pointed to Harmi who was curled close to the entrance, looking larger than ever. 'Harmi made you sleep to heal faster,' Tam explained.

'No thanks to him,' Chasse said, glaring at Natias who was exercising a few paces from Harmi.

'He is a hard taskmaster,' Tam said, 'but you are getting stronger. He is ready to continue your training as soon as your ribs can take it. The break is not as severe as when Suran injured you, and Harmi is speeding the healing process.'

Chasse raised his eyebrow, and he asked, 'You still approve of what he's doing?'

'Harmi approves,' Tam replied. 'I trust her.'

Chasse looked at the dragon. 'Can she fly?'

'She's waiting for the snow to ease,' Tam explained. 'She tried to fly while you were training with Natias.' Tam grinned. 'She looked like you, floundering up the slopes. She fell down so many times, like a baby goat trying to stand.'

'Maybe Natias should train her to fly,' Chasse said sarcastically.

'He wants to help you become what Eric promised you would become,' Tam reminded him. 'A great warrior.'

Sensing movement, Chasse turned his head to watch Natias carry a large stone to a flat section in the cave. He had three stones already in place, each larger than the next. 'What is he doing?' Chasse asked.

'Ask him,' Tam said.

'I can't speak whatever language he speaks,' Chasse replied.

'He speaks four languages,' Tam said. 'And ours isn't one of them. But you have communicated, so go ask him.'

'He points. I do,' Chasse said. 'I know "Moff" and "Ana" and "Oosh-oosh", and I don't like any of those words.'

Natias straightened from placing the fourth stone, looked in Chasse's direction and approached. 'Ask him what the stones are for,' Tam urged.

'I think he's going to tell me,' Chasse replied.

Natias bowed at the waist to Tam as he approached and stood over Chasse. He pointed to his own ribs and asked, 'Kai du amoy?'

'He wants to know if you feel better,' Tam translated.

'Apart from being smashed about by him, yes,' Chasse said. Tam translated, although her brevity told Chasse that she didn't repeat his entire message.

'I – sorra,' Natias said, bowing his head.

'He meant sorry,' Tam said. 'Jaysin's been teaching him our language.' She turned to Natias and said, 'So-rree.'

'So-rree,' Natias repeated, nodding.

'So, you've all ganged up on me,' Chasse said. 'Great.' He stood to face Natias, and asked, 'What do you want me to do?'

Natias looked to Tam who translated Chasse's question. He grinned acknowledgement, pointed at Chasse, then to the stones in turn in the cave and to a point ten paces from the stones, as he spoke. 'He says your challenge is to carry each stone –,' Tam began to translate.

'To the spot over there,' Chasse interrupted. 'I get it. Easy.'

'Not quite,' Tam said, correcting Chasse. 'The challenge is to carry each stone back and forth thirty times, three times a day: morning, midday, sunset. Natias will do the exercise with you when your rib has fully healed.'

Chasse raised an eyebrow and he crossed the chamber to inspect the stones. He lifted the smallest one gingerly, as he tested his rib, and said to Tam, 'Thirty times.'

'Thirty times,' she repeated.

Natias joined Chasse and spoke again, and Tam said, 'He says that, until you are stronger, you will take turns. You carry first, then he will carry, until you reach thirty. Then you move to the next stone.'

Chasse glanced at the other stones, before he put down the first and lifted the second, discovering it was heavier. Curious, he went to the third and tried to lift it, but he couldn't budge the stone. Straightening, he said, 'I can't do this. If the next one's even heavier, how can I do this?'

Natias patted Chasse's shoulder as he stepped up to the fourth stone, wrapped his big hands around it, bent his knees and lifted it. He walked steadily to the destination point and back again, holding the stone to his broad chest. He replaced the stone in its position, patted Chasse's shoulder as he walked past, and stood by the first stone.

'It can be done,' Tam said, grinning.

Chasse's anger rose at his sister's mocking observation. He wanted to argue there was no comparison between a hard, massive, exceptionally strong trained man and himself, but his pride as a dragonwarrior also saw the challenge and refused to admit defeat. He glared at Tam, bent and picked up the first stone defiantly and completed the first circuit, dropping the stone at Natias' feet.

Natias picked up the stone and completed the task, dropping it at Chasse's feet with a smile on his face. 'Good,' he said, and added, 'but get better.' He patted Chasse's shoulder gently, grinned, and walked away.

His legs, lower back, arms and shoulders burned worse than ever before because the trial of stones was harder than any training drill Natias previously devised. The lightest stone grew heavier and heavier with each journey across the cave, Chasse's legs tiring faster than he anticipated, and the second grew in weight before he even picked it up to begin the repetition. The first days, when his rib no longer ached, he struggled to complete all three daily turns of the exercise, collapsing before finishing thirty repetitions on the second stone. Lifting the third stone wasn't an option. Exhausted, he sat, sucking in his breath, reeling from the pain in his legs, while Natias completed his repetitions alone on the third and fourth stones.

The snowstorms came intermittently for three weeks, the snow almost sealing the cave mouth. Between the stone drills and other exercises, Chasse watched Jaysin and Tam practise their magical skills by making light spheres, warming stones, purifying water, healing, and Jaysin and Natias continued to learn each other's languages. Chasse secretly wished that he could learn magic. What his siblings didn't have to do was the physically demanding, almost cruel training he was being forced through. They had it easy.

Jaysin began teaching Chasse Natias' language, but Chasse found the learning difficult and frustrating because every time that Jaysin taught him a sentence or phrase in Natias' language Chasse struggled to translate the words individually into his own before anything made sense and the process was laborious. Jaysin was amused by Chasse's mistakes, but Chasse felt humiliated that he could not learn language as easily as his brother and sister.

When a break in the snowfall came one morning, accompanied by a burst of brittle, encouraging sunshine, Harmi and Tam dug away the snow at the cave entrance. Chasse dropped the stone he was hauling across the cave, shook his head at Natias, using a foreign word that he learned from Jaysin – 'chuss', which meant 'enough' – and approached Tam. 'Where are you going?' he asked.

'Harmi is keen to try flying again,' Tam replied.

'Can I come?' Chasse asked.

'Have you finished the morning exercises?'

Aggravated by her question, Chasse replied, 'I'm finished whenever I want to be finished.' Seeing Tam's disappointment, he added, 'I want to come.'

Tam called to Natias' in his language and Natias nodded, replying, 'I understand.'

Chasse followed Tam and Harmi onto the mountainside and the trio trudged through the deep snow, Tam and Chasse following in the dragon's wake as she ploughed a path with her bulk. Walking between the trees across the mountain slope, Chasse was fascinated by how much larger the dragon had grown in the winter weeks. Her scales were a deep rich red, fading to metal grey as they reached her underbelly. He also noticed that her body shape was changed. She was more elongated than chubby, sleeker, her neck, wings and tail longer. 'Will she be able to fly?' he asked.

'It won't be easy,' Tam replied. 'Dragon flight isn't like bird flight. You can see that. Birds are light because their bones and bodies are designed to minimise resistance to the earth pulling them down. Dragons are too heavy. Dragon flight is a delicate act of physical effort and magic. Harmi has to learn how to balance the two. Her wings and tail are like a boat's rudder, allowing her to change direction and guide her flight, but staying in the air is the outcome of complex magical spells that she has to apply and adjust to stay aloft.'

Struck by a possibility, Chasse asked, 'Can you fly?'

Tam stopped to look at her brother. 'Why do you ask that?'

'Well, it seems obvious if the two of you are bonded as one. You understand flight, I mean the magic aspect of it. It makes sense that you could fly too,' Chasse said.

Tam grinned, and replied, 'Oh, that would be amazing! I hadn't considered that. I assumed, because I don't have wings or anything like Harmi, flying wasn't an option.' She paused and shook her head, before continuing. 'I really hadn't realised that, if Harmi can fly using magic, then I could too.' She took Chasse's arm in hers to continue following Harmi, and said, 'I will have to study what Harmi and I know about flying and see where it leads. My brother is a very clever young man.'

Chasse appreciated his sister interlocking arms, and her compliment warmed his heart. Maybe he couldn't learn like Jaysin or Tam, but he could think of possibilities and that was just as useful.

Harmi reached a jutting ledge and walked to the end. The ledge faced the gorge and Chasse could hear water thundering down rocky falls. The drop below the ledge was easily the combined height of ten men, ending in a large snowbank on a slope that angled towards the gorge's lip.

Chasse stood with Tam a few paces away from the dragon. 'If it doesn't work, that snowbank will break her fall,' Chasse observed.

'That's the least of her worries,' Tam said.

'What do you mean?' Chasse asked.

'If she gets it partly right, but doesn't complete the spell sequences, she will overshoot the bank and she could end up anywhere in the valley. There are so many variables.'

'Like what?' Chasse asked, but Tam waved her hand to silence him as her expression became intense.

'I can't explain. We have to concentrate.'

Chasse shifted his attention to Harmi. When the dragon extended her wings, for the first time Chasse saw in the morning sunlight how gossamer thin the webbing was between the wing tendons as Harmi's wings angled and twitched, responding to currents and fluctuations in the mountain air. Harmi slowly rose onto her hind legs, lifted her head and neck high, bent her legs to spring – and launched. And plummeted into the snowbank, sending a white plume almost to the ledge's lip.

Chasse gasped. Tam sighed. Harmi struggled out of the snow and shook herself. 'Is she all right?' Chasse asked.

'Embarrassed,' Tam replied, as Harmi commenced climbing the slope. 'But she's fine.'

'What happened?' Chasse asked.

'Wrong spell sequence, we think,' Tam explained. 'And nerves.'

'Nerves?'

Tam laughed. 'You're not the only one who questions whether or not they can do something. Of course Harmi and I are nervous. We've never flown before. We've tried, and we know we can because of all the collective knowledge we have, but we have never done it ourselves.'

Harmi reached the ledge and peered over the lip. Tam fell into concentration, leaving Chasse to watch in silence as Harmi repeated her routine, flexing her wings, coiling to spring, leaping into the air – and falling. Chasse's heart fell with the dragon.

'This might take a little longer than we imagined,' Tam said. 'You better go back to your training.'

'I'll stay a while longer, if that is all right,' Chasse said.

'We don't mind if you stay,' Tam said as she looked down the slope at Harmi trudging up towards them. She turned to Chasse and said, 'I can't be certain, but I think it's almost time for Blitzart's Feast. We should at least celebrate it. When you head back to the cave, can you ask Jaysin to forage for what he can find? I'll make a soup and a stew when I return.'

'I'll hunt for meat,' Chasse said. 'I know you won't eat it, but I'm certain Natias will enjoy what I enjoy. And Harmi will need a good feed after this.'

Tam shrugged, and said, 'Harmi and I are considering what we are getting wrong. Sorry, Chasse, we have to focus.'

Chasse watched Harmi take her place on the ledge again. She tested each wing individually, sniffed the air and paused to look across at Tam. She stretched her wings, adjusted her balance, leapt and plunged into the snow. 'That is a long fall,' Chasse said. 'Are you sure she's not hurting herself?'

'Dragons are tough,' Tam said, 'but, yes, she's gathering bruises. You know how that is.'

'Maybe she's trying to fly too early,' Chasse suggested.

'You begin learning something as soon as you believe you are ready,' Tam replied. 'Harmi knows she's ready. She has to try and fail, and learn from failing, and try again, until it comes together. That's how we all learn. Getting it right first time means the learning was easy, not hard, and easy learning doesn't make us resilient.'

'You sound like the Herbal Man again,' Chasse said, smiling. He watched Harmi climbing the slope. 'How many times will she try today?'

'As many as she can, until she flies or she runs out of energy,' Tam replied.

'Natias would be pleased,' Chasse noted satirically.

Tam looked him squarely in the eyes and said, 'Yes. He would.'

Twenty-Seven

Chasse stood before the fourth stone, studying where to get the best grip on its rough edges, estimating how much heavier it was than the third stone, and sucked in his breath. He mastered lifting the third stone a week after they celebrated Blitzart's Feast, although it took another three weeks before he managed to ferry it back and forth thirty times. After completing that feat for the first time, he couldn't walk properly for three days. When he recovered, he tried lifting the fourth stone. He couldn't budge it. He knew he was stronger because he could see and feel muscles in his biceps and quadriceps and his core and pectorals, but the stone refused to be lifted – except, of course, by Natias. Chasse smiled wanly. The weeks of training slowly made him wiser, and he now saw the changes in himself that Natias wanted to make. He was stronger, much stronger than when he left Harbin.

'Du ma arga,' Natias said beside him, and again in halting words that Chasse understood, 'You are ready.'

Chasse bent his knees and squatted, sliding his hands beneath the stone and bracing himself. For an instant, he remembered Harmi perched on the ledge, preparing to spring into flight. *I am ready*, he told himself. *I am ready*. He strained, grunted and the stone rose – past his knees, to his waist, His legs shook. His arms screamed with the weight, but he held it long enough to make his statement before he dropped the stone.

'Yes!' Natias exclaimed and clapped Chasse on the shoulder. 'Yes!' he repeated in his new language. 'Good! Good!'

Satisfaction flooded Chasse. The next challenge was to carry the stone across the cavern and back, even once, but he had lifted it. He finally did what he believed was impossible. He had to tell Tam. He smiled at Natias and said, 'I will keep training, but first I must find Tam. Understand?' he asked, pointing at the cavern entrance. 'I will be back.' He wasn't certain the big man understood. Natias was making remarkable progress learning the language from Jaysin, but his vocabulary was limited and his expression was stilted, like a small child speaking in a deep voice.

He was about to repeat his explanation when Jaysin interrupted from the cave mouth. 'Chasse! Come on! You have to see this! Quick!'

Chasse jogged to the entrance and into the sunlight, and he followed Jaysin who was wading through the deep snow. He realised Jaysin was headed for the ledge where Harmi kept unsuccessfully attempting to fly, but the flash of a shadow across the slope and over him drew his gaze to a red dragon sweeping overhead, wings spread wide, grey underbelly shining and hind legs tucked beside her long tail. His heart leapt. Harmi was airborne.

He watched Harmi sail across the valley and slowly turn as she reached the far side, and she glided to land on a flat patch of snow. She wobbled awkwardly as she touched down, but she straightened and sat upright, staring across the valley at the ledge where Tam was clapping excitedly.

Sensing a presence behind him, Chasse discovered Natias staring at Harmi, his face locked in awe. 'She's learned it!' Chasse said. Natias responded by prostrating in the snow and reciting a prayer in his tongue.

Chasse trudged on to join Tam and Jaysin, but when he reached them Jaysin pointed across the gorge. Harmi rose, her wings straining to add lift, red scales glinting in the sunlight. She rapidly gained height to soar overhead, dipping her wings to turn and fly past the faces of the mountains encircling the valley. The vision of Harmi reminded Chasse of Claryssa's golden flight over Dragon Mountain.

'She is beautiful,' Tam said serenely.

'She makes it look so graceful and effortless,' said Chasse.

'Oh, she is concentrating really hard,' Tam replied. 'I can feel her fear and her exhilaration. But this will become second nature. It feels so liberating.'

I can't even begin to imagine, Chasse thought. *To fly. Amazing.*

On the ledge outside the cave mouth in the sunlight, Chasse used his hunting knife to whittle a lethal point on the end of an arrow. Winter was losing its grasp on the mountains and the snow was melting. Soon animals would emerge from their dens, trees would recloak in bright green leaves and birds would flock in readiness for spring mating. Back in Harbin, the people would be talking of Fler and how she was preparing to sprinkle buds and blossoms and flowers across the land. They would gather and share the first celebration after winter, glad to be released from Blitzart's ice and snow shackles and Shaddho's darkness. His mother, Eesa, would be energetically organising the women to decorate the Long Hall and prepare the feast. Or she might be, depending on Mikane's treatment of her and the villagers.

A sharp sting on his left shoulder startled Chasse and a pebble clattered on the ledge. As he turned to see from where it came, another pebble struck his left arm. Natias was twenty paces away, juggling a pebble. He threw and struck Chasse's left shoulder again. 'Ouch!' Chasse yelped, and he rose, demanding, 'Are you mad?' Natias produced another pebble and threw, but Chasse dropped what he held and ducked, letting the missile disappear past his head.

'This one catch!' Natias called. He tossed another pebble in an arc. Chasse caught it. 'You throw at me,' Natias called. Chasse tossed the pebble once in his palm and threw it at Natias, who caught it. 'Soft,' Natias said disparagingly. 'Throw harder.' He tossed the pebble back to Chasse.

You want harder, Chasse thought. *Try this then.* He aimed at Natias' chest and threw hard.

Natias caught the pebble in front of his chest and tossed it in an arc back to Chasse. 'Harder,' he urged.

Chasse bunched his strength and threw the pebble as hard as he could at the big man. Natias caught it, walked five paces forward and tossed the pebble to Chasse, repeating, 'Harder.'

Chasse hurled the pebble at Natias' chest. Natias caught it. 'Now I throw you,' Natias said, whipping his arm back. Chasse's eyes widened in alarm and he braced to dive aside, but Natias laughed and lowered his arm. Chasse warily straightened as Natias came to him. 'This now you learn,' Natias said, tossing the pebble to Chasse. 'Nothing afraid.' He picked up the arrow that Chasse dropped, examined it and said disparagingly, 'Boy's arrow.' He tossed it away, and said to Chasse, 'Come. Make warrior's arrow.'

The sun slipped over the mountain crest as Chasse and Natias returned with a bag of rocks. Inside the cave, Chasse found Jaysin reading under a light sphere and Tam practising a spell. 'Where's Harmi?' he asked as he lowered his bag.

'Flying,' Tam replied, frowning at being interrupted.

'It's evening,' Chasse pointed out.

'Yes, Tam agreed. 'She's studying the stars.' She looked at the rocks that Natias tipped from this bag onto the floor. 'Why the rocks?'

'Natias is going to show me how to make arrowheads. He says we need a very hot fire,' Chasse explained.

'I can do that!' Jaysin exclaimed. 'There's a spell. You want to make metal. I read about it yesterday. Did you find ore in the rocks?' He scrambled down from his stone seat to examine the rocks, the light sphere following and hovering above him. 'You need a mould to form the arrowheads. The hot metal is poured into the mould.' He rolled the rocks on the ground. 'Yes, these are good. That orange-red stain. That's the ore. You have to scrape and chip that out. Then you need lots of heat. You need to build a furnace.'

Natias stepped between the rocks and Jaysin, saying, 'Natias know. Make chancel. You back.' Jaysin stepped back obediently and retreated to his reading space, making Chasse grin. 'You make landin,' Natias directed at Chasse, using his hands to mime what he meant.

'Arrow shafts,' Chasse replied. 'Landin. Shafts.'

'Shafs,' Natias repeated. 'Make. Must be this. No long. No short.' He used his knife to scratch a measurement on the floor. 'This.' he emphasised. 'Make this.' He held his ten digits up and open and closed five times. 'Make nadi.' He repeated his number instruction. 'Nadi.' He looked across at Jaysin and called him over. When Jaysin returned, Natias said, 'Make light me.' He pointed at Jaysin's sphere. 'Light,' he repeated and pointed at himself.

Jaysin focused, murmured a phrase in a language unfamiliar to Chasse, and a sphere appeared beside Natias. 'Satisfied?' he asked.

'Good,' Natias replied. 'Now, go.' Jaysin shrugged and returned to his reading.

Given a task, Chasse rummaged at the fringe of light in the cave through the small pile of wood that he gathered to make arrow shafts, as well as the shafts he previously constructed, and measured lengths against Natias' gauge, learning that his shafts were inconsistent and generally shorter than Natias required. When he was done, he went to see what Natias was doing.

Natias was near the cave mouth, chipping at a stone, hollowing the middle. Beside him was a small bag with a variety of implements made of hard metal like the spear and armour that Chasse owned. Fascinated, Chasse watched the warrior methodically gouge the stone to create a small triangular shape. Natias looked up and said, using his hands to demonstrate, 'You make chancel. Stone. Stone. Stone. This.' he held his hand from the floor to indicate waist height.

Chasse searched within the cave and in the night outside until he gathered sufficient stones he estimated would form a stable platform and arranged them where Natias indicated, outside the cave entrance. When he was finished constructing, he returned to watching Natias toiling at his stone.

After more chipping and shaping, Natias put down his project and approached Chasse. 'Make chancel wall,' he said. 'Come.' He picked up two bags and handed one to Chasse before leading him into the night with Jaysin's light sphere hovering above them as they climbed the slope into a stand of trees. Natias knelt in the mud and slush beneath a tree and pointed between the tree roots. 'Dig. Find husha.' He mimed squeezing. 'Husha,' he repeated.

'Clay,' Chasse said. 'We call it clay.'

'Clay,' Natias repeated. 'Ah. Find clay. Make wall.'

Chasse dug between tree roots, filling his bag with clay until it was full, and he followed Natias back to the cave under the moonlight. As they reached the mouth, Chasse heard a rush of air and a huge shadow descended, scales glinting red as Harmi entered the circle of Natias' light. Natias lay on the ground as Harmi landed twenty paces shy of the pair.

'You should learn how he respects dragons,' Harmi projected to Chasse. 'How is your training going?'

'He's teaching me how to make better arrows,' Chasse replied as the dragon sidled into the cave. He noted that she was almost too large for the opening as she crouched to enter.

'Learn well,' Harmi told him. 'And then I will teach you other matters you need to know.'

Natias rose after Harmi entered and directed Chasse to place the bags of clay beside his stone construction, before announcing, 'Enough. Tomorrow more. Sleep.'

Dismissed, Chasse headed for his bedding, casting a glance at Harmi and Tam to discover that they were already asleep. Jaysin, however, still sat beneath his glowing orb, reading. His brother was growing. He was lanky, already as tall as Tam, and Chasse knew Jaysin would be taller than himself by manhood. He was surprised that Jaysin was beginning to imitate Natias' practice of braiding his long auburn hair, practising adding intricate knots and beads, with Tam's help. Harbin men wore their hair long and loose, sometimes tying it in a ponytail for convenience while they worked. That's how Chasse wore his hair. As always, his little brother was going against what was considered normal.

Chasse stood beside his sleeping space and flexed his arms. Natias' daily intense training was changing his body significantly, and when he rubbed the stubble on his chin and jaw he knew he was entering true manhood. This next summer would be his eighteenth. Back home, he would be a respected warrior − if things had not changed. On this mountain, he wasn't sure what he was.

He sank onto his bedding, dragging his bear pelt over for warmth and comfort, and he watched Natias chiselling another stone. The big man knew so many things and seemed to have a raft of skills beyond anyone he encountered. He wasn't sure what Natias was teaching him other than the big man was focussing on making better arrows. Harmi's cryptic comment also played in his mind. What was the dragon planning on teaching him?

He lay on his back waiting a long time for sleep. The escape from Harbin left so much undone. He wondered how his mother was faring under Mikane's leadership. She was used to a position of leadership and respect as wife to the Dragon Head. Was Mikane recognising this? Galt reassured Chasse that Eesa would be safe, but how could the goatherder be certain? When the time came, and he was ready, he had to return to rescue his mother and the villagers from Mikane and Marron. It was his duty.

When will I be ready? he silently pondered.

And Banni. He thought of her every day and every night. Was she thinking of him? He rolled onto his side. 'I need sleep,' he told himself, but his mind continued to race through the past and sleep eluded him.

The same dream. Trapped within a dark, swarming press of warriors, being forced towards a wall of raging flames, he was never sure whether he was really hearing screams and battle cries or just believing the noise should be there. Because the dream was familiar, he knew what was happening and what would happen next and he did not want to repeat the events, but he could not escape. He was afraid, and yet he remained mildly curious, as if part of his spirit had to know what transpired. But the dream was not the same. He was not the boy thrust into battle. He was a warrior, strong, experienced. The press parted, and a bedraggled woman reached for him with desperate arms, eyes begging, mouth open as if about to speak, but as the axe went to cleave her he swung his sword and knocked the blade aside. And an old man looked up from the ground, face caked in dirt and blood, and Chasse caught the spear meant to impale him and hurled it back into the flames. The dragonship's prow loomed out of the smoke and mist miasma, taunting him to reach it, but he turned to face the swarm of warriors charging at him and he knew he was ready.

Instead of the familiar gruelling exercises and training routine, Natias made Chasse form and pack clay onto the stone structure while he fashioned an object out of wood and hide with handles and a long, hollowed limb at one end. When Chasse asked what Natias was constructing, Natias made puffing sounds and moved his foot up and down, which made no sense to Chasse.

'He's making a bellows,' Jaysin explained, putting down his book. 'The fire inside the bloom that you're building must be hotter than an ordinary fire. The bellows blow air into the fire, making it burn hotter, and that will melt the ore in the crucible making the rock like water.' Jaysin stooped to pick up one of the stones Natias was gouging the previous night. 'This is a mould,' he told Chasse. 'He will pour the liquid ore in here and it will take the shape within when it cools.' He handed the mould to Chasse who studied the shape.

'You read this in your book,' Chasse said.

'No,' Jaysin replied. 'Tam explained it to me because Harmi knows how it works. I wanted to know because I think I can help Natias make the flames hotter with magic.'

'Have you told him?' Chasse asked.

Jaysin shook his head, saying, 'He hasn't exactly wanted me to help out.'

'Then, I'll tell him,' Chasse said.

'No,' Jaysin said. 'Wait until the time is right.'

'And when will that be?' Chasse asked.

'You'll see,' Jaysin replied. 'I'm going to help Tam collect herbs.'

Around midday, Natias said to Chasse, 'Now we make aryn,' and he showed Chasse how to chip ore from the rocks and crush the chips into smaller fragments. Natias carefully assessed Chasse's work before he set a woodpile alight outside the cave.

Mid-afternoon, Natias put wood and charcoal from his fire into the gap in the clay bloom, lit the wood, placed the bellows at the base and filled the opening until only a hole for the bellows was available. He scooped a handful at a time from the pile of ore that Chasse mined from the rocks and fed the ore into the bloom from the top, before adding a handful of crushed charcoal to the mixture. 'You push,' he told Chasse, pointing at the bellows. 'Up. Down. Up. Down.' Chasse obeyed, while Natias gathered ten small stones and laid them beside the bloom, each with a shape chiselled in it. *Moulds*, Chasse remembered Jaysin calling them. Natias produced two tools, familiar to Chasse, with wooden handles but metal instead of stone or wooden heads, and said, 'This mahdoo. Hit. Hit. Hit.' He mimed hammering an invisible object. 'Make sharp in –' He paused, thinking, and said, 'Make sharp in mould. Hit. Hit. Hit.'

Chasse pumped the bellows while Natias checked the heat and contents for most of the afternoon, until Natias announced, 'Done. Now, break.' Chasse stepped aside and Natias smashed open the base of the bloom with his hammer and released a rush of heat. He used a branch to scrape out the slag and retrieved the glowing chunk within, the wood smouldering and catching alight frequently, before he extinguished it, and then he set to hammering the chunk, breaking away smaller pieces. 'In mould,' he said, and encouraged Chasse to scrape small red hot fragments onto the rock moulds. 'Now. Hit. Hit,' he announced, and he began beating the first chunk, belting it into the shape in the rock before moving to the second. 'You hit,' he ordered. Chasse started on the third chunk.

By the time Chasse was hammering his last piece, the crude metal was cooling and beginning to resist easy shaping, but ten raw arrowheads were lined up in their moulds. Natias produced another metal tool and began working around the edges of the first arrowhead, chipping away the loose and ragged metal. 'You make rest,' he said, handing the chisel to Chasse. 'Hit. Hit. Hit.'

Chasse pulled on the drawstring, arrow nocked and resting across his fingers around the bow, and he sighted along the shaft at his target. Natias' metal arrowheads changed the entire flight dynamics of his arrows and it was like learning to shoot all over, but he appreciated the significant improvement. The arrows, fired correctly, travelled faster, further, and bit deeper, complementing his greater strength earned from Natias' training.

His target was a wild mountain goat. The animal hesitated from nibbling a cluster of Speargrass and lifted its grey and white head, listening and testing scents, ears twisting, before it returned to enjoying the early spring fodder. Chasse released. His arrow sped to its mark.

Chasse carried his hunting prize proudly to the cave, enjoying the warming touch of the midmorning sunshine on his shoulders and face. Natias was practising his sword technique under a large tree and Jaysin sat in the shade under another tree on a flat rock, reading. Jaysin looked up, saw the kill draped across Chasse's shoulders and shook his head. Chasse ignored his brother's disdain and lowered the carcass onto a rock in readiness to skin and gut the animal, but he spun quickly when Natias called his name, right hand extended, and Chasse deftly caught a pebble aimed at his chest.

'Good!' Natias yelled, and he pitched a second pebble, but Chasse caught that one as well, the stone stinging his palm. He was about to throw the pebble back, but wing beats drew his eyes as Harmi descended and alighted twenty paces away. She shook, her red scales rippling along her side and back, and she sat on her haunches, gazing at Chasse, and he noticed, for the first time, that her eyes were no longer blue but amber.

Tam emerged from the cave and walked towards Harmi, acknowledging Chasse as she passed, saying, 'The weather has turned. The world is coming to life. Birds are nesting, and the blossoms are bursting from their buds. Your goat meat will complete what I've organised. Tonight, we will celebrate Fler.'

Twenty-Eight

Sweat running down his nose, salt stinging his eyes, Chasse ducked and dodged and rolled to avoid each swing and sweep of Natias' sword. *How much longer*, he thought, and he dived as the blade sliced past his shoulder and he rolled when Natias stabbed – once, twice – and pushed to his feet. Natias lunged, but Chasse stepped back and ducked as the big man swung high, exposing his midriff. Exasperated, Chasse charged into Natias, knocking him onto his back. He stood over the big man and waited for the big man to remonstrate with him about patience and discipline. Instead, Natias remained on his back and laughed. Then he extended a hand and said, 'Help.' Chasse pulled him to his feet and Natias said, 'Too long. I am tired,' and he chuckled and shook his head.

'You're not angry I attacked?' Chasse asked.

'I wonder how long you persist,' Natias replied. 'Good discipline. Fetch sword.' When Chasse picked up his sword, Natias held out his hand, so Chasse passed the sword to him. Natias held the weapon, rotated it, and lifted the blade to study the runes. 'Old sword,' he said, pursing his lips. 'Natias study while you sleep. This sword made by Menuii.' He looked at Chasse. 'How you get?'

'It was with the armour the Herbal Man left for me,' Chasse explained.

Natias cocked an eyebrow and asked, 'What is Herbal Man?'

Chasse hesitated, thinking of how to describe the Herbal Man to a stranger, and said, 'Like Tam. He was a wizard. His dragon was mother to Harmi, our dragon.'

'Ah. Dracoshaza,' Natias said as he returned the sword to Chasse. 'This is the weapon of a Dracomenu. Good for you to have. Now, I teach you how to use.'

Recognising that he was about to enter a new phase of training, Chasse sighed with disappointment, but Natias leaned forward and patted Chasse's shoulder. 'I make you warrior, good warrior. Sword best use.' He paused, sniffed and said, 'Ai, but you stink. Must wash. Follow.'

Unsure of Natias' intent, Chasse followed his mentor down the slope into the gorge where Natias searched until he found a section of the river less agitated by current and flow, and he stripped off his clothes. When he realised Chasse was not following suit, he gestured that Chasse should also disrobe.

'The water will be freezing!' Chasse protested.

Natias grinned. 'Good for you,' he replied. 'Wake mind.' He stepped in and let loose a bellow as if emphasising the water's brutal chill, which only heightened Chasse's disinclination. Face washing was a daily ritual, but in Harbin a full body bath was only taken in the hot springs of the Dragon's Cauldron leading up to Procra's Dance and Ecg's Feast festivals. Only unlucky fishermen, forced by accident or necessity, swam in cold water. 'This you do every day you can!' Natias called from the water. 'Clean! Fresh! Sharp!'

Chasse stripped, breathed deep, stepped into the water, and retreated when he felt its cold bite. 'Ha!' Natias taunted. 'Chasse not man yet. Afraid of water!'

Urged by the mocking comment, Chasse braced and waded in, dropping to his neck. The sharp chill shocked his senses and he yelped, making Natias laugh. 'Clean warrior fight better,' Natias said. 'Dirty warrior lost in own stench. Also, good for when hard work. Muscle better after.'

The ripple and wash of the flowing river surrounded him and Chasse slowly adjusted to the icy water's embrace as his aching muscles eased their tension. He followed Natias' example and ducked his head beneath the surface, the chill thrilling down his neck and across his cheeks.

Natias climbed out and used his outer jacket to wipe away most of the moisture, and he beckoned to Chasse, saying, 'Not too long. Too cold.'

Chasse joined Natias on the bank, feeling the cool air sparkle on his skin as he copied Natias and dried himself. Dressed, he followed Natias to the top of the gorge, where Natias selected a rock and sat and waited for Chasse to sit with him.

As Chasse sat, Natias asked, 'You have woman?'

'Uh, no,' Chasse replied, surprised by the question, although he immediately thought of Banni.

'Good,' Natias said. 'To guard dragon, you have no – distraction. Only honour dragon.'

'And you?' Chasse asked.

Natias stared into the distance as he replied. 'Long time ago. Natias have Ephrena. Three children. One boy, Atros. Two girl, Hemna and Kinna.' He lowered his head. 'Gone.'

'What happened?' Chasse asked.

'Dragon killers come. Kill. Burn. Everything gone. Natias away. Fight war for Kermakk. Come home. All gone.'

The big man's sorrow was palpable and Chasse did not know what to say, so he sat silently beside Natias and stared at the snow peaks, watched an eagle soaring and retreated into his own pain. His father was dead and his mother prisoner in her own village. Banni was alone to look after Jara. He should not have left.

'What make Natias angry,' the big man continued, 'was that dragon killers work for Kermakk. This I learn after. No more fight for Kermakk. Fight only for dragon. Menuii way.' He rose and held out his hand to Chasse. Chasse took the offer, and the big man pulled him to his feet, saying, 'We brothers, now. Soon, you be Menuii.' He ruffled Chasse's hair before saying, 'Come. Practise sword.'

Chasse crouched behind the Hardberry bush, listening, observing, his hands trembling, while Natias stood on the path, leaning on his staff. Harmi's warning echoed in Chasse's mind: 'It's the Jenic war party. They tracked us to the cave.' With their sanctuary discovered, Chasse knew that they would have to move to another hideaway. First, however, they had a threat to resolve, although Natias was confident that he could turn the war party back when they recognised him. He said that he knew the Jenic from previous encounters.

On a training flight three days earlier, Harmi spotted the Jenic warriors sacking a village across the gorge and shared her discovery.

'Jenica is a collection of villages on the eastern slopes of the mountain range,' Tam explained to Chasse after Harmi alerted the group. 'Harmi's memory comes from encounters Claryssa and Eric had with them a very long time ago. Rather than farm or live in harmony with the environment, they chose to become skilled warriors so they could take what they want from others. Various kings and queens and warlords sought them to serve as mercenaries in wars because of their ruthless fighting prowess.'

Tam's description of the Jenic reminded Chasse of the purpose of the dragonship's summer journeys. Raiders. Men who only found purpose in attacking others. The memory sickened him. 'There's no easy way across the gorge,' he said. 'We are safe.'

Despite the terrain and natural barrier, the Jenic did cross the gorge. Harmi spotted them close to midday and Tam raised the alarm outside the cave, interrupting Chasse and Natias who were practising fighting moves.

Natias outlined a simple plan. 'They know Natias. I meet them. They go.' He added that Chasse would stay out of sight with his arrows ready. 'They make mistake. We fight,' Natias said.

'How many are there?' Chasse asked.

Tam communed with Harmi and replied, 'Thirty-three.'

The number made Chasse's stomach churn. 'Really?' he asked. 'We can't fight thirty-three.'

'Natias says we won't need to fight them,' Tam reassured him.

'If they listen to him,' Chasse said. 'But what if they don't —'

'Jenic listen Natias,' Natias interrupted. 'Jenic know Natias,' and he ended with a statement in Menin.

'What did he say?' Chasse asked.

'He said if the Jenic did not remember him, they would remember very soon,' Tam replied.

Chasse studied Natias waiting on the path. The man carried himself with arrogant self-assurance, as if he believed that no man was his equal. Trask was like that. And Suran. And Mikane. Trask and Suran were dead because of it. Natias was choosing to confront thirty-three warriors with the same attitude. Chasse knew from experience that the man was bigger, stronger and perhaps more skilful than any man he met, but size, strength and skill would not matter against an overwhelming number. And if Natias was slain, the consequence for his family would be terrible. 'If Natias' plan fails, you have to make sure the three of you are well away from the cave,' Chasse advised Tam and Jaysin. 'Maybe climb higher and head north.'

'Harmi will be fine,' Tam replied. 'She can fly.'

'And I will set up an illusion, so they won't find us,' Jaysin said. 'Like I did in the Herbal Man's cave.'

'And we have a few more tricks up our sleeves, now,' Tam said. 'We will be safe.'

Chasse had little choice. The plan was in motion. If events turned sour, he would run to protect Tam and Jaysin, but he was afraid.

'They're coming.'

Harmi's telepathic warning was appreciated, but it amplified the fear in his gut. He raised his bow and took aim along the path to where he expected the Jenic to appear and focused on breathing slowly and rhythmically to allay his fear and stop his hands trembling. Natias was motionless. The spring air was cool, and the sky a sharp blue pocked by white clouds. A pair of brilliant yellow butterflies danced between the branches of a nearby bush.

The leading Jenic warriors appeared on the path. Braided dark hair and bearded, they wore clothing that blended into the greenery and no decorative jewellery. All three carried spears and curved swords. At the sight of Natias barring their way, they stopped. Chasse took aim on the lead figure.

Natias spoke and his gestures clearly demonstrated that he was recommending to the Jenic that they return from whence they came. The Jenic responded to Natias, but their body language revealed they had no desire to leave, so Natias shook his head and pointed skyward.

Chasse followed his direction to see Harmi circling overhead and he grinned. The ruse was obvious and simple. The dragon's presence would convince the Jenic to leave. But when he looked back at the Jenic, to his shock the lead warrior launched his spear at Natias and more warriors burst from the undergrowth. Natias knocked the missile aside with his staff and dodged two more that whistled towards him.

Losing sight of his target in the erupting brawl, Chasse loosed his arrow in frustration, but it fortuitously struck another warrior who inadvertently ran into its path. He loaded and released a second arrow and wounded a second target and he nocked a third arrow.

As he raised his bow, three warriors diverted from the melee around Natias and headed for him. Chasse released, wounding a man in the thigh, but there was no time to fire again. He drew his sword and met the foremost attacker, sidestepping his spear thrust to slice the man across the shins, before he spun from the sword sweep of the second man. He struck him hard across the back of the head with the flat of his blade and twisted to catch the first man a sharp blow under the chin.

Attackers down, Chasse ran to the group surrounding Natias. The big warrior was standing head and shoulders above the Jenic warriors, amid a ragged ring of men on the ground, some bloodied and still, others grasping at wounds and injuries. A quick glance down the path revealed to Chasse that more warriors were coming, but as he turned to stand with Natias a dark shadow skimmed overhead and the path was flooded with flame.

Inspired by the dragon's unexpected intervention, Chasse laid into the nearest warrior with his sword, beating him down until the man dropped to his knees and covered his head in submission. A warrior ran past Chasse and bolted through the flickering flames on the path and Chasse's opponent scrambled to his feet and followed his colleague. Chasse turned, preparing to confront a new opponent, only to find no one standing except Natias. The big warrior laughed, and said, 'Good fight. We win easy.'

Chasse and Tam stood on a stone ledge in the late afternoon to watch the Jenic warriors ferry their wounded and dead along the rim of the gorge. 'They won't come back, but they will certainly tell others where we are,' Tam said quietly. 'We can't stay here.'

'I agree, but where will we go?' Chasse asked.

'Natias' community will welcome us,' Tam replied. She looked up at Harmi who was preening her wing on a ridge above them, before adding, 'All of us.'

'We should leave as soon as we can,' Chasse suggested. He glanced at the late afternoon sun. 'First thing tomorrow morning.'

'Harmi will appreciate a sleep. She needs time to recover her energy,' said Tam.

'I didn't know she could breathe fire,' Chasse observed.

'Neither did we,' Tam replied. 'She remembered the dragon fire spell, but, it takes a lot of practice before a dragon can do it while flying.'

'It's a spell?' Chasse asked.

'It's more a chemical reaction and a physical action,' Jaysin intervened. 'Dragons have highly acidic salivary glands that enable them to eat almost anything, including a special kind of rock called Gwibani that's found in the mountains. They can rapidly increase blood flow to heat up the temperatures inside their throat and mouth and they also have a respiratory system that hyper-oxygenates their airway –'

'I get it,' Chasse interrupted, annoyed by Jaysin's detailed explanation. 'They can make fire in their mouths.'

'But it takes a lot of discipline and breathing exercises and learning how to control the reaction,' Tam added. 'I'm surprised she learned it so quickly.'

'I'm glad she did,' Chasse said. 'She saved us.'

A hand grasped Chasse's shoulder, and he turned his head to find Natias looking at him with a serious expression. 'You are man, now,' the big warrior said. 'Make Natias proud. Make dragon proud.'

Chasse blushed at Natias' compliment, but he was filled with a surge of pride. For the first time, he did not run and was not beaten. He overcame his fear. He was a real warrior, one who could face his enemy. The vestiges of an old nightmare flickered in his memory.

'I think you and Natias would have beaten the Jenic even without Harmi's help,' Tam said. 'I'm proud of my big brother.' She smiled at Natias and said, 'Am nusa o si chekka mashea.'

'Ha!' Natias responded with a broad grin and he patted Chasse's shoulder. 'Chekka mashea!'

'What was that?' Chasse asked.

'Learn Natias' language and you will know,' Tam replied, winking.

Tam's taunt irritated Chasse, but he recognised the challenge and he guessed at his sister's purpose. *Too much like the Herbal Man*, he mused.

When the old nightmare came again, he wasn't as rigid with fear as he was before. The dragonship materialised in the fog and smoke, the mud gripped his boots, and shadowy figures closed in with axes and spears, but this time he was waiting, prepared to face them. Behind the enemy loomed the larger silhouette of a dragon and he knew the dragon was no longer Shaddho coming to claim him, but Harmi, and she was there to save him. He tightened his grip on his sword and gritted his teeth. Death was nothing to fear. Courage would overcome. And he felt a presence beside him, and a voice calmly said, 'If your courage and skill hold true, and your luck, the death weapon will not find you.'

Twenty-Nine

Shadowed overhead by a vigilant Harmi, Natias took the party northwest across the mountains for six days, following narrow tracks through ravines, deep valleys and along sharp ridges. Every so often, Harmi warned Tam of the presence of other people – hunters, small mountain villages, raiding parties – and Natias deviated around or past the potential encounters.

Despite Jaysin's insistent complaints, Natias urged them to maintain a steady pace, stopping briefly only for water and food refreshment and overnight rests. The weather vacillated between mild and cold, but there was no rain, for which Chasse was grateful because most nights they slept in makeshift shelter under trees and narrow overhangs. Tam and Jaysin conjured warmth and light as they needed, and Tam foraged for plants and roots suitable to eat raw or cook while they walked. Chasse wanted to hunt game, but Natias insisted there was no time to waste, so Chasse's bow stayed on his shoulder, his new iron-tipped arrows lodged in their quiver.

On the seventh afternoon, Harmi swept down to land and Chasse watched the exchanges, first between his sister and the dragon, and then between Tam and Natias. 'What is happening?' Jaysin asked.

Tam turned to Jaysin and Chasse and said, 'Harmi found the town that Natias is leading us to. It is half a day walking distance across the side of that mountain.' She pointed to a peak lit by the late afternoon sun. 'That's where we are headed.'

'One more night's sleep and by midday we will be there,' Chasse said, unhitching his bow.

'Not quite,' Tam said. 'Natias will go down first to prepare the people for us.' She smiled, before continuing. 'There are many descendants of the Menuii in the town, and Natias assures me that they worship dragons as much as he does, but none have seen a dragon in their lifetime. Harmi will be a revelation. I agree with Natias. They need to know that a dragon is coming.'

'Natias go now,' Natias said. 'Chasse stay protect. I take one day.'

Chasse wanted to argue that Natias should rest and leave before first light in the morning, but he accepted that the warrior knew where he was and what he was doing. 'I'll protect them,' he assured Natias.

Chasse sat on a log in the moonlight quietly polishing his sword blade, pondering if anything else made it special other than it was originally owned by the Menuii. He rotated the blade, letting it shimmer in the moonlight, and he inspected the edge, marvelling how, like the axe he once had, it was undamaged by use, before he stopped to listen to the night. Owls hooted and a wolf howled in the distance, its echoing call answered by a second, and then a third, and a fourth, all deeper into the mountains. Tam and Harmi were asleep at the campsite in the glade and Jaysin was playing with levitating a stone when Chasse left to be alone to do his exercises and hone his blade.

Natias was a strict instructor, but Chasse appreciated what he learned from the man and he was adopting Natias' habits and discipline, exercising three times a day, and searching to exercise harder, faster, longer.

'Warrior will fight and not back down and will die,' Natias told him in one session. 'Good warrior will fight and not back down and sometimes not die. Great warrior only fight to protect but knows when not to fight. Great warrior does not die except when death gives life to others.'

Chasse spent time deciphering Natias' meaning before he understood the difference that Natias was explaining. He was sure that his father and the dragonwarriors would have taught him similar discipline, in time, but no one he knew in Harbin had Natias' fanatical attitude to daily training. Perhaps Thados came closest.

Memories of Harbin sent pangs of loss through his chest. He wanted to see his mother and Banni and his dragonwarrior friends. He wished his father was still alive. He regretted running instead of fighting, but he knew he could never have beaten Mikane or his warriors. Perhaps now, with Natias' training and his growth in strength and speed and experience, he could go back and reclaim his father's title. Perhaps. Discipline. He ceased his reminiscing and concentrated.

The night fell silent before he sensed the change. His bracelet tingled. Jaysin yelled his name and the cry raised the hairs on his neck. As he rose, the moonlight exposed three dark figures closing in on him from the direction of the camp. He readied his sword and balanced on the balls of his feet, and challenged, 'Who are you?'

A voice advised, 'Don't be stupid.'

Fear sluiced through his sinews. The language was Harbin. He knew the voice.

'Put it down, Chasse,' the voice warned. The figures rushed at him.

Chasse dodged, ducked, and swung, metal clashing on metal, and a weight thumped against his side. He spun, stabbed and his sword bit. A man screamed. He felt a sharp sting across his left arm, but he stepped right and swung again, and his sword cut deep. Arms wrapped around him. Remembering Natias' training, he jerked his head back hard against a face, relaxed, and slid free, spun again, and caught his assailant under the ribs with his elbow. The man grunted and fell and Chasse stabbed at the shadow.

Spurred by another cry from Jaysin, Chasse sprinted through the trees to the camp and discovered men pegging down a rope net that enveloped Harmi, Tam and Jaysin. He attacked the closest man, striking him across the shoulder, and then set onto the next before he lost the advantage of surprise. Others turned to confront him as he beat down the second man, and a spear arced towards him, so he caught it with his left hand, spun it on his palm as Natias taught, and flung it back at the thrower. He smacked aside a second spear with the flat of his sword blade and charged the next two men in his path. He forced one backward and stabbed the second, but a blade sliced his thigh, and he winced as pain sparkled across his leg. More figures surrounded him, shadows like his nightmare, closing in. He was outnumbered, but he was ready.

Bright blue light flooded the landscape, blinding his assailants, and a stream of fire ripped across the scene, followed by desperate screams. Seizing his advantage as the men retreated from the flames, he stabbed two more and slashed the chest of a third before Harmi emerged at the edge of light to spray a second flame stream at three hapless men in her path. To panicked cries of 'Run!' the attackers bolted for the trees as the dragon waddled to the centre of the glade and the blue light sharpened to bright white while it formed a dome over the glade and became a barrier. The terrified warriors tried in vain to break through the barrier, hacking and punching and kicking.

Tam's voice ordered above the pandemonium, 'Stand still and drop your weapons!' and she strode out of the trees, passed through the barrier and joined Chasse and Harmi at the centre.

'Where's Jaysin?' Chasse asked.

'Safe,' she said. 'Thanks to you.'

One by one, the warriors ceased their futile efforts to escape and faced the centre, with those closest to Harmi shuffling fearfully away from the dragon.

'Now what?' Chasse asked.

'This,' Tam replied. She faced the terrified warriors and asked, 'Who will speak for you?'

There was a moment of hesitation before two men came forward.

Chasse recognised one-armed Marron carrying a short spear. The other man, with his wiry build, his swagger and his long dark hair and beard, had a familiar presence.

'You don't learn, do you, Marron?' Tam remarked.

In response, Marron's good arm flexed to launch his spear, but Chasse's hand whipped up and caught the missile before it reached Tam. He dropped the spear and raised his sword, but Tam grabbed his arm and shook her head, saying, 'This is my fight.' She turned to Marron and said, 'There is nothing between you and me. There never has been. It's sad that now you seem to want to kill what you kept telling everyone you wanted to have.'

'I wanted you, you she-wolf! And you could have had me and all that I have,' Marron snarled. 'But you humiliated me. And no one humiliates me.'

'You might be wrong about that,' Tam taunted. 'You must really want to kill me to come all this way over the mountains.'

'I will have you, one way or another,' Marron scowled.

'This is not just about you,' the second man declared, stepping forward to confront Chasse. 'I came here to kill your brother.'

'And who are you?' Chasse asked.

'Your nemesis,' the stranger replied. He glanced at Tam and Harmi, before saying directly to Chasse, 'If you are a warrior of any honour, you won't need your sister or that beast to defend you. I challenge you to prove that you are more than a coward.'

'You don't have cause to make a challenge,' Chasse replied.

The stranger spat and said, 'I have great cause, Chasse, son of Kevan, murderer of my brother, Suran.'

Chasse realised why the man was familiar. He was the same build and features as Suran, perhaps a little older. 'Where is Mikane?' Chasse asked.

'Waiting for me to return with your head in this,' the stranger replied, and he held up a dark grey bag to emphasise his intent. 'Do you have enough courage to accept my challenge?'

'You don't have to accept,' Tam quietly advised. 'He and his men are beaten. We can drive them off and be done with them.'

Chasse glanced in Harmi's direction and assessed the situation. As soon as the magical barrier opened, he knew the others would flee, but he also knew from the man's attitude that Suran's brother would pursue him until one of them was dead. 'I don't know your name,' he said.

'No,' said the man, 'you don't. And you won't know it, unless you get lucky and beat me.' He unsheathed a sword. 'And you won't beat me. I will have vengeance for the murder of my brother. He-Who-Cannot-Be-Named will guide my arm to justice.'

'Mikane already took revenge,' Tam interjected. 'This is wrong.'

'What was wrong was your father telling a lie to save your cowardly brother from justice,' the stranger said. 'I know that your father didn't kill my brother.'

'No,' Tam replied calmly. 'I did.'

The stranger sneered, saying to Chasse, 'First, your father, and now your sister tries to save you. I'm surprised you have any self-respect or courage at all.'

Chasse stepped forward and said, 'I accept your challenge.' He gritted his teeth, raised his sword, and said, 'If I win, your men leave and they will never come after us again.'

'You won't win,' the stranger retorted, and he drew a second sword.

'Chasse,' Tam whispered.

'I have to do this,' Chasse replied. 'Let me.'

'I won't let him kill you,' Tam said.

'Keep an eye on Marron,' Chasse urged. He stepped away from Tam to face Mikane and Suran's brother, fear swirling in the pit of his stomach threatening to rise and consume him, but he recalled his father's words and Natias' teaching and calmed his breathing. 'When you're ready,' he said.

Encouraged by the prospect of a fight, the men at the perimeter of the dome eased forward, remaining watchful of the dragon, while the stranger twirled his two swords artfully as he moved into position, attempting to intimidate Chasse with his skill.

I am stupid for doing this, Chasse reflected.

'No,' Tam's voice said in his head. 'You are a warrior, brother. Be what Natias and Father have made you.'

Chasse assessed his opponent. Like Suran, he was balanced, strong, agile, and likely to be fast. He would strike quickly in succession with two swords. Chasse's defence had to be precise and equally as quick. Two swords looked lethal, but he guessed the man's strength could be compromised when making two strikes. He rose on the balls of his feet and waited for the first attack.

'Scared?' the stranger taunted. 'You know justice is with me. He-Who-Cannot-Be-Named will judge you and I will strike you down.'

The stranger feinted a lunge and, as Chasse stepped back, the man charged, swirling his swords in a lethal pattern, driving Chasse further back while he warded the twin blades. The stranger increased his fury, so Chasse timed his move, met a sweep of the blades, and released pressure before his opponent could adjust. As the stranger staggered forward, Chasse slipped past and took the centre position.

'I am relentless,' the stranger declared, turning to Chasse. 'I will wear you down and cut you apart, slice by slice,' and he moved in on Chasse again.

Chasse blocked what he could, dodged and ducked what he could not block, and retreated again, waiting for the moment to repeat his move and step past the stranger – only this time the stranger anticipated his strategy, swung low when Chasse dodged and caught him across the calf. Chasse yelped and spun to meet the flurry of blades, parrying as he ignored the pain in his lower leg. A blade nicked his forearm. Another cut his cheek. He gripped his sword in both hands and blocked the blades as the stranger swept high, forcing them down, pulling the man with his weapons and rolling his body in the same direction, releasing his left hand and swinging his elbow to hit his opponent across the forehead. Stunned, the stranger faltered, and Chasse used the hesitation to hobble away and catch his breath.

The stranger charged. Chasse straightened, as if he intended to meet the stranger's slashing blades with his own, but in the last instant he dropped to his knees and rolled to his side, swinging his sword as the stranger overstepped. As the stranger tried to regain his balance, Chasse's blade sliced neatly through the back of the man's hamstrings. Howling, the stranger collapsed, dropping his swords to clutch his bloodied legs.

Seeing the unexpected outcome, Marron charged Tam, but he erupted in a fireball when Harmi spat a stream of flame. Writhing like the stranger and screaming, Marron collapsed five paces short of his target and kicked and struggled until his life spark extinguished. The remaining warriors backed away and when they discovered the dome barrier had dissolved they escaped into the darkness.

Chasse stood over the stranger, wrestling with a strong compulsion to kill the man because he was Mikane's brother and Mikane had killed his father. He spoke of justice and revenge. If he lived by that creed, then dying by it wouldn't be wrong for him. Chasse lifted his sword.

'Chasse?' Tam queried.

Chasse hesitated before turning to answer, 'Yes?'

'You're bleeding,' Tam said. She approached and daubed his cheek and arm with a green cloth.

'Nicks and cuts,' Chasse replied, and he gestured at the stranger. 'He needs more help than me.' He glanced at Marron's glowing corpse and shivered before he looked at the dragon who was sitting on her haunches surveying the glade. Two wounded men were helping each other limp into the fringe of trees, skirting three charred bodies that lay where Harmi burned them. Another two wounded men, one sitting, one on his back, remained in the glade. 'What will we do with them?' Chasse asked.

'Jaysin and I will heal who we can,' Tam said. 'We can't stay here. If the others find their courage, they might come back.' She looked at the wounded men. 'In fact, we need them to come back to bear these away.'

'I will bring them back to do that,' said a voice from the tree shadows. A warrior emerged, holding his left arm in his right, and he stopped a few paces short of Tam and Chasse. Chasse recognised Alan.

'You are not the children we thought we were chasing,' Alan said, exhaustion wheezing in his voice. He glared at Chasse. 'You nearly killed me back there,' he accused, nodding at the trees. 'Whatever you have done since we last met, you are a dangerous warrior, Chasse Wolf's Bane. Your father would be very proud.' He glanced at Harmi and Jaysin, before he spoke to Tam. 'They would never have guessed that you were capable of this,' he said. He looked at Harmi. 'They did not expect you to have a dragon.'

'They?' Tam asked.

'Marron. Mikane. Shamsha,' Alan replied.

'Shamsha?' Tam asked.

'Mikane's brother. The man Chasse defeated,' Alan clarified, indicating the wounded warrior.

Chasse looked down at Shamsha, and said, 'He's bleeding badly.'

'I'll attend to it,' said Tam, stooping to inspect Shamsha's injuries.

'You will see that they return to Harbin safely?' Chasse asked.

'There is no more Harbin,' Alan replied.

Tam turned to Alan as Chasse asked, 'What do you mean?'

'After you escaped, Mikane and his people wintered in Harbin, but as soon as the weather settled they put everyone on their ships and abandoned the village,' Alan explained. 'They left our party to hunt you down because Marron was desperate to claim you as his wife and Shamsha wanted revenge when he learned that it wasn't your father who killed Suran.'

A gasp and sound of struggle brought Chasse around to find Shamsha pulling Tam by her hair across his chest with one arm and raising a knife with his free hand. Chasse swung his sword and sliced the knife hand away. Struck with new pain and shock, Shamsha released his grip on Tam and as she rolled off his chest Chasse drove his sword deep into Shamsha's heart. He wrenched out the blade and hesitated, watching the man convulse as he died, before he turned to Alan, sword ready to strike.

Alan's eyes widened, and he raised his hands, yelling fearfully, 'I have no tricks!' He regarded Shamsha's body and said, 'By killing him, you've done us a favour.'

'And you will do the same for us,' Chasse said.

Alan lowered his hands and bowed his head respectfully, replying, 'I will do as you ask, Chasse Wolf's Bane.'

Thirty

'Are you sure they won't follow us?' Jaysin questioned as he hitched his pack onto his shoulders.

'They have too many injured men to care for and no real cause anymore,' Chasse told him. He adjusted his calf bandage. 'Their journey will be hard enough.' He looked up at the sunrays gilding the western snow peaks, and then east to view the rising sun peeking over the mountains. 'The weather might hold for them.'

'I healed who I could,' Tam said, 'but there were men who did not come back. Some will not make it through the mountains.'

'Sorry I not here to fight,' said Natias. 'But I not needed.' He patted Chasse's shoulder. 'You have good warrior to protect you.' Chasse felt pride swelling in his chest.

'I was not needed,' Jaysin said, correcting Natias.

'I was not needed,' Natias repeated. 'Good?'

'Better,' Jaysin said.

Harmi spread her wings, flexed, hunched, and launched into the air. A few wingbeats later, she was soaring overhead, basking in the morning sunlight, her scales shining. She tilted west and sped away. 'Where dragon go?' Natias asked.

'Harmi is flying to our village,' Tam explained. 'She won't be long. She'll be back before we reach your town.'

'What is your town's name again?' Jaysin asked.

'Machutzka,' Natias replied. He paused in thought, and added, 'I think, in your tongue, would mean "Last Place."'

'I hope they have soft beds,' said Jaysin.

'We go,' Natias announced. 'Half day down mountain. People waiting.'

Chasse checked that Tam and Jaysin were packed and unnecessary baggage was abandoned before he followed the trio onto a narrow path into a valley. When he caught up with Tam, he asked, 'How did you escape the net they threw over you?'

'Oh, that was easy!' Jaysin replied, turning to answer. 'Harmi and Tam used that same spell we used in the mountains to move from one place to another. We translocated.'

'It was confusing to wake up with the net over us, but Harmi knew what to do,' Tam said. 'Humans used nets to capture her ancestors for many, many cycles, until the dragons learned how to escape them.' She glanced at the poulticed cut on Chasse's cheek and asked, 'How is your leg coping with walking?'

'You did a good job on all the cuts,' Chasse replied. 'It's numb around my calf, but I'm fine.'

'Don't be too much of a heroic warrior and not ask to rest,' Tam advised, smiling. 'I'm sure Natias will stop.' She chuckled. 'He's very proud of what you did last night. As are we.'

'You and Harmi made the difference,' Chasse said. 'You didn't need me to save you.'

'But you faced Shamsha alone. You acted like a true dragonwarrior. Father would be very impressed,' Tam said. 'We each do what we can, and when we can. Eric and Claryssa would have been proud of you, too.'

Chasse did not continue the conversation. He let Tam move ahead, and he trailed behind, deep in thought. If Harmi returned and confirmed Alan's divulgence of Harbin's fate, there was no hope of returning to rescue their mother, or Banni and Jara, and that deeply saddened him. Becoming a warrior was a step towards restoring what was taken from his family and him – Harbin's future – but, if that was lost, he was committed to Tam and Jaysin more than ever. No matter what the journey ahead brought, he would stand with them and for them against whatever lay in their way. Until the encounters with the Jenic and Shamsha's men, he felt that his fortunes were a combination of luck and the intervention of others, like Tam and his father, but now he was a true warrior, one with victories and scars, a man worthy of respect. Tam's compliments and Natias' approval quietly warmed his spirit. He only wished that he could show his father how much he had grown, not only in height or muscle, or in prowess, but in heart.

Natias set a steady pace as the party descended through the long, forested valley into a narrow gorge where they followed a rocky path beside a fast-flowing river, spray dampening their faces and clothes, grey and white cliffs towering over them. The river's roar made conversation difficult, but Chasse was content to be enveloped in the sounds of the water and wind and remain lost in memories of his Harbin world.

As they emerged from the gorge, Harmi drifted down to meet them, folding her wings along her back after she landed. Natias lay face down reverentially and Tam, Jaysin and Chasse greeted her.

'I will speak so that you all hear,' Harmi projected. 'It is exactly as the one you call Alan told you. The village is abandoned and your people are gone.'

'Everyone?' Chasse blurted. 'What about the fishermen and Galt?'

'Everyone,' Harmi repeated. 'Even the animals were taken.'

The finality in Harmi's news cut Chasse's heart, confirming his fears that he had failed his village, and he fought a deep rising despair. Hearing Tam sob and Jaysin start to cry, he placed a hand on each one's shoulders.

Tam looked up. 'There will be a time when we can fix this,' she said. 'I believe that.'

Chasse nodded, but even as he considered what was possible he could not see how they would reverse what was done. He understood what Harmi's news really meant. 'Our old world is gone,' he murmured. 'This is our world now.'

'What about Mother?' Jaysin asked. 'Can't we save her? You could fly on Harmi and rescue her,' he said to Tam. 'Isn't that right, Harmi?' he asked, turning to the dragon.

Tam put a hand on Jaysin's shoulder. 'There is nothing we can do, now,' she said. 'Perhaps a time will come, as I said, but it isn't now.' She turned to Natias, who had risen, and asked, 'How much further?'

Natias shaded his eyes as he looked up at the sun and replied, 'Not far. Sun at highpoint. We there.'

'Then we best keep moving,' Tam said. She patted Jaysin's shoulder. 'Come on. I'm getting hungry. Aren't you?'

Harmi took flight, and Chasse watched the dragon gain altitude before he fell in behind the trio as they followed the river into a thick forest. He reverted again into a reverie of his memories of Harbin. The world and people of his childhood were lost, stolen. What could he do to reclaim them? And was that even possible?

Natias halted on the crest of a wide bluff where the trees thinned beside a waterfall and the vista opened across a deep valley ringed by high ranges and steep cliffs. They were at the edge of the mountains. Rugged snowy peaks towered behind them and curved to the north and south, but the world east softened into forested undulations.

Chasse joined Natias, Tam and Jaysin on the crest, while Harmi circled overhead. Natias gestured with an extended arm, saying, 'This Kala Barep. Beyond mountains is Kermakk.' He pointed to the valley centre where thin smoke columns rose above the tree canopy, and he announced, 'Machutzka.' He faced the group. 'Jaysin make fire, smoke. People come.'

Jaysin turned to Chasse and said, 'Can you get some wood? I won't need much, but enough to make smoke. Damp wood is good.'

'Damp wood doesn't burn,' Chasse responded.

'Trust him,' Tam said.

Bemused by the request, Chasse headed to the trees to find branches to suit Jaysin's purpose, collected four pieces and carried them to the edge of the bluff. As he dropped his bundle, he asked, 'Is this enough?'

'Perfect,' Jaysin exclaimed. He shuffled one branch across the others, held his hands above the pile and began chanting a phrase. 'Gba igni ma gbaa ignum.' After three repeats, a green flame appeared and spread rapidly across the branch. White smoke curled skyward. Jaysin grinned at Chasse and asked, 'Can you fetch a couple more?'

Chasse strolled into the trees, found three branches, and hauled them to the fire. As he heaved the branches onto the pile, the smoke thickened into a swirling solid column.

'Now, wait,' Natias said.

Chasse sat on the grassy bluff, unhitched his quiver and checked the metal arrowheads for bluntness. He studied Harmi drifting against the backdrop of light blue sky and strings of white cloud, musing on how his father, and even the legendary Nakiades, would be feeling if they could see Harmi. Even though the Dragon Fang never fought dragons, it was etched into their psyche, through the telling of Nakiades' story, the founding of Harbin and the pantheon of Harbin gods and goddesses, that dragons were evil. Yet, the only two dragons Chasse had met were highly intelligent creatures of good intent, although, like their evil friends of lore, they were incredibly powerful. Even as an immature dragon, Harmi was more than capable of routing an army with her flame breath and spells. He was still astonished to know that she had a vast store of knowledge passed from generation to generation. *How far back does that knowledge extend*? Chasse pondered, as he watched her gliding on the currents. *How much do you know*?

And then there was Tam, changed dramatically by the dragon; not only her physical difference – the whitening of her hair – but in her maturity. He teased her for speaking like the Herbal Man, but she had become wise as quickly as her red hair faded. How was she adapting to everything that the dragon knew? He couldn't fathom what so much knowledge would feel like – to know everything that happened in the past, to have all the memories of his father and grandfather and great-grandfather, and even further back.

'They come!' Natias called, pointing along the bluff to a party winding through the trees.

Chasse stood, hitched his quiver, and strode to stand with Natias, and Tam and Jaysin joined them. Chasse counted fifteen men and eleven women approaching, dressed like Natias with weapons strapped to their sides and backs.

'Chaika!' a man at the forefront yelled, and the rest echoed his yell.

'Chaika!' Natias replied. 'A te shema vek atun du! Gada! Gada!'

Chasse looked at Tam, who translated. 'He said it is good to see them and he's welcoming them.'

Chasse assessed the people. Natias was definitely the biggest, but all of the women and men were strong and fit, hardened warriors. All had dark hair like Natias, except one man whose hair was the colour of dry grass. He also had one eye green and the other blue. Natias eagerly introduced all twenty-six people and they circled Tam, Jaysin and Chasse, perusing them, until Natias indicated Tam and said something that made the group step back and bow their heads.

'What did he say?' Chasse asked.

Tam translated. 'He said this one is the Dracoshaza. I don't have a word in our tongue for what it means, but I guess it means wizard.'

Natias said to Tam, 'Meysa draco.'

Overhead, a short screech made the heads of the gathering turn up to watch Harmi descend, her extended wings fluttering to soften her landing, and the entire Machutzkan party, Natias included, dropped to the ground in supplication as Harmi landed. She surveyed the scene, and casually began preening, as if the human obeisance was expected but unworthy of her attention. 'I think she takes too easily to being worshipped,' Tam remarked to Chasse.

'Now what?' Chasse said.

'They escort us to their town,' Jaysin said. 'I like this.'

Chasse glimpsed portions of the town through the tree canopy as they descended the escarpment into the valley, but only once he stepped into the open ground when the party emerged from the forest did he comprehend Machutzka's scale. He saw the great iron gates and the tops of spires and towers beyond the mottled stone walls and the walls were at least the height of ten men. 'How many people live here?' he asked, without directing his question to anyone.

'I'll ask,' Tam replied. She spoke to a young woman who lowered her eyes when Tam addressed her. 'She thinks there may be seven thousand people within the walls,' Tam told Chasse.

The number astonished Chasse as he tried to imagine thousands of people in one place. Harbin had two hundred people or more, he guessed, although he never really knew the exact number. The village they raided on his only dragonship journey was a similar size to Harbin and he glimpsed larger towns, like Jebaran, from a distance aboard the ship, but they did not have the dimensions of this place – not the walls, the towers, the great gates. He was also aware of the wooden hovels and pens nestled against the base of the stone walls, where people and odd animals and flightless birds milled and made alien noise amid mud and muck, and he wondered why they were not on the inner, protected side of the wall. He spotted a goat herd in the menagerie, the only familiarity in the chaotic scene, but the sounds and odours and sights overwhelmed him. Beyond the great dark grey and rusted iron gates, a gong boomed in a slow rhythm.

Natias stood before the gates and called to figures on the ramparts and the gates creaked in response and swung open. When they were wide enough, Natias ushered in his people, but he held up his hand to ask Tam, Jaysin and Chasse to wait. 'Must be done right,' he said. 'Dracoshaza, Draco, Dracomenu, boy. To end of place.'

'How come I go last?' Jaysin asked.

'Does it matter?' Chasse countered, grinning.

Jaysin looked at Tam before he shrugged and replied. 'No.'

'Natias last,' Natias said. 'Not boy.'

'There,' Chasse said. 'Resolved.' He scuffed Jaysin's long auburn hair, much to Jaysin's annoyance.

Rustling air drew Chasse's eyes to Harmi as she landed beside Tam and the people outside the walls bolted into their ramshackle buildings. 'They don't seem too reverent,' he noted.

'Pushka!' Natias remarked with a blunt gesture of his hand. 'Not good people,' and he spat for emphasis. 'Pushka adeh oh jemah!'

Despite the foreign language, Chasse understood Natias' intent, and he saw a man holding up a defiant fist in response to Natias' words before disappearing into his hut.

'Chasse,' Tam urged. 'We're moving.'

Chasse looked up at the towering iron gates as he followed Harmi's tail through the opening, wondering how anyone made metal objects so large. Then he focussed on the dragon. On all fours, she was as tall as Natias, but when she reared on her hind quarters, as she did when she confronted Shamsha's party, she was the height of three men. Compared to Claryssa, he estimated that Harmi was already, perhaps, a quarter of her potential full growth.

The gong steadily reverberated from the walls and the buildings as Chasse cleared the gate, and the space between the sounding of the gong was filled with murmuring voices. The buildings, a mixture of stone and wood construction, varied from single to three storeys high, and many along the boulevard were trading houses with signs proclaiming the goods sold within.

A long and wide tree-lined boulevard stretched ahead to a jagged grey stone structure and people of all ages and statures lined the boulevard, four and five deep. As Tam and Harmi reached them, the people sank to their knees and lay face down in silence and they only rose again after Natias passed. Behind the crowds, here and there, Chasse spied strange large animals with big bodies and long heads on skinny legs, and on them sat men and women dressed in shining metal armour holding long spears with heavy, ornate blades. His head was spinning with so much detail to take in and comprehend. Natias' world was strange and complicated.

The boulevard walk took longer than Chasse anticipated, but when they reached the end Natias called from the back, 'Dracoshaza and Draco must take place on Dracovamin.' He tapped Chasse's shoulder. 'We stand here.'

'Where do I stand?' Jaysin asked.

Natias looked momentarily perplexed, but finally he said, 'Stand here,' indicating the space between Chasse and Natias.

Chasse took his position, but he peered over his shoulder at the monument that Tam and Harmi ascended. Sculpted in the shape of a giant upturned dragon's claw, black talons glistening, it was smooth at the centre and near the front a mound loosely resembled a seat.

Harmi took her position at the centre of the sculpture, sitting regally on her haunches, red scales glowing in the sunlight, and Tam sat before Harmi, her white hair highlighted against the black sculpture, and Chasse was filled with a surge of awe at the majesty of his sister and the dragon perched on the sculpture.

'Wow!' Jaysin exclaimed, echoing Chasse's emotion. 'They both look amazing!'

'People come,' Natias said, drawing the brothers' attention to the gathering crowd.

The gong kept its steady rhythm and Chasse located a large bronze gong atop a tower behind the dragon claw sculpture. Natias waited until the people assembling before them were prostrate and quiet before he held up his right hand, silencing the gong. Slowly, the people rose and they gazed on the spectacle of Harmi and Tam.

And then a company of people appeared from the left, riding the strange creatures with the skinny legs, and the crowd parted to create a path for the arrivals who approached the Dracovamin and reined in before Natias, Chasse and Jaysin. Natias bowed.

The man and woman at the head of the party dismounted and advanced. The man was short and stocky, but muscled under his brown jerkin and breeches, and his hair and beard were braided and coloured with beads. The woman, lithe and taller than the man, wore a brown, flowing dress and her hair was braided like her companion's.

The woman spoke first, touching her chest with her hand and opening it towards Chasse, as she said, 'Sharm, Dracomenu. A te e manu itay gad e draco nemin sha yee harma.'

'She is welcoming you,' Tam translated telepathically for Chasse. 'She said it is a very long time since a dragon last blessed her people.'

The man spoke next, and Tam silently translated. 'He welcomes us to Machutzka and hopes that we will stay to bring hope and prosperity. He said the town and its people are ours and he asks you for permission for them to talk to me.'

'I have to give permission?' Chasse queried.

'You are the Dracomenu, our protector,' Tam projected. 'Without your permission, they have no right to speak to me.'

'What do I say?'

'Step aside,' Tam said. 'They'll understand the meaning of your action.'

Chasse nodded to the man and the woman and stepped aside to let them ascend the dark stone steps leading to Tam.

'You have to learn Natias' language,' Jaysin whispered. 'I think we're staying here for quite some time.'

Sunlight angling through the orange and blue window glass created dappled patterns across the light grey stone floor. Chasse watched dust motes drift in the light rays before he rose from his morning push-ups and stretched his arms. He crossed to the window and opened it to let the air refresh the room.

His room was on the second floor of the building belonging to the Dracoshaza and her family and servants. Tam's chamber filled most of the upper storey, a second chamber belonged to Jaysin, and Chasse's room sat strategically at the top of the stairs, one floor below, to ensure he could keep protective watch. The first floor was a huge meeting and eating hall with smaller rooms for simpler settings and the ground floor contained a cooking area, storerooms and sleeping quarters for the five people assigned to serve the family. A set of stairs rose to the roof where Harmi could roost in the open air, but Chasse knew that Harmi was searching for a cave in the surrounding mountains to serve as her indoor den. The Mena – the Machutzkan leaders – offered to construct a stone den for Harmi in the town to whatever specifications Tam chose, but Harmi wanted privacy away from the curious and the faithful, so Tam declined on the dragon's behalf.

Since arriving in Machutzka, everything that the family wanted was provided – food, clothing, even trinkets that Jaysin discovered in the central market. Chasse mused on his little brother's audacity in acquiring things. Once Jaysin realised that his wish was a command to the vendors, he walked through the market and pointed at everything he wanted and the vendors ecstatically gave them to him, and they carried his goods home, thanking him for letting them be of service. The novelty wore off after several weeks, but whenever Jaysin needed an item for his experiments and conjuring, or to adjust his choice of clothing, he enjoyed exploiting his privilege. He seemed to take to authority with a natural and greedy appetite.

Tam, on the other hand, found her new status stifling. She was expected to attend regular meetings with the Mena who sought her for advice on the city's laws and business, but when she wasn't in meetings, or studying a spell that Harmi shared, she escaped with Harmi, using the translocation spell that allowed them to disappear and appear elsewhere.

'It's all right for Harmi,' Tam told Chasse one afternoon. 'She spreads her wings and flies away. If I walk along the street, everyone stops and prostrates on the ground, and the Mena insist I have you or a squad of their finest warriors accompanying me wherever I go. Sometimes, though, I just want to be alone. The translocation spell lets me come and go as I want, without the fuss.'

Chasse looked from the window across the town with its mixture of flat and slanted wooden slat roofs, its stone walls and towers. The dragon seat – Dracovamin in Menuii – dominated the town's central plaza, which was approached from east, west, north and south by boulevards. Harmi alighted there only one more time after the arrival and her presence sparked a riot as citizens stopped what they were doing and rushed to the dragon seat to shower their affection on the dragon god and to hear what she might have to say to them. Embarrassed by the fuss, Harmi took flight. As much as she appreciated the adulation, thereafter she avoided the Dracovamin seat.

For Chasse, the town was both a fascination and a threat.

He was fascinated by the inventions and the animals. Whole buildings churned out pots and jewellery and metal products that were sold in the market or sent by people called merchants on the backs of the thin legged creatures called horses to towns and cities further east, south and north. There were smaller animals, the Machutzkans called dogs and cats, that accompanied or lived with people, and they helped the people hunt and catch other animals. Vendors in the market sold birds that people bought to hang in cages in their houses. Keeping a bird in a cage made no sense to Chasse. He was used to bartering and exchanging goods in Harbin, but he observed that the Machutzkans eagerly swapped their goods for metal discs that they seemed to prize as much as anything. The more discs a vendor received from a person seeking to swap discs for goods, the happier the vendor seemed to be. The Machutzkans had odd but fascinating behaviours and interests.

The threat to Chasse came from an unexpected source. Women. Because he was the Dracomenu, the dragon protector, he was accorded high status in the town and he appreciated the respect it generated, but it also brought women who offered themselves to be his wife or his mistress, and he was accosted by men who wanted him to take their daughters, and when he showed no interest in the offers he sensed that he was offending people.

'You go from our home, where Kerryn was once your prize, to this place where you can have any or all the women you want,' Tam teased when she saw three women outside the house asking for Chasse. 'There are men who would do anything for this much adoration.'

'It's not what I want,' Chasse replied, irritated by Tam's comments.

'What do you want?' Tam asked.

'I wish that I stayed with Banni.'

Tam took his hand. 'I wish that was possible too,' she said. 'Perhaps it might be possible one day in the future, when we return home.'

Tam's hope gave Chasse little comfort. Harmi confirmed there was no home to which they could return, and that Banni, like all the others, lived somewhere to the south, perhaps in Jebaran. He understood that she would forget him and choose another husband when the time came, but he longed to change that situation. No one in Machutzka could heal that wound.

Like Tam, Chasse felt trapped in the house, unable to leave on his own because of the tiring attention from the Machutzkan population, so he was grateful when Natias invited him to join daily training with the Menuii warriors, especially because it was a refuge from pursuing and persistent women. There were female warriors in the barracks, but they were focussed on their training, not on him, and he could train without undue social attention or pressure beyond the Menuii exercise regime.

He was impressed that Machutzkan women could choose to pursue the path of warriors. His sister would have fitted into the Machutzkan world when she was younger, because Tam was always challenging him to duels and testing her strength. He sighed. That all changed when the Herbal Man drew her entirely in another direction. And he was drawn in a whole new direction, too.

Hearing his name, Chasse looked down from the window to see Natias and a squad of warriors waiting outside the house to take him to training. 'Gadai,' Chasse called in the Menuii tongue and he closed the window.

He couldn't complain. In the space of a few moon cycles, Machutzka had become his home, a safe place where Tam and Jaysin and he could be the people who Eric, the Herbal Man, said they would become. They were living in a place where Harmi the dragon was not being hunted but was venerated by the population and as the Dracomenu, the protector of the Machutzkan dragon god, he held authority exceeding his wildest boyhood dreams. The boy who wanted to be a dragonwarrior was now a man on a different life path than the one he expected to follow in Harbin. He had respect. He had purpose. And he did not have to hide a darker truth of his role from the people he loved. He was one with the Menuii who were protectors, not raiders, not ego-driven warriors looking for fights. If his father could see him, he knew that Kevan would be proud.

Chasse smiled contentedly as he descended the stairs, thinking of the grand title bestowed on him by the Machutzkan Mena – Chasse Wolf's Bane, Dracomenu of Machutzka. At the end of his eighteenth summer, he finally knew who he was meant to be.

ABOUT THE AUTHOR

Tony Shillitoe is a multi-genre author of fantasy, young adult, historical romance, science fiction and contemporary novels and short stories. Fantasy novels *The Last Wizard* (1995) and *Blood* (2003) were short-listed for the Best Fantasy Novel category in the Aurealis Awards and the teenage fiction *Caught in the Headlights* (2003) was listed as Notable Book for Older Readers in the Children's Book Council of Australia Awards.

A former high school educator, part-time TAFE and university lecturer and tutor, writing workshop convenor and writing mentor, International Baccalaureate teacher trainer, sports coach and player, amateur actor and radio show guest and very poor guitar player and singer, Tony is committed to fulltime writing to complete an array of projects while enjoying coffee and good times with family and friends.

BOOKS BY THE SAME AUTHOR